Beautiful Revolutionary

For those who were lost,
and those who feel the loss.

Laura Elizabeth Woollett

Beautiful Revolutionary

SCRIBE

Melbourne • London

Scribe Publications
2 John St, Clerkenwell, London, WC1N 2ES, United Kingdom
18–20 Edward St, Brunswick, Victoria 3056, Australia
3754 Pleasant Ave, Suite 100, Minneapolis, Minnesota 55409 USA

Published by Scribe in Australia 2018
Published by Scribe in the UK and North America 2019

Printed and bound in the UK by CPI Group (UK) Ltd, Croydon CR0 4YY

Scribe Publications is committed to the sustainable use of natural resources
and the use of paper products made responsibly from those resources.

9781911617594 (UK edition)
9781947534636 (US edition)
9781925713039 (Australian edition)
9781925548952 (e-book)

CiP records for this title are available from the National Library of Australia
and the British Library.

scribepublications.co.uk
scribepublications.com
scribepublications.com.au

We found sometimes that the peace was cruel
In spite of the young white wine from the hills

— Louis Aragon

Characters

THE LYNDENS

Evelyn
Lenny

THE JONESES

Rev. Jim
Rosaline
Su-mi
Jin-sun
Paolo*
Martin Luther
Jimmy Jr.
Solomon Tom (Soul)

THE LUCES

Eugene
Joya
Roger
Danny*
Bobbi
Dot
Hattie

THE BELLOWS

Isaiah
Petula
Minnie
Alice

THE BURNES

Rev. Thomas
Margaret
Vicky
Sally-Ann

CHILDREN OF THE REVOLUTION

Wayne Bud*
Tish Bud
Eric Hurmerinta*
Flora Armstrong
Che Brodsky
Darl Patterson*
Hedy Gore

INNER CIRCLE

Terra Lynden
Frida Sorensen
Phil Sorensen
Mona d'Angelo
Dr Harry Katz

OLD TEMPLE

Phyllis Clancy
Ike Dickerson
The Buds
The Hurmerintas
The Harrises

SECURITY

Billy Younglove
Quincy Watson
Terrence

Also on security

Book One

Alone in the Garden

1.

They were married in the Summer of Love, when it seemed like everyone was either getting married or getting laid a lot. They were married in the campus chapel, with her father officiating, and then it was back to her parents' house for cake and champagne, and then it was flowers, and then it was honeymooning in Mexico, and then the summer was up and they were students again. He was the same boy he'd always been, smoking dope and sweating over his senior thesis, and she was the same girl, underlining in red, re-typing everything he wrote, sleek-haired and oppressively brilliant. And even though the world was changing, it wasn't changing the way they hoped, wasn't any more loving or beautiful.

But now is the second summer of their loving and they are going to the new life, and it will be new, and it will be beautiful. They are going with their boxed history, slamming the station wagon, shaking the ringing from their ears. They are watching the old streets float away like balloons until there's only cloudless blue and highway, the bright void where her heart should be. He is the boy she chose. She will make him the man she needs.

'Hey, Evelyn—'

Lenny likes saying his wife's name like it's a Beach Boys song, musical and sunny. Always Evelyn; never Eve. Because it feels good on his lips, yeah, but also it's the name she answers to and saying it means she will answer to him. This haughty French-looking woman, so neat in her beads and blouse, brows dark as her lips are pale. His woman. His wife. Sitting in his station wagon with his marijuana plant in her lap. That's her, looking out the window, face drawn, and she isn't answering. Why isn't she answering? *Evelyn, hey-Evelyn-hey …?*

'Hey, Evelyn? Did you see? Back there?'

Her eyes slash in his direction.

'Yeah, Lenny. I think they must grow grapes here or something.'

Already she's staring out the window again, or tilting her face toward it anyway, her sharp nose scrunched. Out the window where the vineyards are, rows and rows of rigorous vines, like something planted by aliens. Or that's how they look to Lenny, who's spent more time thinking about aliens than farming. But it's not the vineyards he wants to show her.

'You didn't see? It was, like … a tent.'

'Oh, you're seeing tents now?'

She's looking at him now, smiling her witchy not-quite-straight sneer of a smile, and he doesn't even mind if she doesn't believe him. She's so pretty, and he's so lucky, and the white tent seems like a lucky sign, too. He's thinking of white flags, white sails, some folk tale about a soldier who's dying in bed and the soldier's wife looking out to sea for a ship with white sails. Only, the wife lies about the color of the sails and the soldier dies, so maybe it isn't lucky? Lenny tries to remember more, but all he can think of is that the wife had beautiful white hands, and Evelyn's hands are also beautiful and white, and he's very lucky not to be a soldier.

Evelyn laughs. The air crackles. His heart is a paper cup drained and crumpled in her hands. 'Jesus. Those fumes are getting to you,' she says. Then she's turning her head to the window again, as if it's a radio and the breeze a song playing too low.

If there really was a tent, Lenny would like to know what's inside it. Trippy things are always happening inside tents: circuses, weddings, fumigations, revival meetings. But Evelyn doesn't care about that kind of thing, and when he glimpses her from the corner of his eye, holding his plant, there's a smallness about her that makes him sorry. Like all he wants to do is bundle her up and get her to that white house and lay her down someplace soft. His woman. His wife.

Almost a year now since their wedding and it's still a revelation to Lenny: having a wife and having it be Evelyn. In a lot of ways, they haven't really lived like husband and wife, only played at it — Evelyn catching his eye over wine glasses or telephone receivers and telling her single friends, 'Oh, married life is fine', and her parents just a bike ride away across campus. They'd shared a house with another married couple and there were always friends trickling in and out, borrowing books and records, forgetting shawls and little bags of grass. Friends of her parents, too, cool olds who spoke against the war and dotingly read through his paperwork and letters to the draft board. They've had so many people looking out for them, there's hardly been any need for *them*; any time alone or chance to be that eternal thing: a man and woman living together.

But they will live now. They will live. He feels it with a buzzing certainty. *I am alive and she is with me.* There's a daub of sunlight on the dash. He watches it dance as the bright road unfolds and, yeah, maybe he's going a little fast, but he's eager. Like any guy in his position would be, seeing that sign ahead, the surest lucky sign in the world:

↑

EVERGREEN VALLEY

This is the place where their new life begins, and he just knows with a name like that it has to be beautiful, like the garden of Eden, just him and Evelyn. But he doesn't say this; he knows it's one of those things that'll make Evelyn roll her eyes, just as she's doing now, rolling them and groaning.

'Oh, you've *got* to be kidding me!'

And then there's the siren and then she's all action, unbuckling and hiding the plant away in the back seat, digging through boxes and, by her organized magic, locating towels, blankets, even a bottle of Guerlain perfume. She's spritzing and flapping at the air and giving him that look, *what-are-you-waiting-for* and *you-can-thank-me-later* and *do-as-I-do* all rolled into one. It's this look that tells Lenny the siren is more real than anything he's ever dreamed of, even Eden, even that white tent.

Officer Eugene Luce knows the kind of people inside the station wagon without knowing them. It's a sun-faded DeSoto, more than ten years out of make, piled high with bikes and suitcases like some kind of gypsy caravan. From a used car yard, he'd bet, or handed down from their parents. That's how their kind get things: pure luck or scavenging, these moneyed kids refusing to buy into the American Dream.

Sometimes Luce thinks there could be something noble in their scavenging. He's from common folk, after all — down-home Hoosiers who weren't above using old socks as dishrags and melding together slivers of soap. But there's nothing noble about the way they go about it, hurtling down the highway with that music blaring and those strident stickers on their bumper — *Hell No, We Won't Go!*; *We Shall Overcome*; *Make Love, Not War*. Sure, he appreciates the message, but do they have to shove it in your face everywhere they go?

Luce doesn't think too hard about turning on the siren, veering off that highway shoulder. Through their back windshield, he sees movement, a shadow play of gestures and shifting boxes. Then the station wagon comes to a stop and its music pulses on the air like a mirage, and, for an instant, Luce is unnerved. Twenty years on the force without incident, yet there are moments of silvery fear that come upon him, the way a knife might in the dark or the tingling before a heart attack.

He is forty-one years old.

He's in good health. He has a good heart.

He's spent his whole adult life in uniform.

It's an effort for Luce, stretching out his long limbs after so long sitting. He's a tall man; he's aware of this. Aware of the numbness of his legs and buttocks, the ticket pad in his back pocket. Aware of the authority strapped to his belt and the unfortunate softness above it, like a scarecrow's stuffing. There's pain in this awareness. Weathering the blast of their music, picking up fumes of cannabis and whatever strong smell they're trying to cover it up with. Pain.

'Afternoon.' The ticket pad is out, the window open.

At the wheel is a good-looking kid. Really good-looking, actually — fine-featured, angel-mouthed, and, most surprising of all, *clean*. He's wearing Wayfarers and has his hair pushed back like James Dean, a white T-shirt that shows off the whiteness of his skin. Luce doesn't know why, but there's a dry-mouthed agitation in noticing this. Listening as the kid stammers through the music in reply.

'G-good afternoon, sir.'

'What's that? Say, could you turn down that radio there?'

Luce's words come out brusque, and the kid is jumpy like a rabbit. 'Yes sir,' he's saying, grabbing for the dial. Meanwhile, the young lady watches, just watches, her arms crossed, and she's clean, too. So clean she could pass for a Sunday school teacher if it wasn't for the beads around her neck and a certain cold spark in her eyes.

'Excuse me, but what is this in regard to?' she chimes in.

Luce isn't in the habit of answering to uppity young women, and he isn't about to start today. It's the kid he addresses himself to, the kid who's easiest on his eyes and the easiest target, besides. Wayfarers or no Wayfarers, the symptoms are there: perspiration, fumbled speech, slow reactions. A good-looking kid, but high as a kite, no question.

'Going pretty fast there. In a hurry for some reason?'

'No, sir. I mean, we're eager to get home, sir.'

'Excuse me, but this is a fifty-mile zone, and I think you'll find that we weren't speeding.'

Luce has heard of high-pitched sounds inaudible to human ears that can make a dog go crazy. He isn't a dog. 'Home?' He leans a little closer to the kid. 'I don't remember ever seeing you around here.'

'We're new to town, sir. We're renting a place on Vine Street?' The kid swallows. 'We've just come from Davis, sir.'

'College town?'

'Yes, sir. The University of California, Davis.'

Luce allows himself a smile as his gaze slides from the kid to the books in the trunk. 'That explains the library back there.' *The Communist Manifesto. Guerilla Warfare. The State and Revolution.* Luce isn't a reader, not like his wife, Joya; still, he understands the meaning of those titles. 'Real Red library you got there.'

The kid blushes. 'My wife … She's a Political Science major, sir.'

'I am,' the wife interjects. 'And I'm also a certified teacher, if you're looking for an education.'

Luce grimaces at the kid. 'And you? Got a major?'

'Yes sir. Sociology.'

'Socio-what-now?'

'S-sociology, sir. It's the study of social structures? Like … societies?'

'And you're gonna get a job as a — sociologist?' Luce wets his lips.

He knows the kid is unlikely to appreciate his humor, but there's sport in watching him squirm, and he's already looking forward to telling the story tonight. *This kid … you know this kid was so high, he couldn't even remember his own major!* 'Here in town?'

'No, sir.'

'*No sir.* Quite the soldier.'

At this, the kid turns a bright shade of pink and looks away.

'Excuse me, but unless we were speeding, I really don't see *why*—'

That's the young lady again, leaning forward and gripping her elbows, a glint of righteous indignation in her eye. The kind of woman just begging to be dragged by the hair. Luce holds up a hand. 'Now just a minute, little lady. We're just talking.' He looks to the kid. 'But you got some kinda job lined up? In Evergreen Valley?'

'I — I've got a placement, sir. At the state mental hospital.'

'Placement?'

'Alternate civilian service, sir. I'm a conscientious objector.' The kid glances at his wife and seems to gain confidence. 'I'm fulfilling my service requirement as a non-combatant nonviolent civilian. Caring for the mentally handicapped. Sir.'

'You're one of them pacifists?'

'Yes, sir.'

'Is that a problem … *sir*?' The young lady has got her tongue back and is looking at Luce like she wouldn't mind seeing him on fire. He's still holding the ticket pad, but by now they seem to realize it's no more than a prop, flammable material. Luce slips it back in his pocket.

'Wouldn't say a problem, exactly. Not something I'm gonna write you up for …' Stage fright. Luce clears his throat. 'I can see you kids are new to town and maybe unfamiliar with our roads here. Now, you say you weren't speeding, but from where I was looking? Looked mighty close. I'm gonna have to take a look at that license, son.'

'If you're not writing us a ticket, *why*?' the young lady challenges.

But the kid is already reaching into his pocket, his shoulders hunched and frail-seeming. 'It's okay, Evelyn,' he says quietly. The young woman re-folds her arms and glances out the window. She has her long hair pinned up and something about the back of her neck reminds Luce of his wife, Joya, and the way she used to go to bed those first years of marriage with her hair in curlers and would so often weep

10

by the window of their tiny Indianapolis apartment.

By the time Luce gets his hands on the kid's ID, the whole scene has the feel of a tossed cigarette butt. He spends a long time looking at the photo, the kid wide-eyed and stunned without his sunglasses, and learning his stats. *Lynden, Leonard Henry. 5'7". 135 lbs. 1–16–1946.* With a frown, Luce passes the license back.

'You got any priors?' he asks, doing his best not to blush when their fingers brush.

'No, sir.'

'He doesn't,' says the young woman. 'My father is the Methodist minister on campus at Davis. He can verify that.'

'Speeding. Gotta be careful on these roads. Pacifist like yourself. Don't wanna be causing any accidents.'

'No, sir.'

'You'll take it slower from here?'

'Yes, sir.'

Yes sir.

Luce doesn't know what it is about young men obeying orders, but he can't help feeling short of breath, watching the station wagon roll forward. His uniform damp at the collar, tight as a skin.

2.

It's one of those stories they'll tell again and again: the story of the redneck cop who welcomed them to town with a cross-examination but failed to notice the Mary Jane in their back seat. To the friends they left behind and the friends that await them, and maybe even to her parents, in a slightly censored version. Once her rage subsides, Evelyn is able to see the humor of the situation, as they cart the plant and everything else into the bare white ranch-style house on Vine Street. 'Aren't pigs supposed to have a tremendous sense of smell? Better than bloodhounds?' She can still smell it on her clothes, but where before it was a reminder of her acquiescence to Lenny, now it smacks of their united victory.

But after a while, the smell starts getting to her again, like the sweat does. While Lenny is planting the Mary Jane, Evelyn showers and puts on the first outfit she finds, her *Funny Face* black leggings and turtleneck combination. He's still crouching in the dirt when she emerges, his hunched back visible through the kitchen window, and she makes a conscious decision not to tell him she's taking the car. Because of course he'd want to tag along, want to make himself useful or at least keep her company, and suddenly a simple series of chores would become a prolonged excursion.

There's probably more to Evergreen Valley than Evelyn sees that afternoon, but she's worried if she drives too long she'll somehow end up miles and hours away. She sees the Methodist church from afar, its snowy-steepled perfection. She sees the sign for a market with red-white-and-blue flapping in front. She parks and steps out to feel the heat soaking through her clothes like blood.

Evelyn sweeps through the aisles with studied leisure, like an actress incognito. Chooses a loaf of bread. Fruit. Sponges. Soap flakes. Bleach. Tea-light candles. Toilet rolls. A box of sanitary napkins, and, in the local produce section, jugs of wine. Another woman, years older, is also browsing the wine and tuning out her kid as she does, a blond boy of five or six who gapes at Evelyn until she smiles.

'Ma, is that one of the nigger-lovers?' the kid whispers loudly.

The words are a cold splash of water. '*Kenny*, that's *rude*,' the woman hushes, a flame of amusement in her voice. Of course, the kid is right. Evelyn's father's first parish was in a black township. Her first doctor, her first babysitter, her first Santa Claus. What hurts isn't the label so much as the way it doesn't hurt her at all, the way no words will ever mar the white skin she moves around the world in.

But Evelyn isn't one to be deterred by small-minded people. She won't waste her hate on those who don't know how to love. She turns to the mother and boy with a smile so lovely, it's disarming.

'What a beautiful child,' she says, then whisks out of the aisle.

Evelyn wants to believe in love, its power to dissolve boundaries and combat hate like an antivenom. She wants to, but she doesn't know if she can. *Make Love, Not War*, she reads as she loads up the groceries, and she can't resist slamming the trunk with all she's got. The trouble is, she was born at the wrong time. Too late for the ballroom love of the films she grew up with and too early to swallow all the flower-child stuff. The world has a way of making her feel too young and too old at once, both impossibly naïve and impossibly cynical.

She barrels the station wagon out of the parking lot and up Main Street, slowing outside Evergreen Methodist. Its clapboard whiteness is pretty in a trite, wistful way, which chafes against her cynicism. Why should she find white church buildings pretty? What's so pretty about being white? '*Jesus*,' she curses to herself, and jolts the car back into motion.

The house is still there on Vine Street, placid in the sinking gold light. Maybe she was hoping to see it razed by the time she returned, the surrounding vineyards flattened and Lenny waiting for her in torn clothes. She makes do with parking. The silver music of the keys and brown rustle of grocery bags. This is the new life. This is the beautiful life. This is the time for loving.

It's there as soon as she walks in the door, a wafting garden funk.

And then there's Lenny, her beautiful boy-husband: barefoot, white shirt dirty with yard work, smoking a joint and tuning her old peach-pink radio.

'I wasn't sure when you were coming back ...' He looks sheepish. Then, signaling in smoke, 'There wasn't much to do.'

Evelyn is about to say something about the fort of still-unpacked boxes but stops herself. Puts down the bags instead. 'I bought wine.'

'Righteous.'

Lenny holds out the joint and smiles, an innocent glimmer that makes her heart wince. She loves him so much, or wants to. Does it really matter which?

3.

Lenny is bemused when Evelyn tells him she wants to go to church the next day, but a lot of things she does are bemusing to him. Talking back to cops, for instance, or dressing like an existentialist to buy groceries, or setting up a groovy little picnic on the living room floor, complete with tea-light candles in jars. They've got running water but no electricity until Monday — no phone, no television, only the barest bones of furniture. The portable radio runs on battery and they tune into the Kennedy-McCarthy debate for a while, but it only makes Evelyn roll her eyes.

'They're not talking about anything serious,' she says. 'And Bobby Kennedy looks better than he sounds.'

So they turn it off and agree that Kennedy should win the primary regardless; he has more *heart*, he's more *dynamic*, Evelyn says. Lenny doesn't know why exactly he likes Bobby Kennedy — whether it's his politics or just something about him, the way he always looks sort of alone and afraid. There's so much in the world to fear, maybe the best thing they can do is show how scared they are, all the politicians and all the soldiers and all the students and everyone else.

'Ah!' Evelyn cries out suddenly, a strange, small cry, more of surprise than fear. Lenny sees, as if in slow motion, the thing that has made her cry out — a large flying insect moving through the candlelight and then disappearing into the darkness with a thud. He sees her eyes, strangely dark and glistening, and feels an overwhelming powerlessness.

'Should I … try to make it go outside?' Lenny says after a while. It's the best he can offer; he never kills insects. Evelyn shakes her head and takes a swallow of wine.

Not long after that, Evelyn uncoils herself from the carpet and starts fussing with the boxes. He knows she is afraid of the insect; it can still be heard thudding against the walls and there's something extra small about her movements. How strange his wife seems to him sometimes. There's a mechanical trilling of cicadas that's been going on for hours, but it seems louder now that it's dark and she is afraid. He wishes he could help. He doesn't want to kill.

Lenny doesn't know when exactly Evelyn slips out with one of the candles in the jars. He hears her rustling in another room. He hears her singing 'John Riley' very softly:

Fair young maid, all in her garden
Strange young man, passerby
Said, fair maid, will you marry me?
This then, sir, was her reply …

How strange his wife seems, singing about marriage in another room while he stays glued to the carpet. He wants to move but doesn't know how. The cicadas make him think of guns clicking in faraway jungles. There's so much to be afraid of.

'I want us to go to church tomorrow,' Evelyn tells him, just like that, when she returns from singing in the other room. There must be some practical reason why she went there, but all Lenny knows is that she sang, and it seems as if she came to the decision that way. He says okay. Whatever she wants. Because although he knows she doesn't believe in God and was never rigorous about attending her father's services, if it makes her less afraid, he wants it too.

After that, Evelyn holds out her candle and looks warily in the direction of the insect. 'I put our sleeping bags in the bedroom,' she says. So he takes up a candle just like hers, and they blow out the others and like children or mourners they go down the hall. Alone to the solitude he's dreamed of — a man and woman living together and a garden of their own — yet how solemn it all seems, how small. As the movements of her hips walking in front of him are small, her beautiful body in its black clothes, everything that is and everything he loves.

I am alone and she is with me. Lenny looks at the candle. *We are alone.*

*

It occurs to Lenny that his wife is having fun, making enemies in the church parking lot like it's her new favorite hobby. He's given up trying to follow her conversations but from where he's standing she looks almost playful, like a cat in tall grass hunting low-flying moths. His little hunting-cat wife, who was so afraid of that insect last night and this morning under the cold shower so pale and shivery. Sure, he doesn't understand it, and kind of wishes they could leave already, but it's good to see her having fun, and he likes the way she smiles at him, circling back every time she finds some new provincialism worth reporting.

'*That man*—' Evelyn's pupils are twice their normal size, her lips as joyous as a bride's, '—He says "negroes" are stealing jobs at the timber mill.'

And then she's gone again, back to the hunt, with movements so light and a smile so lovely anyone would think she really was out to make friends. Just like a cat, dropping half-dead moths at his feet and disappearing on him. Lenny comes from a family of cat people. He knows the reality of owning-without-owning, warm purring sweetness one second and cold absence the next. He knows Evelyn is a 'liberated woman' as well as a wife, and not so much to be owned as accommodated. Yet he also likes to think she really does belong to him, deep down, and she seems to like reassuring him of this — breaking away from her latest plaything just a few minutes later and returning with lowered eyes.

'Let's go,' she says, slinging her purse and letting herself into the station wagon.

Lenny remembers that floral tapestry purse from when he and Evelyn first started dating. It was there the time they turned on together in the crowded house she shared with her girlfriends, a bright little reassurance of her presence, even as she drifted out on him. He'd enjoyed staring at it for a long time, the psychedelic swirl of its patterns, and was always happy to see it on later occasions. It was as if he and the purse had had a private conversation, which added to his knowledge of Evelyn-apart-from-Evelyn the way conversations with her parents did, or dreams in which she spoke to him, or certain isolated impressions he'd had of her before he knew her: a sophomore with bobbed hair, talking too loudly in a library; fast-walking on a spring day in a striped sweater and sunglasses; standing by a rosebush with her father, Reverend Burne, the cool and kindly campus minister.

It's not until they're both in the station wagon and rolling onto Main Street that Lenny suspects there might be something wrong. They've got chores at home and in town, and he's asking her what she wants to do next, but she isn't answering. Not answering, just sitting there playing her thumbnail over the chain of her purse as he calls her name. 'Hey, Evelyn? Do you want me to drive home or …? Evelyn?'

She's upset. He sees it now. The set of her shoulders and uncharacteristic silence and that chain she keeps playing with. It dawns on him that what was going on back there wasn't fun for her at all but an obscure form of social self-mortification. And he didn't see it. Though he has communed with the patterns of her purse and cherished those stray memories of her talking and walking and standing by the rosebush, he doesn't know enough.

'Hey … it can be one of those stories we tell people …'

Lenny tries to sound upbeat, but even as he's saying it, he knows it's the wrong thing. Because Evelyn's eyes are flashing and the patches on her cheeks are darker than before, and of course they don't have a working phone, let alone any friends in town to talk to.

'Who am I going to tell, Lenny?' Evelyn snaps. 'The only other person here is *you*.'

4.

It is better with electricity, a telephone connection. Her father's voice on the other end telling her she will find her people soon, like she always does. She doesn't want to confide in her father, yet somehow, in not so many words, that's what happens, and she is comforted by his voice, thin and resonant and intelligent. He reminds her of all the places she has spent time in her short life: the black towns in South Carolina; the suburbs of Sacramento; dry Salinas; big-skied Davis; beautiful Bordeaux, France. Of the importance of not being isolated. Of her ability to make a home, wherever she is. By the time Evelyn puts down the receiver, she is ready to believe that Evergreen Valley is an essential stage of her development, as much as her year on exchange in Bordeaux was.

She will make a home for them. She is more than a homemaker — fluent in French, on the dean's list all through college, still dreams of someday working for the UN — yet her present challenge is to make a home here, and to make it beautiful. Beautiful, and also rich with their shared history; for they have history, she and Lenny, have been through so much already, though not even a year married. There was a day not long before Lenny proposed to her when they stood and watched some guys Lenny's age burning draft cards, watched the flames and held hands. If that isn't history, she doesn't know what is.

In the doorways, Evelyn hangs the Mexican bead curtains, bought on their honeymoon the year before. She hangs landscapes by Matisse and Van Gogh, Frida Kahlo with a necklace of thorns, pictures of herself with her parents and sisters and girlfriends and Lenny. She even hangs a psychedelic poster of Lenny's, though she finds it ugly, and puts his bong with the glassware. She spends a long time sorting through their records, arranging them in his 'n' hers piles on either side of the player: his *Fifth Dimension*, his *Odessey and Oracle*, his *Electric Music for the Mind and Body*, her *Odetta Sings Folk*, her *Joan Baez in Concert*, her *Chansons Populaires de France*.

When Lenny returns from the mental hospital early that evening, there's a casserole in the oven, Joan Baez warbling in Spanish on the record player. Barefoot and gypsy-skirted, Evelyn rushes to meet him through the beads, like some kind of housebroken *gitana*. Loops her arms around his neck and kisses him, though he smells of antiseptic and doesn't look all that appealing to her in his all-white, tight-fitting uniform.

'Evelyn … you've done so much,' he says, holding her by the waist. 'This is beautiful.'

And though she knows he has probably had a strange day, seen frightening things in those waxed hallways, his eyes are so wide and blue, and his smile so innocent, that everything in her wants to cry out in protest. *No, it isn't. None of this is beautiful.*

Lenny likes coming home to the white house on Vine Street, surrounded on all sides by greenery. He likes the way the hallway has smelled of Evelyn's cooking two days in a row, and the way she has kissed him, tugged at his clothes, melting away the craziness of the hours before. Crazy hours with crazy men. He is frightened of the men at the mental hospital, even the ones who don't seem so crazy; maybe especially those ones. Through the day, as he draws baths and lathers faces, sets down meals and changes channels, it occurs to Lenny that there's a line that separates 'normal' from 'crazy', and that it's possible for a normal person to trip over this line. He wonders what it would take to make him go crazy and thinks maybe it wouldn't be much, maybe just some bad acid or seeing some lights in the sky or a week in a Vietnamese jungle. But Evelyn is sane. The very definition of sane, with her sleek hair and nice cooking and lovely frisking hands, and she would never marry a crazy man.

They've been alone and afraid in the Vine Street house, but those days are over now and the house is a home, filled with their things and also some new things Evelyn has conjured in his absence: a velvety green sofa, a small black-and-white TV, a double bed that looks as wide and luxurious as an ocean liner. He likes the bed, being pushed back onto it by Evelyn, and later watching her pull on a turtleneck and smile her crooked-sexy smile and tell him, 'The *coq au vin* will be ready now,' as if the melting joy of the past half-hour was just a way of killing time.

It's nights like these that being married is all about, Lenny thinks, lounging on the green sofa and listening to Evelyn clatter through the bead curtains. Eating the *coq au vin* she spoons out of a heavy cast-iron pot and drinking the Pinot Noir, and afterward there are brownies for dessert. 'I figured I should learn to cook this stuff, if we're going to have our own crop.' She looks skeptical. 'Honestly, I don't know if I got the measurements right, so don't eat too much.'

'These are really good, Evelyn.'

She nibbles a corner thoughtfully. 'You know, the man who delivered the bed today? I think he was coming on to me.'

Evelyn talks for a while about the man, the good deals she got on the furniture, her plans for their new home. He forgets to answer a couple of times, and she says, 'Oh, sorry. Am I boring you,' in a flat voice, then starts cleaning up. Lenny thinks she looks cute playing maid in her turtleneck and underwear, watches her butt, her legs, her bare feet. He wonders if he should help in the kitchen, but it's been a long day and his stomach is full and he's had hash *and* wine *and* sex. He decides he'll just tell her she looks cute when she returns, only it's a long time before she does, and by then she's got a new glass of wine and wants to bitch about their college friends.

'I just phoned Joan. She and Peter are flying to Europe on Friday. Can you imagine?'

'That's nice.'

'Yes, but *can you imagine?* Leaving the country at a time like this? And with Peter a 1-A now? It's even worse than running off to Canada.' She takes a swallow of wine. 'It's so much braver what you're doing. Anyone who truly cares about changing this country would stay.'

Lenny doesn't feel especially brave, just lucky. He knows that Evelyn has spent time in Europe, was even engaged to and 'practically living with' some guy in France, and that they wouldn't be married if she hadn't decided such a life wasn't for her. They wouldn't be sitting on the soft green sofa and watching the polls together, and she wouldn't be grabbing his arm suddenly and saying, '*Oh*, Lenny,' because the final count is in. She gives a surprised little laugh, and he laughs too, though he knows nothing has really changed yet. He laughs and puts his arm around Evelyn, and she says, '*Oh*, Lenny,' again and snuggles into him. 'This is *good news*.'

After that, they're both feeling the effects of the brownies and it's nice; she's in a warm, purring mood; says her shoulders feel funny, wants them rubbed. She sits on the floor in front of him as he kneads her shoulders and tosses back her sleek head and says, 'Don't you feel it in your shoulders? A tense feeling?' and he tells her, *No, just relax.* It's funny, Lenny thinks, how drugs always affect Evelyn differently than him, how he's never seen her fully relaxed in all the times they've turned on together, though she's often giddy and touchy-feely. He stops rubbing her shoulders for a moment, and she says urgently, 'Don't stop,' and he likes this urgency. Then she points at the TV where people are celebrating and says, 'It's making my head buzz. Isn't your head buzzing?'

'Do you want me to turn it off?'

'No. I want to see the speech.'

So Lenny keeps doing what he's doing until Bobby Kennedy appears, at which point Evelyn scoots forward to turn up the volume, then joins him on the sofa, practically curling up in his lap. They listen to Bobby Kennedy. They laugh when Bobby Kennedy thanks his dog Freckles, and when he peaces the crowd before moving offstage. Evelyn says, 'Isn't he cute?' and Lenny yawns, and this too seems funny. In not so many hours, he'll be getting ready for work at the mental hospital and maybe still high, but for the present there's just him and Evelyn and the sofa and all those happy people screaming on TV. Screaming and clutching their faces and standing on chairs like there's a mouse scurrying under them, and wouldn't *that* be funny? A mouse in that big crowd? Only Evelyn doesn't think so.

'Lenny,' she says in a faraway voice. 'They *shot* him.'

5.

Evelyn knows it isn't Lenny's fault that she has a hangover, yet in a way, she reasons, it is *exactly* his fault. Because if he wasn't the kind of guy who liked getting high on weeknights, she wouldn't have made the brownies, and if it wasn't for the brownies, the wine wouldn't have affected her so badly.

She keeps her eyes closed as Lenny passes in and out of the bedroom like a ghost in his white uniform, doesn't acknowledge the touch of his lips to her temple. When next she opens her eyes, she's aware of a sore, clenched feeling deep inside her, and thinks: *Of course.* The brown spotting on the sheets confirms what she already knows, and wearily she strips the bed and then herself, and showers, and dresses, and pins her hair, and does everything she can to feel normal. On the front page of the paper, Bobby Kennedy is splayed out like a broken puppet, and the write-up says the man who shot him was a kitchen worker, Mexican or Arab.

She turns on the TV. She makes herself a cup of chamomile tea. She lies down with her tea and a heat compress and feels herself shrink before the sweeping blood-tide of ugliness. On the screen, the students and blacks and Chicanos are mourning Bobby Kennedy who, though shot in the head, neck, and back, still isn't dead. At least when JFK was shot, it happened quickly, skull and brains exploding like watermelon. Martin Luther King, just two months earlier, when she was completing her teaching credential. Never will she forget the way her students had cheered when the announcement came over the PA, nor how she had sat in the car and wept once school was out. But at least she didn't have her period then, and at least she hadn't been in Evergreen Valley.

The blood gets heavier as the day progresses. Evelyn cleans the oven, the floors, the bathroom, until her fingers are puckered and she can think of nothing else to clean. She sits on the toilet and wipes herself and is shocked to see a clot of blood on the tissue, the exact shape and color of a leech.

Evelyn turns the TV back on. She makes more tea. She takes up a picture of herself in bridal white standing with her parents and sisters, Vicky and Sally-Ann, both younger and prettier and fairer-haired than herself. She puts it down and hefts a pile of *National Geographic* from the shelf, occupies herself with the photographs of more beautiful places and people: sherpas in Nepal; Tongan children in flowers and beads; Czech peasant women cycling through yellow fields; Nuba tribesmen with scarified torsos and painted faces; red deserts; green lakes; turquoise icebergs; earth captured from orbit, just a milky blue marble in so much blackness. And that's when she glimpses the insect on the wall.

'Oh!' she cries out — a feminine hobble of a cry, like an ankle twisted in high heels.

Is it a cockroach? A beetle? A cicada? Evelyn can't tell; only that it is large and winged and has been watching her from the wallpaper for hours, as far as she knows. Fear spikes within her. She rises from the sofa and creeps toward it with a rolled-up magazine; she manages to knock it off the wall without killing it, then shrieks as it comes sputtering across the carpet toward her. Then she's striking at it blindly until she feels the crunch of its exoskeleton, sees the smeared brown proof in the carpet fibers, and it's so ugly and so typical of everything, and the house so empty, and being married so lonely, she can't even find the heart to weep.

'Hey, Evelyn—'

Like always, Lenny's wife doesn't answer when he calls her. Wouldn't even if she was within earshot, and she isn't. Where is she? Not in the bedroom or the living room, not in the kitchen cooking. The silence and cleanliness of the house unnerves him, as do the beads that clatter every time he enters another room. Mexican bead curtains from their honeymoon. Where is she? *Evelyn?*

And then Lenny sees the sheets flapping outside on the clothesline, his wife stepping out from behind them. She is wearing something long and loose-fitting and looks, from that distance, like a woman from another century. Lenny feels a surge of tender relief and goes outside to meet her.

'Oh,' Evelyn says. 'You're home.'

The whiteness of the sheets and the greenness of the yard shows him just how red her eyes are, and many other flaws: that her hair and skin are sort of greasy, her complexion too pale, her nose too sharp, the dress not one of his favorites, but one she only seems to wear when she's sick or in a bad mood. He feels bad for thinking these things, and, as if she has read his mind, Evelyn sneers, making him suddenly embarrassed of his white uniform.

'Did you hear?' Her tone is harsh, almost accusing. 'They say the gunman is an Arab.'

'Yeah.'

'Of course that's what they *would* say.' She unpegs a sheet corner and tugs it off the line. 'The worst thing is, we'll never know what really happened.'

'Yeah.'

'You know, it's the blacks who'll suffer most.' She is dragging down the sheet like something caught at sea and showing him her witchy profile, the schoolmarmish knot at the back of her head. 'Our grief doesn't even come close.'

'Yeah.'

'I mean, we're the lucky ones. We get to choose our battles. You got to *choose* your uniform. Have you seen any black men walking around that hospital wearing white?'

'I don't know, Evelyn.'

'No.' She rolls her eyes. 'I guess you don't.'

Lenny watches his wife fold the sheets and bundle them in her arms, then squint at the distant hills and sunset. 'God,' she says, 'I almost wish we were somewhere with sirens.'

He thinks he understands what she means by this. He tries to think of what they'd be doing at this time of day in Davis: of the house they shared with their married friends, and music playing as the women cooked barefoot, and smoking grass at the kitchen table, or maybe Evelyn's parents coming by with covered dishes and funny stories. Davis was fun. She wasn't so uptight in Davis, was she? He catches sight of the Mary Jane across the yard and is hopeful.

'Want to get high?'

'*No, I do not* want to get high. Is that all you ever think of?'

'Sorry. I just thought … if it makes you feel better …'

Evelyn laughs, a snapping-cold sound. 'Has it ever occurred to you that maybe I don't *want* to feel better?' Before he can say anything else, she's pressing the sheets into his arms and slipping her hand into his trouser pocket, so sinuous he doesn't know whether to be frightened or aroused. 'Take these and give me the car keys. I want to go for a drive.'

'I don't know, Evelyn …'

But she's already jangling the keys in the air and giving him one of her dirty looks. 'A week in this damn town and you already think women can't drive? *Salut*, Leonard.'

And with a flounce of her dress and a slam of the gate, she's out of the yard, and he's still holding the sheets, and then he's hearing the thump of the car door and the rumbling of the engine and the screeching of the tires and nothing. He listens to the silence. He hears a mewling and looks around to see a white cat near the Mary Jane. 'Here, kitty kitty,' Lenny says, but the cat won't come, so he goes inside and takes off his shirt and pours a saucer of milk and scoffs two brownies without thinking, and by the time the milk is being lapped up he's already feeling regret.

How is it that things are always changing so quickly from good to bad? Has it always been this way or only since he's had a woman in his life? Is it this way with all women or only *his* wife? Lenny drinks some milk. He thinks deep thoughts: how perfectly round and white the milk looks in the mug, how white that cat was, how he's more truly himself when things are good with Evelyn, and less himself when things are bad.

Lenny smokes. It's a bad idea in the long run, he knows, but he also knows that it'll make him feel better in the short term and more like himself. He switches on the TV. He feels his mind slide into that more comfortable place — detached, but wiser, more empathic. Bobby Kennedy isn't dead yet. It's sad and bewildering what happened, but not that surprising; similar things are happening all the time. Lenny remembers how when Martin Luther King was shot Evelyn came home from her TA job distraught. 'There's no hope,' she had said dramatically. 'I wish I was dead.' And yet, she had let him hug her, and they had gone to a candlelit vigil where Reverend Burne spoke, and had sat in her parents' kitchen until late, talking about the world and how there was still hope after all.

Lenny wonders why Evelyn couldn't have just called her parents this time.

He tries not to think of Evelyn driving alone; of the scenic, winding roads in and out of the valley, and how the walls around him are getting darker. He lies back on the sofa. He thinks instead of the summer before, driving down to Mexico; giant rocks in the sea, her bright dresses and her hair still with the bangs, and how good the music was the whole time — 'Incense and Peppermints', 'Somebody to Love', 'Happy Together'.

There's no hope. I wish I was dead.

The white cat doesn't come inside, though Lenny wishes it would. He closes his eyes and sees the white cat, white sheets, white sails, or are they black sails? He opens his eyes and the walls are black. He is trapped by the walls, and by knowing time has passed, but not how much time. Where is she? Evelyn?

Lenny realizes he is hungry.

Lenny is glad to be hungry, since it means time has passed since he ate the hash brownies, and Evelyn will probably be home soon. Lenny is terrified to be hungry, since it means time has passed, and Evelyn should be home already. Lenny imagines Evelyn buying them take-out somewhere, like a regular young wife who hasn't figured things out yet. He imagines the keys jangling at the door, a smell of fried food.

He is only imagining.

If the phone were to ring, Lenny doesn't think he'd be able to get up and answer it. If too much time were to pass, he doesn't think he'd be able to get up and call the cops or Evelyn's parents. His heart hurts, and his eyes. He tries in earnest to close his eyes, to concentrate only on the good feelings radiating through his body, and he does, and he sleeps, and when he awakes it's to a sudden sense of weight and whiteness, like a ghost walking through him or that cat landing on his chest … But in fact, it's Evelyn kneeling before him with folded arms and eager hands and her face close to his.

'*Oh*, Lenny,' she says. 'I've just met the most wonderful group of people!'

6.

'I was unhappy in my marriage: young, isolated, lonely, oh so desperately lonely! Intimacy, communication, these were things I never knew. Never! My husband, he just didn't love me. There was something so wrong between us, we were living a lie, I couldn't understand it. If you saw him before, what a gentleman, dancing all night, flowers, you name it! I felt like the luckiest woman on earth. And then, wowee, it was like a different person! Wouldn't talk, wouldn't touch me, wouldn't except, well, late at night, if he'd been drinking …'

Officer Eugene Luce has heard this story many times, but it's still hard to know how to take it. Hang his head in shame? Hold it high, for all to see? He settles for sitting up straight, hands clasped and shoulders squared. With the shooting of Martin Luther King and now that new Kennedy, attendance has boomed, more black folks and hippy-dippy youngsters than ever, and being the cause of Joya's misery doesn't feel so good with all those new eyes looking on.

'We had children, one after another. Sons, two perfect sons! They shoulda been my happiness. But, Lord, I was so alone! Every time they cried, I blamed myself. I had … thoughts. They were so little, I thought, if I just put something in their food or, y'know, left the oven on. I thought, heck, it could be *painless*.'

Luce's sons, Roger and Danny, are nowhere to be seen; off flirting with girls from Oakland, no doubt. But his daughters are at his side: tomboy Bobbi and pretty Dot, both ash-blond with freckles on their noses, only Bobbi with his big nose instead of Joya's cute pert one. He passes a hand over the nearest silky blond head, Dot's, and she smiles at him placidly, then turns back to her mother's histrionics. Daughters, they're easier than sons.

28

'*Those were the thoughts I was having.* I was pregnant again and *those were my thoughts.* I was so goshdarn miserable, I couldn't see another way. Till you showed us, Father.'

Through her tears, Joya is smiling radiantly, and, thirty-odd pounds aside, she hasn't changed much from that fresh-faced, worshipful blonde who thought he was the man of her dreams. Did he ever dream of her, someone like her? Well … no. But she was small and soft and looked good in pink, knew how to waltz and jitterbug and flutter her lashes like she was having a pleasant seizure. A virgin, too. How was he to know it wouldn't all work out in time?

'Father, you showed us another way. You showed us our piddly little selfish lives. I was so selfish, Father. So caught up in my petty misery, I didn't spare a thought for the suffering of my brothers and sisters. I deserved every scrap of loneliness in my life. But you forgave me. You forgave us! You showed us, Father, how to open our hearts to love.'

Here, Luce's wife looks around the tent, white and peaked as the hoods of Luce men who came before him. Uncle Hugh, his mother's brother, had kept a photograph on proud display of himself atop a horse in full Klan regalia, looking like a cross between a ghost and a fairytale knight. 'Love of fellow man,' Joya continues. 'Nobody embodies this so completely as you, Father. No people were ever so loving as these people here. We are so thankful, Father, to be here today with our beautiful brothers and sisters!'

It's true, they are indeed loving people, applauding Joya with a loud cracking like Midwestern thunder. Applauding Luce as he rises from his fold-out chair to meet her. There is still a target on his back. He is a tall body and a short haircut and years of emotional neglect, but he's a changed man, surely they can see that. He holds out a large hand and Joya slips her smaller one into it, steps down from the stage with a smile to rival Doris Day: gum-pellet teeth, orange chipmunk cheeks, hat like a dollop of strawberry ice cream.

All eyes on him, Luce takes his wife in his arms, kisses her long and deep.

Lenny didn't think his first week in Evergreen Valley could get much weirder, but trippy things are always happening in tents. Grown men and women crying into microphones, hugging each other, clapping and bopping along to songs not at all like church songs — 'Glory of Love', 'Oh, Freedom!', 'Turn, Turn, Turn'. There are teenagers in blue singing onstage, white and black teenagers, which is another weird thing for Lenny, who hasn't mixed with black people the way Evelyn's family has. But trippiest of all is the man who bursts on the scene as suddenly as an A-bomb, a handsome black-haired man with a voice like moonshine.

'*That's him*,' Evelyn whispers, touching Lenny's arm.

After that, Evelyn doesn't say anything, and neither does Lenny, since listening to the black-haired man is like listening to rock music turned way up. Lenny feels alive listening to the black-haired man, and also like there's a bomb ticking somewhere on his body. The black-haired man is talking about Vietnam. He's talking about the Bible, 'thou shalt not kill' and young men taught to murder by the US government, Bobby Kennedy murdered, napalm, fear, all the things that make Lenny's heart beat rabbit-like. He's talking fast and croony-slow and up and down and all around, and yeah, a bit like a black person, Lenny can't help noticing, though he isn't black. And now and then someone in the crowd hollers in agreement, warlike cries that make the back of Lenny's neck prickle.

'Mmm-hmm!'

'Damn right!'

'Amen, Father!'

It's a trip to be in this place on a Sunday morning, but whether it's a good trip or a bad trip, Lenny doesn't know. He looks at Evelyn, as if he might find the answer in her face: eyes glazed, skin dewy and flushed. Her white hands are clasped over the tapestry purse in her lap, yet its swirly patterns aren't speaking to Lenny today, for after all he's completely sober, sitting in the uncomfortable chair in his uncomfortable church clothes and listening to the black-haired man preaching.

'Father loves you! *I* love you! And, in this spirit of love, I want you to close your eyes and open your minds. Open yourself to receive this loving remedy!'

Again, Lenny looks to Evelyn. She purses her lips and flutters her eyelashes down, so pretty and peaceful he'd rather keep looking at her than receive the loving remedy. But he closes his eyes.

'You must open yourself to love. You must not be afraid. Brothers and sisters, nothing can harm you here. I won't let it.'

And it's funny, but without even trying, Lenny already feels less afraid. Not a bad trip. Not a bad man, this black-haired man, speaking as if from the depths of Lenny's consciousness a name he doesn't know, but a musical name, a woman's name, 'Phyllis'.

'Sister Phyllis … You been suffering. An enormous stiffness in your joints, so that even the smallest movement brings you agony. Can't even bend your knees, sweetheart? Phyllis, do you dare — will you rise for us? Stretch out your limbs?'

Lenny is dimly relieved when the woman called Phyllis stutters, 'Y-yes Father,' and when, through a slatting of eyelashes, he sees her shadowy form rise. The black-haired man says, 'Mmmm,' and then, quietly, 'I love you, sister. The people love you. They're sending loving thoughts your way. How does that feel?'

'Ah!'

'Can you move, sister? Can you move without pain?'

'Ah … Father … Yes, Father!'

'Show us, Sister Phyllis. Move your arms and legs together.'

Lenny widens his eyes to see Phyllis pumping her doughy arms and legs like a gingerbread figure magically animated. Should she be moving like that? Should anyone be moving like that? There's a loud flutter of applause. Someone shouts, 'Hallelujah!' and Lenny is embarrassed. The black-haired man shouts, 'Hallelujah!' too, like he knows it's a corny thing but saying it anyway. Then he smiles down at Phyllis, who's still moving, dancing almost, and tells the crowd, 'She move damn fine for a honky, don't she?' and then, out of nowhere, a young black guy comes forward and takes Phyllis's hand and starts doing a jazzy little two-step with her, and the black-haired man shouts, 'Yeah-hh!', and Evelyn laughs sweetly.

Evelyn *laughs*.

Lenny looks at his wife, waits for her to make that rare sweet sound again, but she only smiles until the dancing stops and the black-haired man holds up a palm. 'Peace. Close your eyes, darlings. It's time to meditate. Meditate on the love that surrounds you.'

Evelyn closes her eyes again, and Lenny wonders what it is about the black-haired man that makes her so soft and trusting. He wonders if maybe it's that the black-haired man is handsome, but of course Evelyn has been around handsome guys, tramped around campus with a whole string of them, and never lost her sharp edges. It's something else — something Lenny feels as well when he closes his eyes, like there are no walls between him and the black-haired man. And he's guessing others feel the same, the way the black-haired man keeps reaching into the dark and pulling out things he has no way of knowing.

'Brother … Cecil. You been short of breath, wheezing, a sensation in your chest like crackling fire …'

'Sister … Thelma. You got spots in your eyes. Can't hardly see for all them spots moving 'round your eyes, big dark leopard spots …'

'Sister … Diane. You been hearing a thump-thump sound from the engine of the red Volvo …'

'Brother … Leonard …'

Leonard: a name Lenny still gets called sometimes by his father, by older relatives seen once a year, by people behind desks and people wearing gloves and people holding clipboards. An icy name, but intimate as having his chest palpated, urinating in a plastic cup, being naked all day in a room full of other naked young men who don't want to go to war. *His* name, insofar as he's a human male with human parents who named him in a hospital twenty-two years ago.

'Brother … Leonard. You got yourself a garden. Lush garden. Planted l'il something in that garden. Brother, you know what plant I'm saying?'

If Lenny is 'Brother Leonard', does that mean he has to open his eyes? Stand up and speak like those other people? His face is hot and his tongue tingly and thick in his mouth. Is the black-haired man a good man or a bad man, looking into Lenny and telling the whole crowd what he sees?

'Don't be ashamed, Brother. I ain't judging. Nobody here — we don't judge our brothers and sisters. Open your eyes, friend.'

Slowly, Lenny blinks his eyes open.

'I ain't judging, brother. I care about you *deeply*. Sensitive, peace-loving soul you got. Dove's soul. Ain't nobody here wanna see you imprisoned, which is why, gotta tell you, friend … Where you at, friend?'

Lenny is aware of the black-haired man looking in his direction through the flashy-dark sunglasses. The black-haired man seems tall to Lenny, and maybe sort of dangerous. Lenny shifts in his chair. He wishes he was somewhere else, back at the white house on Vine Street. Or Davis. This time of day in Davis, they'd be sleeping off their hangovers, or getting ready for Sunday lunch with Evelyn's parents.

'Brother Leonard, you safe here, but I seen — I foresee great trouble for you. 'Less you act soon. Let me look upon you.'

Lenny has a sudden urge to cry, or to be a soldier without thoughts or feelings. Soldiers at least know how to stand to attention. A surge of heat runs up from his belly to his throat, and he finds himself rising on jelly-legs; not a soldier at all, unless a soldier who's been napalmed.

'I see you, brother. I see where you at and where you been. Trouble with the law. You had a small taste already, last week when the highway patrolman stopped you?'

The cop. Almost Lenny had forgotten about that cop, leaning so close with the hot breath.

'I seen that. Like I seen there's trouble in your garden. Great sorrow gonna come from that garden, gonna tear you from your pretty white house. Mm-hm, mm-hm. *Unless . . .*'

Here the black-haired man lets out his breath, low and whooshing, as if the thought of Lenny's pain truly does pain him. The black-haired man loves Lenny; somehow there's no doubt about this. Loves him like a father, and maybe more than a father, for wouldn't Lenny's father disown him if he knew of the marijuana plant? Wouldn't Lenny's father be mortified if he could see him standing here, trembling and pink and tears stinging his eyes and wanting only to do what he's told, as long as it means keeping the white house and Evelyn?

'Only one thing for you, brother,' the black-haired man says. 'You gotta go into the garden and dig it up. Dig it *all* up.'

7.

There's only one name on their lips, and that name is Jim Jones. Moving among his people in the happy after-church hours, and eating from paper plates, and drinking from paper cups — sweet, swirly fruit punch that stains her mouth pink. Watching the sun sink lazy and gold into the hills, and stars winking out of the evening blue, and other people's children dashing after fireflies. *He is a father to so many. He works tirelessly. There is not a creature on this earth too small and insignificant for his love.* And later, packing themselves into the bright station wagon, leaving behind the flapping white tent, it's his name beating in their blood.

Jim Jones.

Jim Jones.

Jim Jones.

They go to the garden together. They go barefoot, under the big country moon. They go to the dirt and jungle-like green and he digs and she watches. She watches until he's finished digging, and when he smiles at her and holds up the wasted Mary Jane, she smiles back. It is the second summer of their loving. He is the same boy she married, the same blue-eyed boy, and she is the same girl, but this is the new life. This is the beautiful life, and in this life they will never be alone again.

Black Is the Color of My True Love's Hair

1.

Evelyn Lynden isn't in love with Jim Jones. Though he is the most brilliant man she has ever met, the most generous, the most dynamic. Though she likes the way his voice sounds, and the way he looks, and his tender way with children and animals and the elderly. Though she thinks about him when he isn't around — things he has said and things she might say to him, about religion and politics and even her most private hopes and dreams and fears. Though she thinks about him more than she thinks about her own husband in fact, her first thought waking up and last thought going to sleep some nights. Evelyn isn't in love with Jim Jones. It doesn't even occur to her that she might be in love with Jim Jones.

Except ... it *does* occur to her. Early on, within their first week of meeting, in some secret part of her that doesn't speak but thinks and frets and understands that she has never been content in her relationships with men. He is a minister. She is a minister's daughter. Of course this is significant, as the fact that he is married with children is significant. Evelyn has seen Jim Jones's wife around Peoples Temple enough to know that she's attractive in a wan, rustic sort of way, and always well-coiffed and well-dressed and well-liked by the people, some of whom call her 'Mother'. Evelyn is aware of Jim Jones's children, too, without knowing their names or how many of them there are, only that they are different races and mostly adopted. All these things are significant. All these things combine to reassure Evelyn, in that secret not-quite-conscious part of her mind, that she isn't in love with Jim Jones.

And because Evelyn isn't in love with Jim Jones, there's no reason why she shouldn't think of him, speak of him, praise him as she brushes her hair and the fan beats and Lenny sits up shirtless in bed, reading a paperback. Lenny, who agrees with all her praise; Lenny, who looks sweet and soft and clean; Lenny, who she's happy to fool around with on a beating-hot Sunday night after setting down her hairbrush, even with Jim Jones still on her mind. Going to him and laying her hands on his hairy boy's chest, touching noses like a pair of cubs, recoiling inwardly at how predictably he gets hard and sets aside his book. *The Moon Is A Harsh Mistress*. She'd hoped he'd read more serious things now that he's been off drugs for a whole month, but what does it matter? The fan is loud. She's thinking of Sundays, church potlucks, grinding herbs in the mortar and pestle, hips grinding. Baking something.

'I think I'll bake a cake tomorrow,' Evelyn says, and when Lenny says 'Mmm', she noses his cheek and elaborates, 'You've been clean a month now. I think we should thank Jim somehow.' Feeling the catch in her voice, breathy and false, yet also the whirring fan and Lenny's dumb lust and how the dark hairs prickle with an electricity that's all their own. Evelyn isn't in love with Jim Jones. Evelyn isn't in love. She's just very, very thankful.

Thankful for the sun and thankful for the valley and thankful to be pedaling through smooth blue shadows past vineyards, as if she isn't in America at all but the south of France. The Haut-Médoc with Jean-Claude, springtime, just before they broke up. She had already known that she would break up with Jean-Claude yet had enjoyed the weekend anyhow, cycling from one village to the next, glancing down at her engagement ring and thinking it was a shame she had to give it up, really a shame. *Je regrette, mais je ne peux pas t'epouser, Jean-Claude.* But she is happier now, more truly and deeply happy, because it is not simply the selfish happiness of loving a Frenchman and planning a life with him, far from the ills of American society. She is living beautifully and meaningfully here in Evergreen Valley, and if she thinks of France now, it's only as a barometer for her current happiness.

There's nothing special about the evergreens near the Jones property, but Evelyn recognizes them somehow, the morning sun soaking their foliage like champagne. Her bike slows; the front wheel wobbles. Then the dirt path and the hump of the white tent like a mountaincap. She has baked a cake for Jim Jones, but if Jim isn't around, she will leave it with his wife, Rosaline. Or she will leave it on the doorstep of the parsonage with a thank-you note, something lighthearted yet courteous that's signed from both her and Lenny. A note could not be misconstrued. *Dear Jim and family: thank you for making our first month in the valley so beautiful …*

Only, Evelyn won't need to write a note. She knows this as soon as she sees the figures of the three men standing by the tent. The men are black and white and in-between. They are making rectangles with their hands and prodding the earth with their feet and frowning over blueprints. They are Assistant Pastor Isaiah Bellows and Officer Eugene Luce and Reverend Jim Jones, but the last is the only one she really sees: Western-style blue denim shirt, blue-black hair, sunglasses. Her insides clench. She alights.

The sun hurts her eyes. The men look up, then at each other.

Sometimes Evelyn thinks there are too many men in the world. Gene Luce, for instance, standing there in brown, just the type to think a uniform makes a man. She sees the familiar way he scans her body, the deliberate way he looks away. She knows a chauvinist pig when she sees one, and doesn't at all regret being a bitch to him that day on the highway. But she's here today as an ambassador of 'Mr and Mrs Leonard Lynden', and she won't be deterred. She rolls the bike forward, drily raises an eyebrow.

'I didn't realize I'd be riding into the scene of a crime.'

There is a blue-skied silence. Then Jim Jones laughs, and his laugh is the contagious kind, high-pitched and a little manic. Isaiah Bellows rustles his blueprints and chortles, skin furrowing beyond the rims of his thick spectacles, and even Luce smiles sheepishly into his shirtfront. Evelyn parks the bike and swiftly takes the moment to lift the cake from her basket, a round shape covered by a blue check dish towel. The men's eyes follow the shape.

'What have we here?' says Isaiah.

'Mmm-mm,' says Luce.

'What the hell is this?' says Jim Jones, once she has placed the cake in his hands. He mugs at the dish towel, like he couldn't possibly know what is underneath it, like he has no reference point for round shapes covered in dish towels. He mugs at Evelyn, and her heart dashes against her chest like a rock to a baby's head.

'I wanted to thank you — *Lenny and I*,' Evelyn corrects herself. 'We're so thankful for everything you've done for us this past month.'

'This got nuts in it?' Jim Jones lifts the tea towel and sniffs.

'It's a French almond cake.'

'Almonds from *France*?'

'They're from the market,' Evelyn says, not with her usual laugh, but a high, tinkling thing. 'I was just thinking yesterday: it's a month now since Lenny last got high. This probably doesn't sound so impressive, but I've never known him to go more than a few days.'

'Ain't nothin', baby.' Jim Jones sniffs the cake again, smirks, and passes it on to Luce without a word. Then, with the suddenness of rising water, he takes her in his arms, kisses her cheek, and leaves her breathless. 'Thank *you*. But, ah, you don't need to go baking me no cakes. I mean, you got more to offer than that. Having you here, that's sweeter. Huh?'

At that, Jim Jones lets her go and motions cordially at Isaiah's blueprints.

'You come at the right time, darlin'. Tent days are *over*. Ask these gentlemen, they'll tell you. Isaiah?'

'These ain't final,' Isaiah says carefully. 'You sure, Jim?'

'I thought we weren't announcing it 'til Sun-dee,' says Luce.

Jim Jones wets his lips. 'Show Evelyn.'

And so the tall gaunt black man unfolds the blueprints, and the tall potbellied white man in uniform holds them steady. Evelyn steps forward, feels a hot shiver of excitement as Jim Jones touches the small of her back, speaks close to her ear. 'Now, this's only the beginning …'

When Lenny returns from the mental hospital that night, his wife is exactly as he last saw her — sifting flour in the kitchen, as if she's been chained there all day. But of course she hasn't. Of course he has no way of knowing where or how she spends her days, or why she looks so flushed, except for what she tells him. Thankfully, she seems to tell him everything.

'I'm making *pissaladière*. I'm only just making the dough now, so you're going to have to starve for a couple of hours, unless you want those grapes over there.' Lenny looks at the grapes; they look small and unappetizing. 'They aren't very good, but Jim is tearing down some of his vines, so it was either that or have them go to waste.'

Lenny plucks a grape dutifully. 'Why is Jim tearing down vines?'

At this, Evelyn beams. 'You're lucky I'm telling you this; the announcement isn't until Sunday.' She rolls the dough into a ball and plops it into the bowl, stretches over a layer of Saran wrap. 'Construction starts on a new Temple building next week. I saw blueprints!'

'Oh.' Lenny eats another grape. He wishes Evelyn was cooking something other than her French pizza thing, which always takes too long and isn't very filling. 'No more tent?'

'Honestly, Lenny, do you really think Jim Jones belongs in a tent? He could be in Congress.' Evelyn slips the bowl into the fridge. 'The amazing thing is, he's doing it all on his own terms, no outside funding. And he wants to be involved in every stage of the process, down to the bricklaying. He really is a maverick.'

'Yeah.'

'It isn't just going to be some elitist place of worship either. He's planning a clothing bank, a kitchen, offices. A swimming pool, for the children ...'

Evelyn talks some more, a *lot* more, and with great enthusiasm, about the building-to-be. At Davis, it had been easier for Lenny to keep track of his wife's enthusiasms, yet now she is unconstrained by a curriculum, he never quite knows what he will come home to. In the past weeks, he has seen her doing everything from conjugating French verbs to writing letters for illiterate black seniors. But there is generally always something cooking or about to be cooked, and she generally seems pleased to see him, and generally they're having more sex than ever, now that there are no housemates or in-laws to contend with. And if she talks a lot about Jim Jones and Peoples Temple, he understands it's because these things make her happy, and because she likes talking more than he does. So he listens.

While listening, Lenny takes off his white uniform and folds it up neatly, causing Evelyn to raise an eyebrow. Another thing Lenny likes about living alone with Evelyn is that he doesn't have to wear much if he doesn't want to. Lenny likes being shirtless, especially now it's the middle of summer. Lenny likes being shoeless. Lenny would like to spend a day shirtless and shoeless by the water with Evelyn, like on their honeymoon swimming in the Sea of Cortez, or just after their honeymoon, lounging by the poolside of his parents' mansion in the Berkeley Hills. 'We should go swimming sometime,' he says, as soon as there's a break in Evelyn's patter, and she slits her eyes at him, for of course this has nothing to do with anything she's been saying. He notices for the first time since coming home that the bridge of her nose is sort of red, dotted with tiny freckles; that her cheeks have flame-like patches; that her arms and even her clavicles seem to be blushing. She didn't look this way in the morning, did she? How does she spend her days? It strikes him that he should listen more closely.

'Well,' Evelyn says carefully, 'I guess we *could* go to Lake Mendocino this weekend. We might not get a chance to go again this summer, with all our Saturdays on construction crew. At least, not together, anyway.'

'Work … Saturdays?'

'Yes, Lenny, *Saturdays*. My God, do I need to start sending you memos?' Evelyn shakes her head, but his shirtless chest seems to distract her from being truly mad. 'It's a minimal commitment. All the able-bodied members will be doing it, Jim included, and he's obviously busier than anyone.' She smiles. 'I hope you listen to the construction crew leaders better than this. You don't want to, I don't know, cut off a hand or something.'

2.

They pack the station wagon and head to the lake around noon that Saturday, with their hats and sunglasses, their towels and books, a basket full of sunscreen and picnic foods, and it's all very *A Summer Place* in Evelyn's mind, very lightweight and bourgeois, and reminds her intensely of the weekend she lost her virginity in Santa Cruz. That was the year she was living away from her parents, with family friends in Salinas, finishing twelfth grade where she began it rather than following her father to the next parish. She was almost eighteen. The boy was called Percy. She has to grapple for the name, but it's there. *Percy.* His face isn't. Only that he had dimples and was good-looking in a bland sort of way. He was someone else's friend on the weekend trip. A whole group of them went, white girls and white boys with wicker bags and convertibles. He courted her for a whole day, up close and from a distance; smiled at her when he caught a football and sat with her at lunch and asked her questions about her family and interests. Later, when it was dark and everyone a little drunk and the two of them walked to the sand dunes, probably neither of them was expecting anything more than some heavy petting. She remembers lying on her back. How soft the sand was. How dark the sky. Looking past Percy at the stars and thinking, *Am I really too good for this? Am I really so pure?*

It was giddy and hot and hurt a bit, but it didn't make her bleed. She wondered about that afterward, whether there was something wrong with her for not bleeding, something insensitive and unfeminine. She and Percy stayed on good terms for about a month and went out a couple of times, to a concert and to a dance, but both times she had treated him with blithe friendliness, like a visiting cousin. By the end of the second date, he had been completely subdued, and never called her back for a third, though he said he would. A little while later, she found out he was dating another girl, and the news left her feeling disproportionately rebuffed, used-up, so that she wept in private and swore off boys for the rest of the summer. Then she was a freshman in college and then JFK was dead, and it all seemed connected somehow to the same misery, which stretched across her life as stickily intricate as a spider web.

Evelyn sits in the evergreen shade with her book. She won't get sunburned again. She watches Lenny bounce to the lip of the lake, wade in to his knees, and look back at her, then take to the water. The next time she looks up, he's just a dot in the middle of the lake, near the boats. If he were drowning, would she notice? She returns to her book, and later sees Lenny sitting in the shallows, trailing his fingers through the water like it's a rare substance, apparently deep in thought.

It isn't *love* when two animals of the same species sniff each other out and mate successfully, but it's seen as a good thing nonetheless. Evelyn and Lenny are of the same species. Percy, too, had been of the same species, and every other young man she went out with and withheld sex from between her freshman year and her exchange year in Bordeaux. There was a certain dry pleasure in withholding what she knew to be good and easily obtainable; in going to the trouble of putting on nylons and ratting her hair and dancing in high heels, and then giving absolutely nothing. In her own way, Evelyn lived ascetically, though she 'had fun' and 'dated a lot'. She sublimated her desires. She got good grades. She had many female friends, who she talked with incessantly about women's rights and whose menstrual cycles fell into sync with hers. And perhaps once every six months, she would drink a little more than usual and let some quiet, attractive fellow take her home and tell no one about it, with the hope that he wouldn't either. For though she wasn't ashamed, it would've looked bad for the daughter of the minister-on-campus to have a 'reputation'.

It would've looked bad for the daughter of the minister-on-campus to be anything but what she appeared to be.

She is reading Camus. She is wearing a black bathing suit, with full black briefs and a black bra. She likes the way reading in French makes her mind feel impenetrable, and the time lapses between one scene and the next. Lenny is there, and then he is not. The trail up from the beach is empty, and then there are two teenagers walking along it; a boy and a girl, short-legged in shorts, with towels slung over their shoulders. Evelyn looks a little closer and sees that the girl has straight black hair and golden skin like an Asian; *is* an Asian; is probably, on that assumption, Temple, and now that she thinks of it, may actually be one of Jim Jones's children. The boy and girl seem to sense her gaze and look up, and the boy calls out from the trail, and Evelyn waves and wonders about Jim, if he is near. She feels a stab of desire, involuntary as a fart, and is embarrassed. She reads some more Camus, and then Lenny is on dry land, toweling himself off and wearing Wayfarers.

'Who were those people?' he says.

'Temple people, I think.'

Lenny nods and shows no further curiosity. He sits on his towel and interprets the title of her book aloud, 'Happy Death', then looks proud of himself for understanding French. He plays with the grass and after a couple of minutes, he says, 'The water was good.' And, not for the first time, Evelyn thinks to herself that *this* is the man she is married to.

Even though the thought of running into Jim Jones and his family recurs throughout the afternoon, it's still a shock for Evelyn to see the messy, many-colored lot of them, loading up a big blue Pontiac in the syrupy end-of-day light. Boys, maybe four of them, all chirping happily, and the smallest of them a black boy, very cute, following after Jim Jones, and Jim Jones with a dog under one arm, a decent-sized sheepdog she wouldn't have thought could be carried like that. Other dogs, too, one of them nosing an empty Coke can, and collapsible sun-chairs, a collapsed umbrella. Jim Jones notices the dog with the can and frowningly says something to one of the white boys, who trots over dutifully and takes the can away and places it in the trash. The teenagers from before are there, too, and what about Jim Jones's wife, Rosaline? At first, Evelyn thinks she must be absent, but then she notices a plain-pale face with cat-eye sunglasses, a sleeveless blouse, a hive of faded reddish-blond hair, a homey female voice running like a creek beneath the commotion. *Why is he with* her? The thought comes unbidden and painful, and Evelyn understands that she's a terrible person and Rosaline isn't, that's why.

'Hey, look,' Lenny says from by the trunk he's just prised open. 'That's Jim.'

Evelyn turns to her beautiful shirtless boy-husband with a smile she hopes is nonchalant and nods, so her still-damp ponytail bobs. Her black bathing suit, though mostly dry, is patched with dampness, and the man's shirt she's wearing over it has two comical dark spots where her nipples are. She passes the basket and towels to Lenny and he puts them in the trunk. A breeze shakes the evergreens. Evelyn shivers. Lenny slams the trunk, comes up beside her, and puts an arm around her shoulder.

Together they watch Jim Jones and his family.

After a while, Evelyn becomes conscious that they've been watching too long, and that Lenny wants to speak to Jim Jones as well, but is feeling the same shyness she is. Lenny likes Jim, she knows: likes him like a foreigner likes Mickey Mouse; has said he is 'cool, like a cowboy or Elvis'. She turns to Lenny with a helpless shrug, and they laugh and wordlessly agree to get in the station wagon without making themselves known, and, fastidiously, they shut the doors and wind down the windows and reverse.

But … Maybe it's the fact that they have to pass the Pontiac anyway, or maybe it's that most of Jim Jones's family are already in it, only the teenagers and Jim still chatting, and the black boy on Jim's shoulders, and one smiling dog. Or maybe it's Jim himself, how good and dazzling yet somehow reassuringly normal he looks, barefoot and wearing shorts, nice tanned feet, nice tanned muscular legs. Evelyn feels a spike of giddy entitlement and, without really thinking about it, she leans out the window and purrs, '*Just look at that bourgeois family.*'

Jim Jones turns, grins hugely, doesn't miss a beat.

'Lousy sonofabitchin' longhairs, get the hell outta here!'

3.

Their life has come to revolve around Peoples Temple in strange, small ways. Friends from before are 'non-Temple friends' and their calls not always returned. Food Evelyn makes is often 'Temple food', for potlucks or midweek meetings, or sometimes cakes or cookies to be sold. When they get in the station wagon to go anywhere, there is always three minutes of meditation first, and the one time Lenny forgets to do this he almost runs over that white cat. When Evelyn is offered a position instructing girls' P.E. at Evergreen High, in addition to the French teaching job she secured even before graduation, she comes home starry-eyed and gushing, 'I can't wait to finally be earning some real money for the Temple!' When Lenny is told of the 'groovy night classes' Jim Jones teaches a couple of towns over, he doesn't like the idea of being away from Evelyn, but she says he *should* go, says it's important not to neglect his mind with all the days spent with crazy people and he'll no doubt learn a lot, can come home and tell her what he's learned and save her the trouble of going herself. So on Thursdays, Lenny packs a change of clothes and drives thirty minutes from the mental hospital to the high school in Moontown, and for two hours or usually more, he'll sit in the over-filled classroom and try to follow as Jim Jones zips from topic to topic: Mao Zedong, the Spanish Inquisition, reincarnation, the execution of the Rosenbergs. Mostly Lenny likes the classes and the people in them — at least half of whom are Temple and the rest hippies or rednecks from all over the county — but the long hours are difficult and he has trouble articulating anything he learns to Evelyn and on these nights they never have sex.

Saturdays are no longer days of leisure but Temple days as much as Sundays, days for Temple construction work, which isn't easy for a

Berkeley Hills boy unaccustomed to physical labor and not so good at taking instructions. The old Temple people from Indiana are often common people, who've made their livings on farms or in factories, and are quick to shove Lenny away or take the tools right out of his hands when he does something wrong, and will sometimes even cuss at him — folksy cusses like *for-pete's-sake* or *goshdarnit*, but their facial expressions mean, snarling.

Evelyn never seems to mess up. He sees her from a distance working and talking in an old shirt of his and wonders how she does it.

Late in July, Evelyn turns twenty-three, and Lenny is proud of his pretty smart wife, so grown-up, always growing. Her birthday is observed early as part of the Temple's communal July-births celebration, a barbecue after one of those hardworking Saturdays, but he would like to get her something nice. So he calls her parents in Davis and speaks for a long time with her mother, whose name is Margaret and who knows better than anyone the sorts of things Evelyn likes. They talk about books, blouses, a delicate but practical wristwatch so Evelyn can keep time when she starts teaching, but in the end, they agree on some earrings: Mexican silver like on their honeymoon, and with little dangling roses. When he describes them to Margaret, she says yes, silver roses, how Evelyn.

'I mean, they're lovely *of course*,' Evelyn says on the morning of her birthday, having unwrapped the tiny jewelry box, 'But I meant it when I said I don't want you wasting money on me. I'd rather help the Temple than accumulate material vanities.'

She proceeds to tell him emphatically not to get her anything for their first wedding anniversary in August, that she won't get *him* anything, and he feels hurt, disconcerted. Yet she does wear the earrings, seems to like them and touch them frequently, and looking at her bare neck and pinned hair, he thinks she is even more beautiful than when he used to see her around campus, walking around like a rare thing that he would never know.

'He *is* bright in his own way, it's just not a lot comes out and not a lot gets through.'

'Mmm-hmm. I seen that.' Jim Jones takes a sip of coffee, swirls it around his mouth, and swallows. 'Thing is, I think, he been *sheltered*. By privilege, parents, women. 'Course, I don't blame you. He got that sweetness, makes a woman protective. Just, ah, honey, don't be fooled into thinkin' you got all the power, on account of he depends on you. Male dependency, that's a form of chauvinism.'

'I never thought of it that way,' Evelyn says.

'You think on that, darlin'. I want you to think on that, 'cause it's my feeling ... Socialism ain't about weak takin' from strong. We all wanna be freethinking, striving individuals, workin' for the greater good, and Lenny can't be doin' that if he's dependent.'

'Perhaps I've been living in bad faith all this time.' Evelyn looks at her coffee.

'Hell, honey, I know you're tryin' hard to live the honest life. Meaningful life. Ain't easy. Hope you don't mind me askin' ... Man you with before Lenny, you love him better?'

'I ... didn't realize I had mentioned ...' Evelyn feels her cheeks burning — that characteristic sense of shame that always comes over her when anyone mentions Jean-Claude unexpectedly. 'I suppose I did, if romantic love is what you mean.' She sees Jim Jones frown and tries to explain herself. 'I was younger then, and it was a new world, and he was the first man of any substance I was, well, *with*. I was vulnerable, I think, to that kind of romantic attachment.'

'You were vulnerable.' Jim Jones chews over this fact and extrapolates quietly, 'You allowed yourself to be vulnerable, like never before. He was, uh, older?'

'Not very much older. Twenty-four. I was twenty. I was you-ng.' Evelyn's voice cracks queerly, and her face suddenly feels like it might shatter. She is still young.

'He taught me things, showed me things. He was a Marxist, and a very good lover.' Evelyn takes a deep breath. 'We read poetry ... French poetry. We only spoke French together. I spoke like a child when I met him, but then I was fluent and then it was over. I could have married him.'

There's much more Evelyn could say about Jean-Claude, but already she suspects she's said too much. Jim Jones is silent, staring somewhere behind her. She has bored him. Her problems are boring and insignificant and not real problems. She brushes her hand over the table and makes her voice clear and shallow. 'It would've been a very different life. But it's not the life I've chosen.'

At this, Jim Jones looks at her. He has his sunglasses tucked into his shirt pocket, and his eyes without them are very kind and very brown, almost Oriental. She likes his eyes. 'That vulnerability, made you love the Frenchman …' Jim Jones starts thoughtfully, then smiles like he's telling a joke and reaches across the table. Her hand. 'You keep that. You *need* that. Where you goin', this life you've chosen, you're gonna need to be vulnerable.'

Later, after they have risen from the table and he has kissed her, a visiting pastor's kiss by her ear, nothing more, and he has complimented her earrings — 'Them's nice roses there' — and she has thanked him again for the paperwork — really she likes it, she isn't suited to being a housewife, anything for the Temple that uses her mind before the summer is up — and after he is gone, and there's only the white emptiness of the house and empty white cups to be rinsed, cups that remind her of eggshells, and her hands on the cups, that hand he held, and her voice humming softly, a song she doesn't consciously choose but so appropriate: *Black, black, black is the color of my true love's hair, His lips are something wondr'ous fair …* And, yes, his hair is black, and, yes, she loves him truly. To the devil on her shoulder, she's smiling *yes*, thinking of the man who just left and smiling, for is it so bad to love him? To love this man so wondrous and black-haired? And anyway, she isn't serious in the thought, can dismiss it any moment, is a freethinking woman with free will. Dismissing it and drying her hands, she sees, outside the kitchen window, the garden where two months ago they were growing marijuana — two months is not a long time, two months is not true love. But love, *she* loves, she knows, and no angel to whisper otherwise, no punishing lightning bolt, only the garden, which somehow breaks her heart, and the white cups drying upside-down and her white hands on the dishtowel and a sudden muddled feeling in her brain, because of course it's true, of course she is, and there's no hope for her: she is in love with Jim Jones.

4.

Jean-Claude was twenty-four when Evelyn was twenty. He was a graduate student of economics, rabidly critical of the free market, pale-faced and pale-eyed when rabid, and capable of talking very fast, in sibilant tones that she found both distressing and sexy. Though his mind was rational, he liked poetry; he'd even had a couple of poems published, which he showed to her early on, wandering off while she read them and later only shrugging and saying, '*N'importe quoi*,' when she tried to talk about them. She didn't think much of his poems, perhaps didn't understand them, but she liked the other poets he read to her. Pressing her ear to the bones of his chest and listening to his voice, lazy and lovely and rumbly, reading Louis Aragon. He would play a harmonica sometimes when bored, and the sound of that had a similar effect on her. He would sometimes draw detailed building façades, craggy faces, including once the face of a vagrant he saw outside the Bordeaux-Midi, which was so sensitively rendered she found herself wishing she'd kept it after they broke up.

It was a very painful breakup.

Jean-Claude was taller than her by nine inches. She felt small walking beside him. She felt small and special when he called her *Ève*, rhyming with *rêve*, and as if she could stumble and fail around him in ways she hadn't with others. When she didn't know the name of something, he provided it. When she came to his apartment hungry, he cooked. When she had a sore throat and went mute before the woman at the counter, he announced good-naturedly, '*Elle a mal à la gorge*,' and some beautiful orange lozenges had appeared, paid for from his own pocket. When she didn't understand a joke or some bit of slang and seemed excluded, he would explain in slower, simpler French, knowing she had a social aversion to speaking English.

She started having fragile, miraculous new thoughts in his language.

Jean-Claude smoked, like most French people. She sometimes did, too, in the beginning, but couldn't help feeling a little false and couldn't get over the sense that it was unhealthy. Like most French people, he liked wine. He was an atheist but had been brought up Catholic. He would take her to cathedrals or to look at religious art, like an urbanized farmboy who still knows how to milk a cow, and would prettily point out obvious things — *La Vierge Marie, Jean le Baptiste, la résurrection du Christ.* Like most French people, he punctuated his conversation with funny contemptuous puffs and splurts and growls, which she eventually learned to imitate.

He used dirty language often. His mind was often dirty.

Sometimes Jean-Claude's eyes were green and sometimes gray or blue. Sometimes he reminded her of a lynx and sometimes of a hawk and sometimes of a python. His face was often patchily unshaven, which she didn't like at first, but later loved. He was uncircumcised, which alarmed her as she mentally compared him to her high school boyfriend Elliot Goldberg, a Jew who had been too gloomy and prudish to sleep with her but whom she had once persuaded to undress in her bedroom while her parents were downstairs entertaining some people from her father's church. She had looked at Elliot for a long time then gone on her knees and tried to kiss him there, and he had told her fastidiously, '*Don't do that,*' and then she had stroked him once and he'd made a mess on her rug and gone home sulking like she'd done him a great wrong.

With Jean-Claude, Evelyn never had this problem.

They were lovers within three weeks of meeting, and she was irreparably in love within four. She liked making love. She liked to believe she was good at lovemaking, as she was good at everything else. She liked to look at the two of them in the mirror that shone across from his bed while making love. They always looked so beautiful together, even more than they did apart, like a pair of actors or very good-looking siblings. Once, Jean-Claude had noticed her looking, and he'd laughed and said, '*Oui, nous sommes les plus beaux amants,*' and it had been so perfect to hear it spoken.

We are the most beautiful lovers.

She was still the girl from the generous Methodist Church family, who could never accept the grace of God. She was still the girl who lost her virginity to a boy whose last name she didn't know as black waves broke somewhere close by. She was still the girl who, working one summer as a bellhop at a San Francisco hotel, had gone up to the room of a businessman who propositioned her, hoping it might cure her to be with a man her father's age. She was still the girl who since the age of fifteen had occasionally thought of killing herself. All of this was still true, yet seen as if looking down from the moon, and no longer painful to her, now that she was beautiful and somebody loved her.

She had been miserable and then she wasn't. She had been a house of mirrors and then she was a sun-filled room with views of lavender fields. Jean-Claude loved her, and the best thing was, he also seemed to know her, to know what she wanted, as American boys never did. For it wasn't all just poetry and lavender; he would refer to her body with crude names, comment on the way she smelled, whittle away at her with his tongue for what felt like hours then tell her she was a *putain* for wanting it so much. Once, she arrived at his apartment after a day of classes, looking windblown and plain, and had innocently asked what he wanted to do.

'*Je veux te violer*, ha-ha,' he said, laughing with perfect Gallic coldness.

And one day, in the February of 1966, he asked her to marry him and she said, '*Oui.*'

She said the thing that seemed most natural, and then retreated into herself like a mollusk, because the happiness was too raw. Jean-Claude, too, had seemed lost for words, shaken his head and smiled in a dazed fashion and said, '*Ah — bon!*' and patted her arm like an awkward male relative. After that, he'd paced and clapped his hands and said, '*Alors ...*' and looked at her as if she was a new toy he couldn't figure out how to play with, before going for his coat. She had tried to follow, but vehemently he told her, '*Non, non. Attends,*' and left the apartment. When he returned, he was very cool, with a cigarette dangling from his lips and many paper bags, and he cooked, and she helped him, and later some friends of his came by and urged them to get drunk.

She sat among his friends until late with his arm around her chair — the American minister's daughter who looked French, who could've passed for Jean-Claude's incestuous French sister, who had done such a good job of breaking free of her homeland.

Perhaps the doubt was with her already. In the time that Jean-Claude was gone, she had stared into the void, smiling. She had seen a slip of scrap paper with a series of call numbers, the word *'allumettes'* without context, a severe-looking man in profile. She had thought to herself, *The man who will be my husband did this*, and then simply, *My husband*. She had thought she was happy, but maybe it was only the absurd emptiness of the world.

They tried to call Evelyn's parents long-distance, but they weren't home — they were busy and popular people — and instead she spoke cryptically to her teenage sister Vicky: 'I have important news, but I shall send it in writing.' Jean-Claude, who was huddled in the phone booth with her, had then asked for the phone, and with endearing solemnity had told Vicky, 'Ev-Lynne, I like her very much,' before Evelyn snatched the phone back, laughing.

He was with her when she wrote the letter announcing her engagement, a letter that said things like: *This is the hardest letter I've ever had to write*, and *Jean-Claude treats me beautifully*, and *I am very happy living here in France*. Then the letter was sent and a cold feeling of security settled over her, as if she'd just cleaned the last speck of blood from a crime scene. She had resumed her wonderful French life, bragged to her American friends, dashed off brilliant essays, spoken to the university administration, dreamed, planned, read the newspapers. News about America was often upsetting, the unjust war that America was waging, US troops totaling 385,000 — but her life, wasn't that everything?

Evelyn's parents wrote back; they were happy for her, if this was the life she wanted. They asked for a photograph. They enclosed a generous check and a letter to Jean-Claude, welcoming him to the family. Jean-Claude only read the letter once before passing it back to her, but he had liked the check very much, said that she should write to her parents more often, and helped her spend most of it on records and leather goods. Other relatives wrote and were encouraging, with the exception of her great-aunt Gracie, who sent a six-page polemic denouncing the French as lazy, dirty, decadent, a nation of communists and sexual deviants. At the next dinner party, Evelyn stood in her black turtleneck with a wine glass in one hand and Aunt Gracie's letter in the other, provoking Jean-Claude's friends into squawks of red-faced laughter.

Yet Aunt Gracie's letter obsessed her. America obsessed her, without her fully realizing it. She found herself speaking often of her father's church work and being met with nonchalant French noises. She argued with Jean-Claude about organized religion, was irked by his pronouncement that all churches should be replaced by socialist collectives, and offended when he denounced all clergymen as opium-pushers. He saw that she was offended but made no apologies.

She met his large family, and found things to dislike about them. His mother refused to speak anything but English with her and was forever talking about Jean-Claude in an offhand, infantalizing manner: *Ee is only a boy, All men is same, Always ee must win ze argument*. His father was considerably older than his mother, quiet like her own, yet with nothing to say about the fascinating period of history surrounding Jean-Claude's birth except that the Germans were swine. His brothers were less attractive versions of him, hook-nosed and running to fat, with a tendency to get very drunk and play fight. His sisters were too young and pretty, prone to giggling over things she didn't understand, and she was disconcerted by his fondness for them; *she* was meant to be his incestuous French sister, no one else.

There were tones of Jean-Claude's voice that Evelyn got to know and dislike: a princely whine when speaking to his mother, which almost always resulted in more money; a high, schoolboy-ish laugh with his brothers; a faint American accent when he wished to mock her without being especially clever about it. She began being plagued by a sense of total anarchy when she imagined living with him forever. Many nights, she woke with her heart scrambling inside her, like a clawed creature wanting to get out.

They took their arguments into the bedroom. They had heated, apologetic sex that left her feeling smothered. More and more, she craved structure, her father's church, fundraising, volunteer work, the challenge of being kind to people she had little in common with. She convinced herself that she was a good person because she longed for these things. She started plotting the breakup, and did not think she was a bad person for letting Jean-Claude continue to cook for her and improve her vocabulary while she did so. She told the university that she would be returning to America.

On a warm day in June, she went to Jean-Claude's apartment and made love to him, knowing it would clear her mind and muddle his. Afterward, she had spoken her lines without expression: *Je ne peux pas t'epouser. Je ne t'aime pas. Tu n'es pas l'homme pour moi.* He had told her that he didn't believe her. She had said some more things — that she didn't want a life with him, had never loved him. No, he said, he didn't believe her, they were lovers, until his green-gray-blue eyes drew tears and his voice cracked. She had the impression of a python, a hawk, a lynx, but pitifully injured, and knew she had to finish the job. She took off her little ring and attempted to put her clothes on but he confiscated them, sat her on the bed in her underwear like a hostage, wept, stroked her, tried to jam the ring into her closed fist. '*Je ne t'aime pas*,' she said, over and over, and it gave her pleasure to say, the truth of it, almost holy, though she couldn't remember why she didn't love him or what there was in the world besides this love she was rejecting. *Je ne t'aime pas.* After a while, he had been too distraught to even weep, and she had taken the moment to stand up and dress and fix her hair. Her face was very composed; she did not in the least feel like crying. Somehow she became aware of Jean-Claude watching her in mute disbelief, shaking his head as she gave her hair a final pat, and she glanced at him coolly, and what he said next she'd remember always as more hateful for being said in English, not the language of their love.

'*Bitch*,' he said.

5.

If Lenny worries about Jim Jones visiting his wife when he isn't home, he doesn't worry for long. Evelyn is always ready to explain the reasons for the pair of used coffee cups, the newest pile of paperwork, why she hasn't started cooking yet. By the time she starts teaching in the fall, it has become so usual for them not to eat until eight or even later that he begins stopping some nights for French fries and cheeseburgers, eating them furtively in the car and worrying about stains on his white uniform, but if Evelyn notices she never says anything.

If Lenny is disappointed that Evelyn's work for the Temple doesn't let up by the end of summer, he doesn't let himself stay disappointed for long. Evelyn is doing *good work*: helping Sister Joya, the cop's wife, organize several letter-writing campaigns to county officials; helping Sister Diane, a social worker and an *actual lesbian*, put together an education package for juvenile delinquents; helping Sister Molly, a florid-faced medical secretary, maintain the Temple's membership files. Sometimes, Evelyn goes straight from her job at the high school to meetings with Temple ladies, and actually gets home later than Lenny, apologetic but happy, slipping off her heeled shoes, sighing about her long day.

If Lenny questions whether he is as happy as Evelyn, he never questions for long. Evelyn always seems to surprise him with nice things at exactly the right time: cookies left over from some Temple ladies' bake-diplomacy effort; a clipping from the latest *National Geographic*; asking him for a massage, which usually leads to more. They still have sex, maybe not as much as they used to, that's normal in marriage, but once during the week if he's lucky, and again on weekends. The sex is good, too, though it's true she hurries him more than she used to, and she rarely cries his name like she used to, and the last time he tried to use his mouth on her, she made a face and told him to please stop messing around down there.

'We've found God,' Lenny tells his older brother, Ned, one evening when Ned calls from Harvard. 'We raise our hands in the air to feel his energy.'

Evelyn laughs when she hears that, and, when Lenny gets off the phone, she tells him Ned will think they've gone insane, for sure.

But Lenny hasn't gone insane. Though life confuses him sometimes, life in the Temple, life with Jim Jones. Lenny is still attending Jim Jones's night classes, and while Jim Jones rarely asks about Evelyn, he almost always gives Lenny bizarre, friendly greetings — 'Hey, baby', 'Lenny-husband', 'Fly in, dove' — and a manly hug, smelling like Brut and Brylcreem. One time, Lenny happens to be walking behind some girls on his way out of class, and one of those girls in a miniskirt, and sees Jim Jones lingering by the doorway and looking up the girl's skirt. Then Jim Jones sees Lenny and smiles in a way like nothing else needs to be said, and Lenny smiles, too, and Jim slaps him on the back, and though Jim sometimes visits Lenny's wife when he isn't home, it doesn't matter; Lenny and Jim have a special friendship.

So it doesn't immediately occur to Lenny to be suspicious one evening in September when he comes home to find two used coffee cups, but no explanation from Evelyn. He's about to ask her, yet something about her attitude stops him, the congested expression with which she seems to be regarding her lesson plans. He notices then that her eyes are puffy, her nose pink. Instead, he asks, 'What's wrong, Evelyn?'

'I'm sorry,' she says quickly, and gives him a strange, helpless look. 'I was just chopping onions.'

She gestures at the stove, where indeed there is something oniony bubbling. Then she gathers her shawl about her and gets up to stir the pot, her flimsy dress casting shadows on the backs of her legs. Lenny decides to believe her.

6.

There is nothing unusual about the afternoon. It's not unusual that there's music playing when she steps out of the shower — French music, Jean Ferrat. It's not unusual that her breasts are naked under her cotton-gauze housedress, or her hair wet, or her elbows stark as baby bird wings, working the towel through her hair. It's not unusual that her feet leave ghostly imprints walking down the hall to the kitchen where her paperwork awaits. Yet the moment she passes through the bead curtains, she has a sense of wide-open panic, as if she's just smelled smoke or heard a window shattering. Then she sees Jim standing in the backyard and knows this is what has made her stomach dip, and she thinks: *Oh.*

He is stroking a white cat that is not theirs but that comes around sometimes. She would like to be the cat. He looks up. *Oh.*

And even after she lets him in and apologizes for making him wait and he says, 'It's alright, sweetheart,' things are strange, frantic. She would like to excuse herself and fix her hair, put on a bra maybe, turn off the French music, which now seems ridiculous, but Jim's voice keeps her roped near, making coffee. He is asking after Lenny. They often talk of Lenny when they are alone together; it makes 'alone together' somehow less problematic. What kind of woman listens to French music and doesn't wear a bra at four-thirty on a Tuesday, anyway? Oh, oh, she must get herself together.

'That pussycat … Ever put milk in a saucer for that cat?' Jim asks as she takes out the milk, and the question seems disconcertingly intimate, that knowing little smile, why must her mind keep flying off to dirty places?

'Sometimes.' Forlornly, Evelyn looks at the milk. 'I don't know if there's enough.'

'Cat's *gone*, baby.'

How she loves the way he talks, his Indiana accent, which somehow manages to be both a Yankee clip and a Southern drawl. 'Gimme some sugar, huh,' he blurts as her hands hesitate on the canister, and even this isn't rude but charmingly direct. He watches over her shoulder as she spoons the sugar and tells her, 'L'il more … Mmm … Thank you, darlin',' and briefly holds his hand over hers so they both feel the warmth pulsing through the mug like a tiny heartbeat.

'Please — sit,' she says with quiet desperation.

But he doesn't seem to hear her, just raises the mug to his lips, and when she edges diplomatically toward the kitchen table, he placidly follows. 'Been meaning to run by you, uh, idea, for the, uh … *newsletter*.' Jim takes another sip and lists closer and again she is cornered, this time against the table. 'Interviews with local pacifists. "Peace in the Valley", somethin' like that. Your husband, could do a profile on him, print a picture maybe …'

'Of Lenny?'

'Hell, sure. He's photogenic? Few lines 'bout his college education, moral opposition to warfare, work … fine work he doin' with the mentally ill. That's a nice story there. Print a nice picture to go with it. Ain't all about riots and homemade napalm. We wanna raise awareness of the quiet protestors.'

Evelyn has a sudden image of being lifted onto the kitchen table, her legs pushed open. She hates herself. 'Well, I probably have a picture you can use,' she says, then has a bright idea to get away. 'I can look now. There's a box of photos in the bedroom.'

Jim's smile widens.

It will be okay, Evelyn thinks, setting down her untouched coffee. Though it feels good, too good, to brush against Jim on her way out of the room, it will be okay. Though the bead curtains also feel good, too good, shivering against her naked arms and shoulders. The curtains knock and sway behind her. She will be alone soon. He will not follow her. A married minister wouldn't follow a married woman down the hall and into her bedroom while she is so damp-haired and obviously braless, would he?

'Nice curtains.' Jim's voice blooms behind her. 'Did I ever tell you … nice bead curtains?'

Evelyn feels the absurdity of the things she says, words plucked and strung together with the ordered randomness of a code. 'Lenny looks cute here, but his hair is a bit long.'

'Oh, that *is* cute,' Jim murmurs, taking the photo and adding it to the pile of contenders on the bedspread. It was not Evelyn's idea to sit on the bed, and this makes her feel less guilty about being there.

'Well, I suppose this won't work. He's shirtless again.'

'Probably he needs a shirt.'

Evelyn shucks a series of photographs showing her without Lenny: sometimes smiling, sometimes not, sometimes with her hair piled high, sometimes with bangs and a bob. In one snapshot, taken just after her return from France, she stands beside her fairer-haired mother and sisters, looking plain and utterly miserable. She notices Jim peering closely at this picture and tells him, 'As you can see, I've always been plain-looking,' and he nods gently, smiles and hums in gentle agreement.

'Mmm-hmm.'

They are not touching. His hands in his lap are beautiful and golden like lion paws, his sideburns thick and black, his head as compelling as the head of some noble black-haired animal — yet they have not touched. 'Lenny after graduation. Perhaps,' she says, and her lips feel dry, her bones like glass. There is a beauty spot on his cheek and he smells strongly, sweetly of himself. *Ilovehim Ilovehim*, she thinks in a tumble. *If only I could touch him … just once.*

'Mmm,' Jim says, taking the photo from her. 'Perhaps.'

He proceeds to add the photo to the pile, to shift his body closer to her. Then he does something both unexpected and expected: lifts the box of photos from her hands, sets it down, and turns to her with an expression of complete benevolence.

'Ev-e-lyn,' he croons.

She sees it coming. Like a rushing train. Like tear gas in a crowd. In the eternal seconds before it happens, she's hearing the whistle, seeing the hand reach for the grenade, and she can't stop it happening. Everything in her holds itself sharp and tense in expectation of catastrophe; everything is steel tracks, stinging eyes, bone waiting to be compressed. It's happening and she can't stop it happening; Evelyn by her knowledge tree and that moment of radical innocence before the lightning strikes. Jim. *Jim.*

It's the way he holds her face, like a delicate thing, and the indelicacy of everything else. Tongue to the brain. Pleasure smoke in the belly. An incomprehensible burning all over her skin, like chemicals. She's gone blind or she's seeing into the flames that know her future, seeing a madness of bitter, swirling red, and she has to say something.

'This isn't right,' she says.

'Bullshit.'

He kisses her again. Again, a bitter taste, and sore little thumps of pleasure from within, like people knocking to get out of a burning building. His hands gliding over her body, flicking at her nipples, teasing her, hurting her. It hurts, oh, it *hurts* to feel this good.

'I can't …' she says.

But of course the words seem false with her smell so frank between them and her lips still wet from kissing. He isn't holding her face anymore but the place where her ribs meet her waist, and she feels he could break her right in half, crush her whole body like grapes, without any consequence to either of them.

'You want me,' he says matter-of-factly. 'And you ain't hiding it well, baby.'

It's hard to argue with this. Evelyn closes her eyes and lets his hands roam to her hips, her haunches, feeling less like a human being than a well-formed female animal, all heat and response. His face is buried in her neck and hair. There is panting, groaning, the delightful friction of their bodies through layers of clothing. 'I'm gonna fuck you like you never been fucked,' Jim rumbles in her ear, and her insides twinge in anticipation, and then it is like a light has been switched on.

'Jim,' she says, her voice thin and urgent. 'Don't. Please.'

He raises his head with an expression of faint annoyance, a black forelock hanging over one eye. 'Well, hell, honey.' He laughs grimly. 'You really tellin' me there ain't a, ah, *overwhelming* attraction here? You sayin' you don't think about me?' He strokes her thigh, softens his voice to a purr. 'I think about *you*, sweetheart. All the time.'

'I think about you,' Evelyn confesses. To deny such a thing would be like denying the blood in her veins. 'It's just, my father is a minister.'

As soon as she says it, she knows how stupid it sounds, that she has surely diminished herself in his eyes, because he starts laughing. Not cruelly, but laughing, sitting up and wiping his crinkled eyes and shaking his black head. She feels all at once like a little girl, lying back on the bed; her flattened breasts a little girl's breasts, her mind as prim and useless as a dollhouse. If she could fly from the room, from her body, she would. Yet all she can do is listen to Jim's laughter and know it is her due; she's a white girl with white-girl problems.

'Don't wanna be laying down with Daddy? That's fair, that's fair …' Jim smirks down at her, then straightens his face. 'Can't say I didn't anticipate this kind of resistance, honey. I just hoped you were, uh, more mature, more *advanced* than that. I guess that's my mistake.'

Evelyn opens her mouth.

'Oh, don't *apologize*. That don't do me no good. I *love* you … bitch. Nobody ever loved you so much as me, not even your daddy. Someday you'll see that. But not today. *I'm* sorry, *I* miscalculated.'

Jim sighs and rises from the bed, and Evelyn is overwhelmed by dread: of being alone with herself, permanently unworthy. She sits up. Her hands are pale and empty. In a faint voice, she says, 'Jim.'

'Nothin' you can say, baby. You ain't ready.' He takes his sunglasses from his shirt pocket. 'Should probably get yourself together before Lenny-husband comes home. If I didn't know better, I'd think: that's a woman who's just been screwed.'

Within a few minutes of Jim's departure, Evelyn has her hair pinned up, a shawl on over her house-dress, the photo box stowed away, the bed remade. She stands at the edge of the room, touching her lips and trying to grasp the enormity of the situation. Did he really say 'I love you'? Did he really call her a bitch? Are they really both married to other people? Is she free or not free?

All these things, Evelyn considers, before bursting into tears.

7.

If the phone rings once after midnight, she is to go into the kitchen and wait for it to ring again. Usually, it rings within the next five minutes, but there are nights that test her faith — twenty minutes, thirty. On these nights, she stands motionless, observing the moon over the backyard, afraid of doing anything more lest she wake her sleeping husband. And when the call comes, she swiftly brings it to her ear and murmurs, '*Hello*,' in a frail foggy voice like she has a cold, and waits for Jim to respond.

'Mmmmmm. Evelyn. Tell me …'

He is counseling her. He has counseled others, in his time as a minister, though never under these circumstances. It is important that they remain objective. He does not trust them to speak in the flesh and not give in to temptation. To give in to temptation prematurely, Jim says, could be disastrous to her psyche, as well as her commitment to the Temple. Her commitment means more to him than their personal relationship, as much as he desires to see this relationship fulfilled on all levels.

Jim tells her that he needs her to be honest. Honest and vulnerable, 'like with the Frenchman'. He knows vulnerability does not come naturally to her, that she is a woman who has never truly 'been mastered'. He expects the process will be especially painful for her. He wants her to remember always that he loves her, and that nothing she reveals to him during these sessions can possibly change this.

'Tell me 'bout the girl,' Jim requests the first night they speak. 'Tiny girl Evelyn.'

So she tells about the girl that she was: a bright, responsible girl with a nice smile for photographs and strangers, nice manners, clean clothes, clean hair, not a lot of imagination. A girl who was kind to her dolls and little sisters, who took genuine pleasure in keeping her bedroom neat, pleasing her parents and teachers, dressing up for church and school in saddle shoes, bobby sox, plaid skirts. She was a girl who never made up stories but liked when her parents read to her, as she liked reading to her sisters when she was old enough. She liked the fairytale worlds: green jungles, purple mountains, vast oceans, the triumph of good over evil. Life seemed full of good things, an essential optimism, until she was in junior high and suddenly it wasn't.

'What happened to you, baby?'

It wasn't anything that happened. It wasn't anything that was said or done. It was just as if she woke up one day and her skin was thinner, the world sharper, all the wind knocked out of her. She took to crying privately about things she had no control over — the Holocaust, Hiroshima, slavery, genocide. She stayed back after classes and asked questions of her teachers that caused them to praise her sensitivity. She felt instinctively that this praise was false, that they were missing the point. One week, IQ tests were done, and the results were read aloud and there were gasps when it came to her own; this, too, seemed false, filled her with a grand sense of injustice.

'You didn't feel you deserved it.'

'I never felt I was intelligent, in any way that mattered. I was never good enough.'

'And Mommy-Daddy? What they say 'bout that big IQ?'

Not much, but they must have noticed the change in her. She remembers a lot of hushed discussions, displays of warmth, encouragement, hugs. She remembers crying facedown on her bed and her father sitting beside her, consoling her. There is shame in this memory. After that, she remembers going places with her father — a retirement village, an orphanage, a home for amputees — and feeling gradually stronger. She turned thirteen and became more self-conscious about hugging her father, even brushing her arm against his, but she was proud of what a good man he was, found him brave and true and handsome in his clerical robes, loved him.

'I loved him too much. I guess I always knew that.'

Jim lets her cry. She tries to be brief and quiet about it, but cannot get rid of the feeling of constraint in her chest. 'You're doin' good,' he soothes her. 'I thank you for your honesty.' He asks her to speak more about the love that was too much.

She loved her father more than she felt was right. That's all. She developed breasts and underarm hair and grew to her adult height of five feet, three inches. There was a pressing need to distance herself from her father, physically and mentally. Boys liked her; this helped. Girls liked her, listened to her, elected her president of various clubs; this helped, too. She was independent, vocal, never cried in front of her parents again, knew how to argue and intimidate others with her intellect. She challenged her father about religion and, while never having the courage to declare herself an atheist at his table, made it known that she did not think the Methodist Church was the pinnacle of morality.

'Tell me, honey … Was rejecting God just a way of rejecting Daddy?'

Evelyn considers the moonlight, the silence like a coin dropped down a bottomless well.

'To be honest, I think I stopped believing in God the day I stopped believing life was a fairytale.'

Night after night, they trot 'tiny girl Evelyn' into the dark kitchen, have her smile her bunny-toothed smile and pirouette, and then rob her of her innocence. Sex is something they must discuss in her presence, but also things *like* sex — self-pleasure, suicidal thoughts, the general desire for oblivion. 'How old were you, baby, when you started …?' Eight or nine. 'What did you think about?' Oh … men. Men's hands. Men's shadows. The looming presence of a man above or behind her. 'Were you ashamed?' Not ashamed, really. She knew that it was private, a thing only for alone in her bedroom after dark, but really it felt too good to be ashamed of.

Jim is pleased to hear this.

Jim wants her to talk about her misery, so she tells him about Elliot Goldberg, the gloomy Jewish boy she dated as a high school junior. She tells him how Elliot's gloominess appealed to her, how they spent hours talking about the Eichmann trial, Babi Yar, Mengele's experiments, dark and tortured regions of the human soul. She tells him how sometimes she felt flashes of what might be termed 'anguish', 'anarchy', 'absurdism', and would soothe herself by contemplating the shelf of household poisons. Yet she never did anything more, couldn't justify the selfishness or the pain it would cause her parents, or perhaps was just too attached to her privileged existence.

'I'm glad you've thought about it, baby. Shows you serious 'bout life.' Jim's voice is tender, understanding. 'But the only reason to lay your life down is if something's worth dyin' for. Anything else, that's self-indulgence.'

He has her tell him about the boys and men — too many to count on one hand, though not so many that it takes all of two. She tells about Percy, the faceless boys and men after him. She tells about the middle-aged businessman when she worked at that hotel in the summer of '64, how strange it was to be accosted in her boyish bellhop uniform, how she felt like Joan of Arc stripping naked for him, how she had given his twenty-dollar tip to a panhandler. 'You liked that?' Jim asks about certain things she tells him, and if his voice registers mild astonishment at times, he quickly covers it up by talking about 'ass-fucking', telling her she's anal retentive and will need to be fucked up the ass at least once if she's to become a better human and socialist.

She tells about Jean-Claude, in more detail than she has before. How, though it was she who broke it off, she's never gotten over the sense of having been wronged by him; of having revealed herself too much, without truly being seen. How she still thinks from time to time of what might've been, if Jean-Claude *had* seen her a little more clearly, cherished her more, fought harder for her. How she had lugged her suitcases dutifully to Switzerland, Italy, Spain, in the weeks immediately after the breakup, realizing only later that she had been hoping he would turn up somewhere, had, in fact, been expecting him to come after her; slowly coming to terms with the fact that he would not.

'All sisters gotta learn someday, men only care 'bout what's right in front of them.' Jim hums sympathetically. 'Course, I can't live that way. I see *everything*, darlin'.'

Sometimes they are not completely objective. Sometimes, talking about sex, he gets carried away telling all the things he'd like to do to her and she says, 'Oh,' in a small startled voice, and he says, 'Don't play so fucking innocent.' Sometimes he cusses at her for whole minutes at a time, and she doesn't know whether to weep or to moan with gratitude.

Once, for reasons unclear to her, he becomes infuriated, tells her he can't deal with a bitch like her always intellectualizing everything, and hangs up the phone. She waits for him to call back, but he doesn't, and so in her forlornness she goes to the bedroom and tries to make love with Lenny, but it's hopeless — there's only one man for her.

Jim knows, in his mysterious way, about her going to Lenny, and the next time they speak, he tells her he would prefer if she were celibate. He tells her he hasn't slept with Rosaline in seven years, and that a similar vow on her part could bring them closer.

They talk about her beliefs: her atheism, her Marxism, her existentialism. He tells her, 'That's all nice and sophisticated, honey, but there's things beyond that. I mean, things like destiny.' He asks her how she feels about past lives, reincarnation, and she tells him she doesn't know, honestly has never given it much thought. 'I only mention it, sweetheart, because I cherish your soul. Beyond this life. And, uh, I can't help feeling, we got unfinished business. Last time we were together, see, you died too soon.' He wants to know if she's willing to go back with him, way back, and she says yes, she will go, anywhere, as far as he can take her.

'Close your eyes, sweetheart.'

He does things with his voice, low dark things that make the air tremble and the spaces within her widen like pools of rain. She knows that she is in the kitchen, holding the phone, yet also that there are other places she could be, and when he asks her to tell him what she sees, she says, 'A cold place.' When he asks her what she's doing, she says, 'Traveling somewhere,' and then, after considering the rocking motion within her, 'I am on a train.' He asks where she is going and she tells him, 'Where the people are.' What people? 'The people, the workers.' She tries to elaborate on the fluttering feeling in her chest and says, 'I am not alone,' and also, 'Something is going to happen when we reach the station.' He asks if he is with her and she says yes. He asks if she is a woman.

'I am a woman, yes,' she says. 'A revolutionary woman.'

She is a revolutionary woman. She has been a girl with parents and boys and sadness, yet her true identity is as a revolutionary woman, and as his lover. He tells her that she was once the lover of a great revolutionary leader, and in her own right an educator, an organizer, a reformer of systems. He tells her that she was French and beautiful. She is still beautiful. 'You're a beautiful revolutionary,' he croons. 'This is your past, your future, your highest being.'

They have been speaking for perhaps three weeks, perhaps three nights a week, for several hours at a time. She has been sleeping little yet performing well in her everyday work, maintaining a distance between her day-self and night-self. On the last night she and Jim speak, she does not sleep at all but remains in the kitchen, making herself coffee and watching the dawn so beautiful, the pink and green dawn, and knows she is exactly where she belongs.

That afternoon, Jim comes to the white house when Lenny isn't home, and they do everything they want to do.

8.

Lenny has begun to have bad dreams. Strange, imprisoning dreams set in the half-built Temple or the mental hospital or some hybrid of the two. In these dreams, he wants to work but can't find what he needs, and he has to ask Jim Jones, who is always right there, smiling and clapping his shoulder and telling him things that make no sense: *It's alright. You'll be a bird soon. Don't forget your clean uniform.*

Evelyn doesn't appear in the dreams. In fact, she's conspicuously absent.

Lenny doesn't want to admit to himself that Evelyn is absent from his waking life, too, especially since he still sees her every day, talks to her, shares a bed with her. He doesn't want to admit that he has woken several nights and found her side of the bed empty, or heard the phone ringing, just once, a lonely and blood-curdling sound. These things are also dreams, he tells himself.

One night – he is sure it must be a dream. Getting up from the empty bed, he shuffles to the kitchen, and, though his eyes are still weak from sleeping and the kitchen dark, he sees very clearly Evelyn in her nightgown, clutching the phone with tears in her eyes, like a teenager whose boyfriend has just broken up with her. He sees her and he's certain she sees him, for her wet eyes meet his through the darkness and there's a flicker of recognition. Yet it isn't a real kind of recognition, not a human kind, more like she's a pet cat he's just disturbed eating the guts of some rodent off a garden path. And he feels nothing human for her, either: only a desire to unsee what he has seen.

Another dreamlike night, she comes to him dressed in her moon-colored nightgown, her breasts beneath it small and peaked like meringues. Her hair is in that rare state of freedom, not a single pin in sight, and it's *long* — to her shoulder blades and ticklish in his face, catching in his mouth. Because she's on him before he fully realizes it, kissing him, touching him, her mouth very wet and bitter tasting. He's feeling her before he sees her, bitter sucking kisses and hands so bitter cold. Thighs cold, too, the way silk is cold. He's surprised to feel such coldness. So surprised, like a falling dream, and is it really Evelyn? *His* Evelyn? Come to him in the night so beautiful and coldly purposeful, like a fantasy he'd be embarrassed to tell her about in the morning? She's turning him loose with cool, brazen tenderness, and he's making it easy for her, not resisting and dreamy-hard and wearing only boxer shorts, like every other night. She's taking him coolly and placing him in that familiar bracing warmth and for some moments there's only sweetness, the sense of a well-deserved windfall.

Then the awakening. Her hands cold on his chest, her hips and thighs doing all the work. He's seeing her more clearly, her closed eyes and gritted teeth and body in motion, and what's striking is he's never seen her this way before. Never in all their time has he seen such a look on her face, like a riddle, or her eyes so tightly shut yet somehow all-seeing. She's *inflicting* pleasure, pinning him down and drawing it out, and the sweetness of it has nothing to do with him. This panting sighing straddling sweetness is neither for or about him, so even in his pleasure there's a sense of being hoodwinked, like watching a magic show and having his pockets picked.

'Evelyn …'

He says her name softly, at the same time touching the small of her back. He doesn't want her to stop, just to come closer — his little dark-haired wife in her moon-colored nightgown; he knows the nightgown, likes it very much. He doesn't want her to stop and is looking into her eyes to make sure she understands this, caressing her gently through the nightgown. And she understands; seems to. Her eyes gloomy but half-open, her face docile and young-looking. Breathing with him, staring back into his eyes, and how beautiful to have her with him. How beautiful to be woken this way, his little dark-haired wife in the middle of the night, hot for him, wanting him, in love with him.

But the coldness. Such coldness. It shouldn't come as a surprise and yet it does, so painfully sharp he could burst into tears. She has taken it all away as suddenly as she gave it — those hips, those thighs, that ticklish hair — and like a wounded animal is huddled out of his reach. At the foot of the bed, all elbows and bare feet and faceless dark hair. A cold woman and also a woman feeling the cold, cast out in the night like a serf or a sinner. So cold, just looking at her is like being exiled.

'Evelyn …'

She doesn't answer. He wonders briefly if maybe *she* is dreaming, or was dreaming and has just woken embarrassed of whatever unconscious need made her come to him this way. How he wishes it could all be someone's dream.

It's a long time before Evelyn speaks. In a flat voice, without turning. 'Just go back to sleep, Lenny.'

Around the same time, Lenny hears something funny in one of Jim Jones's night classes. Actually, he's always hearing funny things in Jim Jones's classes — most of them stories told by Jim Jones himself, but some of them stories from his fellow students, hippie and redneck kids who always seem to be getting into trouble with hitchhiking, swimming holes, other people's horses. This particular story comes from some guys Lenny is pals with, Johnny Bronco and Dale Alport: both white and longhaired, both unmarried, both guys who've smoked pot enough for it to show in their mannerisms. 'Hey … You hear about Jim and Lenin?' Dale, the squeaky-voiced surfer, asks as Lenny slides into his seat, and when Lenny shakes his head in bemusement, long-limbed Johnny slips him an open textbook and points at a photo. 'You dig?'

The photo shows Lenin before he went bald and grew a moustache. He has high cheekbones and a pug nose. Lenny looks across the room at Jim Jones, who also has high cheekbones and a pug nose. He smiles and shrugs, passes the textbook back.

'Yeah,' he says.

They've been learning about Lenin in class, his exile in Siberia, his mobilization of the Bolsheviks, the sealed train, the October Revolution. Jim tells the stories so vividly it's almost like he was there himself, like they're *all* there with him, like they'll never be left out of anything important ever again. 'We gotta enter the next phase of history,' Jim confides. 'This most human phase can only be achieved through the breakdown of capitalist America.'

All through that lesson, the textbook picture is passed around and there are whispers about Jim Jones and Lenin until Jim interrupts the class to make an important announcement.

'It has come to my attention that there's been speculation on my, ah, former incarnation.' Jim looks around the room with the soulful brown eyes of a dog, a bear, Lenin. 'I say only this: I am a socialist and a man of destiny.'

'*I told you* he was Lenin,' a girl sitting in front of Lenny whispers loudly to her friend. The girl is wearing a see-through blouse but isn't pretty.

When Lenny returns home late that night, there's no sound in the kitchen except the ticking of the wall clock and the clacking of Evelyn's fingers on the typewriter, where she sits so skinny and hunched. He feels sorry for her. He thinks it must be boring to be her. 'Did you know Jim used to be Lenin?' he asks her hopefully, but she barely looks up, just says, 'If you say so, Lenny,' then wants to see his notes from class, then tells him off for his poor handwriting, then tells him he should go to bed if he's tired, she will join him later. Lenny doesn't know how much later it is that Evelyn actually joins him, only that the night is filled with bad dreams, before he wakes up to a cacophony of birds.

Of course, Lenny knows there is only one real explanation for Evelyn's behavior; has known it perhaps from the first time he came home in the summer and found her having coffee with Jim Jones. And many times after that, Jim Jones inside the house, looking far too at home — his shoes off, his feet up, once even Evelyn coming through the beads with her lips pursed and eyes down and handing Jim his watch. Most times, Jim Jones has a smile and some words for Lenny, so many words sometimes that Evelyn appears to grow bored and drifts out of the room or sits down with her paperwork. Yet there are other times when Jim Jones passes him by with nothing more than a shit-eating grin, a slap on the shoulder, and goes into the night, sunglasses on and a bounce in his step that Lenny wishes he didn't notice.

But she is still his wife. She still wears her wedding band and the silver rose earrings, and she is still nice to him sometimes, still does his laundry, still surprises him one day by showing him a picture of himself in the latest Temple newsletter with a column underneath that calls him a 'bright young altruist', a 'soldier of peace', a 'patron of the insane and mentally handicapped'. She stands right next to him as he reads, her arm resting lightly against his, and he feels his throat closing up, his eyes stinging; it's the closest they've been in weeks.

'This is really nice, Evelyn,' he says eventually. 'And … unexpected.'

'It shouldn't be.' Her voice is soft and reasonable, her face expressionless. 'You're doing good work. It deserves to be acknowledged.'

They haven't been lovers since that strange night in September. It is October, then November. Though her body is no longer his, he hopes at least that she will continue living with him like a sister: mocking him, managing him, leaving her things around the house for him to touch and sniff. He hopes the new Temple building, once completed, will somehow make things better, and looks forward to the grand opening on Thanksgiving weekend. He is proud of what they've made together, even if it has destroyed them.

And then, one evening in mid-November, Lenny comes home in his white uniform and finds Jim Jones and Evelyn together, only it isn't like the other times, because there are other people, too. Men and women from the Temple, and all of them seem to be waiting for him. The men are middle-aged, old Indiana men Lenny is obscurely fearful of: that tall white cop, that tall black assistant pastor, a round bald engineer called Brother Ike. The women, too, are older: Sister Joya, the cop's corn-fed Doris-Day-lookalike wife; Sister Diane, a lesbian social worker with short chestnut hair and the mouth of a movie starlet. Evelyn is sitting between the two women at the kitchen table and looking almost middle-aged herself; severe, though also very frail. She doesn't look at Lenny. Jim Jones does.

'There's the man,' Jim Jones says with a wide, dog-like smile. 'Lenny-husband.'

The kitchen feels very crowded. Lenny smells cake.

At that, Jim Jones circles his arm around Lenny's shoulder and leads him through the beads to the den, where there is indeed cake. Evelyn follows, and the women after her, and then the men. She sits on one edge of the green sofa, Jim Jones beside her. Jim Jones pats the cushion beside him and in a deep, fruity voice says, 'Sit down, son.'

Lenny sits.

Joya and Diane start serving cake.

'I gathered this small committee here today,' Jim Jones begins theatrically, 'on account of we've observed a, ah, distance between you and your wife. Kind of distance ain't normal for a couple so early in their union. Son, you care to comment on this distance?'

'There has been a distance,' Lenny admits. Jim Jones nods and puckers his lips like a chimpanzee until Lenny goes on. 'I guess ... she's been sort of cold and distant.'

'*Cold and distant.* Uh-huh, uh-huh ... Evelyn, darlin', you agree with that?'

'Yes,' Evelyn says quietly, only to Jim. 'I have been distant.'

'Can you, uh, elaborate on this distance? Tell us why you been so cold on him?' Jim is leaning forward, his fingers steepled together. There's nothing ardent or overly familiar about the way he looks at Evelyn, sits beside her. She is still Lenny's wife.

Evelyn purses her lips, keeps her eyes lowered. She looks so pretty and demure to him, her hands in her lap so neatly folded, her hair so sleek, those roses dangling from her ears.

'Well, first of all, I don't love him.' Evelyn raises her eyes, looks at Jim and only Jim. 'Second, I want a divorce.'

With the exception of Evelyn, who has retreated to another part of the white house that was briefly their home, everyone hugs Lenny at the door. Jim Jones hugs Lenny first, and for the longest, puts his whole body into the hug, strokes Lenny's face, Lenny's hair, calls him a good son, loves him, smells of Brut and other manly things. Next the women, their tangy perfumes, cushiony breasts. Then that cop, Brother Gene, an awkwardly tender hug that surprises Lenny and more than any of the others makes him want to cry. Brother Isaiah and Brother Ike give him curt, clapping hugs, and curt words — Brother Ike, who Lenny is to go with for the next few days, will help him with the Nevada divorce. Everyone is kind to Lenny, everyone wants to help him, everyone is sorry for his loss.

There is a suitcase that Brother Isaiah hands him; it has clean clothes and a shaving kit. Sister Joya asks him if he wants some reading material, and Lenny says he does, he guesses. So he's given an armload of books, chosen seemingly at random; some science fiction, Emile Durkheim, a history of the tsars, a volume of French poetry. He's on the doorstep, about to leave, when Evelyn comes swishing through the beads, bearing a pile of linen.

'I almost forgot,' she says. 'I cleaned your other uniform.'

Stranger in Your Land

1.

He gives her a cabin. He gives her a gun. He gives her a barking dog. He gives her multiple orgasms.

He gives her four nights a week in the cabin between Evergreen Valley and Moontown, and on these nights, they seldom sleep.

He does things to her, things that stop time and make the moon fog over, and sometimes she will open her eyes and find herself weeping, singing, quoting French philosophers, as the dog barks and barks.

He cherishes her. He wants her dead. These two things are one and the same, on the hard, rustic bed with the embroidered linen. 'I should kill you, ugly white bitch,' he says, but also, 'Mmmm, sweetheart. Your skin is *so soft.*' She sees her own body from afar — the flattened breasts and nipples like berries and glacier of white skin over sternum. She sees him licking, sucking, biting, burrowing, his black head between her thighs as powerful as a totem. She is alive, but how and when and on what planet, she cannot say.

He tells her stories from before she was born, about a boy called Jimmy Jones whom nobody loved. He tells her how little Jimmy once healed a cat he found maimed in a ditch. How he once killed a cat, because he felt sorry for it and to see if he could. How he almost drowned a rich kid once, because he could and because that rich sonofabitch deserved it. He tells her of the dust, the crops that failed, the screaming freight trains and lone water tower, the pain that comes whenever he thinks of that miserable one-horse town in Southern Indiana.

He tells her stories from the future. How the ghettoes will be fenced in barbed wire and converted into concentration camps. How America will set fire to itself, mushroom clouds over every major city and years of no sun. How they will find themselves a hot green paradise somewhere by the equator, and eat fruit off the trees, and care for all the animals and the children and the elderly.

He tells her other things: 'We're the same, honey,' and, 'I never had nothing like this,' and, 'Nobody else understands.' He holds her dark hair up to the firelight, admires the secret threads of red, closes his eyes and smells it, sighs, croons. 'I'd be here all the time, baby, if I didn't have so much on me. So many askin' for me ...' He kisses the downy hair at her temple, the pulse of her neck, squeezes her white hands, loves her, loves her. 'I'd like, oh, I'd *like* to marry you. That's what I'd do. Only, baby, *I know you know* we're married in a deeper sense.'

He asks her for things: cold water, warm milk, little white pills. He asks her to check his car, to check the locks, to check that rustling outside, to take the gun. He asks her to rub his feet — 'If you'll do that small thing for me, darlin',' — to rub his shoulders — 'I got a crick, goddamn crick in my neck,' — to suck his cock — 'Your lips, honey, oh your lips right now would be *so sweet*.' He asks her to pour pretty words into his ears — poems, hymns, folk songs — and dozes off while she does, waking with a start minutes or hours later and in the mood to talk again. He asks her questions that have just one answer: does she love him, has he given her life meaning, would she die for him?

'Yes,' she says, without hesitation. 'Yes. *Yes.*'

Then there is the morning where she wakes from two hours of sleep with a black eye, because of things that had happened the night before. Miraculous things. A miraculous thought that came unbidden at the sight of his strong, ministering hands on her body: *How beautiful it would be to have him hurt me.* And just like that, he'd brought the heel of his hand briskly down on her cheekbone, cuffed her hard enough to elicit a strained-startled cry, like no sound she'd ever made before. She could see from his face that the action had given him no personal pleasure; that he was simply responding to a need in her, deep and wordless.

In the raw-wood kitchen, Evelyn applies a bag of frozen peas to the swelling, shuffles around in her shawl and slippers as the dog snuffles over his breakfast and the coffee brews. Just a few months earlier, all she and Jim had shared was coffee on his pastoral visits. Now they share everything: meals, dreams, fluids, a black-and-white dog named Picnic. They share past lives and futures, a Temple where more gather every week to hear him speak, unspoken communication, a god who isn't in the sky, a higher plane, a *Cause*.

Water wells beneath her eye. In this life, she will only cry tears of bliss. She lifts the bag, dabs the wetness away, smarts, smiles. Then she catches sight of the Christmas card on the windowsill and feels something stone-like and brutal in her chest. *Hurt me.* She takes the coffee off the stove, takes up the card. There are impulses that will only cause pain, if indulged.

Merry Christmas Evie & Lenny!

The card shows a cute seasonal scene: apple-cheeked child in mittens, snowflakes, deer, other woodland creatures. Evelyn likes the card. She likes 'Evie', the name only used by her closest family. But she doesn't like 'Lenny', not in this context, and hasn't yet brought herself to read the three-page letter that Sister Phyllis forwarded with it.

Picnic has licked his bowl clean and is scraping it noisily along the floor when Jim lumbers in, looks her up and down with something like pride, and crows, 'G'mornin', Sonny Liston.' Evelyn laughs, feeling something like pride herself: his black hair is perfect, despite the night they've had; his body, though dressed quite absurdly in Y-fronts and a striped pajama top, is perfect; those lovely muscular thighs and calves, so perfect. *Every woman in this church wants you, Jim. Every man, too.* He pulls up a chair and sits back as she sets down the coffee, the eggs, the piled toast, the grilled tomatoes, the bottle of ketchup — a breakfast fit for a king or a truck driver. Then, just as she's about to double back to the kitchen bench, he catches her jaw in his hand, tilts it up to examine her under-eye. 'Mmm. That's *red.*'

'It's not so bad,' Evelyn says quietly. He presses the thin skin and she flinches.

'You need some healing, honey.'

'Oh — no.'

'Father's gonna make it better. Sit tight.'

He scoops her onto his knee, and she sighs his name, '*Jim,*' almost ready to let his fingers perform another miracle. But there's a mental picture that stops her: the Temple, Sunday morning, packed full of people screaming for his touch. Evelyn turns her face away from his caress and slips off his lap, escapes to the bowl of lemons and the citrus squeezer. 'You need to conserve your psychic energies. And your eggs are getting cold.'

'She don't wanna be healed 'cause the eggs might get cold. Goddamn woman.'

Evelyn smiles. She likes 'goddamn woman'. She likes the weight of the knife in her hand, the precision of the blade through skin and flesh. She likes the Kremlin-like glass dome, pressing the lemon halves into it until they're slack and furred with pulp. The citrus squeezer was a gift from her parents, like so many things in this cabin and the white house before it.

Merry Christmas Evie & Lenny!

Picnic has abandoned his clean bowl to beg off Jim. Picnic loves Jim. Picnic knows Jim is a friend to all animals. Evelyn adds a touch of honey, ginger, turmeric to the lemon juice and places it in front of Jim: a nice, healthy tonic, good for his metabolism and immune system; he truly does need to keep up his strength. He ignores the tonic; dumps ketchup over his meal, spears a tomato, slurps his coffee. He's as intent on his plate as he was on her body last night, and as impassive as when he hit her. But he feels her gaze, and Picnic's. He sneaks a crescent of toast under the table, then wipes Picnic's drool off his hands using the 'L.L.' monogrammed napkin — not a gift from her parents, but from Lenny's, who are just the kind of people to give monograms.

'You got the agenda for the meeting tonight?'

Evelyn looks into the neatly-lined notebook of her mind. 'We're collecting Christmas gifts for the orphanage at seven. At seven-thirty, we'll open to discussion of seasonal events. After that, confrontation. We're bringing up Oscar Hurmerinta for wife-beating, Johnny Bronco for womanizing, Kay Harris—'

'Horse-faced bitch.'

'— for racist comments. Also Ike Dickerson. He needs to take a share of responsibility for Lenny's relapse, though we mustn't discourage people from reporting that kind of thing. You might want to commend him on that.'

Jim snorts. 'Lenny needs a reason *not* to smoke, and Ike ain't it.'

'You're right, of course.' This topic isn't on the agenda, but Evelyn knows where it's going. 'And of course she's a beautiful girl, and has made wonderful progress. It's just, what Lenny really needs is someone who can keep him grounded—'

'Are you being objective?'

'I've been considering this objectively, yes.' Evelyn straightens her face. 'My concern is, she isn't ready for a relationship. It's quite clear she has issues with men, what with her making a pass at Gene Luce *and* his son.' She smiles wryly at the incredible fact that anyone would want to make a pass at Eugene Luce. 'Besides, she and Lenny are far too similar. How do we know they won't both just spark up and float off to space?'

'*Are you being objective*, baby?'

Jim is smiling, a crooked sideways smile she's seen often, usually while he's wearing his sunglasses and usually in the presence of less intelligent people. Or in the bedroom, before calling her 'white bitch'. Lenny never smiled at her that way. Such a smile wasn't even in Lenny's repertoire. Perhaps it's this thought, or perhaps the sight of the L.L. napkin stained with ketchup, that makes Evelyn lower her eyes. 'I guess I'm not completely objective.'

Jim nods his beautiful black head. 'Thank you, darlin', for being truthful.' He leans forward and smiles a different sort of smile, calm and soft-eyed. 'Ain't easy, I know. And I know you want what's best. Now, I'm not gonna send blondie to Reno 'less you're on board … but I happen to think they'd be well-matched, and I'm told I'm a fair match-maker.'

He's watching her face with his soft eyes; her soulmate, her perfect match. 'Well,' Evelyn tries, 'if they can be anywhere nearly as happy together as we are—'

'Nobody's gonna be happy as *us*.'

It strikes Evelyn that this isn't a very socialist thing to say. Jim reaches out and touches her under-eye again. This time, she doesn't flinch. 'I want Lenny to be happy,' she says, and already she's feeling more distant, objective, fluttering her eyelashes against Jim's fingertip. 'And, of course, I will assist with all the necessary arrangements …'

2.

In the month he's been in Reno, Lenny has begun to believe in aliens. Actually, he's always sort of liked the idea: hyper-intelligent beings communicating in wavelengths and beams of light. At the long dining table in Berkeley, Lenny's physics-professor father used to speak of UFOs flashing through desert skies. How a disc-shaped aircraft from alternate angles might resemble a sphere, a donut, a cigar. How it might skip across time folds like a flat stone skipping on a lake. How intelligent life elsewhere in the universe isn't only a mathematical possibility, but practically a certainty. How human minds will never quantify the majesty of time and space without end, the ever-expanding cosmos where God and truth reside.

These thoughts are a comfort to Lenny, slumped over the sink at the Silver State Steakhouse. At least, they're thoughts that keep him from thinking about the contents of the sink or the scrim of grease on the water or the injustice of having to wash dishes in Nevada when he has a college degree. Other injustices, too, so raw and private he can't name them, not without feeling ungrateful for the truth that has come into his life and that's connected in some essential way to God.

Father loves you. I love you. Receive this loving remedy.

Lenny doesn't think about his wife, almost ex-wife, as he washes dishes. He thinks of flying saucers, how far-out it would be to take one of those dishes and make it fly across the kitchen, how he'll never do this far-out thing unless someone tells him to. He thinks how not doing things is sometimes truer than doing them; how somewhere there must be a planet where no one does anything, where there are no wars or broken hearts. He thinks of doing nothing, just *being*, and the water lapping at his wrists, and the steam and the sound, and the silence beneath all sound and time and space swirling, endlessly swirling …

But there *is* an end to time at the Silver State. There are young men just like him, greasy and unshaven and skinny under their kitchen rags, pulling off their gloves and muttering — 'Ohh, man,' 'Fuckin' at last!' 'You comin' to see some titties?' Most of them, like Lenny, have bandanas over longish unwashed cowlick-y hair. Some have bloodshot eyes, and Lenny is envious of these guys, enough to steal a glance at one of them, a rangy, long-faced dealer who goes by 'Wile E. Peyote'. Wile E. catches Lenny looking and, with a smirk, makes a series of signs that can't be misinterpreted: fingertips rubbing against thumb, pressing against pouted lips, invisible plume of smoke escaping lips. Lenny grimaces, shrugs, shakes his head.

'*Pussy*,' Wile E. mouths.

Lenny can't argue with the word 'pussy'. It's what he is, pussy and broke — and, worse still, stone-cold sober. Ever since Brother Ike found the quarter-ounce, Lenny's allowance has been reduced to just three dollars a week, and all that's left of his last high is a stale whiff on his gray pea-coat. There's a twinge inside Lenny's skull, a pimple swelling hard and headless by his eyebrow. His sneakers are squelchy with dishwater. He's as dirty and ugly as a rat, pushing out the back door and into the parking lot. There are actual rats cavorting in the dumpster, those same kitchen guys already there, sparking up. Lenny passes them by with barely a nod and looks to the desert sky, thinking maybe tonight's the night those lights will beam down and take him away.

A sharp sound cuts through the air, makes the back of Lenny's neck prickle. 'Hey, baby!' one of the guys calls out, and Lenny remembers Jim Jones saying the same thing, slapping him on the back, grinning. But the wolf-whistle isn't for him, he sees; sees the chick perched on the hood of his station wagon slipping off it when she sees him. She bounds up to him like she knows him; fog coming out of her mouth, blond hair framing her face, a cute heart-shaped face with eyes that are all pupil. She's *cute*, Lenny sees with a jolt, and smiling like a beauty queen, putting her hand right on his sleeve … what the hell?

'It's late, Lenny, so I'll just say one thing,' the blonde whispers the words in his ear, foggy and excited, like the opening of a joke that's all on him. 'Father loves you!'

*

Lenny doesn't know what to think, so he doesn't think. All through the drive back to the boardinghouse and the dark trudge up the staircase, his mind may as well be a moonrock. In the communal bathroom, he sheds his smelly work clothes and turns the taps with a rusty squeak, which does something Pavlovian to his body. Fog. Lips. Hot breath. An impression of yielding warmth. He steps under the spray, closes his eyes to the dart of hot droplets, and, finally, has a thought:

Evelyn.

He tries to grasp her imperfections, squeeze as much out of them as he can. That her teeth were kind of crooked. That she couldn't handle drugs, never more than a few tokes and miserable both times they dropped acid together. That night on their Mexican honeymoon when she got sick and left the bathroom smelling foul, worse than cat litter. Those French songs she liked, oddly stupid and infantile: one about lollipops, another about bicycles, another about a 'hippopotamus woman'. Why love her. Why cry for her. Not a perfect human being by any means, not an actress on a silver screen, not an angel, not as beautiful as his throbbing heart wants him to believe or that choked-stinging feeling in his brain, and, quite frankly, a bitch. God, she was a bitch, and there was that prim school-teacherly side to her as well, which turned him off more than anything, made him feel sometimes like he was living with his mother—

Lenny jerks off. It's quick for such a poisonous thing, and afterward he feels shaky but okay. Like he's just been shot and bandaged up by some backstreet doctor and sent home with a sweet dose of morphine. With trembling hands, he dries himself off and wraps a towel around his waist, and it's only in his room that he realizes the towel isn't his, and that it has yellowish stains that he didn't put there. But it's hard to find the will to care, confronted with his miserable quarters: the bare lightbulb, the rusty radiator, the single bed that no woman has ever shared. And, face-up on the gray floorboards, a note in his landlady's longsighted hand:

Call 'Pastor Jim' tonight!

Lenny wishes he could pretend not to have seen the note, wishes he could simply climb into bed and read Robert Heinlein until his eyes hurt. Yet even the thought of ignoring a summons from Jim feels risky. So he pulls on a pair of drawstring pants and creaks back down to the breakfast nook, practically stepping in a bowl of kibble, practically dropping the receiver, practically misdialing the parsonage. Jim answers after two rings, almost languorously.

'Is that you, Lenny, my son?'

'Hi, Jim … Sorry to call so late …'

The apology comes instinctively, and Jim accepts it as his due. 'Any time, darlin'. You need me, you call me any time.' There's a whooshing of breath before Jim speaks again. 'I know some things lately maybe seem like punitive measures, but it's only 'cause I care and 'cause I know you stronger. I don't like to say it all the time, but, son: you're a born socialist. Which is why it pains me so much to see you squander yourself on drugs and ego relationships.'

'Sorry,' Lenny says again, his face already turning pink.

'Everything I do, I do 'cause it's best in the long run,' Jim explains. 'I see the socialist you can be, and I see you'll never be that so long as you're distracted. Evelyn—' Lenny feels his pulse quicken at the sound of her name; still the loveliest he knows, and still hot with betrayal. '— I mean, *Evelyn*, she got a lotta qualities, but she's not a born socialist. Everything with her, it's gotta be intellectual. And she got that ego hang-up. We been workin' through it, but she still needs a great deal of personal attention.' Jim sighs. 'I don't trust she'll ever have an honest connection with the Cause. That's why she gotta be kept close. You understand?'

'Yeah,' Lenny hears himself saying. 'I get it.'

'That woman … I'm glad I can talk to you. God-*damn*.' Jim gives a bark of black laughter. 'She's *needy*. Probably never showed it with you, but once you take away all that pride and intellectualizing, she's the most insecure, fragile —'

Fragile. The word brings to Lenny's mind a night from early in their engagement, dining with his parents in Berkeley. Dr. Lynden had been speculating loudly, and at great length, about Apollo-1 when Evelyn interrupted in her dear, sharp voice with some opinion of her own. Evelyn was often interrupting. It was one of the many things that endeared her to Lenny, though Dr. Lynden apparently felt otherwise. *'Excuse me, but I'm talking here,'* he brushed Evelyn off in his most professorial tone, and across the table Lenny saw her looking like she'd just been struck. A little while later, he found her wiping her eyes in the upstairs hallway and was bemused by her explanation: 'I'm sorry, but no man has ever spoken to me that way.' Yet it had felt good to put his arm around her and tell her it was okay, his old man had always been a jerk. It felt good to know she could be fragile, too.

How fragile they were. How fragile it all was. Their fragile, young marriage that never really stood a chance.

'— She likes to play strong. It's only 'cause I'm the most empathetic man on Earth that she lets me see otherwise. You should be thankful, friend, ain't you gotta be holding her up. It's *tiring*.' Jim laughs again, and for a moment Lenny wonders if he's actually expected to thank him. 'Course, I'm thankful for the sacrifices you been making. Shows a great maturity. Forbearance. Don't think I haven't noticed. Fact is … fact is, I think you're ready for more responsibility. That's why I wanted to talk tonight.'

'Oh?' Lenny squeaks, relieved by the change in topic.

'I've made arrangements for someone to visit. Someone special,' Jim says coyly. 'I know you've grown fond of Brother Ike, but I think you're gonna like this change. In fact, could be the best thing ever happened to you.'

'Oh?' Lenny tries not to sound too dubious of the pairing of 'fond' and 'Brother Ike'.

'Ain't no small responsibility,' Jim elaborates. 'This … visitor, see: they're new to socialism. Any questions they have, I need you to answer. Think of yourself as my disciple.'

The word 'disciple' reminds Lenny of longhaired guys breaking bread and drinking wine. Or maybe sophomore year, when he'd started getting worked up about Vietnam and fraternizing with other young men over marijuana. Evelyn hadn't been around that year. She'd been in France, and it hadn't mattered because he hadn't known enough to miss her: only that she was the minister's daughter, that she dated a lot but never seemed to have a steady, that he liked her walk and her voice and the way her dark hair caught his eye like plumage.

'Thanks … Father,' Lenny chokes out.

'I trust you, son,' Jim soothes. 'Your whole life, you been so terribly overlooked, but I see how precious you are. Ain't no part of you that isn't precious —' Lenny lets Jim's words wash over him, words as soft as turtledoves and women's hair and the pillow he wants to be laying his head down on so badly. It's a while before Jim says the other thing, so strange and startling Lenny is sure it must be dream-talk, some hallucination brought on by lack of sleep. '— And, darlin': I forgive you for thinking about Evelyn when you masturbated tonight.'

3.

'*Si vous avez des questions, demandez-moi en français,*' she tells the class when they ask about her black eye, and she smiles at the ducking of heads, the fluttering of dictionaries. Last period of the week doesn't mean a free pass, and they know her well enough to know this, that they're expected to keep translating and conjugating until the final bell. She looks out the window at the milky sky and thinks of the small stretch of hours between now and total darkness.

A girl raises her hand: red-faced, white-blond, non-Temple. It's not Evelyn's custom to have favorites, and if the handful of Temple kids she teaches get better grades — the Luce boys; the Bellows girls; Su-mi Jones, Jim's adopted Korean daughter — it's because Temple kids work harder. '*Oui, Jill.*' Evelyn folds her arms as the girl stammers something about Madame Lynden and her *œil de beurre noir.* She is still Madame Lynden. She still wears the ring Lenny Lynden gave her. No need to draw attention. Evelyn turns to the class and answers Jill's question matter-of-factly:

'*Je me suis pris la portière de la voiture.*'

To demonstrate, she mimes opening a car door, hitting it against her face, and reeling back. The kids look suitably wide-eyed, and she has a reckless urge to toy with them further. '*C'est ce qui arrive quand je ne bois pas mon café le matin.*' There are more blank stares as they try to figure out her joke, if it even is a joke, and she allows herself a brisk laugh before taking out her chalk and breaking the sentence down: *C'est. Ce. Qui. Arrive.* This is what happens when I don't drink my morning coffee. I hit my face on the car door. Do you believe me? How would you express this sentence with 'Madame Lynden' as the subject …?

At the end of the hour, Evelyn hangs back at her desk, chiming out the occasional, '*Au revoir,*' and, '*Bon week-end.*' She is well liked by her students; they don't leave in a rush, and many glance back at her before filing out the door. It's only once she's alone that Evelyn finds herself clutching her desk like a life raft, dizzied by a sudden wave of exhaustion. But the wave breaks, and a moment later she has gathered up her papers and slung her purse; she is twenty-three years old, able-bodied and in love, and these things are stronger than fatigue.

There have been changes in Evelyn's life since Lenny stopped being part of it, some of which she dwells on, and some of which she doesn't. She doesn't dwell on her diminished sleep. She doesn't dwell on the way Su-mi Jones ignores her wave from across the parking lot. She doesn't dwell on her inferior car: an ugly little red Volvo, purchased second-hand from Sister Diane. She does dwell on Jim's generosity in facilitating the purchase of the Volvo; on the beauty of a relationship grounded in generosity, but not indulgence. As she drives toward the Temple's rectangular form, she dwells on its beauty; a beauty that's entirely secular to her eyes, despite the cross on the roof, the sign proclaiming:

PEOPLES TEMPLE CHRISTIAN CHURCH

The first thing she sees when she brings the Volvo around the back of the redwood and plate-glass building is Jim's blue Pontiac, trunk aloft. The next is a tall yet feeble female figure toiling over it. In the pale sunlight, the woman's upswept hair is more gold than ginger, fraying slightly at the seams, but Evelyn would know that hair anywhere, the dip of shame and fizzing of defiance that comes from looking at it.

'Oh, Rosaline.' Evelyn hears her own voice ring out, clear and innocuous, as she cuts the engine and steps onto the gravel. 'You look like you're struggling there.'

Maybe the older woman flinches. Maybe it's only a trick of the light. Either way, Evelyn doesn't let it stop her from bustling over to the trunk and placing her hands just above Rosaline's, on the corners of the box she's straining to lift. Rosaline looks up in a daze, her face mere inches from Evelyn's, and her wide eyes seem to widen further, her thin lips to disappear into the general whiteness of her face. '*Oh,*'

Rosaline gasps soundlessly, blinking fast like she's trying to erase some painful vision, and it dawns on Evelyn that perhaps her own face is the painful thing, Jim's mark beneath her eye. *Hurt me.* Yet within seconds Rosaline has looked down and drawn herself up, and in a steady voice she concedes, 'Thank you, Eve.'

'*Evelyn.*'

'Evelyn. I'm sorry.' And Rosaline does sound so apologetic that Evelyn immediately feels like a bitch. 'If you can just get a grip on that side? Oof. Who'da figured dolls and teddy bears could be so heavy—'

'For the orphans,' Evelyn doesn't ask so much as purr.

'The Health Department people, they surprised me with a whole 'nother collection. Really I wasn't expect—' Rosaline halts as they push through the glass doors and Evelyn steals a glance at her face: ghost-pale, careworn, twitchy as a mouse. There've been days when she has looked at Jim's wife with envy — her silky-bright kaftan dresses, her flower-stalk neck, her lacquered beehive in profile giving her the appearance of a blond Queen Nefertiti — but today isn't one of them. '— Expecting such generosity.'

'Of course, you have a lot of influence over there.' Evelyn intends the words to be complimentary, yet they fall as flat as a bad joke.

They don't speak as they inch past the glass cabinets and through the light-filled sanctuary with its covered swimming pool and many echoes. Soft voices and clangs can be heard from the kitchen, but it's a slow time of day: too late for lunchtime traffic, too early for the after-work rush. When at last they reach the storeroom, Rosaline is blotch-cheeked and shaky. Evelyn looks away as Rosaline catches her breath and rubs her back; embarrassed for her and also, to her own shame, faintly smug.

'This *is* impressive,' Evelyn enthuses, crouching down to peek in the box. She frowns at a crude black woolen doll with clown lips and a minstrel's outfit. 'Well … Maybe not this.'

'Oh.' Rosaline frowns too, still clutching her back. 'I used to have one of those as a girl.' She shakes her head. 'A long time ago.'

'Why don't I get the next box,' Evelyn suggests, in her best attempt at a deferential tone. 'You can hold the door or something.'

Rosaline doesn't dignify this with an answer, just flaps her hands and marches on out. Evelyn slinks behind; if Rosaline wants to play the martyr, that's fine with her. Jim has told her about Rosaline's bad back — one of the many reasons they have ceased marital relations — yet she thinks better of mentioning this as they heft the next box from the trunk. 'I'll ask the youth choir to sort through these tonight. There's no reason they should go to the Gift Wrapping Committee any later than Monday.'

'Ohh, noo,' Rosaline protests, her vowels comically rounded. 'I'll ask the boys.'

Evelyn feels a flash of anxiety at this reference to Jim's sons, sensitive-eyed coltish pre-teens as unknown to her as creatures in a paddock seen through the window of a speeding car. Perhaps Rosaline feels anxious, too, since everything about her face seems to either twitch or droop before she starts laboring with renewed vigor.

A copper-brown coupé turns in to the parking lot. Both women look up to watch Jim hunch out with two non-Temple men. Evelyn flicks through her mental log of appointments: *The Prosperity Gazette, Friday 4pm.*

'… A place all people can call their own.' Jim is gesturing at the building. 'I mean that, *all.* Shelter for the cold, food for the hungry, employment for the unemployed. Proselytizing, that's not important to me. I'm very down-to-earth. I plan to feed hundreds this Christmas and make sure no child, county-over, goes without a gift.'

'And your services? Is it true that you claim to heal cancer, blindness …?'

'Healing, that's just a small part of what we do.' Gentle as Jim's voice is, Evelyn can tell he doesn't like the question — that minuscule sharp note only a lover could perceive, or perhaps a wife. 'Every Sunday, we discuss current affairs. We got individuals testifying. Activities for the young people, music … Children's choir, they'll be here in a little whiles, rehearsing for the Christmas show. Cutest thing you'll ever see,' he says mildly. 'I don't like to talk about healings too much. Gives the impression, for some, we don't believe in medical science. Fact is, we got a wonderful system of care homes. Drug rehabilitation program. My wife, Rosaline, she works for the State Health Department inspecting — well, she can probably tell you better herself.'

Jim shines a smile in Rosaline's direction, a smile that includes Evelyn, but impersonally, like a Labrador dropping a tennis ball at the feet of a stranger. Evelyn sees Rosaline's face become smooth and serene, the face of the woman who stands onstage with Jim on Sunday mornings. 'That's Mrs. Jones?' The reporter tilts his head at Rosaline, and there's no sign he's even seen Evelyn. 'Say, Reverend … could we get a picture of you two together?'

Jim's smile twists. 'Sure, Burt. If Rosaline don't mind.'

Rosaline demurs, 'Oh. Well. Y'know, a picture of Jim and the boys'd be nicer. They'll be back from school any min—'

'We'd love a shot of just the two of you first, Mrs. Jones.'

Rosaline blushes at her feet, pats her beehive, shakes her head; accepts. Evelyn feels her insides ripple like silk, watching Rosaline creep toward the men, the way she allows herself to be directed, shoulder encircled by Jim. The way her pink-and-white coloring contrasts with Jim's tan and blue-black; her doe-eyes with his Asiatic squint; her close-lipped smile with his wide grin. Evelyn thinks what a pity it is that the photographs won't be in color. She thinks of getting some copies made for sale after Sunday services. Thinks of everything, except what she would look like, standing in Rosaline's place.

4.

'Terra. Short for Teresa.'

That's what the blonde says, meeting Lenny in broad daylight outside the shitty diner where Brother Ike used to take him for chicken sandwiches and bottomless coffee. She's wearing the same coat from last night, brown suede and shearling, and, when she takes that off in the red faux-leather booth, a hand-knit sweater the same white as her teeth. She smiles a lot. This, along with the blunt fact of her beauty, makes Lenny feel like he's the butt of some cruel joke.

'Well, short for *Little Terror*, actually. That's what Daddy used to call me. I was just the craziest kid, running around screaming, playing drums with Mom's cookware. One time, I got into Daddy's case files and crayoned all over them! He's a prosecutor, y'know. But at home he was just the biggest softie. I never got spanked or anything.'

She gazes at Lenny expectantly: surf-colored eyes, sand-colored hair. He looks at his menu.

'What I guess I'm saying … I wasn't running away from, y'know, some abusive family situation. My olds aren't *bad people*. Daddy even ran for the state assembly back in '62 — Democrat *of course* — only he lost to this dude Theo Hanson; y'know the one who did that investigation after the Watts riots?' The blonde folds her arms over her menu. '*Anyway*. It's just, as soon as I hit puberty, it's like I couldn't breathe. Everybody treated me different. And I don't mean just guys; but, well … *guys*.'

The blonde leans further forward, lowers her voice confidingly.

'I guess you don't wanna hear about all the guys, but most of them only want one thing. It doesn't matter if you're *thirteen*. It's just one guy after another trying to get in your pants and never anywhere deep-er—'

On 'deeper', a giggle bursts from her lips, which makes Lenny wish he had a shell to duck into. Duck and cover, like Bert the Turtle. The night he met Evelyn, at the party thrown by her many female housemates, they'd had a seemingly profound conversation about those nuclear drills they all went through as kids, ducking under their elementary-school desks. 'Ronnie and me, we were together *two years*. He even gave me this pre-engagement ring, real pretty blue topaz with cubic zirconias. But retrospectfully, he wasn't interested in *me*. Me-me. I was just like some fuck-toy for him and soon as he saw the sea of pussy in Haight-Ashbury … well, he didn't give a thought to throwing me away.'

The blonde's delivery is unsentimental. Still, Lenny feels bad for not feeling worse for her. He's glad when the wide-waisted waitress shows up with her pen and pad.

'Oh! What's good here?' The blonde doesn't even glance at her menu.

'Umm.' Lenny shrugs. 'I like the chicken sandwich.'

'Two chicken sandwiches. And, um, iced tea? Two iced teas?' As soon as the waitress shuffles off, the blonde leans back and goes right on with her story. '… Don't get me wrong, I had fun with the free love thing. I mean, when the grass is good and it's a good-looking guy, there's nothing better, right? Trouble is when the dude starts ordering you around like a maid or wants to pimp you out to a motorcycle gang or something.' She sucks on her lips and catches him solemnly in those blue-green eyes. What color were Evelyn's? It's a pop quiz from his broken heart, which he immediately aces: gray. 'We had this commune near Modesto. It was a pretty bad scene by the end. This little chick Merri, some dude broke her jaw. All her bottom incisors totally caved into the bone. You have beautiful teeth, by the way.'

'… Thanks.' Lenny rubs his jaw, raw and pallid as a freshly plucked chicken.

'Sorry. I used to wear a retainer. Did you ever have one? Seventh grade, worst year of my life.' *Even worse than the bikers?* Lenny wonders. 'Anyway, I ended up leaving with this older dude, Rex. He was stationed in Hawaii in his navy days; said he'd take me. It's stupid, but I really thought he was different. He used to sing me "Aloha Oe" … I called him "King" …'

Lenny wishes the iced tea would come.

'I guess that's a warning sign, a guy wants to be called "King"?' The blonde rolls her eyes. 'He wasn't Elvis, that's for sure. Have you seen what speed does to teeth? Well, they weren't anything like *yours*. And he didn't have your nice blue eyes, either. One was all squinty from this fight he was in where — but anyway, looks aren't important. Socialism taught me that.' She raises her chin prettily, as though to invite Lenny to admire her full-frontal. 'I know the attention I get for my looks isn't the real deal. But I was so desperate to believe I was something special, I didn't care. Y'know, I actually thought Rex was some up-front charitable guy 'cause he didn't want me screwing johns, only blowjobs?'

Maybe Lenny would feel worse for her if it wasn't for his sense of being totally out of touch. It strikes him that she's a different breed from the girls he's used to. Marianne Glover, his sophomore-year girlfriend, had taken months of full-clothed necking before she agreed to go to bed with him, and even Evelyn had appearances she liked to maintain: telling her housemates he'd fallen asleep in her room while listening to records, for instance, and always making sure they were dressed by a certain time on weekends, lest her parents visit.

'Um … how old did you say you were?'

'Nineteen? Twenty on February four.' She laughs. 'Aquarius. What's your sign?'

'January sixteen. I mean … Capricorn.'

'Oh, yeah. I can see that. You're quiet and kinda aloof.' She smiles at him in that disarming way, like she already knows him and is just remembering the details. 'Rex was a Leo. Always wanting his ego stroked. And he had this thing about self-sufficiency. Started saying we should get our own boat and sail to Hawaii like explorers. So Rex found this dude on Lake Mendocino with an old yacht. It had some damage to the deck and stuff, but we figured we'd camp out and work on it. Rex said I could name it "Crystal Ship", paint it up any colors I wanted …'

There's a clatter from the kitchen and Lenny tenses up, though he's still several hours from his next shift at the Silver State. She doesn't seem to notice. 'Two weeks, maybe three, we were on the lake? My memory's kinda hazy, ha-ha. The weather wasn't so good, but there was this bait store up the road; the dude there used to let me bag jerky and candy bars just for smiling at him right.' In demonstration, she smiles just right, and Lenny feels his face glow, despite himself. 'We had this primo acid. Called it Rainbow Snake 'cause you'd see rainbows snaking everywhere. Only downside? It gave us the *nastiest* acid belly.' She lolls her tongue. 'Last time me and Rex tripped together, we were squatting in the bushes all night! I remember we had this campfire going near the yacht, and looking through these branches at these colors grooving outta the flames: reds, purples, blues, greens, better than Fourth of July …'

Last time Lenny dropped acid was back in the spring, after handing in his senior thesis, 'Capital Punishment and the Glorification of Violence in American Society'. Evelyn and her friend Mary-Kay stuck with wine and weed, but were a benevolent presence, adjusting lights and flipping records, helping him put on his shoes before he went out to touch the night flowers and gawk at the gods in the sky.

Lenny doesn't know which fact, of all these, seems most unreal to him now.

'I guess I shouldn't blame Rex for bailing when he did. All those sirens, I mean … he had a record. But it messed me up: everything's cool one second and next second the boat's on fire.' The blonde isn't smiling anymore but shaking her head sadly. 'I've had trips go bad, but never like that. I'm lucky I didn't end up in some loony bin — Sorry, "asylum".' She looks up at Lenny so deliberately he wonders if she's implying something about his mental state. 'I heard about your alternate service, by the way, and just wanna say *I think that's so great*. Most guys I know? They only put on the peace act 'cause they don't want *their* asses on the line. They don't give a shit about helping people. Not like you.'

Lenny senses she's flirting with him, but he's more irritated than flattered. He purses his lips until she resumes her monologue.

'I don't remember much about that night in lock-up. Gene says I was screaming a lot: for "King", for "God"; I guess I thought I was dying … You know, any other cop would've left me for dead. But Brother Gene, soon as he realized I had no one? He sent his *wife* to pick me up. In the middle of the night!' Her words come in a breathless rush, and Lenny is relieved that she now seems more interested in the absent Brother Gene than in him. 'I don't even know if my own folks would've taken me in like Gene and Joya, no questions asked. Cleaned me up. Clothed me. Fed me. You're probably used to how Temple people are, but I just assumed there'd be a *catch*.' She makes a high-pitched sound, more yelp than giggle. 'Gene, poor Genie. He was so embarrassed! I don't wanna gossip but … let's just say he's a real *gentleman*. Said if I really wanted to make it up, why not come to church Sunday? Well, I was never big on church, but …'

She stops. Breathes deep. Lenny worries she's about to cry.

'*Father*,' she intones. 'When I heard him — My whole life up 'til then, it's like he looked right into it and saw how *empty* it was. Not just the guys and drugs, but *me*, the way I used those things to keep from caring about the world. I mean … there's little black babies getting their toes eaten by rats, and here I am high every day and dreaming about Hawaii?' She flicks her hair off her face, a prissy gesture at odds with her heavy words. 'It's not easy to hear you're selfish. Shit, I figured anything I did had to be better than living for straight society. But either way, I was avoiding *enlightenment*. True loving connection. My purpose in this life as a committed and compassionate human being.'

Lenny can't help being drawn in by something zealous in her face, the halo of her blond hair, the fact that she believes everything she's saying. There's a freckle at the corner of her lip. He likes it.

'We're nothing if we're not connected. Working together as human beings for some greater good. I never realized that's what I was missing 'til I saw all these people brought together by Father's love to fight against prejudice and poverty. To feel that kinda love, truly selfless, when you've only known ego and exploitation …' Her voice coils high and wistful. '… It's like coming to an ocean in the middle of the desert. It gives a whole new perspective: on friendship, relationships. How important it is to surround ourselves with people who can be trusted to see past the surface.'

There's a space between her breasts where the wool of her sweater pools like spilled milk. Lenny likes this, too. He likes those round, soft swellings, the way looking at them makes his mind feel just as soft. It's this softness he's thinking of when she fixes him with a pout.

'I want you as a friend, Lenny Lynden, but only if you're a guy I can *trust*.'

5.

On a fine blue December morning, a white family in an old white station wagon stops outside the white ranch-style house on Vine Street. The sun is almost at full height, highlighting the water stains on the windshield as Reverend Thomas Burne squints beyond it. He sees a white cat stalking across the lawn, away from a pair of screaming toddlers. Another toddler spins in dizzy circles and collapses. A baby looks on stoically from a plastic swing.

'Congratulations. Looks like you're grandparents now,' Sally-Ann, his youngest, pipes up from the back seat.

'I don't think this is the place.' Vicky, his second-born, sits forward, bookmarking her *Wide Sargasso Sea* with a Women Strike For Peace flier. 'Looks like a daycare or something.'

Rev. Burne's moustache droops as he frowns. 'Care to ring the doorbell and see?'

'Um, no thanks. You go ahead, Dad.'

'I second that.' His wife Margaret grins, cheekbones flushed apple-like. 'Tom, you need to stretch your legs.'

'Ditto. Women's vote,' Sally-Ann sing-songs.

'Well … who am I to argue with democracy.'

Rev. Burne's daughters have an impulse to giggle as he unpacks his lanky body and traverses the toy-strewn yard, careful as a stork. Instead, Vicky scrutinizes her book. 'Mr. Rochester is a creep.'

'I never liked him.' Margaret grimaces. 'Call me unromantic, but that moody-broody act does nothing for me.'

Rev. Burne raps on the door of the white house. Sally-Ann gives a low whistle as it peels open and a dodo-shaped middle-aged woman steps onto the porch. 'Gee, Evie has sure packed on the pounds.'

'Sal!' Margaret cries. But her youngest daughter's joke has taken her by surprise and she's snickering like a schoolgirl, eyes watering under her round sunglasses. Sally-Ann and Vicky exchange glances as she dabs a tear. 'Oh — Don't laugh! — *Girls.*'

'Mom's leaking again.' Sally-Ann smirks.

'Better call the plumber.' Vicky rolls her eyes. 'Seriously, Mom? It's not that funny.'

'It's not funny!' Margaret agrees. 'Just you wait till you're my age and shedding tears at the drop of a—'

'Looks like Evie got a perm, too.' Sally-Ann peers out at the dodo woman. 'And some gray highlights. Motherhood has really matured her.'

This sets Margaret off anew, and soon the car is humid with cry-laughter. 'You know, I can't even imagine Evie and Lenny with kids,' Vicky says.

'*Lenny.*' Margaret sighs. 'He's still such a boy. I hope Evie isn't cracking the whip too hard.'

'This is so weird,' Sally-Ann gripes. 'Who even is that lady?'

They watch Rev. Burne and the dodo woman exchange gestures. Rev. Burne takes a slip of paper from her and dips his balding head, makes as if to go. Out of nowhere, the dodo woman reaches over and plants a kiss on his cheek.

'Far-out, Mom! You've got competition.'

'And I didn't even bring my dueling pistol.' Margaret tilts her face upward as Rev. Burne re-enters the station wagon. 'Hello, darling. I see you've found an admirer.'

'I suppose so.' Rev. Burne blushes. 'Nice lady from Lafeyette … Indiana. One of those "Peoples Temple" members. She had a Korean baby,' he adds curiously. 'We've got a few miles to go yet. They've moved to a cabin, apparently.'

'Evie in a cabin?' Margaret sighs, shakes her head. 'She's full of surprises, our girl.'

The tires are just a whisper on the dirt road, but the black-and-white dog hears everything. He bounds ahead, barking rabidly, and his mistress doesn't bother calling him back. A squirrel, perhaps, or some kind of bird. Last night she and Jim heard screech owls. The cabin comes into view, and Picnic's barks become shallower. Something slams in the distance. Her chest splinters like glass, target-practice milk bottles in the woods. She freezes in her boots, bloodlessly gripping her .22. Then, scrutinizing the movement through the trees, a pang of recognition:

Oh! MomandDad.

Evelyn has always been thin, but what strikes the Burnes most seeing their firstborn daughter emerge from the bushes is how her clothes swamp her body — the clunky boots and long plaid skirt and chunky sweater. Her whole appearance somehow diminished, in fact, cringing and shadowy, as if she's trying to hide not only what's in her hands but her heart. With a slithery feeling, they realize what she's holding. Sally-Ann cracks a joke about cabins and shotguns. Margaret shuffles forward, mouth o-ed. 'A gun, Evie?'

'It's for self-defense.' As Evelyn steps closer the sunlight brings the shadows on her face into full relief. 'There've been reports of prowlers from the highway.'

'Prowlers?' Margaret reaches to touch her under-eye. 'You mean — somebody came and did — this?'

'Oh, no, that was my fault.' Evelyn gives a rusty little laugh. 'I hit my face on the car door. You know how clumsy I get when I don't have my morning coffee. Speaking of which.'

She throws her head toward the cabin and invites them in. Rev. Burne frowns as she mounts the porch, rifle tucked under her arm. 'Lenny, he's okay with … that weapon?'

'Don't let Picnic in. He's covered in dust.' The screen door yelps as Evelyn tugs it open and continues conversationally, 'He was named by some children who found him on a church picnic. Our church has an impressive animal rescue program. Since September we've found homes for thirty-six animals that would've otherwise been euthanized.'

Though the hall is narrow and rustic, it's also tidy and reverently decorated with art and family photos. 'When I saw that bruise …' Margaret tells Evelyn's nape. 'We worry, Evie.'

'Honestly? It looks worse than it is.' Tucking back a loose strand, Evelyn's fingers brush over her rose earring. She motions her family into the kitchen and taps the rifle's handle. 'Have a seat. I'll put this away and freshen up.'

'About that …' Rev. Burne tries again. 'I never want to tell you girls how to live, but I had hoped, growing up in a pacifist household—'

For the first time since their arrival, Evelyn meets her father's gaze, arms crossed and brows blandly raised. 'It's only a .22. Practically a children's rifle.' She smiles faintly and rolls her eyes. 'Everybody keeps firearms around these parts. It's just for show.'

'All guns cause harm, Evelyn … And I've never known you to do anything simply because everybody else is.'

This is such a typically Rev. Burne thing to say that Evelyn has an urge to roll her eyes again. Instead, she looks to her mother, whose face is soft with concern, and her sisters, who mostly just look curious. 'You're right,' she sighs and holds the rifle out to him, horizontal in surrender. 'I suppose I just got caught up in the hysteria. Here. Take it away.'

Rev. Burne shakes his head. 'There's no need for that. I trust you'll do what's right.'

He gives the crook of her arm a squeeze, in lieu of a hug; his firstborn daughter doesn't like being hugged, and he respects her need for distance. She nods and lifts her gray eyes to his, lowers them and turns back down the hall. That bruise. It bothers him. More than he can say.

In Evelyn's absence, the Burnes seat themselves at the dining table, Margaret resisting the urge to get up and make the coffee herself. 'It's nicer than a typical cabin,' she says. 'The way she's done it up. It's almost how I pictured she might've lived in France.' Sally-Ann plucks a lemon from the fruit bowl, sings, '*They call me mellow yellow …*' Vicky needs to pee. 'It does surprise me that Lenny would agree to keeping a firearm,' Rev. Burne muses. 'Well, it's not as if we were ever in doubt of who the decision-maker is in that relationship,' Margaret rejoins. Vicky creeps back in, brown cords rustling like leaves.

'Evie's on the phone,' she reports. 'It looked kind of … intense.'

'She better be telling Lenny to get his butt over here.' Sally-Ann rolls the lemon between her palms.

Soon enough, Evelyn floats back into the kitchen, her bruise freshly powdered and her sweater exchanged for a chic cowl-neck blouse. She looks both more and less like herself than before, her eyes strangely veiled, high color in her cheeks. Margaret asks how Lenny is, and

Evelyn says, 'Him? Oh, fine,' and shrugs with one shoulder. She busies herself at the stove with the coffee and carries on, 'We're expecting large numbers at our service tomorrow. Last week we had over three hundred. I know Dad will be working, but if you want to stay on, Mom, or even just Vicky and Sally-Ann, you're most welcome. People come from Sacramento and even further to hear Reverend Jones speak. He's truly a sensation.'

'I'm afraid this overworked unenlightened housewife already committed to cooking a feast for a dozen seminary students tonight. And Vicky has a date, rumor has it.'

'Well. You'll meet Reverend Jones soon enough.' Evelyn angles away from the stove. 'He's on his way now. He wants to meet you very much, and I want you to meet him.' Her voice dips, dreamily deliberate. 'You should know: Jim has become very important to me.'

6.

Lenny has a friend and her name is Terra. She works with him at the Silver State, hired on the spot to waitress five to midnight. He sees her early in her first shift through the serving hatch, shadowing a larger girl with a face like a speckled egg and dressed in the same Western getup, all ruffle and bodice. She wears the outfit well, hair in two braids on top of her head. He registers her appearance as a minor annoyance and resolves not to look through the hatch again.

But other guys in the kitchen do.

'Did you get a load of Barbarella waiting tables?'

'Mannn! Dig the jugs on that little blonde!'

'Oh, baby, you're makin' me thirsty!'

He tries to lose himself in the usual thoughts of space and swirling water, but it's as if there's a mosquito constantly buzzing around him, settling on his skin, agitating his blood. Scoffing his free steak dinner in the break-room, he finds himself worrying about Terra out on the restaurant floor, those comments like the snarling of wolves. And yet, exciting.

Because guys never talked that way about Evelyn. Did they?

Time passes slowly, intrusively, a clunking thing of heat and metal. For the first time since he started at the Silver State, Lenny is aware of the Lee and Nancy duets playing in the dining area. He's aware of the locker-room-like confinement of the kitchen, and that just outside these confines, girls in uniforms are bending over for tips, smiling, taking orders. He's aware of those same girls butterflying past the kitchen at closing, when he still has an hour's worth of dishes left, then coming back the way they went in sweaters, jeans, sheepskin coats.

'*Pssst! Lenny!*' Terra sticks her head into the steaming space. 'I'll wait for you out there, 'kay?' She beams. 'I made thirty dollars in tips!'

As soon as she's gone, the guys are on him, eyes aglitter with hungry contempt.

'Dude, you know her?'

'How'd you know that babe?'

'You fucking pussy! *You* know *her?*'

'Yeah,' Lenny stumbles out. 'She's my friend.'

Saying it makes it true, in a way he never would've expected when he woke that morning with a hard-on for Evelyn and dreading his lunch date. And squelching out at one a.m. to find her waiting in the dark among the overturned chairs and cowboy kitsch, there it is again: *My friend.* She's reading to the glow of the aquarium, but as soon as she sees him she shuts her book and bounds over, unfazed by the lurking kitchen crew. 'Have you read this? *The Feminine Mystique?*' She links her arm with his. 'Sister Joya lent it to me. She said it *changed her life.*'

Before Lenny can say anything about the ubiquity of that little red book among the girls at Davis, they're at the back door and Wile E. is holding it open, glowing eyes on Terra. 'Hey there, Miss America … You like to get high?'

'Sorry,' Terra says, in that blithely polite tone Lenny is sure all girls must learn, along with how to hook up a bra. 'I'm high on Jesus.'

She doesn't look at Lenny, but the triumph in her profile, the feel of her arm against his, it's enough. He barely hears the jeers as they walk to the car, barely thinks of the high she just passed up. 'Hey, I know it's out of your way, but could we drive under the arch, real quick? I wanna see it all lit up.'

'Sure.' Lenny opens up the station wagon.

'And over the river? I bet it looks groovy at night.'

The exhaustion is just a fuzz behind his forehead as he tweaks and glides through the backstreets and onto Virginia, its topaz and ruby inferno, ice-slick and lined with empty cars, its smoke shops and glitter fountains and nine-foot-tall Primadonna girls. Terra toys with the radio and marvels in that flat-sultry drone. '… It's like Christmas. How it looked as a kid, I mean? Before you're old enough to know it's all just white capitalist bullshit.' At her fingertips, Motown turns to bluegrass, bluegrass to 'Hey Jude'. '… I mean, the valley is beautiful, but something about this place? It gets my heart beating. I guess — I could be happy here.'

This is unexpected, but it takes Lenny some moments to figure why. He slows the station wagon as they pass under the arch and her face really does look like a little girl's on Christmas morning. 'You mean ... you could be happy without the Temple?'

'Oh!' Terra looks stricken. 'Well, I ... The Temple is the best thing that ever happened to me, Lenny! And *you* ...' She fumbles across the shift for his fingers. 'I just mean ... I think these next couple weeks together here could be full of happiness.'

Lenny glances at her small hand curled over his, her short, buffed fingernails. He thinks of Evelyn's white hands, her oval fingernails with the pointed tips. He doesn't want to be rude, but he also doesn't want to pretend they're the same. He pulls his hand away and stifles a yawn. They cross the bridge in silence, the Truckee just a gutter-like trickle below.

'Father wants you to be happy,' Terra speaks up. 'So does your wife. She told me.'

It's the first time Lenny has thought of Evelyn and Terra together. He says nothing as he turns the car to face the neon treasure trove across the river. 'You can talk about her, if it helps,' Terra offers. 'I don't mind at all. Maybe it would help us both?'

Lenny hopes she can't see him cringe in the dark. 'I only met her once,' Terra goes on. 'I heard you met at college?' She toys with the hem of her sweater. 'I got into USC, if you can believe it. Daddy wanted me to be a lawyer, too. My mind's kinda fucked-up now; not as quick, I mean, and I can't read for a long time. But I'm totally committed to getting an education.'

There's something so tragic about this that Lenny can only smile feebly and say, 'I know.' He's thinking of the redneck kids in Jim Jones's night classes, the un-with-it housewives, the black folks learning to read at seventy, but also of where he came from: that mansion in the Berkeley Hills, with its bay views and laurel trees and kidney-shaped swimming pool. That studious boy's bedroom, encyclopedia shelves and M.C. Escher print overhanging the bed where so often he'd wake from hot dreams drenched in shame. *Sons should be chaste like daughters,* wasn't that what Dr. Lynden said? And: *Sons and daughters should spend three hours a night on study, minimum.* His older brother, Ned, at Harvard. His older sister Beth, Cambridge. His mother always with a fat Russian novel in one hand and a long cigarette in the other.

'I guess you prefer college girls? I guess, at least, you'd have more to talk about?'

'It's not that.' There'd been a time when he and Evelyn had talked about collective conscience, Emile Durkheim, her senior thesis on Marcuse and Schelling, her dreams of working for the UN. But when he last opened up the Durkheim he'd brought with him to Nevada, Lenny found it so boring that he'd let it drop under the bed, to gather dust with a volume of French poems in which Evelyn's ex-boyfriend had left an inscription. 'I just … never dated much before college.'

'Oh.' Terra's face empties politely. 'First love, that's rough. But, hey, sometimes these things don't work out and it's nobody's fault. I know with me and Ronnie—'

Lenny tunes her out and concentrates on the bright words on the other side of the bridge: Harrah's; Nevada Club; Reno, the Biggest Little City in the World. 'There was an attraction, sure. But it wasn't based on any real sense of understanding. How could it be when we didn't understand *ourselves*? I'm not saying that's how it was for you, Lenny; I just want you to know, I *want* to understand. I want to help you be happy, any way I can.'

She is close and warm, smells of stale fried food. Whatever she's willing to do for his happiness, Lenny is too tired to even think about. But she's looking at him again with those eyes, and he's reminded of how she looked in the parking lot the other night, and was that really only twenty-four hours ago? 'I really think it would help you to talk about it,' she says, so softly it's almost an incantation. 'What you liked about her. What you miss.'

'About … Evelyn?'

Terra nods solemnly. He has a sudden hollow sense that they're both just actors. Nevertheless, as if caught in a beam of light, he senses there's a script he should be following.

'She came from a nice family,' he hears himself say. Then, because this doesn't convey the point exactly: 'Her family was really nice.'

Terra blinks, unsurprised as a doll. 'That must be hard.'

'Yeah, I guess …' he muses, 'They helped me out a lot. Last year—'

He wants to talk about his father-in-law, Tom: the hours they'd spent speaking about a future without bombs or firearms. His mother-in-law, Margaret: how stylish and vivacious she was, how like Evelyn, the happy Evelyn who'd smiled at him sidelong and cooked wonderful meals and listened to him like he was interesting. His sisters-in-law, Vicky and Sally-Ann, who seemed cool and clever beyond their years, doodling psychedelic patterns in their notebooks, writing nonsense verse and limericks, marching for peace like summery versions of Evelyn with their long, tanned legs and center-parted blond-brown hair. He wants to talk about how *nice* it was to be part of that, when just two Thanksgivings earlier his sister Beth brutally informed him that he was an 'accident', that if it wasn't for him their mother would've left Dr. Lynden long ago.

'For *her*, I mean,' Terra cuts in. 'Think about it. It's easy for you, getting away from your parents. But what if your parents are nice? How d'you get away from *that*?'

It's Lenny's turn to blink now. 'I never thought of it like that.'

Terra smiles.

'I'm *glad* I can help you see things differently, Lenny. Remember: this is only the beginning. We're entering the new age and, sweetie? Don't take this wrong, but I think you could use some enlightening.'

7.

His arm around her chair is a spiritual presence as much as a physical one. If she were to lean back a few inches, she would feel it skimming the fabric of her blouse, a delicious lightness. Instead, she keeps her spine straight, her rear scooched to the edge of the seat, her ankles crossed. It is important that they do not overstate the carnal elements of their relationship.

'I see so much sensitivity in the younger generation,' Jim reflects. 'A sacrificial spirit and social conscience that all of us, and I mean *all of us*, could learn from. You must have observed it yourself, Tom.'

Evelyn notices her father shift at the familiarity of 'Tom' and feels a prick of annoyance. Her father isn't one to bristle at informality, normally. But Rev. Burne nods and answers mildly.

'I speak with a lot of students. There's a visionary quality to their idealism that, unfortunately, tends to be viewed cynically by those in power.'

Jim inclines his luscious blue-black head in agreement. 'That's what I'm saying, Tom. That's what I'm saying. The idealists, the young visionaries: they're our guiding light. Maybe that sounds cliché, but I can't afford to be cynical.' He glances down, eyelashes flickering delicately against the slightly sallow, slightly sagging skin beneath his eyes. 'I owe the success of my church here in California to two things especially: people power, and the vision of young idealists like Evelyn. I thank you for raising such a finely strung, compassionate young woman.'

He smiles, and though the smile isn't directed at her, Evelyn feels her heart squinch up with the corners of his mouth. He makes her so happy. Why can't they be happy for her?

'Of course, it isn't easy being young in these turbulent times. Being a *sensitive* young person.' Jim unloops his arm from her chair, leans forward, and takes another tuna sandwich from the barely-touched pile. 'And it's a tragedy to see the marriage of these hopeful, sensitive newlyweds fall apart. But I pray you won't blame them for their failure. It's a common situation: two young people have growing to do, and they grow apart. They couldn't have known they were so poorly matched.'

Evelyn hears her mother sniff, and her hackles rise once more. She hardens her face without looking Margaret's way.

'We don't blame Evelyn. Or Lenny,' Rev. Burne says, shining his gray eyes from his wife to Evelyn. 'But I think you can appreciate, it comes as quite a shock: we plan to visit our daughter and son-in-law, and we not only find her living alone, but a married man—'

'Mm-hmm, mm-hmm. I appreciate your point, Tom. And I want to be completely honest with you.' Jim chews thoughtfully. 'I was faithful to a sick woman for two decades. My wife, Rosaline, hasn't responded to me sexually for many years. She supports this relationship.' He dispenses of his sandwich with another large bite and licks his fingers. 'I can't speak for Evelyn, but since she and I have been relating, there's been an improvement, I think. Happier. More confident. And I know she's personally brought me great happiness.'

His arm circles back around her chair. His chest heaves valiantly beneath his cherry-red shirt. 'I look into your daughter's beautiful blue eyes and I think, that's a sensitive, idealistic woman. I'm gonna change the world with this woman. Yes indeed, I love her greatly.'

With a rhapsodic tilt of his head, Jim falls silent, and Evelyn feels herself drawn to his serenity like a trained cobra. His face in repose has something doglike, bearlike, warmly mammalian in its handsomeness that makes her want to lean close and stroke it. *Why can't they be happy for her?*

'If you love Evelyn—' Margaret willfully steadies herself to address Jim, cotton-candy hair sticking to the tear-tracks on her cheeks. '*Why don't you divorce your wife?*'

Jim smiles gently, as if he's been expecting this question. 'I've offered to marry Evelyn. She's uninterested at this time.' He glances at her and shakes his head in bemusement. 'She and Rosaline have a wonderful friendship in their own right. I don't interfere.'

To Evelyn's mortification, Margaret starts to cry again.

'In this situation, it would be honorable to intervene,' Rev. Burne speaks up, and there's a quivering thickness to his own voice that makes Evelyn take notice. 'Coming here, seeing our daughter living this way … it seems it's she who's making all the sacrifices. I can't see anything, on your part, that suggests an equal—' Rev. Burne bows his head and pinches the bridge of his sharp nose. When he looks up, his eyes are red-rimmed and fixed on Evelyn. 'You deserve better.'

Evelyn doesn't know if it's rage clogging her chest or something else. 'How can you …' she tries, but it's all wrong — her voice isn't supposed to come out choked. '*How can you say that*, when Jim sacrifices so much for others? When he has given me so much?'

She is ashamed of the tears sliding down her cheeks, of the makeup that comes off when she wipes her eyes. She is ashamed to have let them shame her.

'I don't know, Evelyn …' Rev. Burne shakes his head. His voice is a pale-pink hatchling. His narrow shoulders begin to shake. 'I don't know …'

It isn't the first time Evelyn has seen her father weep. He wept burying the stillborn baby boy Margaret gave birth to between Vicky and Sally-Ann. He wept receiving the news that Adora, the teenaged girl who'd lived with them for a year in Sacramento, had died in an auto accident. He wept at her wedding to Lenny Lynden. But this time is different, as Jim warned her it would be. This time is like scavenging birds at her entrails.

'I'm happy,' she spits. 'I'm so beautifully happy. Why can't you be happy for me?'

Saying it, Evelyn almost believes the only obstacle between her and total happiness is the dejection on her parents' faces, the water dribbling from their eyes. She tries to focus on the refreshments laid out on the table: the plate of shortbread, the soggy sandwiches, the six coffee mugs — Vicky's and Sally-Ann's abandoned for a game of fetch with Picnic. Everything disappears in a messy blur.

'I told you, darlin',' Jim murmurs, encircling her shoulder. She can feel a smile blooming on his broad, handsome face. 'I told you they wouldn't understand.'

*

The drive back to Davis will take two hours. Vicky has a date with Ivan Babenko, a 'very tall, very pink-cheeked' college freshman. Sally-Ann has to practice a guitar solo for her ninth-grade Christmas showcase. Margaret is weighed down by a bag of lemons. Rev. Burne wants to wash the station wagon.

'It needs a wash,' he mumbles into his moustache, giving the windshield a tap. 'Waterstains. We had some rain.'

'That old car,' Evelyn replies without a trace of nostalgia. 'Try vinegar.' Then: 'Lenny took the DeSoto. It was too large for me anyhow. He'll take good care of it.'

'I know he will,' Rev. Burne says. When he hugs her goodbye, she doesn't flinch in his arms as she often used to. He's unsure what to make of this.

Jim Jones, the married minister, their daughter's Brylcreemed lover, has remained in the cabin to use the phone. Rev. Burne is quietly glad he doesn't have to shake the man's hand again. Margaret is glad and not-glad; she'd been nursing a childish, vengeful hope that she might show Jim Jones exactly what she thinks of him, turn her nose up at him, spit in his face, anything but act the meekly weeping pastor's wife.

'*When life gives you lemons …*' Margaret says in an abstract, annoyed tone, lugging the bag of lemons into the passenger seat with her. 'What if I don't like lemonade?'

Evelyn is already on the porch, facing toward the cabin, glancing back at the station wagon as they honk and stutter out, clapping and working her mouth at the rogue black-and-white dog. From such a distance, she looks pure and put-together, like a woman with a nice life, a nice husband her own age, no bruises, no secrets. Margaret tries to believe that this is how it is. But the thought of *that man* glistens like a gun.

'The way he spoke about his wife. As if she were some madwoman in the attic,' she laments as the highway appears beyond the tree-barred dirt road. 'Evie is so smart! I don't understand …'

'She's independent,' Rev. Burne agrees. 'Stubbornly so. I suspect she needs to make her own mistakes.' He frowns in apparent concentration as he turns the car onto the highway. 'It *is* interesting that he is a minister, and that she's so resistant to marrying him. It shows a certain awareness of the Oedipal overtones. I'm confident it can only be a phase.'

They are silent for a long time, thinking of Oedipus, Electra, the mysterious attachments of firstborn daughters. The valley is blurred, full of winter strangeness. Vicky wonders if her parents ever psychoanalyze her in her absence.

'Evie always had real weird taste in guys,' Sally-Ann blurts. 'Remember that gloomy Elliot Goldberg?'

'Elliot Goldberg!' Margaret manages a laugh. 'I remember him tragically fleeing the house while we were entertaining that party from Modesto United.' She shakes her head. 'Poor Elliot. You'd think there was a dark cloud constantly raining dead puppies over his head.'

At this, they all laugh. Sally-Ann keeps it coming. 'Remember that grad student who wouldn't eat our pineapple upside-down cake? The one who was doing the radiation experiments on beagles?'

'You know it's a good day when we're joking about dead puppies. Good grief!' Margaret throws back her head and wipes her predictably leaking eyes. 'Here I go again.'

'Broken again.'

'Drunkenly blubbering again.'

'I *wish*,' she laughs. 'Oh, Tom. Do you think those seminary students will mind if I just plonk a case of wine and a box of crackers on the table and call it a night?'

Maybe there will be wine. Maybe the lamb shanks will turn out tough. Maybe the potatoes will burn. Maybe the seminary students will stay on too long, and Sally-Ann will make up parlor games, and Vicky will return from her date in her mother's borrowed red trench coat not especially in love and help with the dishes. Maybe the lights in the family home will go out one-by-one to the song of students weaving on bicycles, bumping into traffic poles, and Margaret will lie beside her husband not thinking of their firstborn daughter still standing on that porch, barefoot, lips steaming, watching her lover's headlights disappear because, after all, Saturday night is Rosaline's night; on Sunday morning he must dress for church. Maybe she will sleep and when she wakes in a dry-mouthed hot flash she will already be sobbing into her husband's pajama shirt: *That man doesn't know Evelyn! Her eyes are gray, not blue.* Sobbing, and maybe he will tell her he loves her, and maybe, most likely, life will go on. They are a lovely family; they know how to laugh at life's misery.

8.

'Hey, stranger,' Terra says as she slides into the passenger seat, and the joke is that they're strangers and not-strangers; that they've known each other less than a week but passed every day of this less-than-week together, almost every waking hour. Long, talky lunches she always pays for and after-lunch walks by the Truckee, where they watch a St. Bernard try to catch a fish, and shopping in town where she buys a belt buckle for Brother Gene with an engraving of a mountain and steam train ('Old dudes like trains') and falls in love with a pair of cowboy boots, eventually leaving them with tears in her eyes ('No, it just wouldn't be socialist to spend all that money on shoes!'). Long shifts at the Silver State where the other guys look at him differently, offer him free tokes in the alley and invite him to play blackjack and, when he leaves with her every night, make V-licking signs behind his back. And after these long shifts, driving and parking or, as they've been doing more lately, going to the casinos to order Shirley Temples and talk about the empty money-driven lives of all those gamblers, because actually it's getting harder to sit in a parked car with her and not get a hard-on.

'Hey.' Lenny smiles. 'What's that basket?'

'You know, Dorothea? When she heard we were going to Pyramid Lake. I guess she's worried we're gonna get stranded in the desert and starve.' It impresses him how Terra is already on friendly terms with everyone in her all-female boardinghouse when he can't even remember his landlady's name. She sticks her nose into the basket as he starts the car. 'It's just some fruit and PB&J. Oh, and hot chocolate? I told Dorothea you like chocolate.'

As he drives out of town, Terra talks indiscriminately of the people

115

she likes: 'Dorothea'; 'Carmen', an older waitress from the Silver State; Brother Gene and his wholesome blond family. Lenny is amused by Terra's affection for that same tall white cop whom Evelyn seemed to loathe; sees it as proof of Terra's sweet nature, her open heart. She talks about Gene's horses; his horse-crazy daughters, Dot the Virgo, Bobbi the Sagittarius; about his son Roger who took her bareback riding; wild horses; will they see horses today; will they see Indians? Lenny feels a sting of jealousy at the mention of Roger Luce, who he knows to be tall and handsome, and the sting surprises him, seems like a good thing. Like her voice filling the silence is a good thing, her body next to his, the special glow of being on the road with a woman and somewhere to go. They both took tonight off work, with Jim's permission. Lenny knows better than to think about what exactly is being permitted.

'I think I see the pyramid,' Terra says reverently when the open highway and grayish-tan land gives way to gravel and ochre vegetation. 'Oops. Nope. That's just some mountain.'

'We're almost there,' Lenny assures her, though all he really knows is that she'll believe whatever he tells her.

When he finally sees the expanse of marine blue beyond the crests of rock, he feels unaccountably proud of himself, as if he's responsible for discovering that vast body of water in the middle of the desert. 'Groooovy,' Terra drawls as he pulls off the road, and before he's even drawn the keys from the ignition, she's exposing them both to a burst of fresh air.

As she trips gracelessly ahead of him through the sand, his eyes are magnetized by the curve of her denim-clad butt. 'It's like that beach from *Planet of the Apes* …' he tries to distract himself with conversation, then realizes she probably hasn't been to the movies in a while, between screwing bikers and playing home-on-the-range with the Luce family. Plus, she's struggling with the picnic basket. 'Oh, hey. Let me carry that.'

'Lenny, you're *sweet*.' Terra bats her eyelashes and gives him a smile so saccharine he feels queasy. But he shoves the feelings aside and smiles back.

A minute later, they're on the beach with the picnic basket between them, jeaned legs arched, looking out on the water as blue as Neptune, the sky above it faded like denim and furred with white clouds. Terra is in one of those self-consciously philosophical moods he's already come to recognize, and he isn't listening too closely; already he knows it's okay not to listen closely, she never gets annoyed like Evelyn. 'When I see a place so ancient as this, I'm totally humbled. To think: how many thousands of years those rocks have been here, and all those ancient tribes who've sat in places like this and, y'know, the *pyramids of Egypt* …' Sheer faces of rock point skyward out of the lake, and Lenny remembers that Ancient History class he took freshman year, all that stuff about Egyptians, sky worlds and underworlds, underworld skies of chaos and death and rebirth. He runs his fingers through the sand and discovers it isn't sand at all, but tiny white shells like snail shells, and this makes him inexplicably happy. He lies back, watching the wind blast Terra's sandy hair to one side, hearing her voice as a disembodied drone. '… We're ancient in our souls, same as the Indians and Egyptians. Same as the earth, the water, the sky … Hey, what's funny?'

'Nothing.' Lenny laughs and sits up. 'This sand is weird, that's all.'

Terra laughs, too. A sweet, open laugh, and she's sifting the sand through her fingers like a mermaid, hair blasting in his face. 'Yeah, it's weird,' she agrees, brushing her hands off on her jeans. Then she turns to face him with a tight smile, her blue eyes expectant, and Lenny feels once again nauseous with suspicion, that sweetness so readily offered up. This girl, after all, *is* a stranger. This girl isn't his wife. He thinks of Mexico, rocks in the ocean.

'Hey, where are you going?' Terra cries out as he rises from the sand, shedding his gray pea-coat, pulling off his shoes and socks. 'Lenny … what? You're gonna *swim?*'

He nods and throws a grin her way, already walking backward to the bank as he fumbles with his belt and buttons. He's conscious of the meagerness of his body in the harsh winter sun, radioactive white and goosey with cold, a colony of pimples on his back and uneven swatch of hair on his front. Not godly. Not even manly.

'Well. That's just crazy,' Terra grumbles.

The water is sledgehammer cold. At his knees, groin, chest, shrinking every pore, splintering his lungs. Lenny takes it in one numbing hit, plunging his head and shutting his eyes to the stinging blue. When he surfaces, it's only for a draft of air. Then he goes back under.

By the time he breaks from his strenuous frogstroke, the beach is much further away but the pyramid-shaped rock no closer. He searches the shore for Terra and spies her, a pocket-sized figure in her shearling coat, curves like a Coke bottle. He treads water and squints west at the dusty mountain ranges, up at the blinding sun.

Lenny would've liked to see Terra waiting with his clothes ready, holding the thermos of hot chocolate, yet even though she isn't, he's happy to see her. Standing with her hands deep in her pockets, trembling despite her coat's cozy sheepskin lining, the fleecy collar into which she's tucked her fluffy hair. He guesses she's trembling in sympathy with him. He smiles gratefully as he approaches in his soaked underwear, skin aglow, hair dropping icy beads. 'The water was righteous—' he begins, but something about her face stops him: the quivering lips, the nostrils pinched, the pupils pinpricks.

'*I saw a man with the head of a dog,*' Terra whispers.

What the hell? Lenny is about to laugh when he sees her eyes are welling with actual tears, her body is actually shaking. He swallows instead.

'*I saw a man with the head of a dog,*' she repeats. 'When you went under, he rose up.'

Lenny looks back at the lake.

'He's not there anymore!' Terra cries. 'He only appeared when you … went under.'

'Hey, it's okay. Don't cry.' Lenny rubs her shoulder quizzically, fingers grazing the softness at her collar. It occurs to him that Terra has done more drugs than he ever has, that all that acid has maybe permanently fried her brain. 'What kind of dog?'

'Just a regular big dog. A dog with a big black head.'

Lenny stops himself from swiveling around and searching for the dog-man again. 'It's okay … This place is really old, like you said.' He keeps rubbing her shoulder as he looks beyond her at the station wagon, still parked among the sagebrush, its yellow reassuringly bright in the desert sun. 'Want to go home?'

Terra gives a jerky gesture, maybe a shrug or maybe a head shake, he can't tell. Only that she looks small and afraid.

She looks small and afraid, so he does what seems like the kindest thing: he kisses her.

He kisses her, and he doesn't know if they're freezing or burning, standing on sacred ground or floating in dead space.

The afternoon is already gloomy outside the phone booth, neon signs flickering on one-by-one. He huddles behind Terra, the animal tang and thickness of her blond hair. She is nodding and making solemn noises into the receiver, her free hand blindly finding his and twining around it. Her face still has a dewy, flushed look that makes him feel vaguely dissolute. 'Yes Father,' she mumbles piously. 'Thank you, Father.'

She passes the receiver on to him.

'When I awoke this morning, Lenny, I sensed a great shadow looming over you. It has been a trial, extending my psychic mantle to cover you from this distance. Yet I see I wasn't wrong sending Sister Terra to you. I see that you've found protection in one another.'

Lenny bows his head against the foggy glass. He doesn't *feel* strong; a fuzziness in his mind like fleece and a boneless trembling that's maybe from the lake or maybe from the back seat with Terra after the lake. Or maybe it's listening to Jim Jones, expecting to be chastised at any moment. But Jim remains uncritical.

'I know, Lenny, you will honor this young woman, as no man has before. I know you will cherish her charitable heart.'

'Yes, Father.' He hears himself make those same solemn noises. *I will. Thank you, Father.*

She is still clinging to his hand when they squeeze out of the phone booth, not talking much for once. They drift toward the blue neon of a movie house, and her hands are all over him as they line up for tickets, as they stare at the posters of cowboys and spacemen, under his coat, under his shirt, sizzling against his cold-hot skin. Not letting go even when she slides the money on the counter and tells the ticket guy, 'Two for *Romeo and Juliet*,' though she must know how they look, two young people so stupidly in love the world can't wait to see them kill themselves.

But Lenny is glad, sitting in the dark, that it's a story he doesn't have to think about: fair Verona, star-crossed lovers, poison you can taste while they're still talking about roses. The actress who plays Juliet has hair like Evelyn's, but it's Terra's hair in his face, Terra's hand tucked into his, Terra warm and breathing beside him. It's Terra sniffing over the sad parts, drying her eyes on his shirt, Terra who'd be just as sweet by any other name. Terra, yeah, Terra, Terra …

9.

Dear Mom and Dad:

    Thank you for the candy and the skirt suit and the very
unique wall hanging. I hope your Christmas celebrations went
as beautifully as ours. We had many new faces as well as old and
spectacular performances from our children's choir and talented
Temple band. After there was a heavenly banquet of turkey with all
the usual fixings, just like at home only we fed close to 500. 'Father
Jim' personally handed out gifts to all the children, including a
large group from the county orphanage. It is truly moving to see so
many little ones with smiles on their faces and many from desperate
poverty having the time of their little lives. Jim loves every child as if
they were his own ...

Evelyn places her pen down and drains her mug, casting a wary eye
out at the morning frost. She shouldn't be creeping around the cabin
so early, first day back to work and a long day at that: double P.E., and
staff meetings, and a personal appointment with the superintendent,
who no doubt wishes to discuss the rumors regarding her marital status.
She looks at her bare finger and wonders if it is too soon.

    The hallway is still velvety with shadows, the door to the bedroom
shut. She does her best to silence the swish of her black slacks as she
tiptoes to the telephone. Six-fifteen in Evergreen Valley is also six-
fifteen in Reno. Six-fifteen is not *too* early to make a necessary call.

    Still, navigating the byzantine system of area codes, teaspoon-
voiced operators, the righteous indignation of his landlady, Evelyn
several times considers hanging up.

    'I know you think your boyfriend's the moon and stars,' the old lady gripes as a dog yaps in the background. 'But would it kill you to wait for sunup?'

'Excuse me, no, this is his—'

She realizes she can't say 'wife' anymore.

'Hey, Earthgirl. Whaaaa-*uhhhh*—What?' Lenny comes on the line several minutes later, and she knows from his yawn that he must be shirtless, tousle-haired, wiping the crust of sleep from his eyes. A boy, just a boy.

'This isn't Terra.' Evelyn waits for him to fill in the blank.

'Oh ... Sorry.' He yawns again. 'What ... what time is it?'

'It is very important you're prepared for court today. They're going to be asking lots of questions and, since I won't be there, you need to be clear about what you're committing to record. I've written out some crucial points. Tell me if anything else comes to mind—'

'Evelyn ... My hearing isn't 'til eleven.'

'Then you'll have plenty of time to prepare. Honestly, Lenny. I don't think it's asking too much for you to pay attention for five minutes.' The crystalline, teacherlike quality of her voice sounds harsh, even to her own ears. Hot-faced, she shifts her weight to one foot and eyeballs the bedroom door, lowers her voice. 'Now, in every court, regardless of who's present, there's a "plaintiff" and a "defendant". In this case, you're the "plaintiff" and I'm the "defendant". They may ask you to identify the "defendant" by full legal name, meaning "Evelyn Ruth Lynden". When they ask you for the "plaintiff's" legal residence, this is very important: *do not* tell them Evergreen Valley, tell them—'

'Reno. Yeah, yeah, I know.'

'They will also ask when you began residing there. "November 18 1968" is the date on your lease. As far as your intentions for residing in Reno—'

'"I came with the intention of making it my home indefinitely."' The boredom behind his placating tone is evident. 'Yeah.'

'More importantly,' Evelyn gathers her words. 'They'll ask you to explain your reasons for seeking a divorce. "Mental cruelty" is simply legalese for "incompatibility", so don't be unnerved when they use it. However, you'll need to present some case for "cruelty" on the defendant's part. For instance: "the defendant was critical", "the defendant withheld affection", "the defendant — the defendant ..."'

'It's okay,' Lenny reassures her quietly. 'It's divorce court, not the draft board. It'll be okay.'

The memories flare up like draft cards in a crowd: her parents' house in Davis, huddling over *The Handbook for Conscientious Objectors*, the hope, the vexation, the touching.

'Of course. I suppose. Of course,' Evelyn says mechanically. 'And, of course, you have your witness.'

'Yeah.' His voice comes boyish and breathy. 'Terra's cool.'

'I suppose you're going to marry her.' She doesn't wait for Lenny to elaborate on the squeak he gives in response. 'It's none of my concern, but I think you should consider waiting until summer. Jim will be officiating a number of weddings at that time.'

Lenny says nothing, which is somehow worse than if he had said something to contradict her. She purses her lips; unpurses them to strike again.

'I'm missing a book of poems. *Le Creve-Couer* by Louis Aragon.'

Lenny stays silent, so she goes on.

'You may have taken it accidentally. It's quite important to me.'

'*I don't have your poems*, Evelyn,' he says with undisguised, even exaggerated weariness.

'Well. Please check. I may need it for my lessons.' She allows herself a smug smile. 'Also, I'm donating your records to the Temple's White Elephant Sale. It's wasteful to have such a large collection when you could be raising money for the Cause. Not to mention inconvenient for me.'

'… Fine.'

'In fact, it's probably best if you tell me now if there's anything you need kept, books or whatever. I can ask the Luces to store them along with Terra's things.'

'I have everything I need.'

'Fine. Good.'

'Fine.' Lenny sighs or yawns. 'Bye, Evelyn.'

Evelyn says nothing, just inhales sharply and waits for the line to go dead. It doesn't. Self-consciously, she replaces the phone, wincing at the click of the receiver. From the next room, she hears a stirring, a grunt, a cough. Her name brusquely uttered. She lowers her eyes and goes to it.

'Mornin', sweetheart.' He's sitting up in bed, moistening his lips with his tongue, his hair just as tidy and well-glossed as when he arrived at her door the previous night. Cherokee hair, matinee idol hair, hair that never musses. 'C'mere.'

She comes, but not before filling him a glass of water from the pitcher at the bedside.

'Trouble sleeping?' he murmurs, cocking an eyebrow at her, wide lips slurping.

She settles at the foot of the bed, crosses her legs. 'After a couple of hours my mind starts running a million miles a minute. There's just so much to do.'

'I know that feeling.' Jim sets his glass on the nightstand and she follows the curve of his gesture, sheet slipping down to show the folds of his belly, the breadth of his chest, olive-skinned and surprisingly hairless. She looks at the rifle leaning up against the wall, and maybe it's wrong — in the same way this man in her bed is wrong — yet, by the new order of her life, it is also overwhelmingly right. 'Nothing wrong with it. You're young and strong.' He rests his hand on her knee. 'Just don't think I don't notice you tiptoeing 'round like a ballerina.'

His caress is circular, chilling, like the whoosh inside a seashell. She can't hide.

'I was just tying up some loose ends,' she admits. 'I began a letter to my parents.'

She waits for the gentle reproach: *You don't need to justify yourself to them, honey. They're nice people, but they're bourgeois. Don't kid yourself they ain't bourgeois.* But Jim only smiles patiently. Every reproach has already been internalized, every vow in darkness made.

He reaches for her bare hand, spreads it, encircles her third finger with his.

'You remind me of them schoolteachers who used to beat my ass. All leather strap, no ring. Spinsters at twenty-three.'

Then he leans in and clasps the bun at the back of her head, parts her lips with his tongue, parts her teeth. Opens up the sky in her belly and no sacrifice is too great, she thinks, not when he's offering her hurtling space and fiery galaxies.

Blood Red Roses

1.

When Rosaline Jones's husband came to her all those months ago and informed her he was in love with a brilliant and passionate younger woman, she'd felt as if her insides were bleeding, but she wasn't surprised, not really. For twenty years, she'd lived with the knowledge that she wasn't enough for this man, this lusty, lionhearted man who could make miracles with his hands. For twenty years, she'd lived with the knowledge that this man would cause her pain.

The young woman comes to the parsonage in a white minidress, dark hair piled up on her head. Like a beautiful white cat slinking up the porch, making everything her own. *Eve.*

Rosaline winces away from the window's floating lace. It was wrong of her to shift her head from the stricture of the orthopedic pillow, wrong to look anywhere but the ceiling, those dancing frills of light. From outside, she can hear the slap of a basketball against the driveway's concrete, the shouts of her boys, their blood-sports she will never comprehend.

Because even if she had the strength to lift herself out of bed, to throw off her back brace like one of Jim's miracles, Rosaline has no desire to compete with this other woman.

She comes to the parsonage in that white minidress, doesn't knock to be let in. She is all hunger and pristine purpose. As if wanting him were a virtue, being wanted by him.

'Ev-e-lyn.'

Jim's voice in the hall, his happy crowing voice: it hurts even more than that lace-edged glimpse of *her*. Eve says something in reply, and her crisp voice is just another thing Rosaline can't compete with. The voice of a woman taught to raise her hand in class, to value her own opinions, to believe she might change the world. Jim laughs and

Rosaline feels a flush of irrelevance.

Wondering: what could this young woman possibly have said to amuse him?

Then their footsteps on the stairs, and for a brief time it seems like a reprieve. But before long the ceiling is squeaking, groaning, and when Rosaline shuts her eyes in protest, the lush red behind her lids only makes it more intimate. As if they're in the room with her, bucking up against the furniture, fierce and arrogant as fallen angels.

He doesn't know what he's doing. But, no: she knows Jim. *He knows exactly what he's doing.*

And she knows about Eve, things no wife should have to know. That she plays him records by creaky-voiced folk singers, Bob Dylan, Leonard Cohen; that she recites French poetry, the Song of Solomon. That she believes in past lives; claims to have been his mistress in a former life, when they were revolutionaries in Russia. That she'd rather kill herself than live without him. All these things, Jim has felt the need to tell Rosaline, as if to shock her into silence.

Also, in ecstasy, Eve cries out for God *and* Jim.

'Oh — God! Oh — Jim — God!'

Rosaline doesn't want to think badly of this other woman, doesn't want to think of her at all. Still less does she want to think badly of the father of her children. Yet she has to wonder at their ruthlessness; in her own home, her *children's* home, right above her head.

She has to wonder: do they want her gone, or merely to keep her in her place?

The pain of easing her neck from the orthopedic pillow makes Rosaline whimper, yet her whimper is only a ghost of Eve's cries. Her pain is only a ghost of their pleasure, inching to unstrap the brace from her back, the traction weights from her ankles. Her feet thud against the floorboards, like proverbial trees falling alone in the woods. Her spine sears and then numbs as the adrenaline overtakes her, and it's not hard to imagine how it is for all those sisters on Sundays, cheating age and illness to the cheers of the congregation.

'Jim — Oh God — Jim —'

Rosaline hobbles into the hall, past the framed cherubim of her children's faces. Outdoors. The harsh midmorning sun blinds her, afterimages exploding like gunshots. She closes her eyes and imagines her insides in those same vivid red tones, vertebra grinding vertebra. A dragonfly flits past and she opens to the clear blue, the evergreen hills.

A beautiful morning, despite everything.

In the early days, when she was just a trainee nurse and Jim a dirt-poor schoolkid working nights as an orderly, Rosaline believed he'd heal people someday. Not a faith healer, but a man of medicine, with whom she'd travel to poor brown-skinned nations. It was the way he saw the preciousness of imperfect bodies: bodies that stank, coughed, gurgled, only a weak pulse away from being corpses. It was the way he was unashamed to shed tears over an unwed mother's stillborn baby. Maybe, looking at his gold-hued hands, she'd even allowed herself to imagine his touch curing her of all her ills: her freckled face, her rabbit teeth, her wallflower personality, the rheumatism that made her old at nineteen.

I can't help you, Ro', if you don't wanna be helped. Fool my ass, married to a martyr when I could have anyone.

The sweet smell of roses wafts from below as Rosaline climbs down the same way Eve had come up, every step a reminder that she shouldn't be walking. It hadn't been this bad last summer, had it? Fine summer days, lying in the shade, slathered in sunscreen, as Jim and the boys romped in the lake. Eve no more than a speck on the opposite shore.

The boys are still at war, their scuffs and shouts echoing from around the corner. 'You fucker!' yells one of them — Martin Luther, she's sure, at Jimmy Jr., she's sure of that, too. As the sun hits her back, bones, marrow, Rosaline is glad of their rough noise, their boyish obliviousness to all rivalries but their own.

Eve comes out of the parsonage in that white minidress, smoothing the fabric over her slim belly. A snail-like sheen to her thigh. A look on her face that's almost queasy, like a drunken partygoer about to throw up in the bushes. She closes the door and starts toward the stairs, a mermaid on dry land. She spies Rosaline.

Her face changes.

An ugly look. Ugly in a naked way, which makes Rosaline feel just as ugly. A dozen platitudes dry up in Rosaline's mouth: *oh hi there, good morning, whatlovelyweathermyLord.* She averts her eyes before Eve can.

'Excuse me,' Eve murmurs coolly as she descends.

Then she slips past Rosaline, the feline tang of her mingling with the roses, that dark knot of hair blazing so bright, it's painful to see.

2.

'Tell Mother what you did today.'

It is the blue of evening, a fortnight after Eve's intrusion, when Jim's voice drifts up the porch through the racket of slamming car doors, chirping cicadas, crackling citronella candles. Rosaline's ears prick at her sons' whines of protest; a familiar weariness settles in her chest. *What've they done now?* She sits forward in her cushioned rattan chair, causing Chitters the tabbycat to plonk down, tail thrashing.

'G'on, tell her.'

'But *Daddd*—'

They get louder as they advance up the porch. Chitters peeks down at them, then flees under a chair. Rosaline plucks the glasses from her nose, bookmarks her page, looks up as the boys crowd onto the porch: salty-haired and dressed in swimming trunks, Jim at their tail.

'Well, what've you got to say for yourselves?' She smiles feebly.

'*Hi Mom*,' Martin Luther mumbles.

'*Hi Mom*.' Jin-sun and Paolo hang their heads.

'*Mommy*,' Jimmy Jr. chirps.

'Tell Mother what you did today,' Jim repeats. 'Junior?'

Jimmy Jr. sucks his lower lip, a habit he got from Jim. 'We went to Bodega Bay!'

'Bodega Bay? That's some way aways.'

'Yeah.'

'And what'd you do there?'

'Swimming.'

'Oh yeah?' She looks to Martin Luther, Jin-sun, Paolo, and dutifully they play along: *we climbed some big rocks, we ate crab rolls, we fed seagulls.* Rosaline has the urge to draw them onto her lap and enfold

130

their lanky, sun-warmed limbs. But nine, ten, eleven, twelve: they're getting too big for all that. 'Sure sounds like you guys had a busy day!'

'You forgot to tell her the best part,' Jim cuts in, before the boys can finish bobbing their heads. 'Tell Mother who came with us.'

He's wearing a lime-green cabana shirt from when they lived in Rio, his olive skin darker than she's seen it in a long time. She's reminded of those first impressions of him around the hospital; how in that lily-white setting he could've been Mexican, mulatto, anything, and how it had scared her.

Junior pipes up. 'Su-mi's French teacher came.'

His words perfectly soft, angelic, and looking at her with those chocolate-button eyes that stole her heart at the Indianapolis orphanage nine years ago.

'Her name's *Evelyn*,' Martin Luther hisses. But correcting his brother doesn't seem to give the usual joy; it's like he's just spat poison, his head shrinking turtle-like into his skinny shoulders.

'Sister Evelyn,' Paolo offers with a shrug.

Jin-sun crouches, pinches together his fingertips and clicks, '*Chit-chit-chitters.*'

Jim smiles down at Rosaline; not a mocking smile, but placid, *what-can-I-do?* She feels her face grow slack with this newest hurt; knows the only place to hide is inside herself. Pressing her spine against the cushion, she concentrates on the citronella flames, not letting them blur. But Jim is watching her through his sunglasses, evaluating every weakness.

'Well, I hope you guys were on your best behavior.' Rosaline wrests her eyes from the firelight, looks square at Jim. 'And I sure hope your dad didn't let you fill up on junk.'

None of the boys mention Eve's name again. Not at the dinner table, farting their chairs and giggling between mouthfuls of five-bean casserole, nor feeding the cats and dogs, nor dripping half-naked from bath to bed. Jim hangs around just long enough to eat, exchange a few words about his blood pressure, and put on a pair of slacks, before moseying down to the Temple where the young people are having a sing-along. The boys are tucked in, and Rosaline wrapping chicken gizzards with just the cats for company, when Su-mi comes home, all prettied up from a meeting of the brides-to-be at the Luces' place. 'Do you *have* to do that?' Su-mi scrunches her nose at the gizzards, and shame pushes up inside Rosaline like weeds in dirt. Su-mi must sense the shame since she starts helping, despite Rosaline's protests, and asking after Rosaline's back, and complaining about that bimbo Sister Terra suggesting she get married in go-go boots and a big sunhat like Yoko Ono. Once the gizzards are packed in the icebox, Su-mi asks, 'Is Dad home?' and, at Rosaline's head-shake, gives a bat-like look of disgust. But, no, it's not like that, Rosaline objects; he's at the sing-along, he spent all day with your brothers, don't be so hard on him. Defending Jim until the shame turns righteous and Su-mi drops the subject.

It's a good thing, Su-mi marrying, Rosaline thinks, once she's closed herself back inside her room. Even if eighteen is too young. Even if she could do better than Dwight Mueller, the District Attorney's homely son. Even if the marriage was all Jim's idea. To send her out of the house, away from the craziness, it's about the best she can do as a mother these days.

But the shame. It pushes back up, scratches at her, flames her cheeks as she brushes her pale flyaway hair in the soft lamplight. Shame about Su-mi and the eight years she's been her mother without caring for her as she does the boys. About the gizzards Jim will slip into some poor old sister's mouth tomorrow, to be choked up and passed off as cancers. Most of all about Eve, the outrage every time she thinks of her.

Rosaline doesn't expect to hear Jim return while she's still setting her hair in rollers. His tentative tread in the hall, his voice calling her, 'Ro'?', as you'd call a sleeping child. She stays quiet as his shadow appears beneath her door. He raps softly; nudges it open.

'There you are.' He smiles. 'Quiet as a mouse.'

It's the nervous sixteen-year-old boy he most resembles, standing hands-in-pockets in the foyer of her parents' clapboard house, the one he thought was a mansion because it had an indoor toilet and a fireplace. 'New girl, Flora Armstrong, you heard her sing yet? Seventeen and voice like Nina Simone.' He looks at the can of hairspray on her vanity. 'I gotta make some phone calls. Just wanted to, uh, see if you were up.'

They aren't in the habit of wishing each other goodnight unless the children are around; haven't been since he made a more regular habit of going to Eve's at night. Rosaline tries to blank the irritation from her face as she turns to him. 'I'm about to turn in.' Jim sees the irritation and, more important, the effort to pretend it's not there. 'You should, too.'

At this, he slackens, sighs. 'Antonia Bud's in hysterics. That drunk-ass husband of hers wants to take 'em all up to Chicago. Damn crime, with how well them kids are doin' here.' He shakes his head woefully. 'And there's Isaiah sayin' Minnie's got cold feet. Nothin' some counseling won't fix, but god-*damn*; those kids've been engaged since they were knee-high, and I'm hearing this now?'

Rosaline, like all the original Indiana folks, had been overjoyed when Roger Luce, eldest son of one of their first white families, became engaged to Minnie Bellows, eldest daughter of their first black family. 'But Minnie adores Roger.'

'Ain't Minnie's fault. Roger's been overcompensating. Every time some new young thing bats her eyes at him, he forgets his responsibilities.' If Jim is aware of the irony of his words, he doesn't show it. 'Latent homosexual, same as his daddy.'

Though Rosaline doesn't doubt he's right about Gene Luce, she's skeptical about Roger. Ignoring Jim, she peers at her insipid reflection.

'These headaches, Ro' … It's like wire cutting into my skull …'

He's sensed the drift of her attention, is tugging her back like a child at her sleeve. Agitated, Rosaline gives her rollers a pat and keys open the drawer of her vanity. He lists closer as she rattles around inside and shakes a pair of green-and-gold capsules onto her palm. 'Don't take these too close to dawn or you'll get groggy.'

'Thank you, Mother.'

Jim bends to scrape the pills from her palm and plant a chaste kiss on her cheek. A moment later, he's murmuring, '*G'night*,' and creeping away in his worn-out loafers. Once the door closes behind him, Rosaline feels the sting.

He believes things are fine between them.

She's allowed him to believe what he's doing to her, to their family, is *fine*.

Rosaline welcomes the prospect of turning off the lamp, slipping under her covers. Another man would've offered excuses. Another man would've kept quiet, done all he could to keep those parts of his life separate. But Jim isn't like other men. It's his genius and his cruelty, that he doesn't follow other men's rules; makes up his *own* rules. Rosaline recognizes this is exactly what he's doing by bringing Eve into their lives; that there's no way to condemn the gesture without condemning other things — his inclusiveness, his generosity, his honesty.

Unable to condemn or accept, she sleeps.

She sleeps, and wakes to a tension, like a ringing in her ears. Like the phantom cries that used to get her out of bed, months after Martin Luther and Junior learned to sleep through the night. Matching blue onesies. Twins in different skins. She listens for the source of tension; a whining that seems to come not only from her head, but from the walls. *Inside* the walls.

The plumbing?

The bright sliver beneath the bathroom door is visible from the hall. Wrapped in her pale-lemon robe, Rosaline shuffles to the light. Through the door, she hears a rush of taps, a patter of small feet. She presses her ear to the wood. Muffled yet distinct, there it is:

Sobbing.

'Sweetie?' Rosaline calls, knocking softly.

The sobs stop. The taps keep streaming. She knocks again.

'Is everything …' Her voice falters '… Everything okay?'

It's a long moment before the water ceases; even longer before a chink appears and Martin Luther's damp eyes stare out at her. Her eyes but also Jim's, like the sensitive face with its cleft chin and olive skin. Not for the first time, Rosaline marvels at that cocktail of genes.

'Mom,' Martin Luther says, voice wet as the tiles he's opened out to, and it only takes a heartbeat for her to understand: the soggy sheet, the brimming bathtub, the smell of urine from his alligator pajamas. 'Can you help me?'

'Oh, sweetie, sure.' Rosaline steps in, clicks shut the door, and squeezes Martin Luther's shoulder. 'Oh. Y'know, you coulda woke me?'

'Sorry Mom.'

'Shhh. Don't you go apologizing. Accidents happen.'

Rosaline is aware of Martin Luther keeping his distance, glossy dark head hung, swaying like a sleepy soldier. She frowns at the overfull tub, then winces as she bends to pull the plug. They both cringe as the drainage splats like diarrhea.

'Sorry Mom.'

'I thought there was a baby alligator in here, when I heard all that splashing.' Rosaline again touches Martin Luther's spindly shoulder. He doesn't crack a smile. 'Let's take these down to the laundry, huh? I'm sure we can find you some clean jammies …'

They move downstairs like refugees by night. The laundry is yellow-lit, cluttered with scraps of boyswear. Rosaline finds something clean, dry, blue-striped, Martin Luther's size. She hands it to him, stripes waving before her tired eyes. Martin Luther is too old to undress in front of her without shame; she knows this, but also it can't be the only reason he's sniffling.

'Marjy. Hey.'

An early childhood name, from when he was 'Martin James' instead of 'Martin Luther'; 'Martin' for her maiden name, 'James' for 'Jim'. She knows he hates being called it around the other boys, but she suspects he still likes it, between them.

'Mom.' A strangulated cry. 'I saw—' His face crumples and hides among the blue stripes. 'I'm sorry. I saw Dad kissing Evelyn.'

Rosaline's first instinct is to hide her face, too. She drops her eyes, covers her mouth as if for a tiny belch. 'Oh?'

'He kissed her on the beach when we were climbing the rocks and again in front of the lighthouse and when he drove her home,' he reels off. 'He kissed her on the mouth.'

Having reached the end of his catalog of sins, Martin Luther clams up. Rosaline feels the silence between them as something solid, malign. A cancer to be spat up.

'Well. Your dad and Eve, they've got a special friendship,' she says breathlessly, lifting the lid of the washing machine. 'Sometimes they might hug or kiss. That's how it is.'

'But he's married to *you*.'

It's only child's logic, but the simplicity of it is a blow. Rosaline bends to stuff the sheets inside the metal burrow. 'Married people can't always do those things together, Marjy. It's complicated.' The odor rises to her nostrils. 'It's not easy for your dad when I'm sick. I'm not such good company.'

Rosaline watches his eyes narrow to slits, his lashes flutter with the effort to understand. He looks just like Jim in this moment: dark, wounded, calculating.

'You mean ... Dad kisses her because you're sick,' Martin Luther asks, without inflection. 'If you weren't sick, you'd come to the beach and he'd kiss you instead of — her.'

'Maybe. Like I said, sweetie, it's ... complicated.'

'*If you weren't sick*,' he repeats, 'he wouldn't kiss her.' He rocks on his feet. 'So why won't you just let him heal you?'

It isn't the first time that Martin Luther, that any of the boys, has asked this. It isn't the first time she has had to make excuses for Jim. Her annoyance flares: first at Martin Luther for his difficult question, then herself for not being able to answer it, then the ceiling and everything above it for staying silent. *It should be you*, she thinks. *It should be you explaining yourself, not me.*

'We've talked about this, Marjy. Your dad, he's got so many depending on him. He's gotta put them first. It's not easy, but that's the sacrifice we make — *Dad* makes ...'

Rosaline's voice catches. She's seeing Eve kissing her husband: on a rocky beach, in front of a lighthouse, in the car with the boys looking on. Eve in white. Eve by the roses.

'Don't cry, Mom. I'm sor-ry.' Martin's voice cracks, jerked out of the solipsism of his own grief. 'Please. Just stop crying.'

But she can't, and neither can he. Wiping his nose on her belt, nudging his face against her belly, as if it might somehow open up and let him back in. She thinks of foolish things: bleating lambs; eggs in nests; how scared she'd been when once, just the once, not knowing his strength, Jim knocked her to the floor while she was pregnant and a little blood came out.

'I wish you weren't sick, Mom. I wish you could take us places.'

Martin Luther's voice is wispy, resigned. His shoulders rise and fall deeply. Almost nice, this quiet in the eye of the storm. Almost, she wants to walk out in it, touch the broken stalks, smell the earth, look at the miracle-green sky.

'I'll get well soon. I'll take all you guys someplace,' Rosaline says. 'After Su-mi's wedding ... How's about I take you all to see grandma and grandpa in Indiana?'

'And Dad?'

'Not Dad. Don't say anything to Dad.'

3.

'You're a lucky man, Lynden.'

The hand that claps Lenny's shoulder is large and muscular. He turns from watching his new wife crouching with the flower girls to smile at the owner of the hand: Brother Gene, Eugene Luce. Tall and clean-cut like Paul Newman, with that strong, straight Paul Newman nose and a look of being stuffed into his shirt and tie. Lenny smiles at Brother Gene, as he's been smiling all day at the men who've come to clap him, the women who've squeezed his arm tight like a blood pressure test. 'Oh? Yeah.'

Then he turns back to watch Terra some more.

Her dress is short, tight at her bent haunches, billowy at the sleeves. She's got a crown of some kind of white flowers: apple blossoms, he wants to say, but maybe not; maybe it was Minnie who had apple blossoms? Minnie or horsey-pretty Jo Harris with the chestnut hair, who's marrying Jorge Harrison, a mixed-race guy from Louisiana. Su-mi Jones he knows has no flowers, but a black bouffant like Priscilla Presley, and Donna, Johnny Bronco's bride, a jaunty little hat with a birdcage veil that conveniently hides her big, humplike forehead. Whatever the flowers are, Lenny likes them, as he likes the blond hair down Terra's back, thick as a pelt, bright as a flag. Terra's hair and Terra's dress and Terra's flock of little girls: nappy-haired; daffodil yellow; foxy-red; Pomo Indian. Little girls in dresses as short as Terra's but full-skirted, holding tiny hand-woven baskets, plucking grass to fill them, upturning the baskets over Terra's head and hiding their faces in spasms of guilty mirth.

'Some things never change.' Brother Gene's hand stays on Lenny. 'Young ladies, they may be burning their bras and whatnot, but they all want a special day.'

'Sure,' Lenny agrees.

'Course, the styles are different. Joya had this long, swirly skirt. Like a mermaid's tail. Darn near stepped on it a hundred times. Had a few too many, that day.' Brother Gene gives a short, cough-like laugh. 'Dutch courage. We all need it sometimes.'

Lenny catches a whiff of sweet heaviness on Brother Gene's breath, and the hand on his shoulder makes more sense. Unlike most Temple parties, there's been a steady trickle of valley wines all afternoon. But then, this isn't a typical Temple party. Sister Phyllis broke a chair from laughing too hard. Sister Antonia's kids broke up a fight between her and their drunk dad. And, in the parking lot, enough rows of tables to accommodate anyone who's anyone in the county.

'Twenty-two, 'bout your age. My first year with the IPD. She was the smallest, blondest thing you ever saw, but, Lord, was I *scared*.' Brother Gene, as if suddenly aware of his lingering hand, lets it drop like a piece of wood. 'It was different back then. Never had much to do with young ladies, outside church and family.'

Brass instruments fart from the bandstand, gather voice and soul. Lenny watches as Terra gigglingly picks bits of grass from her hair, blows them like fairy-dust into the girls' faces.

'Shesureisgood with them,' Brother Gene slurs curtly. 'I know my girls? They're gonna miss having her around. More'n they'll miss their big brother, even.'

As if on cue, Lenny notices the younger Luce girl breaking off from the throng near the bandstand and weaving in Terra's direction. A cute kid of about twelve, ash-blond like all the Luces, honey-hued shoulders and happy Hawaiian-print frock. She stops a few feet from Terra, hangs her head and traces a foot in the dirt until Terra looks up, reaches out a belled sleeve.

'See? Practically sisters.' Brother Gene's drink slops as he nudges Lenny.

What can his new wife and little Dot Luce have to whisper about? Lenny doesn't know, but it pleases him to watch them hold hands, the girl ducking to Terra's ear. Terra's mouth moving, her eyebrows upturned. Then she looks over her shoulder, eyes bright as a pair of reef fish, swimming through the corals of suits and skirts to meet his.

Lenny grins.

'*Officer*. Why aren't you out there shaking your thing?' Terra simpers as she approaches, hands on Dot's shoulders, tossing her mane at the bodics grooving to 'I Heard It Through the Grapevine'.

'I got two left feet, Cinderella.'

'They look just right to me,' Terra flirts. 'Anyway, that's not what I heard. I heard you've got moves.'

She and Dot start giggling. Lenny feels his cheeks tighten. Strange as it is seeing his brand-new wife flirt with a man twice her age, he knows this is what she does best; that she was hand-picked by Jim for exactly this reason to meet-and-greet newcomers every Sunday.

'Clever young lady like you shouldn't be listening to rumors,' Brother Gene says conservatively, but there's a crackle of humor in his voice.

'Well, this clever young lady is just *dying* for a dance with her daddy.'

Terra squeezes Dot's shoulders so the girl whips her head around. 'Am not! Terra!'

Terra winks and pushes Dot toward her father. 'I'll be watching!'

Lenny's new wife leans into his shoulder as they watch the pair shamble off. 'He *loves* you,' she sing-songs in his ear. '*And* he's drunk.' Lenny laughs, shivers as Terra skims a hand over his butt. 'Hey, Spaceboy, listen: don't tell anyone, but I just heard the craziest thing. *Listen* ...'

'I'm listening.'

'Dot, right?' Terra lowers her voice. 'So you know Dot Luce has the cutest little crush on Paolo Jones? Jim's Brazilian kid?' Lenny doesn't know why he'd know such a thing, but he nods anyway. 'Yeah, well, they were playing at bride and groom, and Paolo says, "I'll miss you when I go back to Indiana," and Dot's like, "Huh?", and Paolo says, "Mom's taking us to live with grandma and grandpa in Indiana." Not *visit*, Lenny. *Live*.'

'Oh?' Lenny follows the forms of the tall white cop, his little blond daughter, as they merge with the crowd. 'Are you ... sure?'

'I wish I wasn't, but what else could it mean? It must be *serious*, if Mother's taking the kids away? Do you really think Mother could leave Father? Do you think Father *knows*?'

Together, they peer back at the tables. Jim Jones has his helmet of black hair bowed toward the District Attorney, Frank Mueller, a squat old dude with a mouse-colored moustache. To his right sits the DA's son Dwight Mueller, a pimply law student just married to Su-mi Jones; Su-mi herself, looking blasé; the DA's buxom wife and, finally, Mother Rosaline — cleft-chinned, pale as parchment, seemingly burdened by the weight of her red-gold beehive. To Jim's left are Roger Luce and Minnie Bellows; Minnie's parents, Isaiah and Petula; some white dudes Lenny doesn't recognize. Evelyn.

'He must know.' Lenny looks to his ex-wife, as if her pale, crossed legs and talkative hands might hold the answer. 'They must've figured it out together.'

'*Do you think ...?*' Terra repeats, touching her blunt fingernails to her lips.

Lenny wrests his gaze from Evelyn to Rosaline. Mother Rosaline; she's a nice lady, if too middle-aged for him to think much about. The old people love her, and the children. She has all those children, different races. She sings a song some Sundays for her black son — *black baby, as you grow up, I want you to drink from the plenty cup* — with such aching tenderness, it can't possibly be scripted. It's a shame, Lenny guesses, that she might be leaving and taking all those kids with her. Then again, he guesses maybe it's good news for Evelyn.

Maybe, he guesses abstractly, he should be happy for Evelyn.

'Do you think ... maybe we should say something?'

'To Father?' Lenny can't recall a single serious conversation with Jim Jones since getting back from Reno. There's comfort in this, the sunny block of time between now and those draining late-night phone calls. He's had a good appetite, these past months. He's gained a little weight, a little muscle. He's been earning money for the Temple with a weekend job, stacking logs at the timber mill. He's more than halfway through his alternate service. He's been sleeping in a shed on the Harrises' farm, but banging Terra regularly, daydreaming regularly of how she looks on her back, her toes curled skyward, her baked-pink nipples, her brown pussy hairs, her face close and hot, scorching out all other thoughts.

He'd rather not have to talk about anything heavy with Jim today.

'I think we should.' Terra ignores him. 'Father deserves to know they're talking.'

'It's probably none of our business, Earthgirl. Besides, he looks busy.'

Obediently, Terra quietens to regard Jim, talking to the DA in his humble, insistent way. Though it's impossible to know what they're discussing, stray words of Jim's float up: *liberation, self-sufficiency, overpopulation*. It occurs to Lenny that he's been hearing Jim all day, without fully realizing it; his voice beneath the commotion like a hum of traffic, constant.

'Well ... what if we tell someone else,' Terra muses.

A whisper of discomfort rises in Lenny as he follows his new wife's gaze along the table.

'Come on, Earthgirl.'

'I *mean* it,' Terra stresses. 'Lenny, you know how people *talk*. We can't just sit on this.'

He watches his new wife's eyes fix on his ex-wife; hair in that same boring bun, skin bleached by the sun, glaringly plain next to those dusky teen brides. Terra gives a sudden bark of laughter. 'Don't worry, honey. *You* don't have to come. Hey, it'll only take a second, huh?'

And before he can say anything else, she's tilting her face up to his, digging her fingers into his hair, curling her tongue behind his front teeth to tickle his palate. His new wife. What are those flowers anyway? Apple blossoms?

You're a lucky man, Lynden.

Lenny looks off at the bandstand, where Marvin Gaye has given way to tom-tom drums, the hard bass riff of 'Sunshine of Your Love'. Brother Willie, a new recruit with a honey-brown afro and deep cuts on his cheeks, is on lead vocals, and he's *good*. The sun is good, turning Lenny's eyelashes green, beating against his back, itching his shirtsleeves. He watches the crowd: little Dot doing a loose-armed monkey, Brother Gene hunching to mirror her; Sister Diane with her elegant, tulip-shaped ass wiggling circles around Jorge's dad, Brother Hal; Brother Corbin, a skinny red-haired Texan, chivalrously rocking out with Sister Ursa, the white chick with Down's Syndrome adopted by Isaiah and Petula Bellows. They're good. It's all good, better than any old church wedding. He's a lucky man, yeah. And yet ... he can't help turning back.

Evelyn is making room for Terra at the table, smoothing her dress, re-crossing her legs. A satiny dress, high-necked, dappled like a Monet painting, shorter than anything she ever wore with him. The non-Temple white dudes lean in, laugh at whatever Terra says. Then, like a schoolgirl to her deskmate, Terra covers her mouth with her palm. Evelyn inclines her head.

Their two heads, gold and dark, conspiring. Like staring naked-eyed at a solar eclipse.

4.

Most nights, they eat quickly at the Red Creek commune, sopping up lentil stew with home-baked bread. Quickly because their days have made them hungry: long hours at the mental hospital for Lenny, at the Temple daycare for Terra. Because there are chores, allotted and taped up on the fridge: dishes to wash, clothes to iron, animals to feed. Because they haven't had a honeymoon and time alone is precious.

'I can't believe you like me even when I smell like chicken poop.' Terra giggles, stripping off her overalls in the bathroom. For the first time all day, they have a few minutes to themselves. She admires her reflection. 'Well … maybe I can.'

'Are you going to wash your hair?' Lenny likes helping with Terra's hair.

'Nope. I washed it Saturday. Martha'll kill us if we use up another bottle.'

Sister Martha is a white single mom who lives in the back part of the house with her twin sons, Joey Dean and Bobby James. It's Martha who starts banging on the bathroom door within five minutes, yelling about hot water.

'Dried-up bitch was probably timing us.' Terra rolls her eyes, turns the tap off with a hiss. 'Don't you think it's racist how she always sits so far from Nessa at the table?'

'I never noticed.'

'Just watch. Every time they're side by side, she holds her arms like *this*.' She tucks a towel under her armpits, curls up her hands like a cripple. 'Some of these old white people, it's like they're all about integration on Sundays, but when it comes to *living* it …?'

Lenny watches her pat her breasts dry, her belly; twist the towel around her dripping locks and pull it off seconds later. She shimmies into her waiting shift dress; combs out her hair; checks her flushed face. As an afterthought, she steps into her underwear — the wholesale Woolworth's kind they all wear, *T. Lynden* Sharpie-d on the waistband.

She's quick. Why not? They've got a meeting to get to.

Sister Nessa is in the kitchen, mashing something in a bowl. A tiny woman, hair in tiny braids, her belly a boulder between her and the counter. Practically mute and prone to flinching when Lenny or any other white guy comes upon her unexpectedly. But she seems to like Terra; flashes her gums and mumbles, 'Nah, I'm okay,' when Terra fusses over her being on her feet so late in her pregnancy. Not for the first time, Lenny wonders what it'll be like having a newborn around, and then wonders whether he and Terra will ever have one, and then guesses if they do it'll probably be adopted. In the den, Brother Corbin is helping Joey Dean with his homework, and Terra leans over their shoulders. 'You know, *Moby Vagina* is a way better book,' she says straight-faced, then rears up laughing. She's still laughing as they walk under the dark trees to the station wagon, and Brother Eustace is running the engine of his pickup, nodding his head to a murmur of Motown. He looks up when they reach the station wagon and nods, 'Hey,' and Lenny nods, 'Hey … you going to work?' and Eustace nods again, 'Yup,' showing him the night-watchman's cap on his dashboard.

Lenny doesn't know what to feel about he and Terra being the only ones from the commune invited to this meeting. Lenny doesn't know what to make of all the meetings, but he doesn't dwell on it; the drive is too nice, balmy night air blowing and a first-date excitement in his belly. When they reach the Temple, there's fewer cars in the lot than usual, and, in the meeting room, about fifteen young people gathered, all white except for Jorge Harrison and Minnie Bellows-Luce. He wonders if he and Terra are tardy, but Jim Jones just waves them in with a lilting, 'Lyndens,' and keeps advising Roger and Minnie, seated Indian-style at his feet.

'People looking up to you. Means there's people gonna talk behind your back, that's inevitable. I *know* it. Every day. But you gotta be above it. Don't have an ego, you won't be touched by personal attacks. Minnie, you're stronger than most, damn sure stronger than this whiteboy. His weakness, can't let it affect you. Now, I'm not saying total abstinence—'

'I don't care about that, Father,' Minnie speaks up. 'I just thought, now Roger and I are married … we'd make each other stronger.'

'Ideally, honey. And don't get me wrong, you're well-matched. Wouldn't have advised this union otherwise. But Roger's got issues to work through, and you can't let him hold you back. Strong, proud black woman like you — I think you could stand to be more withholding.' Minnie lowers her long-lashed eyes, and Lenny feels a surge of sympathy for the girl, who seems to dislike being singled out just as much as he would. Mercifully, Jim turns his attention to all the young couples clustered on the plush carpet. 'Masturbation, that's fine. But no sex. We don't want any pregnancies at this time and we don't want ego-trips. It's egocentric to waste time on sex when you could be contributing to the Cause.'

Terra catches Lenny's eye with a sexy little smile; they nod in unison.

After that, Jim lectures Roger for a while. Lenny is sort of glad to see Roger Luce in trouble. Roger is handsome. Roger's nose side-on is like a Greek statue's. Roger's eyes are blue ice chips. Roger lived in the same house as Terra, until recently. But the incessant talk of 'overcompensation' and 'latent homosexuality' is boring; Lenny has heard it enough times in midweek meetings, where guys like Roger and Johnny Bronco are often brought up for being vain or playing the field. So Lenny turns his attention to the carpet, pretending it's blue moss; to the children's finger-paintings tacked on the wall; to his new wife and the young women who aren't his wife. Jo. Laura. Minnie, listening to her husband being criticized with a poise that seems almost superhuman for an eighteen-year-old …

It's only when Jim's speech takes a sudden turn that Lenny's ears prick up.

'My marriage ain't no different from anyone's. I trust all you here to understand that,' Jim utters modestly, hands clasped, chin doubled down at the carpet. 'There's highs and lows. Strength and weakness. Rosaline, goddamn I love that woman, never saw a better mother, but she's not so strong.' He shakes his head. 'Physically and mentally, she's unstable. It's not easy for her, living with the burden of my future assassination.'

There's a melancholy hush. It's not the first time Jim has mentioned that he will someday have to die for the Cause, but it's always a bummer to think about.

'Sometimes, darlings, the burden gets too much for Mother. She loses sight — and this is something not many in this church know, but I think you're advanced enough to hear it — loses sight of her destiny as a mother to our people.' Jim sighs. 'Some of you may have heard rumors. Lenny, Terra ...'

They flinch, one after another, as if catching a jolt of static electricity.

'I thank you for your discretion. You've shown yourselves to be deeply worthy of my trust. But we don't got nothing to hide.' He unclasps his hands. 'So long as Mother is struggling, I'll continue to hold her up. I know how much you need her, and she needs you.'

'What can we *do*?' Jo Harris-Harrison pipes up, her voice dopily drawn-out.

'Exactly what you're doing, sweetheart. You keep on putting our Temple family first, that's enough. Mother, she'll regain her strength, but 'til then, we gotta maintain the order. Make sure the old folks, the little ones, they don't worry their heads over empty gossip. Children need to know they're *loved*.' Jim raises his head. 'Terra? Terra, sweetheart ...'

Lenny watches Terra stir; flick her hair and rub her legs, as though cold.

'Sister Phyllis tells me you doin' wonderful work at the daycare. Now, some of us been talkin' 'bout putting together a camping trip for the school-age kids. And we want you to be Head Counsellor.'

'*Me*?' Terra widens her eyes. 'Wow ... Hey, what's "Head Counsellor" do anyway?'

'Well, first order, honey, you wanna nominate some co-counsellors. I'm thinking five sisters, five brothers—'

Terra beams over her shoulder. 'Brother Lenny?'

'Notsofast, there.' Jim laughs. 'I want you to be objective as possible, sweetheart. Bear in mind, Lenny's got his own responsibilities: alternate service, weekend job ... Right, son?'

'Yeah,' Lenny says, feeling the glow of Jim's gaze. 'I guess ... it'd be hard to get the time off.'

'Not to mention, we gotta keep the communes operating smoothly. Both of you gone from Red Creek, gonna put an unfair strain on the other residents, isn't it?' Jim turns back to Terra. 'I want you to consider this socialistically, honey. Don't be swayed by personal attachments.'

Terra frowns and furrows her brow. Then, just as quickly, her face unclouds. 'Minnie?'

'Minnie and Roger, they're both needed down at the college dorms next month. Like I said, don't be hasty. Other responsibilities you gotta consider—'

'Laura?' Terra butts in. She starts counting on her fingers. 'Dale, Donna, Johnny—'

'Sonofabitch, you gonna let me talk?' Jim blusters, and they all laugh. 'I said, not so fast. You see Phyllis tomorrow. Give her ten names and she'll pass 'em on. Got it?'

'Yes, Father.'

Terra straightens her back like a class pet, and everyone laughs some more. Jim's sunglasses flash as he tilts his head, twists his lips. 'Can't get a word in edgeways, that's the truth. Now, all you: don't matter if you're part of this or not; your contributions, they're just as valued. Every letter you write, every toilet you scrub, it helps the Cause ...'

He goes on in this vein for some time, before turning to Dwight Mueller, the desirability of Su-mi taking a secretarial job in the DA's office instead of starting college as planned. Terra rests her arm against Lenny's, mouths, '*Sorry*,' and Lenny smiles, shrugs. Sure, he'll miss her, and sure, there's a feeling inside he doesn't want to acknowledge, like milk left to sour. But a couple of days, her and a bunch of kids in the woods, no big deal, right?

It's nearing midnight when the meeting breaks up, and Lenny's stomach is grizzling again; his legs are tingling and stiff. Jim says, 'Remember, we're in a danger cycle, so don't forget to walk around your car three times,' then embraces each of them as they filter out in hazy, foot-dragging clusters. 'Son,' Lenny notices Jim beckon Roger just as he and Minnie are making a beeline for the door, 'I need you to stay for one-on-one counseling, remember.'

Roger blanches. Blinks quickly and mumbles something Lenny doesn't hear. *Too bad for him*, Lenny thinks, without really feeling bad.

But Minnie, she's got those beautiful dark eyes flashing at the sight of Jim encircling Roger's neck, talking close, his tone at once chastising and tender. Minnie drops her gaze. Shoves her hands deep in the pockets of her India-print dress; willowy body, long neck, lovely oblong face, widow's peak. Hurries past Lenny and Terra through the sanctuary, out to the parking lot, then stops, like she doesn't know where to go.

'Minnie!' Terra calls. 'Wait up.'

Minnie turns. Swipes a tear.

'Minnie, what's wrong?'

She only shakes her head, mutters, 'Oh Jesus.'

And that's all she'll say, no matter how much Terra coaxes. Unease eats at Lenny as he looks away from the girls: at the clouds drifting over the moon like dirty water, the blinds lidding the sockets of the great glass windows. Or maybe he's just hungry. He looks across the parking lot at Laura, Johnny, and Dwight as they laughingly trot in circles around Dwight's shiny Aston Martin — a wedding gift from Dwight's rich dad, frowned upon by the Temple. Terra asks if Minnie's going to wait for Roger. Minnie doesn't know. Terra looks at Lenny.

'Hey … Can we give you a ride?' he offers.

They don't mention Roger during the drive down to Minnie's parents' house in Prosperity. Instead, Terra asks Minnie questions that seem simple but have long, interesting answers, like, 'Did your dad have his own church before he met Jim?' and, 'Do you have much family outside California?' Listening to Minnie talk about her Tennessee aunts, how they thought her dad had become a 'godless northerner' when he threw in his pastorship at a nice all-black church to work wood in Indianapolis, Lenny almost misses the turnoff. When they finally rumble up the drive of the Bellows' farmhouse, Ursa, the white sister, runs out to meet the car in her nightie like a kid from some Amish backwater, and spends a long time admiring the yellow paint job, making Minnie admonish, '*Ursa*, it's *late*.' Then there's the dark, winding journey back to Red Creek, just a hamlet to the northeast, named for the trickle running through its red dirt. Through the ride, Terra talks about poor Minnie, whom Roger shouldn't take for granted; she's so nice, so smart, so pretty, not just 'pretty for a black girl' but, like, prettiest in the Temple — don't you think? On and on until they get inside and have to be quiet, can't wake Martha, and Nessa needs all the sleep she can get before the baby comes. Looking at the strip of darkness under Nessa's door, Lenny thinks of the times he's seen it lit up, Nessa and Eustace's voices crawling out from under it, and wondered if black couples talk about the same things in private as white couples do. In their own room, Terra turns on the lamp with the colorful scarf draped over it, casting psychedelic patterns across the walls, the bed. She sets the alarm for four-thirty. Undresses. Lies down, hands on her midriff.

'I can't believe Father chose *me*,' she says, to Lenny or maybe to the ceiling.

5.

That Lenny Lynden hasn't had much luck with the ladies, that's for sure.

'You haven't had much luck,' Luce says, by way of consolation, when the kid shows up at the end of summer with nothing more than a suitcase and a cursory phone call from Jim.

Marital problems. Just needs a few days to clear his head, that's all.

'Huh?' says Lenny Lynden.

'Nevermind.' Luce points him upstairs. 'You'll be bunking with Danny.'

Lenny Lynden doesn't wear a shirt to bed. Luce learns this early the next morning, bumping into the kid on his way to the bathroom, and it's such a pretty shock, the tousled brown hair and the shallow navel, Luce can only stumble, 'B-breakfast at seven.' Sleep isn't an option after that, so Luce puts on his boots and gets a jump on the chores, the children's chores, and the next he sees of Lenny Lynden, he's eating oatmeal in his white uniform and being interrogated by Dot.

'Are you getting divorced *again?*'

Lenny Lynden shrugs.

'But Terra's so pretty! Like, like, Sharon Tate—'

'Not *Sharon Tate.*' Bobbi slouches back in her chair, long legs spread wide in tight yellow slacks. She tugs at her short pigtail as if that might make it grow. 'Jane Fonda, maybe.' Then, to Lenny, playing older than her fourteen years, 'You know, *Barbarella?*'

'*Ro-ber-ta!*' Joya casts an overwrought look from Bobbi to Hattie, their new black baby foster daughter, drooling oatmeal in her high chair. Joya swats at Bobbi's wide-apart knees. 'Have some manners! And I want you to get rid of those pants. They're pornographic.'

'You Can't Always Get What You Want,' Bobbi backtalks. Yet, no doubt glad to be dismissed, she uncurls herself from her chair and storms out, backside wagging defiantly.

'Honestly … that girl has such an artistic temperament,' Joya sighs, dabbing Hattie's mouth. Artistic being code for difficult. Code for *his fault*. She turns to Dot. 'Of course Lenny and Terra aren't getting divorced! They're just taking some time. Right, Lenny?'

Lenny Lynden doesn't answer.

Mostly, Luce feels sorry for the kid. That Evelyn Lynden, it's true, he thinks the kid dodged a bullet there. But Terra, she's a sweet girl. They made a sweet couple at the wedding, though nowhere near as striking as Roger and Minnie. It seems a sorry thing for the honeymoon to be over already, even if Luce himself never had much use for honeymoons.

Joya thinks so, too.

'We've got to get Lenny and Terra back together!' she declares, after Lenny Lynden has left for the loony bin and the school bus has come and gone.

'If Father wanted us intervening, he'da said it, Joy,' Luce demurs; not because he disagrees but because his wife, like all females, has a habit of coming on too strong.

'Father trusts our influence.' Joya hoists Hattie up in her thick orange arms. Since taking a job at the hair salon in Evergreen Valley, Joya has come to favor sleeveless smocks, capri pants, not the skirt suits she looks best in. 'I'll talk to Terra when I take Hattie to daycare.'

Luce watches Joya touch Hattie's spongy hair. Hattie looks up, burbles, 'Bada-gin!'

Brother Gene.

'I'll take her,' Luce says.

And before Joya can protest, he scoops Hattie up, pets the frizzy hairs at her forehead. Joya doesn't seem inclined to protest anyhow, just flutters her eyelashes like her brain can't quite compute his helpfulness. 'Don't forget Fluck!' she sings after his brown shirt, brandishing 'Fluck' — dubious name aside, just a fluffy toy truck.

It's not quite eight-thirty when they reach the Temple daycare on Vine Street: a white ranch-style house where, funny enough, Lenny Lynden used to live with that she-wolf, Evelyn. Luce gives his siren a whirl for the kids on the lawn, and for Hattie, who likes it just as much as the others did when they were small, debunking Joya's fears about bad ghetto associations.

'Woop-woop!' Hattie squeals.

Luce laughs, 'Woop-woop,' then hands her Fluck.

Terra, out on the porch, is laughing, too, shielding her eyes from the early sun. Blue-sprigged prairie dress and hair in braids on top of her head like a milkmaid. She starts coming down the path as he's coming up, Hattie in his arms. She grins at him, '*Officer.*'

'Cinderella.' Luce grins back.

A nickname, one that stuck, from the first time he saw her looking like a proper young lady instead of the barefoot thing who'd done a shit in the corner of her cell. It took two weeks to cure her of crabs, after which they burned her sleeping bag.

'Man, is she heavy!' Terra marvels, taking Hattie up, giggling. 'Guess I'd be too, if I was still living with you guys.'

Joya's cooking, she means: those big plates of beef and noodles, breaded pork and tater tots that got her looking corn-fed and rosy even before the crabs were gone. Luce sucks in his gut theatrically and Terra laughs, loud and sweet. A sweet girl, not in the least troubled by the business with Lenny Lynden, apparently. Luce considers leaving it at that; convincing Joya to let the kid stay forever, eating oatmeal and walking their halls shirtless. But the guilt kicks in.

'I got time for a coffee.' He tips his hat toward the house.

'Oh?' Terra blinks quickly, reminding him of his daughters, caught out in a lie. '*You betcha,*' she resorts to the mock-Hoosier accent that always makes him and Joya smile. Then she nudges the door open and volleys down the hall, 'La-la-la-laura! The fuzz is here! Get your ass on the grass, stat!'

A minute later, Laura Kana, a husky white girl with big black eyebrows, appears in the doorway, wiping down a toy truck. She smirks at Luce's uniform. 'Oh jeez. Busted again?'

In fact, Luce did bust her once, smoking outside the movie-house in Moontown when she should've been in school. The tomboy daughter of a local wine family, and a couple of years above Roger at Evergreen High — when she showed up.

'Just coffee, for now.'

'Yeah? We don't have any donuts.'

Maybe it's a joke, maybe not; the impertinence of these new young ladies, it rankles, makes the back of his neck hot and taut. But he removes his hat carefully before squeezing his tall body past, and there's pride in the gesture, what it signifies: a man *and* a gentleman.

There's a little Asian boy playing with some dangly curtains at the entry to the kitchen. Terra steps around him, and he stares after her skirts. In the den, a pigtailed white toddler sits on the sofa between a black boy and girl. The TV babbles. Phyllis Clancy is folding laundry, but looks up when she sees Luce and blurts, 'Well, hiya.'

Phyllis is good people. An unmarried woman with a big bosom and even bigger behind, a few years older than him, raised a few miles north of him, just as racist before she came to the light of the Cause as he was.

'Hiya,' Luce says back. 'Should be out there enjoying the sun, Phyllis.'

'Last time I did that, I cooked like a ham.'

'That right?' Luce watches the sun crawl up the wall, watches the kids watching *Captain Kangaroo*. 'Honey-glazed or Virginia?'

Phyllis snorts a laugh.

They shoot the breeze for a couple minutes about the weather: dry California summers and the warm, wet summers back home; summers of cracking lightning over baseball fields. A boy the next town over, Luce still remembers, summer of '37, who got struck down playing ball, and how there were always more reasons to believe in a punishing God than not. When Terra wiggles into the room, she's got Hattie at her heels and a steaming mug in her hands. She passes it to him with a balmy blue-eyed look, the kind he hopes his daughters will never give so freely. 'No sugar or cream! I know you're cutting back.'

Luce drinks with a grimace. Mind-boggling that Joya was never able to teach her to make a decent cup of joe, in all the time she lived with them.

'Who's that? Hattie-hat-hat!' Phyllis puts on a silly, growly voice for Hattie, who's coyly clutching Fluck. Hattie giggles, screams, launches herself at Phyllis.

'That's our Hat,' Luce confirms. He raises the mug to his lips, thinks better of it. Cutting his eyes at Terra, he tries to signal that it's time for serious talk, but her face is a bland and beautiful vault. Cautiously, he tries: 'You're looking well.'

'Yeah?' Terra looks pleased.

'And Lenny?'

'*Oh.*' A well-trained daughter, she catches herself mid eye-roll; makes her voice soft as cotton candy. 'Yeah. Thanks for taking him in and all that. We really appreciate it.'

'Nothing to it.' The kid's white torso ghosts up in Luce's mind. He forces himself to look at Hattie, happily clambering up the couch, babbling, *up, up*! 'Course, y'know, he can't stay forever—'

'He can come back whenever he wants,' Terra interjects. '*I'm* not stopping him.'

Luce looks to Phyllis, who's gone back to folding: one ear trained on the TV, the other on the little ones. Third ear, probably, on him and Terra. 'Well. Some encouragement sure wouldn't hurt ...'

Terra laughs then. Who knew such a pretty, sunny sound could be so callous.

'Oh, Gene! It's real sweet of you to care. But, look ...' She flushes at Phyllis's nearness, takes Luce's arm. He's surprised to let himself be dragged so easily into the corner by the little blonde. 'There's just more important things for me to focus on right now than some boy's feelings. I know that sounds mean, but, well ... *tough tomatoes.*' Another Midwestern-ism. 'This life. Things are changing so fast: there's a revolution coming, we've got to be ready—'

'I don't quite understand,' Luce cuts her short. 'What's that got to do with the kid?'

Luce almost wishes she *would* roll her eyes; it'd be less brazen than that doll-like stare, that blink. 'He *is* a kid,' she says softly, touching her lips. With the gesture, Luce's eyes are drawn to a series of scratches on her arms: from the camping trip, he knows, a survival game involving running through briars; all the parents were consulted and asked to sign consent forms. 'That's the trouble: I'm a serious, socialist woman, and he's a kid.'

'Not a bad kid,' Luce qualifies, feeling a dutiful pity for Lenny Lynden, twice-dumped and too moony to speak for himself. 'He's serious, works hard. Loves you, seems like.'

'*Loves me,*' Terra says, as if the thought is new to her. 'I guess he does? Gene ... you're a doll. But it's different these days. I mean, we don't have to pretend like when *you*—' She stops, seeing his stony expression;

gives him a sad smile. 'Maybe I love him? I *do* love him, like brother and sister, like you and Joya, y'know? And I don't want to *hurt* him. It's just, all that relationship stuff? It's capitalist bullshit; propaganda invented by white church slaveholders to keep us from really loving. I can't be with a man who wants that. Not Lenny, not any man. There's only one who can fulfill me as the beautiful revolutionary I am.'

She's pink in the face, like she's been rolling around in a haystack; those milkmaid braids flashing gold. Quick as a flame, Luce has the urge to pull those braids, twist her wrists behind her back, something. But, no, he's not that kind of man anymore; not the man who used to slap Joya around because she wasn't what he wanted, who took her from behind so she couldn't see his shame. *A gentleman*, he reminds himself, wringing his hat in his hands.

'I can't go back to how things were. Not after Father — His *love*. You wouldn't understand, I guess, but oh wow, there's nothing like it! Painful, yeah, but the kinda pain that makes you stronger? Like … ohh. Just imagine you're a woman giving birth, *hours and hours*, only at the end *you're* the baby, this beautiful shiny new baby, all crying and naked and no sins, just beautiful, beautiful! I've never felt so beautiful. Oh, Gene, honey, if you *knew*—'

One of the babies is crying, as if to illustrate Terra's point. Luce turns in case it's Hattie, but it's the pigtailed white girl. Phyllis picks the girl up, rocks her, and Luce envies her for not being part of the conversation. When Terra reaches to touch his arm, he recoils, like she's the girl from lock-up again.

'*Jim's a married man*,' he reminds her through gritted teeth.

But so was Luce the night she'd slid her hand up his leg, tried to repay his charity the only way she knew how. It occurs to him a longhair doesn't change its spots, and this new generation doesn't care one bit for marriage.

'Father is the reincarnation of King Solomon, you know,' Terra says, and then looks at him expectantly. 'Don't be mad at me, Gene. You'll hurt me so bad if you're mad. I swear.'

Luce hands her his unfinished coffee. 'Here.'

'Are you mad? Genie? Hey?' She puts herself in his path with the insistence of a football player. 'Y'know, I really am grateful Lenny's with you. It makes me feel so much better. You were so good to me, I just know you'll make him right at home. Hey, you're not mad, are you?'

'Alright,' Luce murmurs evasively. 'Whew. Time flies.'

That's apparently good enough for Terra. She presses her body against his, softly mounded as sand through her summer dress; whispers close and quivery, 'Catch some bad guys for me, officer,' so there's nothing to say except, *only if you're home by midnight, Cinderella.* Then he's flapping out his hat and she's baby-talking, 'Say "bye-bye" to Brother Gene! *Bye-bye!*'

'Bada-gin! Bai-bai!' Hattie chirps.

The patrol car is where he left it. The sight of it reassures him; its smell of trapped sunlight, dashboard dust. Luce doesn't have the heart to whirl the siren again, but he waves at Laura Kana on the lawn, thinking after all she isn't so bad, just a small-town kid with a big mouth. Just kids, all of them. He'd been twenty-seven when he first knew Father's love. It hadn't seemed so young then; five years married already, two kids under five, another on the way. And of course, Jim hadn't been 'Father' then, just Jim: a well-groomed, devil-handsome street preacher he'd met while patrolling the black side of town. They struck up an acquaintance, then a friendship; night drives through the Indianapolis suburbs sipping from flasks — wild nights, free-talking nights where nothing was off-limits. They talked of women's bodies and their smells, how it was perfectly reasonable for a man to want no part of that. Of how Luce had never even seen a black person until he left his hometown but had accepted without question the notion of the 'nigger'; the ape-man who, if seen after sundown, could sportingly be chased down and clubbed to death. Of how when he started seeing colored folks with regularity around Indianapolis, just going about their business, lining up for buses, what they reminded him of most were horses: their proud necks, their intelligent eyes. And he never would've hurt a horse. No Luce would've. Though chickens were decapitated like daisies and cats thrown off roofs for fun, to hurt a horse would've been like hurting a good pal.

One of those nights, summer of '55 it must've been, parked out by some railway tracks, Jim had put his hand on Luce's crotch and the universe made sense. Then a night they'd gone to an empty house, an old lady's house by the looks, rose-patterned wallpaper in the style of thirty years earlier, and Jim had fucked him against that wallpaper.

It only happened two more times. Stopped so sudden it was like the world stopped turning, and from then on, they only saw each other together with Isaiah Bellows, or all three of them and their wives at a restaurant, always a whites-only place so Jim could make a scene. When Jim and Rosaline went to work with the poor in South America, he and Isaiah kept things going in their ham-handed way, and all he felt for Jim by '65, following him to California, was a thorny sense of entanglement, like plowing his way through dead rosebushes.

6.

Since it doesn't seem like Lenny Lynden's going anywhere, they put him to work.

Nothing too strenuous. Cleaning the stables. Turning the hay. Some sweeping and scrubbing around the house for Joya, who's got less time for such things, caring for Hattie and working full time at the hair salon, overtime at the Temple Publications Office. Lenny Lynden does what he's told without complaint, often shirtless, which is, well, a nice thing. Sometimes Danny helps him out. Sometimes the girls follow him around without being especially helpful, then report back whatever facts they gleaned: Dot, wide-eyed and breathless; Bobbi, the 'teenager', feigning coolness.

'Did you know that Lenny Lynden's mom comes from *Australia*?'

'*Austria*, not Australia, dumbass. She left because of the Nazis.'

'Did you know Lenny Lynden never kills bugs?'

'It's because he's a pacifist, and *I* think it's admirable.'

'Did you know Lenny Lynden thinks letters and numbers have *colors*?'

'Well, so what?' Luce greets their nonsense. Or, 'Better call the Publications Office.'

But, fact is, he likes these tidbits. The colored numbers, he questions the kid about breathlessly at the dinner table, murmuring, 'Well, I'll be darned,' when the kid tells him five is yellow like a banana, six is violet-blue. Danny leaves the table in boredom. Both the girls get the giggles. Luce sticks to the subject, until Joya finally snaps, 'Gene! Give it a rest.'

When he learns of Lenny Lynden's preference for chocolate desserts, Luce persuades Joya to bake a devil's food cake. When Bobbi takes another tumble off Magic Dancer, her chestnut mare, Luce enlists Lenny Lynden to help pop her dislocated shoulder back in place. When Luce sees Lenny Lynden feeding the goats one morning, he wants nothing more than to creep up on him, touch his bare shoulder, speak words so earth-shakingly tender that all things will be permitted.

Joya sees Luce looking, gives him a disgusted face, and brings Lenny Lynden a robe.

Come Sunday, Lenny Lynden won't go to Temple: doesn't refuse, just keeps sleeping, no matter how Joya yells and the girls clip-clop down the halls and Hattie totters into the room, prods him with her breakfast-sticky fingers. 'It's *his* soul,' Joya harrumphs, slamming the door, and they leave the house as a family, arrive at the Temple just as a busload from San Francisco gets in.

Jim's going to have to start holding more services in the city, Luce figures; it's getting so crowded they can barely breathe.

Terra is around, meeting and greeting newcomers, looking pretty as always with her hair down her back and a minidress Joya sewed her. She waves but nothing more. During the service, the only time he sees her is when she ducks onstage between songs to bring Jim a thermos of something. He hopes for Jim's sake it isn't coffee she made herself.

Jim doesn't notice Lenny Lynden's absence, or doesn't mention it anyhow.

After the service, all the kids skitter in different directions, and Luce does his best to talk to as many newcomers as possible. For the poor folks, it's the usual soft sell: good grub, good music, good clean recreation, free legal aid and medical care and tuition. For the white college crowd, he makes it a little more sensational: ever heard of a town called Greensburg, Indiana; my uncles were Klansmen; see that adorable two-year-old with the plush truck, that's my baby daughter. Getting a rise out of how those smug California boys can't quite figure him out, their credulous eyes, their dreamy-slow gestures, their hair a little too long like something from a painting.

But his mind keeps drifting to Lenny Lynden, how sweet he looked sleeping, how sweet he *is*, with a frequency that makes him get up to refill his punch too often, telling himself: *Give it a rest, Gene.*

Then, by the punch bowl, there's Evelyn Lynden, looking like she's just read his mind.

'Hello, Gene,' she says softly, politely. 'How are you?'

She's wearing a short dress with a high neck. She's well-put-together, he'll give her that. But everything else about her irritates him: her scrawny body; her sharp witch nose; her watery little eyes; her hair bunched neatly on her head like something sentient and eager to please.

''Scuse me,' he says, filling his cup and turning his back.

People start coming by the house for Lenny Lynden the next week.

Not Terra. Not Jim. But others.

Monday is Johnny Bronco, a white California boy about Lenny Lynden's age; not as good-looking but tall, longhaired, with an easy grace and a firm handshake. Danny is friendly with Johnny, too, and after playing with the bongo drums in the garage for a while, the three go off in Lenny Lynden's car and don't return till well after dinner.

This saddens Luce a little, but Joya is pleased. 'His life could use some variety.'

Tuesday is Ike Dickerson, who Luce knows from the old Temple days. A cheerful bald-headed man with a roly-poly body more like a woman's, divorced back in the fifties and never remarried; rumor has it, he's sweet on Rosaline. Met Jim through the Communist Party and used to bore Luce to death talking about commie books he had no interest in reading. But Ike has more to him than book smarts. Standing out by the chicken coop with Luce and the kid, he gives some good advice about how to re-roof it for winter. After that, Luce leaves them alone, goes to see the horses; Candy Cane, Magic Dancer, Bingo. From a distance, he observes Ike scolding Lenny Lynden.

This saddens him, too, though most likely the kid deserves it.

No one comes Wednesday, but Thursday after dinner, a young black man in a night-watch uniform shows up, grinning from ear-to-ear. Turns out he's a buddy from Lenny Lynden's commune, has just become a dad for the first time, a fact that inspires Lenny Lynden to give him a hug and say, 'Nice going, Eustace.' Although Luce is jealous of the hug, he thinks it's nice Lenny Lynden has a buddy; nice, too, that this buddy is so excited about his newborn daughter; enthusiastically seconds Joya's invitation for the buddy to come in for a celebratory grape juice. It's all nice and good around the table, hearing how Jenessa sailed through her labor, how the baby came out a small but perfect 5lbs 8oz, how they're going to name her 'Nzingha', after an African queen. At some point, though, Eustace makes a stray reference to Terra, how she sang 'Bye Bye Baby' to Nzingha right before going to her meeting tonight, and Lenny Lynden looks like he's going to cry, then does.

'He gonna be alright?' Eustace asks in wonderment, seeing Lenny Lynden flee the room.

Luce and his wife look at each other, shrug, start telling stories of the kids as newborns: Roger, who came out long and pale like an uncooked sausage; Danny, born in a blizzard; Bobbi, who gave Joya the most pain; Dot, who tried to hang herself on her umbilical cord.

Friday evening, Luce comes home to find Lenny Lynden slumped on the stairs barefoot, white uniform rumpled, staring into space. The girls are all there, too, Bobbi with her arm in a sling giving orders from above to Dot, who's assiduously threading beads onto a bit of macramé around Lenny Lynden's wrist. Meanwhile, Hattie is climbing everywhere, sticking beads in her mouth. Everything about the scene annoys Luce, and is compounded by the fact that Joya isn't home.

'What in the *heck* is going on?'

Lenny Lynden jumps. Beads go everywhere. The girls whine, '*Dad!*', then, seeing the mood he's in, skedaddle. Luce scoops up Hattie and repeats his question louder, tapping the kid's shin with his boot so he jerks up. His blue eyes are frightened, watery, red-rimmed.

Higher than a kite. High as a spaceship!

It isn't tenderness he feels for Lenny Lynden in that moment, just a desire to get him out of his sights. When the kid stammers, 'N-no sir,' in response to Luce's accusation, it takes all Luce's patience not to shake him, sock him, march him somewhere private. *Son, you're on your last straw. Ever bring dope into this house, I'll lock you up.* Then the kid retreats to Danny's room, and there's only the weight of Hattie in his arms, her watchful brown eyes.

'Roberta. Dorothy. Be ready in half an hour,' Luce barks, setting Hattie down outside the girls' room. He catches a glimpse of dreamcatchers, painted horses, some longhair musician of ambiguous gender — too much flowerchild crap for him to comprehend in his current state. 'Make sure your baby sister's dressed.'

Locked in the bathroom, Luce feels his collar, damp with sweat; his back. He unbuckles with a clank like handcuffs, is throbbing and big with blood, is bent over the sink, is done within a minute with a sweet, whinnying moan he hopes the girls don't hear. He puts his brown uniform in the hamper. Runs the taps. Changes into clean plaid, blue jeans, the belt buckle Terra bought him in Reno. He looks, maybe, clean and casual and a little bit festive; maybe younger than he is.

He raps on the boys' room.

At the Temple, they will eat food, hear music, pass a nice Friday night with nice friendly people. This, or some such thing, is what Luce plans to tell the kid. But when he looks in, Lenny Lynden is already facedown asleep on Roger's old bed.

In the end, the decision to send Lenny Lynden packing is all about blood.

The chicken coop needs re-roofing. Lenny Lynden agrees to lend a hand after his shift at the timber mill Saturday. Wayfarer sunglasses and smelling of sawdust, slow-walking across the grass to where Luce is gathered with Isaiah and a reluctant Roger, up from the college dorms for the weekend.

Not a job that needs four men. This Luce suspected when Isaiah showed up uninvited — proud, laconic, with his own tools and Roger in tow. It becomes crystal clear as soon as they get started, Roger and Lenny both reaching for the same screwdriver, eyeing each other warily, repeating the act with the box of nails. '*Watch it*,' Roger snarls at Lenny, and even though Roger's been moody for months now, walking around like God has personally wronged him, the rudeness surprises Luce and Isaiah both. Wordlessly, they decide it's best to separate the boys: Roger inside on the stepladder; Lenny, smaller and lighter, out on the roof. Meanwhile, they supervise.

Supervising Lenny Lynden. There could be worse things. The kid is in a better state than the day before, smiling in a dazed way when anything goes right; a plank of rotting wood lifted easily as a wet Band-Aid, a new plank set in its place. When anything goes wrong — a dropped nail, a suspicious fissure in the wood, a centipede twisting into view of his elbow — he's equally dazed, but also pained, and maybe even sweeter. *Sweet kid. Good-looking guy. Pretty boy.* Luce feels the endearments rustle in him like autumn leaves; feels cataracts forming when he looks anywhere but Lenny Lynden. Isaiah mentions going to the house for refreshments, and maybe Luce hears the note of warning in his old friend's voice; maybe even sees the tension in his eldest son's jaw. But Luce just nods and keeps right on directing the kid. 'Let me see … Hold it there … Hold it tight … Ah, hold it.' The kid's head of brown hair seems at times to bump against the sky. His back has a nice curve to it, like a swimmer. The dusty seat of his jeans. *Sweet kid. Good-looking. Pretty, real pretty*. Like a prayer, if this was a thing to pray about. Like closing his eyes and feeling the sun on his face — until Luce feels himself grabbed from behind and hurled toward the earth.

For a moment, it seems as if his younger, handsomer self has come back to smite him.

But it's Roger. Tall, towheaded, graceful as a dancer, eyes frosty as an Indiana winter. Fist landing with a soft *biff!* like in the comic books he and Danny used to read before Jim Jones said, *We don't need our kids wasting time on this white savior bullshit*. It doesn't land hard. Doesn't hurt. Already, with a dull astonishment, Luce is calculating his odds, and that they're good. Then, like work, nothing more, getting Roger in a headlock, ready to cut his breath short. Yet not ready for the flinch, the voice hoarse with hate: '*Get your hands off me, faggot.*'

'Hey … what?' Lenny Lynden cries incredulously from above.

Mercifully, Isaiah intervenes, grabbing Roger's arm like he's a ragdoll, jabbing him in the chest. 'You *do not* say that! You *do not.*' Isaiah is a good friend. Isaiah was there when Luce's world stopped turning, reminding him what it meant to be a good man, a father. Luce is thankful for Isaiah as he brushes himself off, feeling heavy as a bag of amputated limbs. He touches his lip and, seeing his rust-tipped fingers, is more disturbed than he wants to admit. Isaiah keeps jabbing Roger. '*Honor thy father!* You don't know that? *Honor thy father!*'

Roger nods, cheeks red, shirt ripped, looking more like white trash than the son of one of the Temple's oldest families. It occurs to Luce that Roger has done badly by Isaiah's beautiful daughter, Minnie; badly enough to come to Jim's attention. It occurs to Luce that maybe they *are* white trash, not the Bellows' equals.

'Hey, man. You okay?' Lenny Lynden, down from the roof, asks tentatively.

Luce looks at the kid's shirtless chest, no longer able to recall what all the fuss was about. Just a young and stupid interloper, an imposition. 'Uh huh,' Luce snorts. Over the kid's head, Isaiah shoots Luce a stern look that says everything: *This is your fault, get your act together, set an example for your piece-of-shit son.* Luce nods in agreement, begins his wounded march up to the house, avoiding his girls and Ursa riding horses, his wife on the porch painting Petula Bellows' hair mahogany. He uses the phone upstairs.

'Jim. You've got to do something about this Lenny Lynden.'

7.

Both of Lenny's wives are at the meeting. Both of them have had sex with Jim Jones. But only one of them comes to the floor when Jim says, 'There's a young woman here who begged me for sex on the children's camping trip last month and who thinks she's something special. You know who you are. You're not special. Stand up and apologize to these people you've hurt. Yes, *you*. Stand up.'

And, like a scolded child in her pink minidress, Terra rises from the carpet, wringing her hands and hanging her head.

'I'm sorry, Father,' she says.

'You're disgusting!' skinny Sister Kay, Jo's mom, calls out. 'Why would you do that to Father? Don't you know, y'know, it *sickens* him to hafta relate to people on that level?'

'Do you really think,' Sister Molly starts breathlessly, 'you're so much more deserving of Father's love than the rest of us?'

'Oh, she thinks it,' Sister Joya scoffs. 'I *lived* with her. I've seen her walking around like she's hot stuff! Flipping her hair, looking in the mirror ... Right, Gene?'

'Right,' says Brother Gene. 'Looks in the mirror all day long, that one. You notice these things, living with someone.'

Terra looks at Gene, mouth agape, pink patches on her cheeks. Her eyes start welling.

'I've seen it, too,' Brother Ike picks up the slack. 'She thinks she's prize pussy! Like blond-hair-blue-eyes makes her better than all the other sisters.'

'White supremacist bitch!' Sister Laura, herself white as curd, yells out.

Jim laughs. 'Ain't no wonder. You give a little girl a porcelain-face doll with gold curls, tell her that's beautiful? She'll believe it. Course, that ain't my idea of beautiful, no way.'

'Father doesn't think you're beautiful!' Sister Diane cries. 'He thinks anyone caught up in the sex plane is self-centered and ugly. *Why* would you ask that of him, when you know his loving energies are better focused elsewhere?'

'I'm sorry,' Terra sniffs. 'I guess … I've always been looking for a loving father figure? I never had anything like that in my life, and Father, he's the ideal man, he's an amazing lover! No man ever made me feel so good, so in touch with myself and, and, meaningful—'

'So what you're saying is, you need to be fucked by my dad to stay loyal?' Su-mi cuts in. 'That's sick, you know that? You know how sick that sounds to me?'

'Yeah, that's real sick, Terra,' Brother Dwight jeers, his acne-reddened face more amused than disgusted. 'That's Su-mi's dad. Don't you know how it feels for her to hear about people like you?'

'Not "dad",' Jim corrects. 'I'm not "dad" here. I'm your leader. And, when you're leader, people make demands, everyone wants a piece of you. I'm not saying — oh, sure, I could take care of every sister in this room tonight like *that*.' He clicks his fingers. 'And not just the sisters, mind, 'cause there's been others. I mean … what I'm saying's, I got the prowess. I'm the only true heterosexual man alive, Sister Terra got that right. But the sexual act don't bring me pleasure. What's underneath your clothes, that don't mean nothing to me. 'Cause that's not my highest love for you. It pains me, darlings, when you're so weak you can't think of anything higher.'

'I'm sorry,' Terra repeats. 'You're right, Father. I've been so weak, so disgustingly selfish. I know it didn't bring you any pleasure when you fucked me, and I appreciate you doing it anyway, for so many hours. I'm so sorry—'

Lenny doesn't feel much as he watches his new wife cry, plead. A blunt, buzzing hurt in his mind like TV static. A punctured feeling in his chest. But not a lot for Terra. She could be a doll tossed around, an actress on a flickering screen.

Someone, Sister Joya, criticizes Terra's hair; it's too long, she uses too much shampoo, has refused every offer to cut it free-of-charge. Someone else, Sister Laura, criticizes her for throwing herself at Jim on the camping trip, with all those children present. Lenny looks again at the children's drawings on the wall, slogans in bright paint: *Brotherhood is our Religion, Black is Beautiful, Christ the Revolution.* He hears his ex-wife say his name.

'Lenny Lynden hasn't said how he feels about all this.'

Lenny's first instinct is to be annoyed. By the clear, chiming sound of Evelyn's voice. By the formality of 'Lenny Lynden', when she once knew him as just 'Lenny', and herself still goes by 'Lynden'. By her face, attentive yet impassive; the notepad in her lap; the silver roses in her ears. Everything about her more unsettling for that former familiarity. There must be a German word for this feeling. His mom would know it.

'It feels …' He shrugs. 'It feels shitty.'

'You don't say, son.' Brother Ike leans forward and shakes his head.

'I bet it made you feel like shit,' Sister Diane commiserates. 'To hear your wife say you never satisfied her as a man? That must've made you feel like shit.'

'Yeah.' Sister Diane is good-looking, for a lesbian: side-swept short hair, long neck, generous mouth and breasts. 'It made me feel … like I'm not even a man. Like I'm nothing.'

'Oh, he wants to feel like a *man*,' sneers Sister Molly, a fleshy woman with Jackie Kennedy hair. Lenny knows from previous meetings that she has a husband who beats her. 'What makes you think you're a man? What makes you think you're *anything*?'

'He's clearly overcompensating,' Sister Joya proclaims. 'Father is the only real man here! All the others are just latent homosexuals.'

'Are you a homosexual, Lenny?' Sister Kay asks, almost sweetly.

'No,' Lenny says quickly. 'I-I like women.'

'I'd like to see him stand up and say that.' Brother Ike chortles. 'Stand up and, while you're at it, why don't you show us all how you make love to your wife, right here.'

Jim laughs loudly at that. But Lenny doesn't stand. He looks at his wife in her short dress and she looks back at him tearfully, like she's just seen a dog-headed man or her whole life burning. He thinks, well … Then she opens her mouth.

'Don't touch me! All men but Father make me sick! It's like insects crawling all over my body. Ohh, don't you ever try to touch me, Lenny Lynden, or you'll be *sorry!*'

The women laugh. So does Jim, then the other men. Jim says,

'Insects?', and laughs some more. 'What insects? Beetle? *Cock*-roach?' He laughs so much his belly shakes, and it doesn't seem he'll ever stop. But he does, after a while, wiping a finger under his sunglasses.

'This sister, she cracks me up. Sisters, they get high-and-mighty, don't they? Don't worry, son. I wouldn't take it personal. Stand up. Let me see you.'

The tide has changed so quickly, there's nothing to do but let it take him out. Lenny stands. He feels Jim's eyes laser through his clothes; wishes he had a fig-leaf to hide behind.

'He's a good-looking guy,' Jim assesses, glancing around the room for confirmation. 'I think most would agree, that's a good-looking guy? Pretty. Gene, don't you think he's pretty?'

'Y-sure,' Brother Gene stumbles, blushing to his ears, giving a short cough. 'He's … pretty.'

A few women titter. Jim smiles good-naturedly. 'Pretty guy, don't have to work hard. Used to women coming along, waiting on him hand and foot. Easy to see how a kid like that can just passively overcompensate.' He lets the argument sink in. 'Plenty of sisters here, I think, can attest to that.'

'He's so passive,' Evelyn chimes in. 'He doesn't know what to do with a woman.'

'He just lies there expecting us to get him off. Like, he's God's gift?' Terra echoes brashly. It's hard to believe she was weeping not long ago. 'Father knows how to please a woman selflessly, for hours at a time. But you're nothing like Father. You're just a little boy.'

'It seems to me more and more men act like little boys these days,' Sister Joya gripes. 'Overcompensating with little girls. Don't think I don't know about you flirting with Bobbi and Dot.'

'You flirted with *my* daughters? In *my* house?' Brother Gene rears up like an angry horse.

'He told Dot she looked good in a miniskirt, and I saw him lying shirtless on the bed with Bobbi,' Sister Joya declares. 'It's obvious he can't handle a relationship with an adult woman.'

'Is that true, Lenny? You told little Dot Luce she looks good in a miniskirt?' Terra looks almost like a wife again.

'I don't know …' But come to think of it, he probably did. Those Luce girls, they're not as innocent as they look: Bobbi sharing joints with him out by the stables; Dot asking him to kill horseflies and stinkbugs, chattering away about murdered starlets.

'If you think you're gonna shrug and smile your way outta this one, you've got another thing coming, Mister!' Sister Joya hollers.

Mister?

The accusations keep coming, and Lenny takes them all with hot-faced incomprehension; hands folded over his groin, eyes stung by the lights above. *What's happening? Why is everyone so mean to me?* His failing seems primordial, like original sin, or at least something from way back in his childhood. When Jim speaks again, in a calm, slightly indulgent tone, it's a relief.

'Alright, alright,' Jim says. 'He's heard enough. Let me talk.' He shines an affectionate look at Lenny. 'People get excited, son. Mothers especially, they get protective. Me, I know you meant no harm when you said that thing to Dot Luce. Innocent compliment. Fact is, our females shouldn't be wearing miniskirts if they wanna be taken serious as socialist women.'

Some of the young women — Evelyn, Terra, Laura, Jo — tug at their skirts. Sister Joya starts to say something, but Jim holds up a palm.

'That's my belief, sisters. We can talk about it some other time. I gotta say now: Lenny, I like you very much. You're sweet, gentle. Not hotheaded, like these others. I value your commitment. It's not your fault you never had a loving father figure.'

Reluctant to agree or disagree, Lenny shrugs.

'I'm so loving, Lenny. I know what you need. You don't have to beg. Your personal relationship with the Cause is more important to me than my comfort. It's true, the sex plane is sickening to me, but I will sacrifice my body over and over, if that's what it takes to bring you people to enlightenment. Evelyn will make an appointment for you to see me for one-on-one counseling this week.'

'I—'

'Don't need to say nothing, darlin'. I forgive you. Sit down.'

Lenny sits. He sits and avoids the glances thrown at him by his brothers and sisters: pitying glances, curious, disgusted. Discussion turns to Laura, who was seen getting into the car of some army dude Friday night, and who admits to having done mushrooms with him in the woods near Fort Bragg. 'We're not against relationships with outsiders if it's for recruitment purposes,' Jim says, 'But, honey, this just sounds like you going back to your old ways. And that's *shameful.* You remember you were a miserable drug addict before you came here?' Lenny looks at Jim's flashing hair, his sunglasses, his golden skin, and tries to tell himself Jim is handsome, like a cowboy, like Elvis. Evelyn gets up from her place near Jim's feet, sits next to Lenny, scratches something out on her notepad and shows it to him.

Personal counseling at the parsonage, 10pm, Thursday.

Lenny gawks. Evelyn knits her brow, underlines the date, gazes at him in that blandly expectant way that isn't new.

Lenny shrugs. Satisfied, Evelyn peels off the slip of paper, hands it to him, rises from the carpet, and walks back to Jim.

In past lives, she sat beside him on floors that way. In the white house on Vine Street. At the party where they met, in the house where she lived with her many girlfriends. Talking about Bert the Turtle and her thesis on Marcuse and how as soon as she graduated she'd go back to Europe, work for the UN, change the world.

He slips the paper into his breast pocket, hot as a burning draft card.

'You're coming back to the commune with me, right?' Terra loops her arm with Lenny's as they exit to the parking lot at the end of the meeting, eyes sore with fatigue.

Lenny looks at Gene and Joya, lumbering hand-in-hand toward the cop car. Depressing.

'Yeah, sure,' he says.

Terra beams.

Mother Rosaline answers the door. She is wearing a yellow robe and looks tired, but her smile is kind as she points Lenny upstairs: 'Jim's in his office. That room with the light.'

Before coming to the parsonage, Lenny showered, shaved, combed his hair, dressed with care; collared shirt, pressed trousers, fresh underwear. Somewhere in the back of his mind, like a lesson drilled into him in childhood — study hard, eat your greens — there's an earnest belief that nothing bad can happen to him so long as he's a clean boy in clean clothes.

But Jim's office has a bed in it. That's one of the first things Lenny notices. Also, although Jim is wearing a pajama shirt, he doesn't have any pants on, only Y-fronts.

'Good evening, son,' Jim says, taking in Lenny's cleanliness like it's a bouquet, something just for him. 'Lock that door? Thank you. C'mere, now. Take your clothes off.'

Like jumping off a skyscraper in a dream and waking to floorboards, bruises. Like drinking something sweet then going into convulsions five minutes later. Like being dropped in the middle of a jungle with a gun and orders to kill. Some things are real before they happen.

With trembling hands, Lenny starts to undress.

He undresses and thinks: this is what it means to be a man. Having soft things taken away from you. Disappointments like tracks in the dirt. Things you can't undo or reclaim. It means always accepting, never fighting fate. And if the same rules don't apply to Jim Jones, it isn't because he's not a man, but because he's God.

Nobody will ever mistake Lenny Lynden for God.

8.

Rosaline is already waiting on the porch, a mug of ginger tea in her hands, when Eve arrives in her red Volvo. She watches Eve slam the car door, sling her smart leather tote. She says, 'Hi there,' and Eve's lowered eyes snap open like a doll's.

Eve murmurs, 'Hello, Rosaline.'

'The boys'll be home from school any minute,' Rosaline says. 'Shall we talk upstairs?'

Eve nods, edges up the porch steps. She is wearing square-toed pumps with shiny square accents, squarish heels. She reaches Rosaline's level, but is not as tall as Rosaline.

She smiles. Lips whitish. Follows Rosaline into the parsonage as though she would never dream of crossing that threshold uninvited.

'Would you like some tea? Coffee?'

'No, thank you.'

They mount the staircase to Jim's office. Rosaline goes straight to his oak desk, puts down her tea, opens a manila envelope. Eve hovers in the doorway, casting a furtive glance at the bed. When Rosaline looks up, Eve swishes over, places her bag on the floor, folds her arms over her chest.

Her collarbones make gullies. Her posture is not good.

'I'm getting Frank Mueller to witness this, but thought you should see it first,' Rosaline says, sliding the paper across the oak surface. Her daughter Su-mi is a Mueller now, lives in a big modern house with the pimply Mueller boy. *Safe*. Rosaline tries to read Eve's reading face, yet all that comes to mind is the coolness of blank paper, her own carefully picked and pecked words:

To whom it may concern:

In the event of my death, I, Rosaline M. Jones, would like for Evelyn Lynden to take over the mothering responsibilities of my children. I would, in fact, hope that she would move into the house and fill any void my absence might leave.

Signed: Rosaline M. Jones

October 16, 1969

Then Eve looks up and there's something. A brief, ugly something, as though she has just been spat on, or is about to spit. Or maybe weep. For an attractive young woman, she sure has a lot of ugly looks. Rosaline wonders if this is one of the things Jim likes about her.

Eve makes a quick gesture, a flick of the arm from which Rosaline instinctively recoils. Only after the fact does it occur to Rosaline that, perhaps, Eve was moving to hug her.

But the moment passes. Eve smooths her knitted blouse, tan slacks; no minidress today, schoolteacher clothes. With impersonal curiosity, Eve asks, 'Is this Jim's request?'

'No,' Rosaline says. 'He doesn't know yet.' She folds her brow, crumples her hands. 'Doesn't need to, necessarily.'

'I think Jim would approve.'

'Well, you'd hope so, wouldn't you,' Rosaline lets slip, instantly regretting what to her seem like harsh words. Eve, however, doesn't seem affected, and this is what unsettles most. 'Anyways, if you approve, I'll get it witnessed, and that's that.'

'I approve, of course,' Eve purrs. 'They're … beautiful children.'

'I know it,' Rosaline says.

'So bright and sensitive. I've never seen children so advanced for their age.'

'They've had an unconventional childhood, that's for sure.' Before her mind can stray to the underside of this truth — the death threats, the wet beds, the night a couple of months back when she tearfully locked herself away from Jim's fury, came out to find him benevolently telling the boys, *Mother is suicidal, she likes to play the martyr, but we'd rather die than not be a family, right darlings?* — Rosaline continues proudly. 'Not many little boys can say they've gone from Indianapolis winter to the beaches of Rio and back again before kindergarten.'

Eve smiles. 'They'll be going to the moon next.'

The smile is genuine enough, a little crooked. There are worse women he could've chosen, after all; women less inclined to honor the parameters of words on paper.

'One thing I don't understa-nd—' Rosaline hears her voice crack, but presses on. 'You coulda stayed quiet? You coulda had him all to yourself.'

'No one can have all of Father,' Eve objects priggishly. 'He belongs to the people.'

'But you coulda been his wife, if you wanted. It woulda been, dontcha think, more …?'

Comfortable? Respectable? Sane? Rosaline doesn't know how to finish the thought, and Eve's face isn't giving any clues; those steady, slate-blue eyes too devoid of self-interest to want anything more.

'I want only what's best for the Temple.' Eve passes the paper back.

'Well … I'm glad we're on the same page.' Accepting the paper, Rosaline smiles feebly at her unintentional pun. 'Thanks for coming by, Eve.'

Eve's mouth opens to correct Rosaline, closes again. She takes up her bag and gives Rosaline a strange, sidelong look. 'Thank you … Rose.'

A strange young woman. Or maybe not so strange. Maybe entirely typical of the new generation. As they walk downstairs, Eve asks after Rosaline's back pain, and Rosaline says, oh, well, the worst is over. Rosaline looks at Eve's smart leather tote again and says, that's nice, very versatile. 'It was a birthday gift from my mother,' Eve explains, then looks bashful: because the gift was clearly expensive, because she has a mother who buys her such gifts, because this mother is probably the same age as Rosaline. Walking out to the porch, Eve predictably refuses Rosaline's second offer of a hot beverage — 'I shall have a coffee when I get to the Publications Office.' Then that crooked smile again, and turning on her heel, treading carefully past the withered roses, down to her red car, and if Rosaline never had to see this young woman again, if she were to fall off the face of the earth forever, she wouldn't mind at all.

But though there are thorns today, there is no blood.

Book Two

Children of the Revolution

1.

They all remember where they are the day Father is shot down in the Temple parking lot.

Fourth of July, 1972. One of those God-sent Evergreen Valley days, so hot the air is wavering, and not just from barbeque smoke. Hillsides scorched gold. Silver-white dime of sun. Sky hard and blue as a vase you want to pitch something at, just to see it break.

The day Father is shot down, Roberta 'Bobbi' Luce is in the woods beyond the Jones's vineyard, riding Magic Dancer. Riding with her butt in the air, since every time it hits the saddle, it's another whack from the paddle. Seventy-five whacks for necking with Wendy from school — not because Wendy was a girl, but because she was *non-Temple*. Seventy-five whacks, agreed on communally and administered by Sister Regina, another lezzie, just to show it wasn't about *that*. At the time, it seemed worth it, thinking of Wendy's black hair waterfalling down her back, her way of shaking it off her face to light a cigarette against Bobbi's, to press her lips against Bobbi's. But now Bobbi's ass is a motley of turquoise and red, and Wendy doesn't want to neck anymore, says it was a mistake, she's no dyke, and nothing seems worth much, everything just *hurts* … like Magic Dancer, hearing that firecracker, POP!, whinnying, rearing up, throwing Bobbi off her back and butt-first against the dirt.

The day Father is shot down, Darnell 'Darl' Patterson is in the Jones's driveway, shooting hoops with the guys as the girlfriends look on. His

181

girl, Hedy Gore, thick-thighed in torn jeans and stringy pumpkin-orange hair and that pert white-chick nose all rimmed with red, same as her eyes. Lately, looking at Hedy, nothing but stringy hair and red eyes, and sure, she's always been a little rough around the edges, a city kid with a surprising knack for farm life, just like him, but Darl hoped maybe she'd make an effort for Fourth of July. Wash her hair, maybe. Put on one of her flowery dresses and show the white slopes of her shoulders, the red fur of her armpits. Show off her body — no baby to worry about ruining it now, and since when did Hedy like babies? Hedy, who's always going on about overpopulation, how humans are poisoning the oceans, tearing down too many trees? Of all the chicks Darl's been with (and there've been *a lot*), Hedy's the last he'd expect to get the blues over an abortion. An abortion they would've agreed on even if it wasn't for that committee of white chicks talking them into it; no way was Darl going to give up his only chance at college to be a dad at twenty. No way, when his own brother Julius got shipped back to Oakland with an opium habit and no legs just last summer, and his cousins Randy and Benji getting shot at somewhere in the jungle right now probably. *No way* is Darl sentimental enough to believe mixed-race babies are going to save the world … you need a revolution for that, and revolution's tough. Revolution means being ready at the first gunshot, POP!, and Darl's dropping the ball to run to it, he's *ready*.

The day Father is shot down, Charles 'Che' Brodsky is trying to make moves on Flora Armstrong around the back of the bandstand. *Trying*, since it's not easy making himself heard over Danny Luce's drum solo, and his version of making moves is arguing with her about Israel. 'Call me a Zionist,' Che says. 'All I'm saying is, Sadat is hostile and Israel has every right to defend its borders.' Flora snaps back, '*Borders*? You mean stolen land?' Flora has eyebrows like Joan Crawford, a kohl-rimmed stare like Theda Bara, earrings that look big enough to knock him out, but just ten minutes ago she sang 'Feelin' Good', and Che could actually see the birds flying high, the sun in the sky, the good feelings. 'I mean defensive depth territory, and we wouldn't need it if the Arabs recognized the State of Israel.' Flora laughs. 'We, Charles? Let's not get ahead of ourselves. You're from Queens.' Che laughs too, adjusts his saxophone strap. 'Flora, you can do better than ad hominem attacks.' But, of course, he *is* from Queens, and she's from Harlem, and here they are in Evergreen Valley, discussing conflicts in the Middle East between sets, and he'd have to be a masochist not to appreciate his luck. Flora says, 'Oh, I'm just getting started,' and starts giving him the stats on displaced Palestinians, and he has to lean close, Danny has stomped on the bass drum, a big hollow POP! that makes the crowd scream.

The day Father is shot down, Leticia 'Tish' Bud-Hurmerinta is hunched over a plate of collard greens at the picnic table, trying to make her sister-in-law Polly eat. Tish isn't normally the kind to make anyone do anything, but Eric's worried about his sis, and honestly, *she's* worried. The way the weight has slid off Polly these past months. The way, sixteen, chubby Polly suddenly looks like a lollipop. 'C'mon, try a little,' Tish coaxes. 'There's no bacon bits. I checked.' Polly shakes her lollipop head. Eric, who's supposed to be staying out of it, cuts his eyes at Polly from across the table. 'C'mon, *greens*. From the earth. *Au naturel, ma chérie.*' Polly's favorite subject at school is French, with Evelyn Lynden. Tish has noticed Polly's green eyes hungering after Evelyn, and other slim white women: Terra, Frida, Mona. 'I can't, Tish,' Polly whispers. 'It's like eating *slime*.' Tish sighs. 'Don't let Antonia hear you say that,' Antonia being Tish's mom, who didn't spend all that time in the kitchen to have her greens compared with slime. 'Goddamnit, Polly!' Eric barks. 'You sound like a privileged bitch!' Tish shoots him a look, though deep-down she agrees; she wouldn't *dream* of turning her nose up at food that way, and not just cause she's skinny. The kind of skinny that can put on a turban and pass for a starving Biafran woman onstage, even if she was stuffing her face with Antonia's famous red velvet cake ten minutes earlier. '*Please*, Polly. You're so beautiful. We just want you happy and healthy.' Polly's eyes flash with tears, same eyes Eric's got, real pretty. Like it weighs a ton, Polly lifts the fork to her lips. Nibbles. Sputters. 'Goddamnit, Polly!' Eric slaps the table, then looks surprised at the noise, an air-puncturing POP!, and across the parking lot, Father's falling.

The day Father is shot down, Wayne Bud is crouching in the vineyard, aiming a rifle at Father's gold shirt. A moment he's been practicing for weeks, but still it seems insane to Wayne, the press of his finger on the trigger, the shattering POP! Then the predictable chaos: women shrieking, dogs barking, Father's gold shirt flowering red. The rush of bodies, wanting blood for blood. A pitchfork waves over the top of the vines, like some kind of parody of a lynch mob. Wayne flattens himself against the dirt, heart rabbiting, mouth watering at the injustice. *Too smart for this shit.* Smart, as in he actually enjoys calculus, chemistry, physics, his colossal pre-engineering course load. Smart, as in maybe he got off a bit too much on the challenge of planning a realistic-looking assassination attempt. *Too smart for this shit*, Wayne repeats to himself as the boots get closer, the dogs. But just in time, Brother Gene hollers, 'Other way, Father says!' and the mob swerves like a cloud of birds, and never again does Wayne want to be in the position of needing a fat old white cop to save his skin.

How long Wayne stays on his belly, sun soaking the back of his shirt, he doesn't know. After a while, the screams turn to sobs, prayers. Smoke curls up from the grill in a hopeful little wisp. Wayne army-crawls to the other side of the vines, cradling the rifle like Brother Gene taught him in last week's training session. At an understated jog, he starts downhill to the woods.

If anyone asks about the rifle, it's to shoot Father's shooter.

No one will ask him in the woods, though. Wayne's reasonably sure about this, and it's what makes that wall of evergreens so desirable. No one to ask questions. No one to see the heave of his chest, the sweat on his brow. Goddamnit, he's not supposed to be so emotional.

The earth is scattered with pine needles, pale green spots of sun. Antonia, his mom, will be weeping, he supposes. His big sis, Tish, comforting the younger ones: Ignatius, Henty, Elly, Shondra, Angelique. Alice, whom he's not dating anymore, never was, if he's honest, will be crying on Billy's shoulder, and though Wayne can't begrudge them this, it makes him feel as though he's standing in the snow outside a well-lit house full of mourners.

The revolutionary life is lonely, he reminds himself, thinking of that poem from Evelyn Lynden's French class about the partisan, traversing shadowy frontiers alone.

Only, Wayne isn't alone. Feet are clopping the earth again, foliage crashing, and he barely has time to duck before the shape emerges: chestnut-brown, big as three men, snorting and whinnying. 'What the …?' he mutters, though in fact he recognizes the horse. When the white girl comes trudging red-faced through the bushes after it, he isn't surprised.

'Magic!' she whistles. 'Here, Magic!' She strides forward purposefully, trips on a branch and falls flat on her ass. '*Ow-wow!* Magic Dancer, damn you, get over here!'

At that, she starts to cry, and this doesn't surprise Wayne either, though in all the years he's known Bobbi Luce, she's never been much of a crier. And he has known her *years*. Since Indiana, epic snowball fights and ball games, Cowboys and Indians; she *always* had to be an Indian, was totally stubborn about it, and totally annoying. An annoying kid in general, Roger and Danny's little sister: too young to be an equal playmate like the older girls (Tish, Su-mi, Alice, and Minnie), too prissy; even if she played the tomboy, it was always in a prissy way, like she wanted to be congratulated on her originality. He remembers her interrupting a ball game once to proclaim she'd seen a sasquatch, provoking a mass hysteria. Another time, gluing herself to him at some church event and telling him everything she knew about Clydesdales, till he snapped back (eight years old, but already surly as hell), 'So what? Do you want a medal?' Wayne never would've talked to his sisters that way, or Alice and Minnie, or Su-mi, but it seemed justifiable with an annoying white girl like Bobbi, and she hadn't cried, just stared at him with those bluey-green eyes and that big nose, almost like a third eye.

But now she's crying, and Wayne doesn't know what to make of it.

He does it because he's bored. Because, even if it was for the good of the Cause, he feels bad for shooting Father, making all those women cry. Because, loner tendencies aside, he's a Temple kid; kind and helpful to a fault. 'Hey, horse girl! Why the long face?'

Bobbi yelps. Then she's cry-laughing. '… What the hell, Wayne?'

Another thing about Temple kids: they're good liars. Have to be, what with Father constantly trying to read their minds. 'Johnny Bronco lost his frisbee,' Wayne bluffs.

'Well *I* lost my horse,' Bobbi harrumphs, wincingly dusting off the seat of her jeans. 'Some idiot decided to let off a firecracker in broad daylight. Did you hear?'

Wayne grunts noncommittally, tactfully stares away from Bobbi's ass, which is shapelier than he gave it credit for. 'She'll be back soon,' he reassures her. Since she kind of looks like she's going to cry again, he adds, '… Want me to catch her?'

'Pshhh. *Good luck.*'

It's not a yes, but he'll take it. He throws a glance at the bracken where the rifle is concealed, then dashes off. It's not long before he locates Magic Dancer — ears pricked, flicking her shiny black tail. Wayne clucks his tongue. Magic Dancer side-eyes him, blinks her long lashes, starts trotting over … then, skittish as a cat, scuttles in the opposite direction.

By the time Wayne gets hold of the horse, the old sweat has dried into a crust at his collar, and new sweat is dampening his neck. He tries not to feel too much like a stable boy as he leads the horse back to Bobbi. 'She's stubborn like you.'

Bobbi is crouched by the bracken, rifle in hands. Wayne is sliced by the apprehension that he *knew* she might find it, and he'd left her alone to do so anyway. Why? So he could bring her precious pony back? So he could get away from her tears? So he could get away from the gun?

You're not as smart as you think, he chastises himself. *And you're not much of a revolutionary.*

Mock-alarmed, Wayne cries, 'Jesus, Bobbi!'

Bobbi looks warily from him to the horse. 'I thought I heard a firecracker.'

He shrugs. 'It's Fourth of July. Maybe you did.'

'It *is* yours, right?' She looks at him with those irritating pale eyes.

'Why would you say that?' Wayne snaps, but he sounds a bit like his kid brother Henty, that time they caught him smuggling snails into the house by the bucket load. Bobbi starts dissembling the gun. Wayne groans. 'What are you *doing*?'

She rolls her eyes. 'My dad's a cop. I know what I'm doing.' With a kind of helpless thrill, Wayne watches her check the cartridge. 'Blanks, Wayne?'

Wayne scowls. 'Do you want your horse or not?'

Bobbi clicks the rifle back together. Flounces toward him, yanks the reins from his hands, and shoves it against his chest. He tries to protest, but she just gives him that stare. 'Tell me it isn't yours, and I'll put it back in the bushes.'

'*I'll* put it back,' Wayne argues, then does. 'Why're you always sticking your beak in everything, anyway? Some things are on a need-to-know basis, alright?'

'You *owe* me,' Bobbi retorts.

She climbs onto Magic Dancer, lowers her ass into the saddle with a hiss. Of course, she had her ass whupped last week. Kissing a non-Temple girl; just the sort of thing Bobbi Luce would get an ass-whupping over. Wayne makes an effort not to stare as she trots past him, bucking and wincing. 'Uh ... maybe you shouldn't do that.'

'I'm *fine.*'

'Yeah, but ...' He catches up. 'Maybe I need help finding that frisbee.'

'Wayne Bud needs help? I'll believe it when I see it.'

'*Maybe.*' Wayne smiles. He isn't in the habit of smiling much, but he knows his smile is effective. He holds his hand out. Rolling her eyes, Bobbi lets him help her down.

It isn't her company he craves; it's being away from the drama of Father faking dead. Or that's what he tells himself as they tie up Magic Dancer and beat the bushes. Eventually, Bobbi declares, 'Johnny can find his own frisbee. Can we go back now? I'm hungry.'

'Me too.' Wayne crouches to untie Magic Dancer. 'So hungry, I could eat a horse.'

'Ha-ha. Nice one, Dad.'

'Just, let's walk slow? Things are kinda crazy back there.'

Bobbi raises her brows but doesn't ask questions; Temple-crazy could mean almost anything. 'If you can't tell, I'm not really in the mood for people.'

'I can tell.' Wayne watches her ass as she leads Magic Dancer ahead. 'So ... do you still see that chick?'

'I wouldn't tell you if I was.'

'I can keep a secret.'

'Yeah, but you *wouldn't*. Everyone knows you're Mr. Perfect.'

Wayne frowns, though he can't argue with the assessment. The only time he's been in trouble in recent memory was back in high school, when the coach called him 'John Wayne' affectionately. He'd retorted that John Wayne was a talentless racist.

It's silent, except for their steps in formation, the cicadas. Wayne asks, 'Do you only like chicks?'

'Do you have a problem with that?'

'Course not. Just curious.'

'Yeah … I don't know. Maybe. Father says we're all latent homosexuals anyway.' Bobbi shoos a horsefly. 'Did you ever think you might be … you know …?'

'No. What?' But actually, he has wondered. Last summer especially, when Alice started going around with Billy Younglove, necking and close-dancing with Billy at every Temple party. In all his years of assuming he'd marry Alice someday, Wayne never did more than kiss her chastely, drive her places, study with her. Never *wanted* to do more, though Alice was easily one of the prettiest girls in the Temple, and, more importantly, one of the smartest.

'Let's put it this way.' Though he can't see it, Wayne can hear the smile on Bobbi's lips. 'Are you staring at my ass right now?'

'What? No. I mean … It's kinda hard not to. You're right in my face.'

'Hah!' Yet Bobbi quickly reddens as their eyes meet, and they both look at their shoes just as quickly.

Further up the path, Bobbi stops. Turns to him with a weird little smile. 'Hey … wanna see?' Before he knows it, she's unbuckling her jeans, peeling them down and flashing her ass, which, he'll remember till the day he dies, is bruised every color of the rainbow.

Wayne starts to laugh. Hard, bone-shaking laughter that feels almost like crying.

The heat is strong but violet-edged, the sun melted gold, when Bobbi and Wayne clip-clop back to the parking lot with Magic Dancer. People are making noise, no longer mournful, awed, and sure enough, Father is hobbling through the crowd — Mother Rosaline on one arm, Sister Petula on the other, his clean shirt unbuttoned just enough to show his taped-up chest. Meanwhile, Brother Ike's sticking two pudgy fingers through the hole in the bloodied gold shirt, yelling like a carnie, 'Lookat the size! Gotta see it to believe it!' Evelyn, plain face tearstained, is shadowing Rosaline, and beside her is her newbie sister, Sally-Ann, who joined a couple of months back, straight out of high school. Bobbi's parents are clap-grinning and hugging little Hattie, her brothers with their wives, Minnie and Clarisse, her sister Dot trailing the Jones boys as they weave toward Father. Wayne's siblings, all leggy and ebony-dark as him, are huddled with their mom and the Hurmerintas.

'My loves,' Father oozes. 'Your prayers have given me the strength to heal myself!'

Bobbi shoots Wayne a look: pity.

He finds her hand and squeezes every feeling he's having into it.

2.

After the 'assassination attempt' of Fourth of July 1972, Father wants things.

Father wants the gold shirt mounted behind glass and displayed in the foyer of the Evergreen Valley Temple. Father wants the gold shirt put in storage when the local police, despite Brother Gene's attempts at containment, start making inquiries. Father wants twenty-four-hour surveillance of the Temple grounds. Father wants, most of all, soldiers.

'Strength. Secrecy. Selfless service.' Father gives Wayne, among the group of promising young men gathered before him, a special look. 'I know you're capable, brothers.'

'Um. Father?' Billy Younglove, a notoriously snappy dresser, raises his hand. 'Do we get uniforms?'

They get leisure suits, matching brown berets. They get semi-automatics — but only after they complete the intensive weapons-training course with the SFPD that Brother Gene recommends them for.

They're a dozen, to start with: four white, eight black. Shortest is Danny Luce, five-eleven; tallest, Darl Patterson, six-five. But they're all under twenty-two; all students at the college an hour south of the valley; all where Father needs them, exactly when he needs them.

Like midnight, dropping Father off at the Sheraton Hotel, watching from the lobby as he checks in under a false name. Five a.m., picking Father up from the airport, keeping straight faces despite his trench coat, low fedora, and sunglasses. Planning Committee meetings, hitherto closed to them, watching the doors and escorting Father outside to piss (no peeking allowed; Father is self-conscious of his unusually large penis) and, on a handful of occasions, firing shots into the night. At services — up in the valley and down in San Francisco — they perform pat searches and stand by the exits with menacingly crossed arms.

Darl, Eric, and Wayne are all on duty when this white guy shows up for a midweek service, too blond, too good-looking; a square jaw like Superman and silver-gold eyes. The guy says he's Frida Sorensen's brother, and they can see it: same jaw, same Scandinavian looks, though Frida is plainer and her accent's a freakshow, Alabama by way of New England. By contrast, this guy sounds comfortingly regionless, like an extraterrestrial disguised as a news anchor. What he doesn't say is that he's a famous photojournalist.

Naturally, they don't let him in. 'Midweek is members-only.'

Next night's Planning Committee meeting, Frida is dragged over the coals for her brother's nosiness, for even *having* a brother when the Temple's her family, and she cries till she's hoarse, says she doesn't give a shit about Phil, is pretty sure he doesn't give a shit about her, where was he when she was living in that hole in Oakland, and if Father wants her to tell Phil to fuck off, she'll *do it*. 'Now, now, no need for extreme measures,' Father chuckles, and the following hours are spent going over the big questions: what does Phil want? Who is he with? Is he worth the risk? Someone brings up the possibility that Phil might be CIA. Someone else brings up the trouble they've been having with that right-wing journalist from *The Examiner*. Someone else brings up the raw humanity of Phil's photographs from Vietnam. 'I remember that one in *Life* of the dead women in the rice paddy,' Evelyn Lynden says, and Lenny Lynden, who rarely says a word in meetings, asks, 'Was that him? I remember that.'

It's agreed that Phil Sorensen will be invited to Sunday's service.

To their list of things to do, Father's soldiers add, *Keeping an eye on Phil Sorensen*. And they do. Between their papers on property law, their veterinary science labs, their lectures on thermodynamics, they monitor the too-good-looking photojournalist: visiting the veterans' medical center in Sacramento; attending a job interview at a newspaper in Sonoma; helping a blue-haired crone cross a street in Moontown. They monitor him at that first Sunday service as he watches the healings with a surprised affability, clapping in all the right places, lining up to shake hands with Father afterward. Shaking hands with Mother, too, talking with her at length, and later being introduced by a sulky Frida to faithful old black ladies, educated whites, gorgeous young women.

'Sorensen wants to do a story on us,' Father boasts next meeting. 'Course, we don't trust him. But wouldn't hurt to keep him close, show him the good we doin'.'

The story doesn't happen, but other things do. Phil moves into a commune in Evergreen Valley, starts giving German and Photography classes in Moontown. Phil begins helping out in the Publications Office, converting the storage closet into a darkroom, writing human interest stories and advertisements, milking his media contacts for positive coverage of the Temple. Phil is invited to join the Planning Committee and, within two weeks, given two new titles: Head of Public Relations and Youth Counsellor.

'Privileged white men like Sorensen gotta be made to feel important. Makes them easier to keep in line,' Father tells Wayne, Darl, and Billy in a deferential undertone, when he sees them looking surly over Phil's latest appointment. 'Don't be fooled, sons. He don't hold no sway. All power to the people, that's my belief.'

They don't believe Father, quite, but they try to. For the greater good, it seems important that they *try* to put their private lack of faith aside.

And it's not like Phil's unqualified, or even unlikeable. Of all the Counsellors who come weekly to inspect the Temple-owned dorms, Phil's the coolest. He's cool when Darl steals a white rat from the lab to give to Hedy. When Che freaks out about the Munich Hostage Crisis, Phil walks him to the phone booth and feeds him an hour's worth of coins as he talks to his mom back in Queens. Phil listens to their complaints, even the petty ones, like how uppity Gail looks when she wears her glasses on the edge of her nose. Instead of yelling at them for not making their beds right, Phil teaches them to do it like he used to in the military. He tells stories about the military; tells Billy, who wants to be a pilot, about flying in tin-can planes six feet above the jungle canopy. They appreciate that Phil has actually *seen* the war they're lucky enough to be studying through rather than fighting, as they appreciate he isn't waiting to be congratulated on the fact that he's obviously spent time around black people before the Temple. In this way, he's different from Frida, who used to screw a Black Panther, and Diane, who did missionary work in Africa, and Evelyn, with her lefty-churchy family.

Also, Phil smiles a lot.

Wayne wonders if he should start smiling more, if people would take him seriously if he smiled as much as Phil. Around the dorms, at meetings, greeting newcomers on Sundays, Wayne makes an effort to stretch his mouth into a Sorensen-like grin. But when he catches sight of his grin in the shiny metal of the tea dispenser, he's reminded of a performing monkey, and well-meaning white people still keep acting surprised to learn he's in college.

Fuck it, Wayne thinks, and goes back to scowling.

Phil doesn't have a girlfriend; doesn't seem interested in pursuing any of the (many) Temple chicks with crushes on him. Yet he talks about past girlfriends, and compliments Danny Luce on Clarisse's beauty, and once says 'Wow!' when Alice leaves the room in a figure-hugging dress, and another time, incongruously, describes Evelyn Lynden as a 'knockout'. When, inevitably, Father brings up Phil's sexuality in a Planning Committee meeting, Phil confesses to having behaved regrettably with paid women in Vietnam, and before that, in college, him and a buddy taking turns on one girl; high school, fucking a fourteen-year-old friend of Frida's.

'Do you know how *disgusting* that is?' Frida seethes. 'Did you ever think what it was like for me, growing up with a disgusting chauvinist for a brother?'

'You're still a chauvinist, and you still disgust me,' Evelyn says solemnly. 'The overcompensation is beyond belief.'

'You make out like you're this totally enlightened guy, Phil. But you need to confront your latent homosexuality,' adds Mona d'Angelo, whose family owns a bunch of factories in New Jersey, and who resembles Evelyn, only younger and poutier, with big spooky eyes.

All things considered, it isn't unexpected when Father asks Wayne to summon Phil up to the men's room after a service in San Francisco, nor when he and Darl hear moaning as they stand guard outside the men's room door. Not unexpected, yet despite himself, Wayne had expected better of these men, who move through the world like they're his betters.

No true revolutionary cares about titles, though, and this makes it easier for Wayne to ignore how quickly certain white men and women rise through the ranks. Wayne doesn't want titles, just progress, and as long as he's learning how to solve block matrixes or convert sewage sludge into crude oil, he's making progress. Sometimes, Wayne can't even sleep, for fear of all the progress he's made being undone during the night. By flashlight, he studies with an afghan over his head, screened from his roommates' snores, farts, furtive wanking.

That's where he is the frigid January night Tish knocks on his window. He knows it's Tish because she's always had this jaunty way of knocking, *rat-a-tat-TAT*, which simultaneously gives him the shits and makes him smile to himself. Back home, she used to knock that way on his bedroom, forcing him to look up from his books long enough to remember chores and meals. But he can't recall Tish ever knocking at the dorm, and neither can his roommates.

'Fucking hell! What the fuck's wrong with you?' Harry Katz, a pre-med student who's older than any of them, but weedy and volatile as an adolescent, lunges for the window.

Wayne drops down from his bunk and intercepts Harry before he can put his fist through the glass or something equally insane; Harry's known for his psychedelic-flashbacks. 'Cool it, Harry. It's just my sis.'

'Yeah, Harry. Cool it,' Terrence chimes in from the lower bunk. Terrence has an amazing ability to wake up whenever someone has food or is ragging on Harry.

'I'm *cool*,' Harry mutters. 'I'm cool. Just minding my own—'

Wayne unlevers the window with a metallic crunch, opens to Tish's face. Her skin is ghoulishly blue and the whites of her eyes shiny like liquid metal. 'Can Eric borrow your car?' she asks, and though her voice is superficially steady, Wayne hears it as a whimper.

'What *happened?*' Wayne scans her face for bruises, blood.

'Eric needs to get to the valley. *Now*,' she urges. 'Polly tried to commit suicide.'

Outside, Eric is clenched, pacing, like he's got to take a dump and the toilet is occupied. 'Give me those!' he yells as Wayne jogs up the drive, jangling the keys to his Ford.

Eris is one of those white guys who's always turning red from cold, anger, exertion. Looking at his wind-slapped cheeks, Wayne can't imagine what it's like having all that blood so close to the surface. He thinks twice about handing over the keys. 'I'll drive, man.'

It's a difficult drive. Winding roads, misted windows, Eric barking orders from the back seat. Tish placating. Mostly, Eric's alright, but it pisses Wayne off to see Tish playing peacemaker like she's Mother Rosaline or something, and part of him keeps remembering all those times Eric's mom has shown up to the Temple with bruises — though he knows judging Eric on this is like someone judging him on his old man's boozing.

When they reach the Hurmerintas' backed-up driveway, Wayne stops Eric before he can storm the door. 'I know you're scared, but watch how you talk to my sister, alright?'

'Yeah. You're right.' Eric nods. 'I'm sorry.'

In the den, Molly Hurmerinta is huddled with Mother Rosaline, Sister Diane, Sister Joya. Danny Luce is standing nearby, arms crossed, but no uniform.

'Where's Polly?' Eric demands as soon as he walks in. Molly Hurmerinta jumps up.

'Oh, my boy! Ricky! You're such a good brother!' She squeezes him against her mountain breasts. 'And look, you brought Tish and Wayne! Whole family's here!'

'Where's Polly?' Eric asks again, extricating himself. 'Mom? Is she … in hospital?'

Molly hauls a handkerchief from her sleeve, blows her nose.

'She doesn't wanna look like me. That's understandable! But starving herself when there's Biafran mothers can't even make milk for their little babies? It's sick, Ricky. *Sick.*'

'I know. Polly's sick,' Eric says flatly. 'Please, just tell me she's—'

'Oh, honey,' Joya interjects. 'She's gonna be just *fine.*'

'Can we get you some cocoa?' Diane rises. 'You look like you just blew in from Canada!'

Mother Rosaline rises, too. Though all the women have obviously been crying, Mother's face is ruined in that way particular to redheads. '*She'll be fine,*' she whispers, wiping a sliding tear, squeezing Eric's arm, then Tish's. Tish looks alarmed; follows Mother out.

'Mom,' Eric pleads. 'You said she tried to commit suicide?'

'No, honey. We said she's *suicidal,*' Joya corrects, like Eric's a slow-learning child. 'Her self-esteem is *zilch.* Says she doesn't care if she starves to death, and your mama should go adopt some orphans from Africa.' The mothers trade a look, eyes-to-heavens. 'Honestly, Polly's heart is in the right place, but she can't see the forest for the trees!'

'Doesn't know her own worth,' Molly agrees. 'How could she, with a dad like yours? If she'd'a just had a loving father figure from the start ...'

Wayne knows there's no love lost between Eric and his dad: a hard, weaselly Finn with the same green eyes and short fuse. So he's surprised when Eric bleats, 'Where *is* Dad?'

Molly flaps her handkerchief. 'He's fixing them houses in Eureka. Anyways, what's *he* gonna do? You think *your dad* knows how to talk to Polly?' She gives a Chihuahua-like yip. 'Only one she wants to talk to is *Father*. Y'know, he'll do anything to make her feel beautiful.'

Eric's red cheeks drain of all color. He jerks toward the staircase.

'Now, don't you do that!' Molly waylays him. 'Let her have some privacy!'

'She's in the middle of one-on-one counseling!' Joya squawks. 'It's *delicate*, you hear?'

Danny comes over and blocks Eric's way. 'Just leave it, okay?'

Eric shoves Danny. 'And what if that was one of your sisters up there?'

'If my sisters ever need counseling, that's their business.'

Tish, Diane, and Mother re-enter with their trays of cocoa. Locking eyes with his sister, Wayne knows it's *bad*; worse than when their own dad was thrown out of the house and entered into the Temple's alcohol rehab program. Eric turns to Mother.

'You're letting this happen? What, your husband screws underage girls and you just stay downstairs making cocoa? Do you know Polly still sleeps with her *teddy bear*?'

'Nobody said a word about *screwing*!' Molly cries. 'Where'd you get that dirty mind?'

'You can't talk to Mother that way!' Danny backs her up, a genuine crack of hurt in his voice. 'She practically raised us! If you're going to disrespect Mother, just—'

But Mother closes her eyes, breathes deep. 'I don't have any claims on Father.' Tears spill down her freckled cheeks. 'My life isn't any more precious than Polly's. She's a beautiful young woman, but she needs Father to help her see it. I'm here for her, and your mom, too.'

'No.' Eric shakes his head, clenches his fists. '*No, no, no.*'

'I know.' Mother lifts her chin, as though to invite a strike. 'I know. *I know.*'

Eric doesn't strike Mother; he isn't like his dad that way. But he does strike Danny, and Danny strikes back, and between the two tussling white boys and the screaming women and the hot cocoa, the only sense Wayne can see is to put his body between them all, then drag Eric outside by the scruff of his shirt. 'You're gonna hurt somebody like that,' Wayne says gruffly, as the night air slaps their cheeks. 'You could've hurt *Tish.*'

Eric slumps down on the porch, looks up at Wayne. 'What if it was Tish up there?'

Wayne refrains from saying the first thing that occurs to him; that Tish isn't the kind to starve herself and threaten suicide; Tish, who was in and out of hospital when they were kids, finding blood in her pee, getting tumors removed from her kidneys. 'I'd be mad, too ... But you have to try to be objective.'

Eric puts his head in his hands and starts to cry.

When it becomes clear to Wayne that Eric isn't going to stop any time soon, he slips inside to find Tish. She isn't there, but Father is, drinking cocoa and talking solemnly with Molly, Joya, and Diane. He tilts his sleek head at Wayne. 'Thank you for being here, son.'

The main thing that stops Wayne from throwing any punches himself is the sight of Danny, nose stuffed with tissues. 'Thanks, brother,' Danny mumbles.

Soon after, Tish and Mother appear on the stairs with Polly, who's dressed in a long frilly nightgown. They're talking between themselves, even laughing. Wayne gives Tish a *what-the-hell* look and in return she rounds her eyes, *who-knows*. Father raises his mug at Polly.

'Hungry, sweetheart?' He smiles. 'Want some warm cocoa?'

During the ride back to college, as Tish's head rolls against the Ford's window and Cat Stevens plays on the radio, Eric tells Wayne, 'The bullet didn't go deep enough.'

Wayne pretends not to hear.

'Whoever shot Father last summer. The bullet didn't go deep enough.' Eric meets Wayne's eyes in the rearview. 'Tell him I said that.

I don't give a shit. He deserves to die.'

Wayne doesn't tell. Since what Bobbi Luce said that day in the woods, Wayne is wary of being seen as a tattle-tale. But somehow word gets out, or maybe Father reads the violence on Eric's mind, because that same week all Eric's security duties are taken over by Terrence. A couple nights after that, Eric shows up at Wayne's dorm asking if he can borrow the Ford again, he needs to get out of the place, just drive, and Wayne goes one better; loads up the trunk and drives the two of them out to the woods to shoot, shoot, shoot.

3.

In retrospect, it makes sense, but until Father orders all the men and women who've ever begged him for sex to stand up in the members-only meeting, Bobbi Luce never imagined her dad could be one of them. Not because he's her dad, or because he's married to her mom, but because she's always imagined those men to be young, hip, college-educated, and her dad is just a dumb old cracker who says things like, 'tough tomatoes' and ''55 was a good year.'

And yet, she remembers things. Snippy remarks from her mom over the years. How he never even looked at Terra when she walked around the house in too-short nightgowns, though Bobbi and her brothers couldn't look enough. How weird he was around Lenny Lynden, and how his weirdness made her mom even more of a bitch than usual.

'That time you fucked me up the ass all those years ago,' Bobbi's dad blubbers, the crude words strange on his lips. 'That was the only time I was ever happy.'

Bobbi hates her dad. Not as much as her mom, but enough to be surprised by how little hate she actually feels, seeing him stand up with all those younger, better-looking people.

'Of course, they're all *white*,' Bobbi overhears Eunice Mosley bitch to Flora Armstrong, a black girl whose style she's always liked, on their way out of the building that night, and she's ashamed she didn't notice something so obvious. Because white skin is the most obvious thing Bobbi's dad has in common with doll-pretty Polly Hurmerinta, and Evelyn's sister Sally-Ann Burne, and Harry Katz, the moody med student, and dreamy blue-eyed Lenny Lynden, and Bobbi's big brother Roger, and every other person who admits to having forced Father to make a sacrifice of his body.

'What do you expect?' Flora catches Bobbi looking. 'White folks always want to think they're something special.'

And it's true, Bobbi does want to think she's special, though all evidence seems to be to the contrary. While her mom says she has an 'artistic temperament', Bobbi knows she doesn't have the talent to match it: she can't sing like Flora, can't turn their sappy Temple stage-plays into genuine tragedy like Tish Bud, can't play drums like her brother Danny, can't even bead and crochet like her sister, Dot, who's got about as much imagination as a filing cabinet. She isn't pretty like Dot, let alone beautiful like Minnie and Alice, and while she isn't particularly interested in being beautiful, at least that'd be *something*. She isn't a good horse-rider, though she's been riding practically since she could walk. She likes writing, but she doesn't trust herself to use big words correctly. Graduating Evergreen High without distinction, it's a relief to no longer worry about being brought up for her mediocre grades, shouted down as a slack-ass counterrevolutionary. Yet it's also clear that now she's an adult, her time for believing she's special is over.

'I'm going to be a nurse,' Bobbi starts telling people, and immediately sees a change in the way they look at her, like she's not as selfish and useless as they assumed.

Nurse is a good job for a young Temple woman. The Temple needs more nurses, and plenty of girls Bobbi looks up to or has crushes on are studying to be nurses: Tish Bud; Sally-Ann Burne, with her pretty oval face and eyes that crinkle small when she laughs (which is often); Junie Crabb, a Pomo Indian girl, with a pretty round face and glossy waist-length hair, who plays flute. If these girls with actual talents are happy to devote themselves to caring for sick people, there's no reason Bobbi shouldn't be, and really, she *is* happy when her mom presents her with a pile of textbooks at the beginning of the summer, when her adopted sister, Hattie, makes her a paper hat with a red crayon cross.

Bobbi packs textbooks with her for the Temple's cross-country bus tour that July, but mostly they go untouched; it's her *last* summer before college, after all, and there's other stuff going on, like Hedy Gore's pet rat Pinkeye crawling from seat to seat, and making up stupid variations on 'Hail to the Bus Driver' with Sally-Ann, who seems like she's been riding buses with them forever, even if she only joined last year. Then there's Brother Ralph, who's the one responsible for those sappy stage-plays, giving her a book about lesbians to read. Brother Ralph is gay — a real slinky gay man with flowy shirts and a degree in Dramatic Arts — and works at a second-hand bookstore in Stanford, which is where he gets all his books, Bobbi guesses. 'It'll probably go way over your head,' he tells her loftily when he gives her the lesbian book, with a little wink that makes it okay, and sure enough it does go way over, but she likes the way the characters are tortured and European, and the pages thick with words like *effulgence, raiment, intaglio*. At one point, when Bobbi assumes everyone around her is sleeping, Wayne Bud reaches a lanky arm across the aisle and plucks the book from her hand.

'Hey!' she whines.

He reads a page. Pulls a face like her dad, gives it back, and pretends to nod off.

Bobbi hasn't had a lot to do with Wayne since the previous summer, but she's seen him around, wearing his uniform and beret like a softcore Black Panther, surlier by the day. It's his surliness that interests her, not his uniform, not his looks, though she supposes Wayne *is* good-looking … for a guy. All the Buds are, with their blackest-black skin and long limbs, which seem built for another climate — the plains of Africa, maybe, though Bobbi knows better than to say this. Until recently, though, Bobbi always preferred looking at Tish, who's got cute buckish teeth, long whipping cornrows, a waist that curves in and hips that curve out. Always, she's preferred looking at women, and she's never understood why other girls don't as well; why anyone would waste time on men when there are waists and hips, and walks that flow like water.

'Alert! Alert!' Bobbi hears her dad's stupid cracker voice come over the bus PA, sees the sleeping bodies stir. 'All buses to evacuate! Father predicts an explosion!'

'*A gas explosion,*' Sally-Ann quips, and a few guys obligingly supply raspberries. Bobbi can't imagine Evelyn ever responding to an alert like that, and that's what she likes about Sally-Ann; how she makes jokes even when it's 'inappropriate'.

But then there's Wayne: Mr. Perfect.

Bolting up from his seat, treading the aisle and calming a few hysterical seniors, wailing toddlers. *He* is *perfect*, Bobbi thinks, and the thought's such a shock, she drops her book.

They empty out at a big dark cornfield, all eleven busloads of them. Wayne and some other security guys start helping her dad and Bob Harris check the engines for bombs, until they find the culprit under bus No. 5. Phyllis Clancy faints. Father says, 'Darlings, stay calm,' and whispers something to Evelyn, who goes back inside Father's bus, lucky No. 7. Terra and Jo Harris-Harrison rally a group of seniors into doing jumping jacks, running on the spot. Dot sneaks into the cornfield with Paolo Jones, and some other young couples follow suit, later stroll out with messy hair, munching on ears of unripe corn.

'We have defused the bomb!' Father, who's been watching over his personal bomb squad, bravely placing his body in as much danger as theirs, announces once they're done. There's a peal of applause, miscellaneous *right on*'s and *hallelujah*'s, which fall flat on Bobbi's ears — because she's watching Wayne. A few paces behind Father, frowning, scuffing his shoe in the dirt. When Wayne's mom, Antonia, and a couple of his siblings go up and hug him, he forces a smile, but Bobbi notices the limpness of his shoulders, how weary he looks.

'Of course Mr. Perfect knows how to defuse a bomb,' Bobbi teases as they're re-boarding the bus, each with a sibling attached to their wrist. 'You should get a medal or something. What d'you think, Hat? Should Wayne get a medal?'

Hattie, who's up long past her bedtime, replies in a stonerish drone: '*Yeahhh.*'

'Defusing a bomb is one thing. But I don't know shit about Clydesdales.'

Bobbi laughs and cries, 'I can't believe you remember that!' Wayne's little brother Henty laughs, probably because Wayne just said *shit*. Hattie laughs, because everyone else is and that's enough for a five-year-old.

Without discussing it, they wind up sitting together, siblings on their laps. Henty blows on the glass and draws a *H*, and Hattie proudly proclaims, 'H is for Hattie,' then falls asleep pretty much as soon as the bus starts moving. Henty keeps drawing on the glass with mousy finger squeaks. Wayne closes his eyes and says, 'Tell me something.'

'About Clydesdales?' Bobbi asks.

'Sure. Clydesdales. Anything.'

So she tells him: Clydesdales are draft horses, they come from Scotland, their feet are feathered, everything. Until her voice is wispy, and Wayne looks like he's actually sleeping.

He isn't though, because he confides:

'I'm sick of his shit. But one of these days it might be for real, and what if I'm not paying attention then, you know ...?'

In Chicago, Bobbi is asked to help with the healings for the first time. She isn't sure what she expects, but presumably something more dignified than accompanying Mother Rosaline into a toilet cubicle to help a Holy Roller shit out a 'cancer'.

Bobbi's job is mostly to sweetly encourage the lady to push as she strains over the bowl, not so different to Hattie when she was potty-training. The lady is sobbing a bit — she never suspected she could have cancer — and Bobbi tries her best to tell her it'll be okay. When the lady's done, Mother slips a red blob from up her sleeve into the toilet. The lady cries in horror but then fans her face, all relieved; she consents to having the cancer scooped into a plastic bucket and shown around the church.

Bobbi scoops while Mother helps the lady freshen up. At the cubicle door, Sally-Ann and Tish take over the bucket. Bobbi hesitates, but they're friends, after all. 'What *was* that?'

Sally-Ann and Tish glance at each other. Their faces are straight, but only just.

'*Chicken gizzards*,' Tish whispers. Then the straightness is gone.

'Gross,' Bobbi says nonchalantly; she's not some squeamish girly-girl like Dot.

Sally-Ann beams. 'The white dresses are a lie. We're real gross.'

Mother shoots them a look from over by the mirrors, and they stop giggling; follow her out to the screaming sanctuary, bucket in tow.

Mother must be embarrassed, though, since she takes Bobbi aside as they're lining up for the bus that evening. 'I know it feels like dirty work, but we wouldn't be doing it if it wasn't for the greater good.' She skims the air between them apologetically. 'Lotsa these folks wouldn't come all this way if it wasn't for the healings. But the real healing doesn't necessarily happen onstage: diet plans, sickle-cell anemia tests, reproductive health education ...'

By the time they reach the east coast, Bobbi can confidently slip a cancer out of her sleeve without any help. The grossness is an okay price to pay for skipping out on services, hanging out with the other nurses and the guys from security, who are the ones to guard the icebox full of gizzards. Darl, biggest of them all, constantly cracks them up by posing with his legs so far apart it's like an invitation to play leapfrog. Then there's Terrence, who falls asleep like a senior, but always snaps his eyes open before anyone can steal his beret or draw a dick on his face. And most of all Wayne, who tries so hard to look serious but gets itchy feet every time a soulful beat pulses in from the sanctuary.

In Boston, Father beckons Bobbi over and tells her what a good job she's doing.

New York City, she doesn't see much beyond the ghettoes where they're pamphleting, but Che and Flora sneak off to a jazz club and come back smelling of smoke, with stories that make her jealous. Somehow, they don't get in trouble for that, but there's a nasty confrontation after Che's mom turns up to the next day's service and takes him and Flora to his favorite deli.

'You think you can just come and go as you please?' Sister Regina shreds Che at the rest stop outside Philadelphia. 'You think it's revolutionary to show off your girlfriend like she's some kinda Hottentot Venus?'

Though Che argues his mom isn't racist — she's been pro-integration longer than he's been *alive,* she's the reason he loves John Coltrane — it's agreed he has counterrevolutionary tendencies, should shave off his moustache, and would benefit from one-on-one counseling.

'You know what that means?' Darl rags on Che as they're re-boarding the bus. 'Father wants to fuck you.'

'Not happening.' Che reaches for Flora, who asks if he wants to borrow her razor.

Bobbi's always liked Flora's style, but she starts paying more attention after that. Flora debating Che about sexism in the Talmud. Flora swapping looks with Eunice Mosley when skinny white women march around with their clipboards giving orders, expecting crowds to part for them like they're Moses at the Red Sea. Flora, most of all, standing up in a members-only meeting to ask Father why he keeps giving leadership positions to white folks, when their membership nowadays is at least two-thirds black.

'Sister, if it was up to me, it'd be different. But society is fucking *racist*. People out there? They more likely to buy our message if we give it to 'em soft. Don't mean you don't got power. You make the message, sister. You *make* it.'

On the homebound bus from Florida, Bobbi hears Flora discussing a book about some bisexuals in Greenwich Village and asks if she can borrow it.

'*You* read James Baldwin?' Flora looks dubious. But, taking pity on her maybe, she tells Bobbi she can have the book once Eunice is done with it.

Back in California, though, there's not so much time for reading, or at least not for reading that isn't study. She's still helping out with healings and, together with some other nursing-students-to-be, Opal, Denise, Janet Lakshmi, starts taking tutoring from the older girls twice a week. She starts taking on more odd jobs: driving seniors to and from their medical appointments; lugging their groceries; tidying their houses — jobs that make her feel as if her whiteness has been smudged away, her selfishness replaced by a guilt-tinged glow. She works in the Temple offices, mostly on the mailouts and letter-writing campaigns, but also calling up prospective members, posing as a telephone surveyor for a pharmaceuticals company.

One night, Terra asks her and Polly to dress in black, gets them to pick through new members' trash cans for anything Father might use during his predictions the next Sunday.

'You've come a long way,' Bobbi's dad says the day they pack her things to take to the dorms. 'I'm proud, Bobcat.'

Bobbi's mom says something similar, in different words: 'The way you're going, you could be on Planning Committee by Thanksgiving!'

Bobbi knows she should aspire to be on the committee like her parents, like Roger and Minnie, like Danny and Clarisse. But from what she's heard, it just sounds like more work and more confrontation.

Then there's Father, one strange afternoon in the Publications Office, coming up behind her at the photocopier, placing a hand on the small of her back. 'You're doin' good work, honey,' he murmurs, breath warm on her neck. 'I'm proud of you.' He doesn't say anything else, but his hand moves, up her back to her neck, the ends of her hair, which was cropped short at the start of the summer when Father said all the Temple girls needed to focus less on their looks. There'd been a lot of crying, including from Junie Crabb, who's self-conscious about her weight and said she wouldn't feel pretty without it, and Janet Lakshmi, who's been to India and thinks her long hair is sacred, and Hedy Gore, who likes to let her pet rat hide among her red locks during lectures, but Bobbi had been one of the brave ones, not flinching when her mom took her scissors to it, laughing and ruffling her hand through it afterward. Father touches this hair, then her summer-bare shoulders, then her tits, and she feels a splintering of feelings — surprise, disbelief, a blunt hurt and blunt acceptance, like falling off her horse — and amid it all, a single overriding thought: *eww*.

Father drops his hand, edges away. *He's read my mind*, Bobbi thinks. Until she notices Wayne, standing in the doorway.

Wayne steps aside for Father as he creeps toward the door. Bobbi goes back to her photocopying, ignoring the shuffling of Wayne's papers at her back.

'You're working your way up,' he says coldly. 'Congratulations.'

With effort, she can keep the photocopies from blurring before her eyes. But she can't keep the crack from her voice as she shoves past Wayne, storms out of the narrow room.

'Fuck *you*. I don't want *up*.'

4.

Wayne knows that, now Polly has transformed from a self-conscious sixteen-year-old into the youngest member of the Planning Committee, the main thing keeping Eric in the Temple is Tish, and the main thing keeping Tish in is family. Temple family, and the other kind, which they're not supposed to think about so much. If he has trouble imagining leaving their little brothers and sisters behind, it's a given his big sister does, too.

Which is why he takes pains to make it easier for her when she gets the chance to take a job at San Francisco General Hospital while Eric starts his first year of law school. 'Don't worry about coming up to the valley this week. Mom says the little shitheads have choir practice,' or, 'Got any notes to pass on to the little shitheads? I'm cleaning Mom's gutters this weekend.' With all his running around for security, Wayne becomes adept at delivering notes, drawings, home-baked goods, frequently enough that no one feels neglected.

After witnessing Father feeling up Bobbi Luce, getting Tish away from the Temple seems suddenly important to Wayne. Not because he's scared for her — it's common knowledge Father doesn't touch black girls — but because it kills him to think that, no matter how hard Tish works, she'll never get as far as all those white chicks with daddy issues.

He doesn't tell her any of this, but when she stops showing up to services in the valley, he's glad for her, and when she stops helping with healings at the San Francisco services, he's glad, too, and when anyone asks why they don't see her around so much, he's ready with excuses about the hours she's working. He lets himself believe, unremarked as Tish's loyalty always was, that her disloyalty will go just as unremarked. He's wrong.

About six weeks into his go-between routine, Wayne attempts to visit Tish's one-bedroom rental near the hospital. 'She's working overtime,' Eric says gruffly, peeking through the door. Then, 'Just leave us alone, okay?' When he gets back down to the street, Wayne notices a carload of glowering brothers from security parked opposite. He hesitates, before casually striding across to them, leaning through the window.

'See anything worth seeing?'

'What's it to you?' Terrence retorts, flashing his gun.

'Hey, man, we're all in this together,' Wayne bluffs, making sure his own gun can be glimpsed as he slides into the back seat beside Billy. He considers saying that he's on a mission, has just bugged Tish and Eric's apartment, but decides to stick with the strong and silent act. After a few minutes of staring through the window, he pulls out the red velvet cake his mom baked for Tish and starts unwrapping the tinfoil. The guys' ears prick.

They wait for over an hour, but the hour passes quickly, since Wayne's thinking of Bobbi Luce. He wouldn't have thought of Bobbi, maybe, if Danny Luce's blond head wasn't in front of him, but there it is, and there she is: swaggering through his brain in her tomboy clothes, short hair, a piercing in her nose like Janet Lakshmi. She's been looking dykier than ever, and acting it, cozying up to anything with two X chromosomes. She's also been, like Tish, skipping services, and getting in trouble when she does show up. Getting in trouble at the dorms, too, neglecting chores, ditching class, masterminding every stupid water balloon fight and weeknight dance party. She doesn't talk to him, and he doesn't blame her; just misses her.

'Hey, sister!' Terrence lets out a low whistle and adjusts the rearview mirror, waking Wayne from his reverie. He glances out to see his sister's white uniform, seemingly disembodied against the night. Then the sheen of her nylons and black skin. He feels genuinely afraid for her, in a way he hasn't since she was six and had those tumors on her kidneys. Terrence rolls down the window as Tish levels with the vehicle and repeats, 'Hey! Sister!'

Tish jerks. Freezes. Stares at the gun Terrence is dangling, just so, out the window.

Terrence motions for Wayne to roll his window down, too. He tries to glare and look apologetic at the same time.

'Sister … you comin' to the valley tomorrow night? Members-only meeting?'

Tish nods. 'Yeah,' she says blithely. 'Should be.'

'Your man, too?'

'Yeah,' Tish repeats. 'Eric's coming.'

Terrence A-OKs her, grins, and rolls the window back up. They drive slowly alongside her until she's inside the building; leave with a shriek of tires.

The next night, Tish is there with Eric to listen to Father's predictions, or threats:

'There are some young people who think they know better than their Father … who think there's something out in the world they can't get here … Young people who don't believe the revolution's comin' fast enough, who choose anarchy over a life of self-sacrifice. I got one thing to say to you, children: the world is agony and you ain't gonna find nothin' out there but agony and death. You'll die out there, children. I know 'cause I *seen* it, and lemme tell you … If you can't put our family first, you *deserve* to die.'

After the service, Wayne watches his mom and siblings swamp Tish. He watches Eric endure a crushing hug from Molly, goo-goo eyes from Polly, who these days looks like a miniature Evelyn Lynden. He watches Father, Reaper-ish in his dark robes, sidle up to Eric, place a hand on the back of his white neck. Eric flinches.

'*You'll die out there, children.*' Darl's big-assed redhead, Hedy Gore, mimics Father's drawl under her breath. '*I know 'cause I'm Death.*'

Darl shushes her, darts his eyes at Wayne. With a barely perceptible smile, Wayne presses an index finger to his lips and mouths: *Shh.*

A moment later, Evelyn stalks by, skinny and haughty as always.

Wayne looks back at them once Evelyn has passed. To his relief, they're grinning.

There are only the three of them who talk about leaving that night — Wayne, Darl, and Hedy — but they agree there must be more, agree they *need* more, safety in numbers. This is during the ride back down in Darl's Chevy pickup, loaded up with crates from the last harvest.

'We told ourselves we'd wait it out. Finish school,' Darl confides.

'But I dunno how much longer I can take orders from a wackjob.'

'A junkie wackjob,' Hedy qualifies.

Trust a white hippie to think everyone's as high as she is. But Darl must notice Wayne's skepticism, because he shoots him a solemn glance from behind the wheel. 'Strictly confidential, okay? I've seen his medicine cabinet. He's got more speed than a racehorse.'

Now that Hedy's opened her mouth, everything's coming out. How she was berated for a whole hour for putting a 'Save the Trees!' sticker on the truck, in case it offended the valley's timber workers. How she was forced to eat SPAM despite being a vegetarian, to show she didn't think she was 'special'. How she was called a whore for getting pregnant, a selfish bitch for mourning her abortion. How she was forced to write fake confessions to working as a whore, doing drugs, dealing drugs to kids, molesting her kid stepbrothers. How her twelve-year-old stepbrother was beaten black and blue for going to see a kung-fu movie the same week that Hedy, earning some sly cash ushering at an arthouse cinema in the city, saw Father sitting in the dark with an arm around Evelyn Lynden.

'They were watching this French film about a workers' strike. I quit that night.'

Wayne's mind suddenly feels like a forest full of dead tree stumps. 'Are you … sure? Father and *Evelyn?*'

'Man, I know you don't got much experience with women, but *come on.*' Darl slaps the wheel. 'You think she's *that* devoted to the Cause?'

'She does a pretty good job of looking like a spinster, I'll say that.' Hedy's bust heaves. 'And *I'm* the whore …'

Wayne imagines the dead stumps burning. 'Have you told anyone else?'

'About Father's movie date? *No way.* I saw how Flora got shredded for even suggesting Father doesn't hate those long country club lunches with Frank Mueller.'

Flora and her white boyfriend Che were two of the most vocal critics last month, when the Counsellers came around collecting their socialist theory books, claiming the college was getting more conservative and they needed to protect the Temple from scrutiny. 'You want good socialists, but when we start educating ourselves, it's a threat!' Flora had raged as Brother Ike loaded the books in his truck, to be incinerated up in the valley. 'Nothing more threatening than black folks getting *educated*.' Wayne, too, had been enraged, wanted to knock the glasses off Gail's nose when she argued that *everyone's* books were confiscated, not just the blacks'. But he kept his cool, and he'd listened when Alice Bellows with her lovely oblong face stood up and said that what was most important was that they lived socialism, and they didn't need theory for that, and they were all getting educations that would allow them to build a better society: as teachers, doctors, nurses, lawyers, architects, engineers. Alice spoke so beautifully, was so *beautiful*, Wayne had swallowed his objections. Remembering it now, though, all he can think is that he'll have to get used to living in a world without Alice Bellows' face.

'Tell Flora and Che,' Wayne instructs Hedy. 'I've got a feeling they'll be receptive.'

The next day, while the others work on Flora and Che, Wayne calls Tish at the hospital, apologizes for his gun-flashing the other night. 'Yeah, you *better* be sorry,' she says, and agrees to meet him in an alley near her apartment, to bring Eric. Waiting in his dark clothes, Wayne feels small; smaller still when Eric shows up, shielding Tish like a bodyguard. When Wayne reaches into his pocket, Eric reaches to disarm him. But it's just a notepad.

I'm leaving, Wayne scratches. *Are you with me?*

Tish reads it and starts to cry. Tears plop over her two-letter reply: *OK.*

There are seven of them, with Flora and Che. Wayne runs into Flora pumping the tires of the communal bicycles and she raises her chin in acknowledgement.

'I'm asking my girl Eunice, and Lanie Younglove,' she says, and keeps pumping.

Eunice is a ballsy chick, with a buzzcut and a mouth that can break into the world's biggest grin or biggest snarl, depending on who you are. Usually it's a grin, with him. But Lanie, Billy Younglove's sister? She's quiet, always hiding her nose in *The Upanishads*.

'Don't worry.' Flora must notice his uncertainty. 'I'm not naming names. I'll just tell 'em I'm moving back east with Che.'

But Eunice has a new boyfriend, Fletcher, and the Temple has offered to pay for his schooling. Lanie wants to stick around for her mom and Billy. They both tell Flora they'll keep quiet, but Wayne can feel the clock ticking. And he still hasn't worked up the nerve to ask Bobbi Luce.

He starts finding reasons to visit the girls' dorm. To sit the next table over from her in the cafeteria. Even to follow her into a nursing lecture. She *notices*. Turns around pulling ugly faces and, when that doesn't work, tries to pelt him with a wad of paper. Her aim sucks.

Later, he follows Bobbi to the library, where she's studying in a group with Janet Lakshmi and some others. They stare as he takes a seat close by; pretend not to as he takes out his books and proceeds to gaze at Bobbi from over the top of them.

This goes on for maybe half an hour, before she shuts her book, storms over, and slams a hand on his unopened cover. '*What the fuck are you doing?*'

He looks at the ring in her nose. It looks stupid, but kind of interesting, too.

'Studying.'

'*You piece of shit,*' she hisses. '*You're so full of shit.*'

The white lady librarian, who resembles a barn owl, gives them a scandalized look. Suddenly, Wayne has an idea to get Bobbi alone.

'No kissing in the library!' Barn Owl screeches at the same moment Bobbi spits in Wayne's face, shoves him away. 'Get out, right now!'

'*What the fuck, Wayne ... You really are a piece of shit,*' Bobbi cusses him out as they're exiled from the library, the jeers of her study buddies loud at their backs. 'You know I don't like guys ... and I sure as hell don't like *you.*'

'Alright, alright. I'm sorry.'

He catches her arm. She rips it from his grip. 'Sorry for what, exactly?'

'I'm not sorry for kissing you ... but I'm sorry for doing it without your permission,' Wayne answers solemnly. 'And I'm sorry for what I said at the photocopier.'

Bobbi folds her arms. 'You're going to have to be more specific.'

'I said something that was untrue, and unfair to you. I implied you were using your body to get ahead.' Bobbi's face, though still skeptical, softens slightly. 'Look, I've had to stand outside a lot of closed doors. I've heard things, and seen things, including how certain white people become more essential to the Cause after an hour on their backs than the rest of us can in a decade. It's fucked up, and it makes me crazy, and I took that out on you. I'm sorry.'

'It *is* fucked up,' Bobbi agrees. She stares at her sneakers. 'I'm sorry. I don't know what else to tell you.'

Wayne stares at her sneakers, too. 'Tell me you'll come with us.'

'What?'

'A bunch of us are leaving. Tell me you'll come.'

Bobbi scrutinizes him with her pale eyes. 'Why are you asking *me*?'

'You were here when things were good ...' Wayne takes a step closer, thinking of the early-early days, when he truly believed it was Father's magic that wiped the tumors from Tish's kidneys, and that there was no limit to what a black boy could achieve, so long as he was smart and loyal. '... You understand how bad things have gotten.'

5.

They will go by night, eight bodies split between the Ford and the Chevy. They will go east, then north, then east again, avoiding main highways. They will go with their firearms in their trunks, and a pool of cash from Che's pawned sax, Hedy's stepdad's civil-war medallions, Eric's dad's furs from Finland, the camera stolen from Phil Sorensen, the petty cash box from the Publications Office. They will live thriftily, as the Temple has taught them, but the road will meander and funds will run low before they can decide between Canada or New York, and they will settle in the next city that comes along: Sioux Falls, South Dakota.

In Sioux Falls, Bobbi and Eric will pose as a nice white couple, rent a nice three-bedroom house from a nice white lady. Wayne, who hasn't touched Bobbi since that day in the library, will feel jealous of Eric, as he has felt jealous of the three girls, seeing Bobbi cuddle up to them by campfires, plant sisterly kisses on their cheeks. He will tell himself that he is twenty-one and sex is no longer counterrevolutionary, but out of habit, he won't believe it.

The three couples will take the three bedrooms. Bobbi and Wayne will take the living room, cringe when they hear the other couples being couples through the walls. They will take jobs: in pizza parlors, supermarkets, department stores. They will earn paychecks and, not knowing what to do with them, spend too much on stuff like cigars and chewing gum.

On the last day of November, Bobbi will turn nineteen, and they will throw a party, inviting new friends from their new jobs. Wayne, though his dad isn't far from his mind, will drink a beer, just one, and that beer will be enough to make him pull Bobbi away from the record player where she's playing 'Willow's Song' for the thousandth time, put his lips on hers and not remove them for the whole night, and by the first of December, they won't be virgins.

They will have a good year, just one, in South Dakota. They will say the word 'love' and mean it. They will disgust their brothers and sisters with the newness of their affection. Two-by-two, their brothers and sisters will leave for other places: Eric and Tish for Chicago, Che and Flora for New York City, Darl and Hedy for Washington State. They will be forced to move out of the nice three-bedroom house and into an apartment on the bad side of town, the only place that will rent to a couple with skins like theirs, but it will be their own, and it will seem like they have a future.

They will talk of becoming teachers, of inspiring children from neighborhoods like theirs with a love of words and numbers. She will offer to work while he studies and he will reluctantly accept, attending classes where he is the only black person, staying late in the library so he can pick her up from her second job waiting tables at a German restaurant.

One night, a patron will complain about the colored man loitering outside the restaurant, and from then on Bobbi's manager will ban Wayne from waiting for her, and she will begin walking home alone, and he will worry, and it will occur to him that he wouldn't worry so much if she wasn't a blond girl in a black neighborhood.

They will argue about stupid things: how late she is getting home, how short her skirt is, how her lamp keeps him awake when she stays up reading novels by dead white people. There will be a day, coming back from the liquor store, when they will argue about some stupid thing, and she will push him away, and he will grab her arm, and a white cop will be waiting around the corner to shove him against the wall and ask, *Miss, is this lowlife bothering you?*

That day will be bad, but not as bad as the day she will come home from work with two black eyes, a cut lip, her uniform torn, purse stolen. She will not say anything about the man or men who did it, and he will not press her. He will make her stop working nights, will stop pressing his body against hers at night until she says, *It's okay, let's just fuck, fuck me Wayne Bud, or what … are you scared or something?*

They will receive an invitation to Che and Flora's wedding, but they won't go, as they won't when Tish and Eric invite them to spend a weekend near Lake Geneva. They will have a desire to hunker down in their apartment, Cold War-style.

Their differences will chafe. He will find her blond hairs in his clothes, hear her singing 'Willow's Song' off-key, and wonder how he could ever be attracted to someone so white. She will see him frowning at her half-read novels, and his lack of imagination will seem like a male thing, boxing her in.

She will cheat. He will freeze. They will end, and it won't be long before they're only phases to each other: *that time she dated a guy, that time he dated a white girl.*

He will marry the first cute sister with an appreciation for differential calculus that he meets. He will anchor. She will drift. She will spend time in Spokane with Darl and Hedy, their baby Forrest, who is the color of a palomino, freckles on his cheeks. She will, without meaning to, crawl back to the Bay Area, and feel her pulse quicken when she sees the Temple Greyhound buses.

She will be living with her first serious girlfriend when she calls him on the number Hedy gives her. He will be pleasantly surprised to hear her voice, and they will talk into the night, about the Temple buses, her girlfriend Marina, his wife Kathy, his students. After that night, there will be nights when they can't deal with all the space around them, the time passing, the schizophrenic burr of Father's voice in their brains. Nights in the years to come, when their stories are no longer theirs, and they can barely hear each other over the screaming headlines. Nights after everything's gone to shit and their dreams are decaying bodies in a distant place. Nights when their voices are the only thing to remind each other that the good things, love, beauty, family, still exist; that the night, endless as it seems, cannot undo their progress.

International Woman of Mystery

1.

'*Bon anniversaire, madame.*'

The customs officer at Charles de Gaulle raises an eyebrow at Evelyn from over her passport, and she raises an eyebrow back. Gives him a taut smile.

'*Vous êtes très gentil, monsieur.*' You're very kind.

The officer looks from Evelyn to Terra and Frida, both giggling and tossing their hair at more men in uniform. He asks, '*Vous fêterez à Paris avec vos amies?*'

Evelyn glances over her shoulder, feeling nothing but the coldness of cash strapped to her body. She says, '*Elles sont mes sœurs.*' They are my sisters.

'*Elles sont belles.*' The officer stamps Evelyn's passport.

His fingers brush Evelyn's as he returns the passport. But he's staring at Terra and Frida.

Evelyn marches ahead with her suitcase, comparing the D.O.B. under her passport photo with the fresh date stamp:

July 22, 1975.

She is thirty years old today.

They take a room at a small hotel in the Latin Quarter. A queen bed with a striped coverlet and a matching sofa. 'I can take the sofa,' Terra offers, eyes shining sanctimoniously.

Frida looks from Terra to Evelyn, chin squared, arms crossed. Most likely, Frida would've made the same offer, if Terra hadn't beat her to it.

'I'll take it. I'm shortest.' Evelyn places her suitcase on the sofa, starts slipping off her sandals. 'Frida, you can have the first shower.

Terra, why don't you get us some maps from reception?'

Once Terra is gone and water is rushing behind the bathroom door, Evelyn unlatches her suitcase, hunts among the precious Tampax boxes for her tape recorder. She slips in a new tape, switches it on, sticks it inside her leather tote. Sets her tote on a spindly table midway between the bed and the sofa.

The early evening light tumbles through the curtains, dusty and yellow as apricots.

'I got us some maps of the city and a map of the Mee-tro.' Terra bursts in, brandishing the maps like a winning hand of cards. 'I don't know, are we gonna use the Mee-tro?'

'*Métro*,' Evelyn corrects. 'We're only here for the night.'

This is news to Terra, but she doesn't ask questions, just bounces over to the window. 'Mind if I open this?'

Evelyn shakes her head. Terra pushes aside the curtains, hoists up the window and, with a sigh, leans outside it. After a while, she asks, 'Do you hear music? Like, harmonicas or something?'

Evelyn looks up from the map, spread napkin-style across her lap. She listens.

'"*Le Chant de Partisans*", I think. Yes.'

When Frida sticks her head out of the bathroom a few minutes later, she is all heat-flushed paleness, dripping hair. 'So … either of you pack any *real* Tampax?'

Before Evelyn can shake her head, Terra is crossing the room to her own handbag, beaming. 'Our moons are in tune!'

'If you need more, there's a pharmacy on practically every Parisian street corner,' Evelyn adds. That *she* has not bled in months is irrelevant. She refolds her map and looks at Frida. 'I want a shower, too, once you're done.'

'Sure,' says Frida. 'Just as soon as my cunt is corked, I'll be right out.'

They laugh. Not just at Frida's dirty mouth, but at the Southern drawl that crops up when she cusses — the result of a rebellious adolescence near Fort Benning.

'Sure,' Terra echoes, though nobody asked her. 'You should have the next shower, Evelyn. I don't mind at all.'

*

In the locked bathroom, Evelyn takes off her blouse, her skirt, her money-belt. She takes off her underwear and considers her body, plastered with US dollars.

2.

The sky is still light when they go out to meet it. Their bodies do not know what time it is. Their eyes see everything: women with naked backs and diaphanous palazzo pants; wizened street pornographers; ragged couples melting into each other like Rodin sculptures. Evelyn leads the way, sometimes pointing out sites — the Place Saint-Michel, the Sorbonne, the Jardin de Luxembourg — but mostly leading in silence.

Frida, an army brat who's lived in Japan, West Germany, and perhaps ten different states, looks nonchalant. Terra gapes.

'Is this where Jim Morrison's buried?' she asks as they pass the ivied walls of the Montparnasse Cemetery. Evelyn smiles, guides them from the green boulevard to the bustling underworld of the railway station. In line for tickets, the press of the crowd makes the girls stick to Evelyn like fabric to sweat-damp skin. They study their fingernails, their wedding rings; peer through lowered lashes at men in hats, men in glasses, men smoking, men with beards or averted faces.

Three tickets to Zurich, departing first thing in the morning.

'The lakes are beautiful in the summer.' Evelyn recalls the brief, unhappy weeks she spent traveling through Western Europe after her broken engagement. 'Imagine wearing a swimsuit while looking at the Alps.'

Above ground, the evening resembles one of those multicolored cocktails: burning Grenadine topped with mimosa orange, drowning in blue Curaçao. It is past cocktail hour. It is nearing lunchtime in San Francisco. They walk down darkening *rues*, boulevards, past smells of ash and fried butter. They walk until they are hungry, and beyond that. At a set of traffic lights in sight of the Eiffel Tower, Frida's grumbling stomach gives her up.

'We'll find a bistro,' Evelyn says. 'Somewhere with fewer tourists.'

The place is small, dark, wood-paneled. They choose a table indoors, with views of the narrow street, people dining under ivy-green and wine-red awnings. Evelyn orders for the three of them: *escargots, duck confit, tarte Tatin.* A bottle of Burgundy. When the waiter comes and uncorks the bottle, they laugh. They laugh, too, when he comes again with the snails in their pretty, striped shells, swimming in green butter.

'*Aw,*' Terra says, eyes brimming. 'I don't know if I can.'

'I can.' Frida reaches gamely for her two-pronged fork.

'Just pretend you're eating shellfish.' Evelyn takes up her fork and shows them how.

They clean their plates. The waiter whisks them away and pours out the last of the wine, asks in English if they want another bottle. '*Oui, le Chablis encore,*' Evelyn says amiably, and notes the girls' faces: surprised, gleeful, a little judgmental. 'It'll help us sleep.' She pushes her chair back. Her face is warm, her legs boneless; it is her birthday. Snatching up her bag, she jerks her head at the *FEMMES* sign at the bistro's rear. 'I'll be right back.'

Bolted inside her cubicle, bidet running, Evelyn takes the tape recorder from her bag, stops it, listens to the thuds and creaks of the hotel room.

I got us some maps of the city—

Evelyn fast-forwards.

Soon as my cunt is cork—

Forward again to her own voice, so high and clear it makes her cringe:

A cardigan will do.

I wish I packed a cardigan. Terra. *Velvet in summer. What was I thinking?*

You've been in San Francisco too long.

More creaks, scuffles, then Frida: *It's all yours, Evelyn.*

This is what she wants. Evelyn brings the device to her ear, listens to her past self shut the bathroom door, start the shower. The girls talking in her absence.

Paris … I can't believe it. Terra. *You know how guys always say they'll take you to Paris?*

Guys say a lot of shit. Frida.

Or Hawaii. I had this guy wanted to sail me to Hawaii and work on, like, a coffee plantation.

Ha. Wonder where he is now.

Oh, Rex was a bum. He's probably sitting in some prison cell. Scoffs. Silence. *But, like, Evelyn looks really good?*

Yeah.

Like, really good? I thought, you know, prison ... Didn't you think she'd be more ...?

Rough?

Giggles. *Oh man. I don't know? Like, maybe they give special treatment to gringas?*

I dated a Mexican once. He didn't treat me special.

Squeaks. Hisses. Street noise.

Why'd they call this the Latin Quarter anyway? Is it, like, the Mission District?

Uh-muh-nuh. Ask Evelyn.

Paris! I can't believe it.

Thunks. Clatters. A whoosh of a door opening, and Evelyn's own voice again, quiet and strained: *Your turn, Terra.*

Hey, Evelyn, why's it called the Latin Quarter?

We're close to the Sorbonne, which was built in the twelfth century. Her classroom cadence. *All the students used to speak Latin, until the colleges were suppressed during the French Rev—*

Evelyn cuts herself short. Slips the tape recorder away. Looks at her pale knees with the heaviness of heart that comes from being talked about but not understood. Yet they haven't betrayed the Cause, and this is foremost. She rises, flushes, washes. When she returns to the table, their duck has been set down.

And that's when she sees him.

Through the window, standing at an outside table, talking with a group of men.

'This is *so* crispy,' Terra gushes, looking up from her plate to Evelyn. It is this alone that tells Evelyn that she's been standing for an eternity, slack-jawed as a class dunce.

She sits.

Quite mechanically, she cracks the skin of her duck with her fork, shreds a bit of dark flesh, lifts it to her mouth, realizes she's forgotten how to eat. She puts her fork down and takes up her wine glass, which is somehow, miraculously, full. Gulps.

She stares.

It's his limbs that she recognizes: the length of them, or the way he holds them. The texture, if not the style, of his hair. He has a briefcase, but his sleeves are rolled up and his blue plaid jacket slung over his shoulder. His limbs, yes, his limbs. She spears a vegetable, she doesn't know what kind. She chews it. 'I've only ever had duck in Chinatown.' Terra. 'Peking Duck? That shit's too sweet.' Frida. Another vegetable. The food is good, but only abstractly; she couldn't describe its taste. 'One of my brother's friends shot a duck with an assault rifle when we were stationed in Virginia. Phil's friends were always sociopaths, I swear.' Evelyn sees the man straighten, wave his arm in the direction of the street, step away from the table.

'I'm sorry,' she murmurs, standing, feeling the girls' eyes flicking to the outdoor tables, the men. 'Eat. I'll be back as soon as … soon.'

Evelyn has become quite good at making herself invisible. Or perhaps it's a skill she's always had and merely honed, as life has demanded. Following the man with the slung blue plaid as he ambles toward Odeón Station, and she knows before it happens that she will have to buy a ticket, if she wishes for any kind of resolution. She is poised at the ticket counter when he slips through the turnstile for the westbound Métro, and her hands almost don't tremble at all, counting her change, and she almost doesn't rush at all, just walks briskly in his shadow. She spies him on the platform at the same moment she hears the train's whistle, and it all has the feel of something predestined, the ease of it, the push of strangers' bodies, allowing her to sidle into the very same compartment. She sees his knees. She sees his briefcase. She sees his jacket. She sees that he is reading but cannot see what. The train thrusts into motion, and everything is black mirrors, ghost faces, time machine flash. Everything is underworld and some dark boat ferrying her toward torture or death or rebirth. *Mabillon. Sèvres — Babylone. Vaneau.* It is a blessing, as more bodies pile off, to be as short as she is; to be on the plainer side of attractive; to be ten years older than the girl he once proposed to. Just before Avenue Émile Zola, Jean-Claude lowers his reading, and she sees it is only a newspaper. He picks up his briefcase. She turns her face; stares with interest at an ad for baby formula. Not until the train has come to an absolute halt and he has absolutely stepped off does she move toward the door and onto the platform.

He is so close.

He has put on his jacket and is walking upstairs with long, lazy strides. An Arab man with clouded eyes stands at the Métro's mouth, shaking a can of coins and rasping. She vows to give him some change, when she is not so busy stalking. Jean-Claude's jacket, his long limbs, making a turn further up the block. No traffic. Plane trees swish in the breeze, casting watery shadows. Apartment windows are beautiful prisons, glowing amber with ornate grilles, trite geraniums in planters. They pass a gated garden. He stops to light a cigarette, and, though her heart flares up in panic, her body stays in the shadows until he has disappeared with a curl of smoke around the next corner.

Her mouth waters.

He is walking with echoing insistence down the winding, narrow street; the kind of street only a local would ever have cause to walk down. They are alone. In a city of millions, they are alone, and this improbable intimacy terrifies her. She could run to him. She could call his name. She is radically free, and her freedom could express itself in any number of ways.

She clings to obscurity, watches as he finishes his cigarette outside an apartment building and flicks it away.

And then he is doing something with keys, dragging open the wrought-iron door with a sound like the implements of her own torture being laid out. And then he is footsteps, and then there is nothing but the street and herself; the weight of herself, too much to bear.

The girls' faces are shiny from drinking, their glasses empty, by the time Evelyn returns to the bistro. Her own glass is still full, her meal and dessert waiting cold and uneaten. Evelyn raises her eyebrows apologetically but doesn't apologize as she spreads her napkin over her lap. She takes a sip of wine, eats a few bites of duck *confit*, a few bites of *tarte Tatin*. She sips again and pushes her dessert toward Terra: 'Have some.' Though their instinct is to refuse, it is a sin to waste food when there are starving children in the world. Terra takes a forkful, passes the plate on to Frida, who nibbles dutifully and returns it to Evelyn. The girls look at each other with round eyes, then at Evelyn, swirling her wine and eyeing her food with detachment.

'*That dude ...*' Terra leans forward, shaking her hair off her face. '*Was he ... an agent?*'

Evelyn raises her brows again, twists her lips in a way that could mean yes or could mean nothing. She drinks. Then, opportunistically, concedes: 'It's too early to tell.'

'*He looks like the type,*' Frida hisses, eyes sparking. '*Exactly the type.*'

3.

'I trust whatever you decide,' she speaks softly into the receiver. 'But, given the circumstances, a change in plan seems prudent.'

'Oh, Christ Almighty ...' He repeats the sentence as a mournful wheeze, 'Oh-h, Christ Al-migh-ty ...' She waits patiently. 'You say Terra and Frida can be trusted to travel alone?'

'They're just girls,' Evelyn says. 'But they understand the importance of this mission. And they're eager to impress.'

'They've been spending too much time together. They may already be forming an alliance.'

'Their allegiance is to you. Believe me, they never miss an opportunity to remind me of how well they've served their Father.' Evelyn lets the words linger, caress. 'If it were more than a day, I'd share your concern. But Mona will be meeting them across the border, after all.'

Mona d'Angelo: a beautiful manic-depressive from New Jersey whose 'depressive' Jim cured back in '72 and whose 'manic' he has put to good use. Jim softens. 'You'll brief them tonight?'

'I'll brief them just as soon as you've reminded them both of their personal relationship with the Cause.'

'I'm so tired of these bitches needing to be reminded.' Jim sighs. 'When I'm loyal, I'm loyal for *life*. Don't matter how much it takes out of me; that's who I am.' There is nothing accusatory about his reference to loyalty. There is nothing disloyal about what she is doing. 'Do what you gotta do to intercept this spook, honey. Find where he's stayin', get access to his files, I don't care how. Use your body, if you have to. Course, it's sooner than I'd like, but I know you're strong, and you're looking good. Better'n ever.'

Evelyn is quite certain this is untrue. But even his lies have the ring of greater truth; in this case, that her body has more importance as an instrument of the Cause than of comfort.

'I doubt it'll come to that,' she assures him softly. 'Do you want Frida or Terra first?'

'Frida,' he says, with a wistfulness she doesn't like but doesn't question. She is about to put the phone down when he speaks up: 'Happy birthday, Little Mother.'

Evelyn looks at the bathroom door. 'I'll get Frida.'

They're kneeling barefoot on the tiles, quiet under the roar of the bathroom fan, counting their assets one Tampax box at a time. Evelyn looks at the old slash marks on Frida's arms as she waits for her to finish her current roll, lock it back inside the tampon applicator, return the applicator to the box. 'I'll take over, Frida. Father wants you.'

Frida's eyes flicker with pride, satisfaction, something. She stands and pulls her sleeves over her scars. 'Twenty-four,' she tells Evelyn. She isn't talking about her age, but she could be.

Evelyn closes the door behind Frida, observes Terra's spaniel-gold head, then crouches to assist. Ten hundred-dollar bills per tampon applicator. Thirty-six tampons per box. Three boxes apiece. Perhaps ten minutes later, Frida takes Terra's place, face bashful and eyes bright. They are counting their 'bodily assets' when Terra returns, tear-stained but triumphant, bearing her blue velvet jacket and her sewing kit. She sits on the lid of the toilet and starts unpicking the lining of her jacket. Evelyn stacks her last ten thousand dollars on the counter.

'The shoulders and the pockets,' she tells Terra, with a nod at the jacket and the cash on the counter. Then she steps out.

The room seems luxuriously large compared with the cramped bathroom. She looks to the window and, despite the drawn curtains, feels watched. She sits on the striped bed. She picks up the phone where Jim's voice was just minutes ago; checks again for wiretapping. She checks the time: eleven-thirty. She checks the bible-thick book borrowed from reception and finds the name. The name is not common. The name might've been hers, in another life.

'*Allô?*' the man growls after five *dring-drings*. '*Allô?*' She listens as he exhales with a hiss, scuffles with the receiver, mutters impatiently, and hangs up.

She lies back on the bed, heart beating. Smiles to herself, just for a moment.

4.

On the striped couch, she sleeps four hours, at most. Curled on her left side, the position she's come to favor. One of the girls is snoring. Evelyn traverses the darkness and uses the bathroom quietly as she can: toilet, bidet, toothbrush. She sheds her nightgown, which fits like a sack but is well-made, with convenient buttons. Cocoa Butter for the pale, lightning-like marks on her breasts and stomach. Earth-toned underwear, blouse, and midi skirt. Hair, thinner than it once was, scraped off her face. Behind her ears and at her wrists, a dab of Guerlain.

She wakes the girls as she used to wake her sisters for school, years ago. Gets them organized in much the same way.

'Beware of friendly strangers. Flirt with officials, if necessary, but if anyone else approaches you, remember: you're married women.' They glance at their rings. 'You'll be using your aliases at the new lodgings. Scarlett, Natasha.'

'Yes, Isabelle,' the girls chorus obediently.

She leaves them waiting for a cab outside the hotel: Terra wearing her blue velvet jacket and clutching her suitcase; Frida with a piece of luggage in each hand. Takes the Métro west once more. On Avenue Émile Zola, she finds a *tabac* and purchases a newspaper and a pack of Gauloises. Stations herself on a bench around the corner from his apartment and watches the sky lighten, the little dogs take their morning shits.

Sometime after eight, he appears, dressed in blue plaid, smoking, completely self-absorbed. By the light of day, she can see that he has grown a moustache. She wishes it didn't suit him; that the morning light didn't flatter him; that she could end it here.

She folds up her newspaper and follows him underground.

*

She follows him east, as far as Grenelle. Changes to a northbound train when he does. They cross the Seine together, get off together at Madeleine Station. The streets seem wider, more sterile than those they came from. She follows him up Rue Tronchet, away from the Napoleonic temple. Past storefronts, hotels, cafés. He ducks inside one, and, though she would like a coffee herself, she remains across the street, smoking. Later, he stalks out, blazer flying up around his midsection, which isn't as trim as when she knew him, but it's too late to care. Further up the street, he pushes through the green door of an entirely unremarkable building.

The thrill of pursuit over, Evelyn stares into the abyss of that bright Paris morning.

She crosses the road. Examines the placard on the green door: *DCP Audit et Conseil.* She feels the burn of contempt for him: his unexciting profession; the small, capitalistic life that would've been hers if she'd tied herself to him for eternity. Yet her desire isn't dulled by this contempt; if anything, it's like a picked scab, prickling with new blood.

She allows, at last, a thought she's been blocking since last night to slip through. *Married? Of course, he must be. Children, too.*

At his café, she orders coffee, a pastry. Takes out her little black book and examines his phone number, like it's a code she might crack. After breakfast, she finds a telephone booth. Calls the number. A woman answers.

She wants to hang up, violently. Instead: '*Pourrais-je parler à Madame Chaudouet?*'

'*C'est moi,*' the woman answers, affably bored. '*Marie Chaudouet.*'

Evelyn gives her the French version of a spiel she's often used to screen members prior to healing services in San Francisco: telephone survey, pharmaceuticals company, five minutes for the chance to win a year's worth of products.

Within five minutes, Evelyn has learned that there are three individuals within the Chaudouet household. Madame, who favors Embryolisse moisturizer. Monsieur, who treats his hayfever with Lomusol. Their little boy, who prefers the cough syrup that tastes of oranges. She doesn't know what to do with this information, except run her mind over it like a blunt knife.

She asks about contraception.

'*Non, nous ne l'utilisons pas*,' the woman responds calmly. '*Nous voulons un deuxième*.'

After hanging up, Evelyn buys a ticket for the next morning's train to Zurich. Buys another newspaper. Takes it to a bench in the Tuileries but cannot read; just keeps sharpening the hurt. *He is married to a woman called Marie. They have one child. They are trying for a second …*

By midday, she is waiting for him to leave his building again.

A bustling café. He sits at an outside table, with an omelet and a glass of something clear and fizzy. He never ordered fizzy water back when they were students, but Evelyn supposes many things have changed. She opts for wine at the cramped bar. In the mirror above the bar, she tries to make sense of the reflected confusion: rattan chairs, umbrellas, suit jackets. Blue plaid like a piece of sky glimpsed from a dungeon.

Her mind has a tipsy film to it, when he comes through the door with a sound like a cat's bell. He waves his wallet at the waiter. '*Dépêchez-vous, j'ai un rendez-vous!*'

Entitled, but good-natured about it. He was always like that with waitstaff.

She arches her back, plays her fingers over the stem of her wineglass. His fingers drum the countertop in time with her blood's beat. *But I know you? Is that really you? Ève—?*

Without a glance in her direction, he pockets his wallet. The bell rings again.

'*Madame?*' the waiter says, looking at her with concern.

5.

In the four-star hotel, Evelyn lies atop the silk brocade covers. Stiff pillows piled around her head. Ceilings high enough to give her vertigo. One hand on her stomach, confirming its renewed flatness through the fabric of her blouse. Brain like a rat in a maze.

The lives she could've lived are amputated limbs, abortions: *Evie, Evelyn Chaudouet, Ève.*

She lies her cheek on the sun-striped pillow and surveys the phone on the nightstand. It is five a.m. in California: too late to call Jim at his apartment above the Temple on Geary Boulevard; too early to call her parents at the Craftsman-style house across the bay in Berkeley. This calms her, for she doesn't truly wish to speak with any of them. She looks from the phone to her tote, then her sandals, waiting at the foot of the bed like faithful dogs.

She has traveled light.

Sinking her feet into the plush carpet, Evelyn thinks of the girls, crossing the border to Switzerland. Of Jim's love for them, no more important to her than a ripple on the surface of an alpine lake. The bathroom, when she slips inside, is cool and smooth as a mausoleum, scented with white flowers. Around the sink, like votive offerings, tissue-wrapped soaps and dainty creams in bottles. Evelyn runs the bright gold taps and chooses a cream that smells of gardenias, washes her hands and dries them off with a soft white towel. She looks at herself, her skin and eyes made radiant by the expensive lighting. She tells herself, *Ève.*

In the boutique on Rue Saint-Honoré, Evelyn lets herself be stripped by an obnoxiously young assistant with over-plucked eyebrows. At their feet, like dead butterflies, a half-dozen dresses. '*Mais le robe rouge!*' the assistant insists, waving a red dress like a matador's

234

flag. Evelyn is close to tears. Her face is burning. Clothes have never fitted so poorly. Yet submitting, with a humiliation so deep it thrills her, to the rough hands on her body, the red straps binding her neck. As though fixing a crooked picture frame, the assistant sticks a lacquered talon between her breasts, centers the plunging neckline. '*Et voilà.*'

A black curtain opens.

Evelyn steps out. She looks and looks. She doesn't look like herself, but who is she, really? The assistant stands behind her, holds her waist like a lover, murmurs things; *silk georgette, very nice, you're a woman, you have a woman's breasts, better to show it.* Evelyn looks from her décolletage to her face, and the two don't seem to match, let alone to express anything of her mind.

'*Je voudrais acheter cette robe,*' Evelyn says quietly. She turns to view her back, notes the price tag; they have fed whole communes for a week on less. '*Je voudrais la porter tout de suite.*'

In answer, the assistant jerks a brow, pulls out a pair of scissors, snips the tag.

Evelyn will wear the dress immediately.

It is late afternoon when Evelyn steps out of the hair salon and onto the street: fresh blow-waves catching the light, windows catching her reflection. She feels her reflection walking alongside her like an emissary from a more beautiful world, drawing stares from men, turning their heads. Entering the café of that morning, she heads straight for the bathroom. Returns to the bar several long minutes later, feeling so unbearably stoppered-up, tense, she can't decide whether to sit or stand.

She lights a cigarette. Orders a cocktail, heavy on the anise. It helps.

The evening sky is a romantic sepia, the air heady and floral. Evelyn strolls in the direction of his office, chest warm with alcohol, mouth spicy. Passing a table of men, she hears a jeering *miaow*. She is conscious of the little rubber dome fitted against her cervix, a need to urinate again, yet also an obscure pride, to be attractive in spite of these discomforts.

A collection of parts is simpler than a whole. At the stationery shop window, a few doors down from his work, Evelyn concentrates on the parts that compose her: *hair, dress, legs.* Simple; it should be simple.

He comes from the building with the green door. Dressed in his blue plaid, tallest man on the block. A sense of wholeness swallows her parts, and just as quickly, a void. Twenty again. Alone in the apartment in Bordeaux, smiling down at her engagement ring, at her own bright emptiness. She hasn't changed. It was stupid to think she could; stupid, stupid.

'*Excusez-moi, Monsieur,*' she murmurs, scuttling past him before he can see her clearly.

If Jean-Claude says anything, she doesn't hear it. If he looks at her, she doesn't look back. *Say something. Look. Something, anything.* She doesn't look anywhere, in fact, until she's turned the corner and is drawing the Gauloises from her purse, chafing her thumb. The lighter won't work. A flame appears from another source.

'*Vous êtes perdu?*' the stranger asks.

'*Oui,*' Evelyn concedes, accepting the light. '*Je suis perdu.*' Yes, I am lost.

She sips in smoke, feels it furring her front teeth, vows to brush well that night. The hotel bathroom with its altar of flowers, tiny bottles. She doesn't look at the stranger until she has uttered the next part, in the same tone of resignation:

'*Ramenez-moi à mon hôtel, s'il vous plaît.*'

He isn't tall or handsome. He blinks quickly, as though he might've misheard her. Falters to accept, then blushes to the roots of his receding hairline. Balding yet boyish. Bright blue eyes that make him seem more American than French, and that make her oddly nostalgic. She doesn't know him, though. He doesn't know her. This is better. Better not to be known, not to be named, not to be remembered.

This is the man who takes her back to her hotel.

He spends a long time on her neck, her breasts. The inevitable happens; her milk lets down. An unambiguous jet that makes him look up in horrified fascination, before renewing his efforts.

He calls her *maman*, mommy.

Afterward, when he asks her to dinner, she declines, lets him show himself out. She showers, remakes the bed. Sits in her hotel-issue robe and checks the phone for wiretapping.

She calls room service, then her mother. She asks, 'How is Solomon Tom?'

6.

The meetings with the Swiss banks are over within the next forty-five hours. Hundreds of thousands of Temple dollars counted out, deposited into high-interest and tax-free accounts, the paperwork signed at shining mahogany tables. No questions asked by the neutral gentlemen in their gold-rimmed spectacles and Italian wool suits.

Mona d'Angelo boards the next afternoon train to Milan. She has a different cover story to the rest of them: family in Verona; returning to the US via Rome. Meanwhile, they change out of their businesswear in the station bathroom and purchase tickets back to Paris; buy magazines and Swiss chocolate; pass the hours before their train, weary of each other's company.

In Paris, they do not linger. They purchase separate flights on separate airlines to separate Canadian cities; wait in separate lounges for stretches of time like mundane crucifixions.

It's not until the earliest, darkest hours of Monday that Evelyn pulls up in a cab outside her parents' house in Berkeley. She thanks the driver. She needs no help with her luggage. She has her own keys, slots them quietly. In the hallway, she switches on the lamp just long enough to slip off her shoes and navigate to the back room.

Solomon Tom, to her surprise, is wide awake in his crib. Silently staring as though he's been expecting her.

'*Soul*,' Evelyn coos, scooping him up.

Evelyn loves her baby. A love as unremarkable as her need to breathe, perhaps, and yet a miracle to her, a startling thing. Of course, she and Jim hadn't planned him. Of course, her first impulse had been to book an appointment to get rid of him, as she would a troublesome tooth. Now, her body shifts to accommodate his weight; her nose hunts for that sweet, rosy smell at the crown of his head. *Soul. Her Soul. Soul-baby.*

'Sleepy baby,' Evelyn whispers teasingly, though she can already tell he isn't, really.

Watchful as a painting, Evelyn's baby follows her with his eyes as she opens her suitcase and puts her soiled clothes in the hamper, finds herself a fresh nightgown. Though she slept little during her flight, during the layover, during the journeys that preceded it, she isn't tired; anyhow, doesn't feel like sleeping; her exhaustion so deep as to seem existential. 'Not sleepy, baby?' She smiles over her shoulder, and Solomon Tom smiles back; he's old enough to do that now. Five months old and his development perfectly in line with the books she's read; she records it in a soft-bound pastel-blue diary.

'Not sleepy, huh,' Evelyn repeats. She notices a dusting of dog hair on the comforter and, annoyed, cracks a window. Checks the clock, then the ceiling.

She puts on a Donovan record, from the pile Sally-Ann left behind when she joined the Temple, moved out of home and into one of the Temple's student communes.

Solomon Tom likes Donovan.

Evelyn curls up on the bed with her baby in her arms, beneath the wall-sized peace mandala painted by Sally-Ann. With insomniac eyes, she gazes at the silky brown hairs on his head, the barely-there brows, the tiny pug nose. He gazes back, his own eyes inky-blue, bottomless. When, after a century of gazing, he lets out a mewl, paws the front of Evelyn's nightgown, she acquiesces gently; tugs the gypsy-like ruffle from her shoulder. He latches on. The feeling is strange, borderline shameful, borderline painful, until he finds his rhythm and that tingling sense of familiarity takes over.

It occurs to Evelyn, even as her mind numbs, her body relaxes, that she would like to put an end to this nursing business as soon as possible.

Once Solomon Tom has had his fill, his inky eyes begin to flutter shut. She tickles him with her fingertips, prods him as she would a warm loaf of bread. She murmurs things, brainless and sing-song. He slides into unconsciousness, just the same; grows heavier in her arms, and her eyelids heavier with him. There are some files in the closet, reports to be read on the Temple's Agricultural Project in South

America, better known as 'the Promised Land'. She feels a grip of hopelessness, commingled with satisfaction, at her inability to move. She closes her eyes. Fragments of song crawl into her mind.

Diamonds in the sea …
I dug you diggin' me in Mexico …

Perhaps it is Mexico she dreams of. Sun-baked stretches of coast. Strange granite outcrops in the ocean. Bright flowers that morph into Sally-Ann's graphic floral comforter. She hears, faraway and cheery, her mother declare, 'Little Mother is hibernating!' Her sleep-fogged brain trips over the comment: *But I can't be a mother yet! I've only just returned from my honeymoon.* Then she notices her breast, milk-large, whiter than milk, hanging loose as in some Renaissance painting. Then, like a rib stolen in the night, her baby's absence. She fixes her nightgown, wipes the sleep from her eyes. From the depths of the house, Picnic barks and Jim's voice resounds, rustic and insistent; his high-pitched laugh.

Her parents dislike Jim. Somehow, the sound of his laugh reminds her of this.

Evelyn is still drowsy, cheeks flushed, when Jim tiptoes into the room. He has Solomon Tom bundled in his arms. He is wearing a maize-yellow guayabera. He has his sunglasses on. He looks, to her temporarily objective eyes, quite fat and a little ridiculous. Within a split-second, however, she has glossed over his imperfections; the chin doubled with his grin, the cosmetically-enhanced sideburns. She sees his pug nose, a grownup version of Solomon Tom's. She feels an overwhelming gratitude.

'Little Mother ain't sleepin',' he tells Solomon Tom, with an indulgent smile at Evelyn. 'See? We knew, didn't we, Soul? Little Mother done slept enough.'

'Too much,' Evelyn agrees, flattening the sheets with her palms.

Jim's weight dents the narrow bed. He places Solomon Tom between them. A fresh scent of baby powder rises up, making Evelyn aware of her own less-than-fresh smell.

'I need a shower.' She shifts aside. 'You shouldn't sit so close. I stink.'

This only provokes Jim to slide closer, nestle his face in her armpit.

'Mmm, you *do*.' He sniffs at her crotch like a dog. 'Little Mother's got her period.'

Evelyn scowls, crosses her legs. She does need to shower, and to pee, desperately. Yet she remains where she is, because of the way Jim is looking at her, mostly; his gaze through those sunglasses as humble and loving as ever, seeming to see everything, and forgive it. He reaches to stroke the fine, glossy hairs at her temple. She waits for him to mention Paris.

'You finished next quarter's budget for the Promised Land yet?' he asks instead.

'I'm still working on it.'

Jim inclines his head at the baby. 'I can get Frida and Terra on it, if your hands are full.'

'*No*,' she says, too quickly. Jim looks smug. She continues, poker-faced, 'If you'd like their input, of course, that's your decision. I do think we should factor in the latest profits forecast though. This isn't a time for cutting corners.'

'Terra did a damn fine job on last quarter's commune budgets.'

'I agree … and her expertise will be invaluable as we move toward complete communalization of our meals service. But there are more complex factors at play, and it'll take time to teach her the sort of long-range planning we need—'

Before she can finish, Solomon Tom gurgles peevishly, smacks his lips. Then he wails and stretches his clumsy half-fists toward Evelyn. Jim catches her eye with a smirk.

'G'on, honey,' he purrs. 'My son's thirsty.'

Evelyn takes up their baby obediently, hushes him. Her fingers fumble to clasp the fragile back of his head, the folds of his neck, and she feels a shiver, just a shiver, of revulsion. She gives Solomon Tom her pinky finger to suck and it quiets him. She looks cagily at Jim.

'I'll get Mom to give him some formula.' Wiggling her finger inside Solomon Tom's mouth, she lets herself feel an appropriate measure of guilt. 'I think it's time to start weaning. He may begin teething any day now. After all, he's very advanced.'

Though Jim shows no sign of disapproval, only that curious tilt of the head, that animal benevolence, she feels compelled to explain further:

'I want to move out of home — Well, not *home*.' She smiles

sardonically. 'This house isn't home, nor is America. What I mean is, I want Soul to know his true home, the Temple.'

There are unspoken things between her and Jim. She feels them, rippling and lurid as sea corals, as the innermost parts of her body: the walls of her uterus, the folds of her intestines, the valves of her heart, the glands of her brain.

'Alright,' he says, with an air of almost-formality. And yet, more inconspicuous still, a note of pride. 'Alright, Evelyn.'

Of course, the moment cannot last. Solomon Tom rejects her pinky, shrieks anew, and she is quick to spirit him away from Jim, so sensitive to noise, bright light. Telling Jim to rest. Telling him: a pill, if he needs it, in the purple ceramic turtle on the nightstand. Her voice calm, though Solomon Tom is attempting to drag her nightgown down her shoulders. She twists her way into her robe, and is immediately glad of the cover, for already upon entering the hall she hears the blare of the TV in the den, the broken voices of Jim's teen sons. Always, on his visits from across the bay, Jim brings a couple of them along for security: puberty has made them tall and strong, and his need for trusted guards has become more urgent since Wayne Bud and all those other young people defected. In the cozy oak kitchen, Evelyn finds her mother cleaning up after the boys' latest fridge-raid, and a look passes between them that encompasses this, and other things. Jim beached on the bed in his sunglasses and guayabera. Solomon Tom's squalling hunger. Evelyn's desperation to shower and relieve her bladder. The certainty that this arrangement cannot go on forever.

'Here, come to Grandma,' Margaret coos, unburdening her of Solomon Tom.

Under the scalding rain of the showerhead, Evelyn's scalp tingles; her skin flushes. She imagines her milk drying in the heat, her breasts shrinking to their former, merely ornamental state. Her mind reels forward to a time, soon, when she will return to the Temple with Jim's baby in one arm, a clipboard in the other. And if the people whisper, it will only be of the tales he has told them. A perilous mission for the Cause. Mexico. Prison. Her body brutalized by enemy guards, impregnated against her will. Her baby born out of wedlock, yet into the holy light of revolution — and what a beautiful baby, beloved by Father, this baby called 'Soul'.

Urban Jungle

1.

There is a night in the February of '77, damp, smudged with moonlight, when railroad officer Eugene Luce, shining his flashlight into an idle box car, sees a man having sex with another man. Almost dropping his light at the shock of it, two pairs of blue jeans rumpled around two pairs of hairy ankles, two pairs of heaving buttocks. Two blue hard hats.

'Railroad police! Stop what you're doing!'

The men cuss. Pull up their pants. Grab for their hats.

'We're mechanics,' one of them says boldly. 'We're just, uh, working.'

'Doesn't look like work to me.' Luce clangs the metal siding with his nightstick. 'Get dressed and get out here.'

By the time they jump out of the box car, into the dirty moonlight, they're both zipped up, tucked in, sheepish. A light-skinned black man and a suntanned white man, both in their late twenties, muscle-bound, stubble-cheeked. The white man does the talking.

'Look, I don't know what you think you saw …' As a wheeze of laughter escapes his buddy, the white man changes tack. '… We had some drinks after work and got carried away. Forgive us, officer?'

'Trespassing on railroad property is a felony.'

'We work here,' the white guy repeats. 'And I *know* this car isn't going anywhere.' He exchanges a glance with the black guy. 'If you wanted to join us, officer …'

Luce can smell their sweat, the alcohol on their breath; can hear the racket of car changes in another part of the yard. Things that *should* put him off. He grips his nightstick, kicks at the gravel so dust flies up in their faces. 'Move it, or I'll lock you up!'

'*Pfft*,' the white guy spits up dust, raises his palms in surrender. 'Alright, take it easy.' The black guy echoes, '*Easy*,' backing away. Then they break into a jog, hard hats slamming against their thighs, giggles ricocheting through the yard. Fading into the fog, so all Luce is left with is the unbearable boil of his blood.

2.

'... Dot Luce, you say you're sorry, but that doesn't change the fact that you've endangered us all with your carelessness. How're we supposed to trust you if you can't even—'

'Not just careless, *arrogant*,' Luce's ex-wife Joya, now 'Joya Mendelssohn', cuts Terra short. 'Plain arrogance, to assume she had the right, without even bringing it to the committee! Where'd you get such a high opinion of yourself, Missy? I sure didn't raise you that way!'

'*We* didn't,' corrects Molly Hurmerinta, with a tug of her chevron cape.

'Dot, you've always struck me as a young woman who puts care into everything you do.' Meyer Mendelssohn, Luce's younger and more with-it successor, sadly shakes his balding, long-haired head. 'I would've thought you'd consider the consequences of your actions.'

Luce has to rack his brain to remember his daughter's offense — showing old snapshots of the Promised Land to some non-Temple friends at her college — but he's not going to let himself be outdone by Meyer, no way. 'Makes me *sick*,' he spits. 'No better than your traitor-bitch sister!'

Risky, even three years after the fact, to mention the traitors. But sure to get a reaction. Dot's tear-stained face turns a deeper shade of crimson, quivers like a foal's legs.

'Now, now, no need for that.' Jim sits up on his sofa, positively glowing. 'Dot, you're gonna have to work to earn back our trust, but I know you ain't no traitor-bitch, honey.'

A caressing quality to Jim's voice that turns Luce's white knuckles whiter. Dot lowers her eyes. 'Thank you, Father.'

'Course, you *shoulda* known better.' Jim's mood switches. 'Dumb white bitch, what were you thinking? Showing pictures around like that?'

'I thought … they're nice pictures. I didn't think anyone would m—'

'*You* thought,' Joya sneers. 'Well, I guess you must be the best mind of your generation or something!'

'*Nice pictures*,' mutters Joseph Garden, their Agricultural Planner. Used to be with the Nation of Islam and has a militant arrogance that Luce associates with those men parading around the local mosque in robes and skullcaps. But Joe is clean-shaven, his muscular forearms shown to full advantage. 'Our work in the Promised Land is better than your blurry-ass holiday snapshots.'

'You should be showing them Phil Sorensen's photography,' coos Lenny Lynden's mother, Liesl, a fine-boned lady about Luce's age, who somehow manages to wear her drab Mao suit like it's made of silk. Like Lenny, she's got the brown hair, but curlier; a staccato European accent — not German, but something like that. Austrian? Austrian-Jew, that's it. Old money, who lost it all in the war but married rich. If it wasn't for the good of the Cause, Luce would feel sorry for the ex-husband she bled dry when she joined the Temple. 'Phil is an *artist*.'

Phil Sorensen, he's something, it's true. Army-brat-turned-Vietnam-photojournalist-turned-official-Temple-photographer-filmmaker. 'I've got some righteous shots from the December expedition.' He accepts Liesl's praise with a square-jawed smile. 'How about I bring the projector to the campus sometime? We could even do a screening of the new film—'

'The film is for members only!' Jim bellows. 'You bring that film on campus, how we know they ain't gonna be making copies? Distorting our glorious footage and selling it to those right-wing media assholes? Vulture bastards, don't give a goddamn what's true and beautiful …'

As Jim launches into one of his tirades, and Phil respectfully bows his head, Luce concentrates on keeping his eyes open. Casting them up to the empty balconies, the pale soar of the ceiling. On the second floor, he glimpses movement: a doll-sized woman in trousers, circling toward the staircase like a figure in a Swiss clock. Descending to the stage and going straight to Jim.

Evelyn Lynden whispers in Jim's ear. Placating him, you'd maybe think, but he keeps ranting and she keeps that same blank expression, stepping back when he waves his hand like he's shooing a fly. Then she walks over to Frida Sorensen, Phil's stuck-up skin-and-bones sister, and taps her on the shoulder, then Terra, who widens her eyes, shakes her head quickly. Evelyn slits her gaze, says something low and fast. Meekly, Terra dips her head and follows.

They go upstairs, pants swishing so urgently you'd think they were about to soil them.

'… We have to keep our babies safe,' Jim concludes, face sluggish. He glances around, flinching at the sight of Dot, still standing there in her pin-tuck blouse and ditsy-print skirt. 'What you doin', Sister? What you people doin', letting her stand alone? Where's your spirit of forgiveness?' He waves his hand again. 'Show her some love, goddamnit.'

Dot's slim legs buckle in relief as they catch her in a loving flop of hugs, arm squeezes. 'That's right. Hug her good. We know how to resolve our conflicts lovingly, hm?' Jim yawns. 'Makes you tired, don't it? Makes *me* tired. Almost, makes me wanna sleep forever.'

Jim lies back, drooping his head in a pantomime of narcolepsy or death. Luce laughs edgily along with the others, for Jim's shirt has crawled up to reveal a strip of abdominal pudge. Jim sits back up, tugs it down. 'No, not time for sleep. We got too much to do, don't we. But a little rest, darlings …' He nods sleekly. 'I know how hard you work. Time you all got to enjoy a token of my appreciation.'

Just in time, the women reappear on the stairs with trays of paper cups. 'Sweet valley wine!' Terra beams, high-pitched like she's talking to a bunch of preschoolers.

'Are we Catholics now, Father?' jokes Sally-Ann Burne. From her snub-pretty face, easy goofball grin, you'd never guess she's Evelyn's sister. But maybe it's always like that — a sweetheart for every bitch.

'Gotta be over twenty-one!' Joya affectionately ruffles Dot's pageboy cut. Of course Dot was always *their* sweetheart, Joya's favorite. 'We aren't *all* over twenty-one here.'

'I'm only twenty, Father,' pretty Polly Hurmerinta raises a hand.

'Oh, you're old enough,' Jim chuckles, and there's a hint of that caressing tone again. 'And you're a good socialist. We're all good socialists here. We *all* drink.'

Evelyn, Frida, and Terra busy themselves passing out cups. As Evelyn bends to Luce, her collarbones gape, and he remembers she has a baby now, wonders where the weight went. As if sensing his scrutiny, she frowns into her blouse, pulls away to serve Phyllis.

'Our vineyards have been blessed with a wonderful harvest,' Jim explains, once all thirty-some of them have cups. 'Dot, honey? Tell me that don't taste like manna from heaven.'

Eyes still tear-bright from the confrontation, Dot sips daintily, sputters. Not the reaction Jim was hoping for.

'It ain't poison, Dot!' Luce swoops in. Jim cackles, and it feels good, that he can still make Jim laugh after over twenty years. Luce drains his cup, grins through the bitterness. 'Tastes like manna from heaven, it does!'

'You heard Gene,' Jim booms. 'Drink your wine, drink it up, drink, drink. When I tell you to drink, I mean it.'

All around Luce, cups tilt up, crumple in fists. Evelyn, by the red stage curtains, looks at Jim steadily and drinks. 'You all done yet? Show me. *Alright.*' Jim knocks his own wine back, wipes his mouth, holds his empty cup aloft.

Frida magics a garbage bag out of thin air, starts making the rounds with Terra.

'I'm out of practice.' Phyllis leans close to Luce, flashing her wine-stained teeth. 'Either there's two of you or I'm seeing double?'

'Just me and me twin brother … Steve,' Luce offers lamely.

Phyllis throws back her head to laugh, and so does Luce's ex-wife, face tomato-red against her cropped gray-blond hair.

'Hiya, Steve! Didn't see you there!'

Drunker than a skunk. She'd have to be, to laugh at his jokes these days.

'Now that you've all had a chance to enjoy yourselves, I have an announcement,' Jim speaks up from the front of the room. 'Funny what Gene said. *Ain't poison.*' He chuckles softly. 'Fact is, the wine you've just consumed contains a slow-acting lethal toxin. Within forty-five minutes, you'll all be dead.' He smiles. 'I have drunk the same wine and will die with you. We will die together.'

*

We will die together.

There'd been a Planning Committee meeting, not long after Luce's traitor-bitch daughter ran off with those Children of the Revolution, when Jim asked if he'd be willing to die for her betrayal. Joya, too, and all the other folks with treacherous blood. All of them, called to the floor, and Luce had been the first to say yes: gripping the .45 on his belt and vowing he'd kill himself, but first he'd kill *her*. Luce isn't afraid of death. Luce is ready for death!

Luce looks sidelong at Phyllis. She doesn't look ready: fingers stuffed in her mouth like cold cuts, muttering under her breath. *Praying.* Embarrassed, Luce glances away. Then his gag reflex kicks in.

Smells like … piss?

Somebody pissed themselves?

Bob Harris has pissed his pants. Bob, who's good with engines and dogs, and whose caramel-colored mutt Luce helped bury after it was found dead (shot by neo-Nazis, apparently). Luce is disappointed in Bob, disgusted … and dreading the moment Jim makes an example of the poor candy-ass.

'Oh God … Oh God … I don't wanna die …'

Distracted by Bob's pissed pants, Luce hadn't noticed Phyllis's rising desperation. Now folks are turning to look at her.

'What're you saying, sister?' Jim asks, in a tone Luce knows isn't as affable as it sounds. Surely Phyllis knows, too. That doesn't stop her repeating herself.

'Oh please God … Help … I don't wanna *die!*'

'Phyllis says she doesn't want to die,' Joya reports, with a sweet, condescending, utterly Midwestern cluck of the tongue.

'You don't want to die, sister?' Jim puffs himself up. 'You don't want to leave this life of misery and injustice? Sister, to leave this life behind is a protest. To lay our lives down, that's the most revolutionary act in this inhumane world. Our deaths won't go unnoticed.' He moistens his lips. 'As your leader, I'm glad to die tonight. My individual life ain't nothing. You think your life has meaning? You think some sky-god's gonna swoop down and save your ass?'

But Phyllis isn't listening. Breathing too fast, in-out, in-out, her face like a sheet in the wind. Could that poison be working already? Luce doesn't feel it. Maybe it works on women quicker? As he wonders, Phyllis shoots to her feet.

'P-lease!' she bleats. 'I have to get to a doctor!'

Maybe Jim nods at Luce. Maybe he doesn't need to. Mongoose-quick, Luce springs up and blocks Phyllis's path, grabs ahold of her fleshy wrist. Phyllis lets out a tiny, '*Oh!*' Then, just like Luce feared, her eyes flutter white; her body falls against his like a tipped cow.

'Looks like she's fainted, I guess?' Luce says awkwardly, doing his best to hold her up like she's a Hollywood damsel in distress.

'Get her out of here.' Jim gestures dismissively. 'We don't want no traitors here.'

'I never trusted that bitch!' Terra bursts out, shaking her hair like an actress. A few folks stare at her and she pinkens, swallows her words.

It's Meyer who helps Luce move Phyllis. Luce would've preferred someone with muscles: Joseph, Phil, even Ralph or Tobias, those fit young queers who're always palling around with Liesl Lynden. They push backstage, where a couple of young guards are slouching around by the musical equipment, Dot's on-off sweetheart, Paolo Jones, among them.

'Jesus!' Paolo, irreverent as his dad, slaps burly Quincy Watson on the shoulder and the two take over, lie Phyllis flat on her back like the world's most well-fed mummy. Meyer finds a sheet to cover her with, then stands by the guitars, pinching his nose-bridge. Paolo flashes Luce a cocksure smile. 'We got this.'

Joya always hoped to see Dot and Paolo married, to be co-in-laws with Jim and Rosaline. Luce guesses that won't happen now.

'Alright, Gene?' Jim asks as Luce wanders back in. Luce nods, 'Alright.' Then, as if in proof that all *is* right, Lenny Lynden lies back, hands behind his head like he's cloud-watching.

'What're you doing, Lenny?' Jim crows. 'That poison can't be working already!'

'Not yet,' Lenny says. 'I'm just making myself comfortable for the next life.'

'How d'you feel about dying, Brother Lenny?' Jim persists, amused.

'I feel glad,' Lenny says flatly. 'I'm glad to leave the pain behind forever.'

Luce looks at Lenny Lynden: over thirty by now, no longer the kid he used to drool over, brown hair already beginning to recede. But stunted-looking, young in the face, like something stopped growing in him at twenty-three. Once again, Luce feels like gagging.

'I'm glad to die too, Father. Oh, you betcha, I'm *glad*,' Joya asserts. 'Just one thing I'm wondering …What about the kids?'

Luce knows she can't be talking about their full-grown kids: Dot, right there in the meeting with them; Roger and Danny, living with their wives in the Promised Land; the traitor-bitch, living wherever traitor-bitches live. Hattie, she means, and the others she's adopted with Meyer since — Tremaine and Alisha. Luce hadn't even thought of them or of his new wife Juanita, fast asleep back at the Potrero Hill commune. He looks at his cheap wedding band and his throat slimes up with guilt.

'What about my wife?' he chokes out. Jim looks dumbfounded. Embarrassed, Luce prompts: 'Juanita and me. We got a full house in Potrero Hill.'

At that, other folks snap out of it. Jim rolls his tongue around his mouth, tilts his head away from their questioning. With a flick of her wrist, Evelyn steps forward.

'All our members will be taken care of.' That high, finicky voice that could give a snake tinnitus. 'The sleeping quarters have been fitted with diffusers containing poisonous gas. Within twenty-four hours, everyone will be dead.'

Evelyn folds her arms, steps back, stares to the side, profile razor-sharp, hair flat against that dainty skull. From Jim, such words would seem necessary; from *her*, they inspire a surge of hate. Luce reminds himself yet again that she has a baby.

Jim looks at Evelyn curiously, then nods.

'You've all been carefully chosen on the basis of things I've seen in your karmic makeup. It is very important that you die with me, so you can realize your full potential during reincarnation.' Jim inclines his head at Joseph Garden. 'Joe, your work in the Promised Land has not been in vain. The project will continue to flourish in the hands of our pioneers.'

Roger and Danny will live. Be fruitful and multiply with their pretty, colored wives. Luce guesses he should feel grateful: lines continuing, seed spreading, all that. Luce guesses he's done his job. Luce would've been fifty next month. *Old.*

'What've you got there, Mey?' Joya swivels her head as Meyer slips back in through the curtain, guitar in hand. 'Oh no, you *didn't.*'

'Thought we could have a little sing-along,' Meyer confirms with a sheepish grin.

Stupid thought, Luce thinks. But nobody's asking him, and Jim is beaming. 'That's nice. We'll leave this world singing. Ain't that nice?'

Meyer takes a place by Jim, starts strumming gently.

'Thank you, Father!' Diane Chatswood rises to testify, clutching her breast, tears in her eyes. 'Thank you for choosing us to cross over with you!'

Molly gives Bob her big chevron cape to cover up his piss-stain. Diane kisses her Temple-wife, Regina O'Neal, a busty real estate broker. Other folks give out hugs. Dot taps Luce on the shoulder and, serene as can be, says, 'See you in the next life, Dad,' wraps her arms around his neck like she's a cuddly seven-year-old again. Terra ambushes Luce with one of her full-body flowerchild hugs, whispers, 'Later, Officer,' her smile wavery. Petula Bellows, breaking away from Isaiah and their younger daughter, Alice, to choke up a verse from Revelations, '… *Neither shall there be mourning, nor crying, nor pain anymore.*' Liesl Lynden and her queers, offering their svelte bodies up to him like he's one of their own. Joseph. Phil. Then Joya, with a canny grin, a gruff little laugh, seizing him in a bear-hug. 'Looks like you're in heaven already, big guy!'

But over Joya's shoulder, Luce has noticed something fishy. Evelyn and Frida consulting, scratching notes. Terra, after finishing a round of hugs, going to them, peering at the notes. Then Terra swoops back to the floor, starts clapping and singing with exaggerated zeal. Evelyn points Frida behind the red stage curtain. Returns to Jim.

'*There grows a tree in Paradise …*' Jim halts his singing as Evelyn withdraws from his ear. 'Forty-five minutes! The forty-five minutes have elapsed, people!'

Everyone stops, unsure if they should be keeling over. Kay Harris coughs uncertainly. Joya's face sags. A group of young people trade glances, then crack up.

Lenny sits up, running a hand through his thinning hair.

'I know you're eager to step over to the other side. But not today, darlings,' Jim announces in a sacrificial tone. 'This was a test. Most of you have made me proud.' At that moment, Frida opens the curtain to Phyllis, leaning on Quincy's arm. 'Phyllis, you are still too attached to life in America. A true socialist would prefer death to this corrupt existence. Until you understand this, you cannot be trusted.'

'Oh! Father—'

'It has been decided, Phyllis: you will go to the Promised Land in two weeks. This is not a punishment, but a chance for you to learn a new way of living.'

'Two weeks, Father?' Phyllis rounds her lips. 'But I … My asthma, Father, it's worse in the heat, and I burn … real easy. Wouldn't it be better, if someone young and health—'

'*How dare you question your leader, after you've proven yourself so unworthy?*' Jim booms. 'How dare you insult our pioneers? Dr. Katz is a medical genius and our clinic will soon be the world's best! Miserable bitch, I shoulda let you choke.' As Phyllis gapes like a fish, he turns conciliatory. 'No, Phyllis, the decision is final. This will do you good, my love.'

Jim rises slowly from his sofa

'It has been a long night. We are weary, very weary.' He beckons to Terra, who beckons Dot, who touches her pale pageboy and dutifully takes Jim's arm. 'Sweet dreams, darlings.'

3.

'*You.* Where'd you put my hat?'

Luce's new wife's face is accusing but her body is polite: hands clasped, two feet's space between them, despite the smallness of the converted laundry that serves as their bedroom.

Juanita likes her own space. Luce knows this because his body takes up too much of it.

'Your red hat?' Back in the day, Joya used to give him points for noticing colors, fabrics.

'Mister, you ever see me in another hat?' With a hiss of impatience, Juanita turns her back, fastidiously points out a bare hook on her shelf. 'I had it *right here.* So?'

Luce is familiar with his new wife's methods of storage: her hooks and baskets and dry-cleaning bags, and stacked plastic tubs strategically draped with tablecloths. Yet he'd never dare touch her things uninvited. 'Sorry, Juanita. Haven't seen it.'

'*He hasn't seen it.*' Tugging the patchwork curtain aside, she bustles out, muttering. 'The man hasn't seen it. *Somebody* did.'

Luce takes Juanita's absence as an opportunity to do what he often does in her absence: look at the portrait of Albert on her shelf. Albert was Juanita's first husband, married to her when they were teens in Tuscaloosa. Albert was handsome. Albert died in an East Bay shipyard accident in 1942, breaking Juanita's heart so bad she tried to jump off the Golden Gate Bridge. Luce would've been fifteen in '42: a tall and pink-cheeked blond boy, hitting home runs, poring over the G.I.s in *Stars & Stripes.*

When Juanita waltzes back in, hat atop her crimpy updo, Luce stops looking at Albert. 'Look at that. You found your hat.'

They're on the next bus to Geary Boulevard within ten, along with half the commune. Rondelle, a big blunt-faced girl who always has attractive boyfriends, takes up two seats while her latest, Ray, a smooth young thing in a velour shirt and striped bellbottoms, does chin-ups with the handstraps. Gina, a shaggy-haired white girl who works at the dry clean with Juanita, leans over her seat and tries to flirt with Ray — 'I know who you look like in those pants! The Hamburglar! Can you steal me a hamburger, Ray?' Across the aisle, Martha is giving Earlene some unsolicited advice on her wayward teen son, Jerome. Juanita sits by her pal Corazon, a hard-of-hearing senior, and starts loudly bemoaning the foolishness of the commune's young people.

Luce stands apart, trying not to look like he's eyeballing some men in tight jeans and T-shirts. When they get off at Castro Street without a glance his way, he strokes his silver stubble.

'Should've shaved,' he says quietly; then, loud enough for Juanita, 'You think I should've shaved, Juanita?'

'Too late now,' Juanita says pragmatically.

'Whassat?' Corazon croaks.

'Too late for the man to shave now.'

'Mm-hm,' Corazon agrees. 'Too late now.'

From behind them, Rondelle lets out a groan over Martha's latest boast about her twin sons, Joey Dean and Bobby James, both pioneers in the Promised Land. 'Lady, Earlene don't give a damn if your boy's the next Tarzan, so how 'bout you give her some peace and quiet?'

'Excuse *me*,' Martha rejoins. 'But how's anybody supposed to find any peace and quiet with the likes of you screaming all over the place?'

'I'm just sayin' what everyone's thinking.'

'Whassat?' asks Corazon.

'Just more foolishness,' Juanita explains.

By the time they reach the Temple, the cafeteria is packed. Juanita and Corazon join a table of seniors while Luce fetches their meals, then returns to queue up for his own. Waiting, his eyes go to Meyer and Joya, sitting to eat with Hattie, Tremaine, and Alisha, and it hurts, if he's honest. He turns his attention to Dot and Paolo at the edge of the cafeteria, looking none the worse for whatever happened last night; piss-pants Bob Harris, a little ways ahead of him in line; Ray and those striped bellbottoms; where *does* Rondelle find these guys? Then, because last thing he needs is to get hung up on another straight man half his age, Luce glances to the back of the line and lands on Lenny Lynden, clutching an empty tray with the miles-away look of a mental patient.

Too depressing for words.

Dinner is some kind of potato-bean mush, soaked up with Wonder Bread. Luce wolfs it leaning against the wall. When something small collides with his leg, pokes him in the belly, he narrowly avoids dropping his plate.

'Shouldn't scare a man when he's eating,' Luce chides Hattie, 'Unless you want to wear his dinner.'

Hattie titters unapologetically, flashing her bunny-rabbit grin. 'Did you work at the railroad today, Brother Gene?'

'Mm-hm. Day shift.'

'I still want you to take me to see the trains.' She toys with the rainbow beads around her neck; a present from Dot, from the days when she still had time for beadwork. 'If I'm going to drive a train someday, you should let me see them.'

Horse-riding was all the rage with Dot and the other one. Hattie's obsession is driving: trains, Temple Greyhound buses, heavy machinery in the Promised Land … you name it, she wants to drive it someday. 'We'll see,' Luce says, wiping his mouth, frowning at the grate of his stubble. 'Should've shaved. What d'you think?'

Hattie stands on her tippy-toes to touch his cheek, laughs uproariously. 'Yeah! Yuck.'

She shadows him through the cafeteria as he returns his tray, happily comparing his hirsuteness with other men in the vicinity. It occurs to Luce yet again that he didn't think of her during last night's death-rehearsal; that Joya is indisputably the better parent; that he shouldn't feel so smug that Hattie favors *him*. They join the shuffle up to the auditorium, passing by Lenny Lynden, who's sitting on the floor, apparently engrossed in his uneaten bread crusts. Terra stands nearby with her arms crossed, looking down at Lenny and the crusts apologetically.

'Lenny needs to shave, too,' Hattie whispers gleefully. '*Why* is Brother Lenny sitting *there*?'

'Likes the view, I guess,' Luce tries to joke, yet there's something so sad about that young couple with nothing but bread crusts between them, he ends up frowning.

'He's going to miss the film about the Promised Land!' Hattie says, in a tone of fastidious concern that owes something to Joya. 'Phil Sor-en-sen's film.' She slips her hand into Luce's. 'Brother Gene, I want to sit with *you* tonight.'

'Sure,' Luce says, flattered, even as his throat threatens to close up. 'Sure, you'll sit with me. Uh … you sure? Sure you don't wanna sit with all the kids?'

He's rambling; he knows it; knows Hattie knows. But even more, he knows something's *wrong*. With his body: too tight-fitting, heavy as an ox, every orifice seemingly shrunken. With the bodies around him, packed like sardines, unfamiliar, though if he racked his brain he could probably name everyone. Someways ahead, he catches sight of Juanita's red hat, floating amid the crowd like a jellyfish. 'That's Juanita's hat,' he says matter-of-factly. He stops in his tracks; places a steadying hand on Hattie's shoulder.

'Um, Brother Gene?' Hattie bites her lip.

Luce hunches down, so his gaze is level with those rainbow beads. 'Just a minute.' He breathes through his mouth, for his nostrils feel like a pair of cocktail straws. He straightens up, pats Hattie's head, walks a few more steps. Can't go on.

'Must've ate too fast.' Through the throng, he can make out the projector screen being set up where, just last night, they were saying their goodbyes. 'I ate too fast … that's all.'

'Are you going to throw up?' Hattie asks with a nine-year-old's peculiar mix of curiosity, concern, and disgust.

Luce shakes his head — though now the possibility has been brought up, it does seem like that, a possibility.

'I just need some fresh air.' Though Juanita's red hat is already some distance away, he points it out, rather than send her back to Joya and Meyer. 'Go to Juanita. Go on.'

Hattie looks at him like she's a puppy he's just driven to the woods, told to run free, and driven away from.

'Go on,' he repeats. He pets her hair, lies through his teeth — the lie of the deadbeat dad who really does only plan on getting that pack of cigarettes from the corner shop. 'I'll be *right back*.'

Whatever his intentions are when he goes to the parking lot, dry-retches by the dumpster, it's the sight of Evelyn Lynden that decides it. Evelyn, whom he's not used to seeing outside meetings, let alone outside, let alone outside after dark on her own with her back turned. Bent to reach something inside her small European car, and though he doesn't want to know what it is, neither does he want to alert her to his presence with any sudden movements. So he stands and watches her pull from the car not the expected box of files but a little boy, her boy, the one they call 'Soul'. About two years old and so adorable it's hard to believe he came from a rape in a Mexican prison, as the story goes. But Luce never believed the story. Doesn't believe it now, watching those chubby arms circle her neck, the round face press against her lapel, something of Jim Jones already about the eyes and nose. She slings her bag, shuts the car. Glides toward the building, creasing her chin to say something to her child. Then, as quick as she appeared, she's inside the Temple, out of sight.

4.

RAINBOW + ARROW, the sign says. Spelled out in rainbow neon. Enclosed in a neon circle with a neon arrow blinking up. Not subtle, that's for sure.

Luce goes in, mostly because it seems wiser than loitering out on Castro Street.

The city has eyes. He keeps his lowered as he navigates the dark staircase, and inside it's dark, with flashes like weather from above, and loud music, padding his mind against the what-ifs. *What if he's been followed. What if he sees someone he knows. What if Jim's already reading his mind.* Music he recognizes from Rondelle's radio; if not the song then the style, racy, beating like a heart, and the singer, a black lady with a soaring voice, singing about needing a man.

Nothing subtle about that, either.

It's the kind of loudness that used to get on Luce's nerves with the hippies —their blaring rock-and-roll and smelly painted buses. But these men aren't dressed like hippies. They're working men: plaid shirts, white vests, blue jeans, overalls peeled to the waist. Some shirtless.

Though it's a weeknight, and early in the night, some men are dancing. Others standing close, talking, smoking, crushing up to the bar for drinks. He'll need a drink. Shuffling to join the mass of men at the bar, he surreptitiously draws his wallet from his pocket, confirming that the five dollars intended for tonight's offering plate is still there.

'Daddy, you're *tall*!'

Luce doesn't know where the words come from or if they're meant for him, but he *is* tall, and old enough to answer to 'Daddy'. He stands a little taller, sucks his belly in tighter, holds his head at a dignified angle, like Paul Newman. Plenty of women have said he has a Paul Newman look. Plenty of women have thought him handsome, and no reason plenty of men shouldn't, too, especially when the liquor's flowing and the lights are dim. As the line inches forward, he lets his eyes rove to a muscle-bound Latino, lifting a vial to his nose. The Latino passes it along to a skinny fellow with a handlebar moustache, and within seconds they're at each others' necks like vampires, and Luce's jeans, to his fearful pride, are tightening.

'What can I get you, sugar?'

The song has changed; something by that Swedish pop group. The crowd has thinned to reveal the bar, and the man behind it: a well-oiled mahogany-wood bar, a well-oiled mahogany-haired man. He's got on a pair of rainbow-striped shorts, very tight, *very* revealing.

'Let me see …' Luce stammers. 'Uh … not wine …'

'I'm only here to give you what you want, sweetie,' the bartender cuts in, with just enough honey to keep Luce from feeling like he's been sassed.

'Let me see …' Luce tries again. 'Uh, whiskey.' Then, worrying his choice isn't flamboyant enough, will single him out as an imposter, he adds, 'Sour. Whiskey sour.'

'Whatever you say, babycakes.'

Luce watches the bartender sashay away to make his drink, his walk pert and bowlegged, and, oh, he's good in those shorts, and, oh, his body's *good*. Slight and not-too-tall; the kind of build Luce likes best, though he's only just beginning to realize he has preferences. Only just beginning to realize that the thing he hasn't considered a possibility in over two decades is more than a possibility; it's low-hanging fruit to be plucked. Another man in rainbow shorts, bigger, broader, leans to take an order, pops a cherry in his mouth, then wiggles saucily over to the liquor shelf, where a bartender in female drag is shaking bottles. This doesn't interest Luce. Men done up like women — what for? But the big guy is whipping her tail with a dishtowel, tweaking a nipple through her rainbow bra. She whips him in revenge. Flicks her Farrah Fawcett hair. Stalks to the counter, breasts jiggling, hips swiveling. Convincing.

'Well. What do you want?' she snaps at a queen to Luce's right, and as soon as that raucous young voice comes out, he knows it *is* female, and not just that. It's *familiar*.

'Get those out of my face.' The queen, who's at least Luce's age, waves dismissively at the barmaid's chest, then inclines his head in the direction of the big guy. 'I want *him*.'

'You Can't Always Get What You Want.' Under its thick makeup, the barmaid's face is disarmingly young, a glimmering stud in her big nose. 'But you can get a drink.'

'I'll drink anything he pours in my mouth.'

'Oh, for-fuck's-sake.' She turns her back, showing a Venus de Milo-esque curve that makes Luce's blood run cold. 'Rudy! Grandpa wants to pay a guy to flirt with him.'

The big guy, 'Rudy', immediately swaggers over to Luce with a grin.

'Hi, cowboy. You're cute! Anyone ever tell you you look like Paul Newman?'

'Not *him*.' The barmaid turns to Luce apologetically. 'Hey, sir, I'm sor—'

She stops: struck by the same bolt that's causing him to grip the bar, white-knuckled.

'… *Dad?*'

Luce doesn't know how they get to his traitor-bitch daughter's apartment. Well, they walk; he knows that. But what turns they take, what they talk about, how he keeps from strangling her along the way — these are things he doesn't know.

Walking alongside her in her tattered lamé coat, waiting at traffic lights with her, he has the sense of being colorblind or partially deaf.

There is a simple answer to why he doesn't strangle her, of course, and that's that she's his daughter — *Roberta, Bobbi, Bobcat* — and that means more than any vows he's made to Jim these past years. He doesn't like to think of it this way, though. Even if he was ready to forget all his responsibilities in the first pair of well-muscled arms that'd have him, he's not ready to think of himself as a *traitor*.

'I think there's some beer in the fridge,' Bobbi says, after she's led him up three flights of stairs, sat him on a saffron-and-rhubarb-striped sofa, and fled to the kitchen.

Luce makes an ineffectual gesture as Bobbi returns with a couple of bottles of Budweiser, still dressed in that ridiculous rainbow outfit and gaudy old coat; probably from the 1920s, probably older than him. She takes a swig, then retreats to the edge of the room.

'I'm gonna change. Be right back.'

Should he kill her? When she comes back, maybe? Luce looks at his sweating beer. Looks around, and is saddened that the room is nicer than the one he shares with Juanita. Furniture that matches the walls. Art on the walls. Arty movie posters: *The Wicker Man, Holy Mountain*. A Trojan horse wearing a feather boa. No TV, but a radio and a Victrola.

'Ow!' Bobbi cries as she collides with a table on her way back in.

The darndest clumsiest kid. How many times did she fall off Magic Dancer?

Luce sniffs the air disparagingly. 'Can't say you're working with much. But you've made it interesting, I guess.'

'... Thanks.'

Bobbi sits as far from him as possible, on the arm of a saffron leather chair, legs wide in short gym shorts. Luce points to the yellow lettering on her college sweatshirt. 'Michigan?'

'Yannis. My roommate.'

'Another homosexual?'

'Uh-huh. Another "homosexual".'

'Can't walk two feet in this city without bumping into one.' Luce snorts, shakes his head. 'That bar of yours. Not helping the stereotype. The self-indulgence, I mean—'

'And I guess you were there for selfless reasons?'

'I mean, not much of a life. Snorting drugs on a weeknight. New partner every night. Not too healthy ...' He grapples for words to wipe the smug look from her face. 'There's gonna be a pestilence, Jim says. Hundreds of thousands of men infecting each other. Maybe millions.'

'Well, Father knows best.'

'Waste of life, all I'm saying.' He punctuates with a swig. 'Nice little revolutionary life you got here, pouring drinks in your underwear. Is that what all you Children of the Revolution are doing these days?'

'Look, Dad.' Like the yank of a dog's chain, the way she says it, *Dad*. 'I invited you here thinking you might be something other than a closet case, and maybe we still had things to say to each other. But if you wanna go back to your meeting, fine. I'm sure Jim hasn't even noticed you're gone yet.'

If this last part is meant to sting, Luce tries not to let it show. 'Alright. I'm listening.'

'Alright. Good.' Now she's been given her soapbox, it seems to Luce she hasn't got the first clue what to do with it. 'You know, my life *is* good.' She looks at him like she wants him to nod. 'Okay, I had some hard years, and maybe it's not everything I thought it would be. But I've got good people; I'm reading, learning … seeing more of the world. Yannis and me, we're saving to go to Europe. The Greek islands. The Acropolis.'

'Gosh. "The Acropolis".'

'There's a whole world out there, Dad.' She pushes a wilting ash blond curl from her cheek. 'It's not perfect, but nobody's telling you what to do every hour. Your life is yours. You're *free*.'

Young people. Always the first to think they understand 'freedom'.

'I'm glad you get to feel free in a world where your black baby sister still gets called "nigger",' Luce snaps. 'Could've asked how your brothers and sisters are doing, maybe. Could maybe spare a thought for someone other than yourself. But that's alright. Good for you.'

Bobbi tosses her head, wipes her eyes. With a giddy sense of victory that goes back to boyhood, putting dead mice in his sisters' beds, Luce realizes he's made her cry.

But women's tears, they tire him. His meanness in the face of them. All of a sudden, he's tired of sitting and exchanging mean words. *If only he could kill her.*

He stands. Walks to the wall with his beer like he's at an art gallery.

'You dumb cracker. I was thinking of *you*.' Bobbi tells his back. 'All the time, working at that bar, I've been thinking someday you'd come in; it was only a matter of time …'

'Should've gone to the bar across the street instead.'

'*It was only a matter of time,*' she repeats. 'Dad, don't you get it? This is *your time*.'

Another thing about young people: stupidly idealistic. 'I've had my time.'

'When? Indiana?' She scoffs, reducing all memories of being young with Jim to something measly. 'We're not in Indiana anymore. This city right now … There's never been anything like it. Men like you are finally accepted.'

'The Temple has always been accepting of —' he hesitates, thinking of Ralph and Tobias, with their slim bodies and loose gestures and arts degrees; are they *really* like him? 'More accepting than the outside, I'd say.'

'Is that why you're still married to Mom?'

She's seen his wedding band.

'Sorry to tell you, but your mom and I have both remarried,' Luce says, not sorry. 'I've got a beautiful black wife. Juanita.' He waits for Bobbi to look adequately impressed.

'She's quite a woman. Has had quite a life,' he continues. 'Not an easy life. Born in Alabama. Lost her first husband young. Second was a no-good man.' Juanita's words, gathered from various conversations during their year together, and waiting to be used as proof that there's more to their marriage than the sad truth: that after all that time with Joya, he doesn't know how *not* to be married. 'Two children. Six miscarriages. Struck out on her own. Worked all sorts of jobs: assembly line, maid, seamstress … Started her own dry-cleaning business, even.'

'Sounds like things have changed a lot,' Bobbi admits.

'Oh, sure,' Luce says. 'Lots of changes … Your brothers, guess you wouldn't know? Your brothers are working for the Cause in South America. Dot, well …' The image of Dot going upstairs with Jim wedges like a bone in Luce's throat. 'She's grown up pretty. No surprises. As for your dad — well, you don't have a cop for a dad anymore. I'm with the railroad police. It's a change. Change, that's life, isn't it? Y'know, wish I could sit here and tell you all the changes, but Juanita, she'll be wondering …'

At that, he gives his daughter a toothy smile, hefts himself from the sofa. If she looks at him oddly, he chooses not to notice. He strides to the door, stops to gulp his beer.

Not finishing his drink — that'd be rude, wouldn't it?

'You're not a cop anymore?' Bobbi marvels. 'Why not?'

One of those committee decisions, like Isaiah's daughter Alice not taking the bar after law school, or Meyer not taking an assistant professorship at one of the big city colleges. Like him proposing to Juanita after a single tepid date at an ice cream parlor in North Beach. 'Got this other job. I like it plenty.'

'But you were always a cop.'

'Not always.'

'As long as I've been alive, you've been a cop. As long as you've been in the Temple.' She shakes her head. 'It's just so hard to imagine … I don't even think I ever asked you why you became a cop in the first place.'

Luce shrugs again. 'Just a thing I did.'

'There must've been a reason.'

'I liked the uniform.'

'Come *on*, Dad.' Bobbi gestures helplessly at the sofa. Obediently, casually sucking on his bottle, Luce wanders back in, leans over the top of the sofa like it's a windowsill.

'I did want a uniform.' He takes another drink; lets it go to his head. 'I was too young for the war. Seemed like the next best thing. Heck, I knew I was … but in uniform? Seemed like I could always count on being a little bit good.'

Luce wishes his daughter wouldn't look at him like it'd be less embarrassing for everyone if he just dropped dead. 'Is that why you joined the Temple, too?' she asks. 'To be "*a little bit good*"?'

'Well. It's complicated …'

'Because of Jim?'

'Maybe.'

'You loved him, didn't you?'

To Luce's surprise, the question doesn't surprise him. Maybe he's been waiting years to hear it. 'That was a long time ago.'

'Do you still love him?'

'It's different.' Luce swallows the bad taste in his mouth. 'I don't think of it like that.'

'How *do* you think of it?'

Just two men. Born in different years and different towns, but close enough to maybe hear the same trains, to watch the same clouds, to smell the same storms hitting dirt, to come together like magnets. 'It's my life. That's all.'

Luce straightens, moves to the window to cool his face. From the street below, men's laughter rises, and further off, the nostalgic *woop-woop* of a police siren. 'I owe him my life.'

Bobbi sighs. 'If you saved someone from jumping off a bridge, you wouldn't expect them to follow you around for life. Would you?'

Juanita almost jumped off the Golden Gate Bridge once. Why didn't she? Jim hadn't been there to save her.

'It's not like that.' Luce comes back around to the sofa, sits. If he sits, maybe his thoughts will stop whirling. 'It's been a good life.'

Good, if he keeps his mind on certain things. Hattie holding his hand. The early years in the valley, when the girls were little and just wanted to ride horses. Indiana, when the boys were little, too: singing in church, church holidays, Roger with his nose painted red, playing Rudolph.

Good things. Not the bitter wine, making him gag.

'… A good life. The only life. I guess I'd die, y'know, if I didn't have this life …'

But something has been uncorked. Things better kept in, they're rushing out in a wine-dark tide, and darned if he can do anything about it, except hide his face as he cries. Big shoulder-heaving, lung-squeezing cries he didn't know he had in him, and wishes he didn't have to know about. Cries like bodies hauled out of a muddy trench, badly decomposing, tainting the air he breathes, so it seems he'll never take a clean breath again.

He does, though.

Breathes deep.

'I'm not ready to die,' he says.

Book Three

Welcome to the Promised Land

1.

The air in the clinic is warm, but the stethoscope is cold, making Clarisse Luce shiver as it passes along her stomach. She laughs. Danny Luce, at the foot of the bed, laughs with her. Rosaline Jones, listening at the stethoscope, smiles and thinks: *A beautiful couple.*

'Little galloping horses,' she says softly.

Rosaline unloops the stethoscope and hands it to Clarisse. 'Make sure you angle it forward.' As the young woman fits the pieces in her ears, Rosaline draws the metal circle back down. 'Baby's ribcage is right here. Listen close and you'll hear the heartbeat. Like little galloping horses.'

Clarisse's eyebrows knit. Danny, watching her, knits his brows, too. Then joy melts the concern from their faces.

'*Oh my God,*' Clarisse marvels. 'There it is.'

Danny crowds over to his wife's side of the bed, presses his ear against hers, his silky blond head against the cushioning black fuzz of her natural. Though he surely can't hear a thing, he beams, face shiny with the morning's heat.

'Oh my God,' Clarisse says again. 'It's *fast.*'

'Should it be fast?' Danny asks, fixing Rosaline with his blue eyes, so pale against his outdoor complexion they have the look of being painted on. 'Is that normal?'

'It's normal for your baby's heart to run a little faster, uh-huh.'

Once the expectant father, too, has had a chance to listen, Rosaline peers through her reading glasses at Clarisse's file, frowns at the notes, then at Clarisse's prominent clavicles. 'I'm recommending Dr. Katz put you on a special diet. Every mother gains weight at her own pace, of course. But protein and calcium are especially important in your second trimester. Some milk and a hardboiled egg, at least …'

Clarisse's eyes light up: *milk, egg*. Yet self-denial is still the name of the game.

'I don't know …' she protests. 'People are already giving me dirty looks.' She drums her fingers on her bump, still little more than an after-dinner bloat. 'I know it's a bad time.'

Overpopulation. Food shortages. A new truckload of people every week.

'Don't even think about that,' Rosaline reassures her. 'It's a good thing.' She turns to Danny, who's also looking fraught. 'It's a *good thing*.'

The young couple look at each other doubtfully, then shake their heads and grin. 'We're really excited.' Danny kisses Clarisse's hand. 'It's all we want to talk about.'

Rosaline raises her eyebrows encouragingly. 'Have you thought about names yet?'

'We like "Libya" for a girl,' Clarisse answers immediately. 'For a boy …' She looks at Danny and laughs. 'We just want a girl.'

Rosaline laughs, too. 'Well, that's understandable. Boys, though … they're not so bad.'

'I guess they're fine,' Clarisse concedes, glancing at Danny. 'I guess we were thinking, for a boy—'

'Eugene,' Danny says solemnly. 'We were thinking "Eugene".'

Eugene Luce. A tragedy what happened to Gene Luce. Even if he was a traitor. Even if his traitor daughter has been slandering them to the press ever since, trying to pin on them what was clearly a matter of wrong place, wrong time. Even if Jim has hailed the death an 'act of karmic retribution'. Cut in two pieces by a train car; not a death she'd wish on anyone. She wouldn't wish *death* on anyone, period … unless maybe that someone was ill and a danger to himself and others.

'That's nice,' Rosaline falters. 'Real nice. Your dad would like that, I'll bet.'

Though the dove-gray sky will no doubt rain cats and dogs later on, for now it's webbed with sunlight. The fields are rippling, banana leaves crumpling in the pale breeze. Standing outside the medical center, Rosaline looks. Looks and breathes.

No matter how busy they get, how her back aches, how her menopause flares, how her lungs sometimes bring up a foul leaf-green sputum — there's always time to look and breathe.

A couple of nurses, Sally-Ann Burne and Elly Bud, come up the path from their morning rounds, chime, 'Hi, Mother!' and duck inside the infirmary. Another pair of girls, grimy and headscarved from garden work, wave as they enter the pharmacy with baskets of herbs. Meanwhile, Eve is ambling up the path from Jim's cabin with uncharacteristic slowness, and toddling ahead of her is her little boy, Soul, and alongside her, curiously, is Phil Sorensen.

Rosaline looks away, as if she has witnessed something private.

But then Soul squeals and, menopause or no, Rosaline is still a woman who responds to children's noises. She turns to see Phil lifting Soul onto his broad shoulders, jogging ahead, slowing to a halt. Glancing back at Eve with his square-jawed grin. Eve stands at a distance, arms folded, looking uncomfortable. She says something to her child, ignoring Phil. Soul squeals again, pulls Phil's fair hair. Phil charges forth, joggling his shoulders so Soul laughs.

Eve watches, the slightest smile on her lips.

Rosaline isn't the kind to feel smug without a simultaneous rash-like spreading of guilt. So she blushes down at her orthopedic shoes, then up again as Phil calls, 'Morning, Rosaline!'

'Morning,' Rosaline answers politely. 'On your way to the playground?'

Eve, who by rights should be the one blushing, gives her such a dirty look it makes her skin crawl. But Phil grins; the same square grin he used on Eve; the grin he uses on everyone; there's a reason he's such a successful PR man. Just yesterday, when the US consul came on an inspection, armed with a list of complaints from interfering relatives back in the States, Phil had done most of the talking, deflecting attention from Jim's slack face, Jim's slurred speech.

'That's the plan.' Phil tickles Soul's dangling legs. 'If Little King doesn't make me run circles around the whole town instead.'

At that, Soul gives Phil's hair another tug and whines, 'Go! Brodder Phil! Go, go!'

Phil laughs and obeys Soul, trotting off toward the playground. Eve hangs back, emphatically *not* looking at Phil. Rosaline diplomatically turns her back, moseys off to inspect a splash of bougainvillea growing along the side of the building. But instead of taking the chance to creep away, to the office, to the radio shed, wherever it is she's going, Eve starts through the long grass with her file in her arms.

'Excuse me! Rose,' she sings out.

A little tenderfooted in her strappy sandals, but nevertheless efficient. Soon enough, Eve is poised in front of Rosaline with her file to her chest; pale face pinched, white blouse bloomy, an elfin point of ear peeking through her dark hair. She smiles at Rosaline, unconvincingly.

'What a beautiful day. I just love this time of morning, don't you?' Having fulfilled her small-talk quota, Eve continues in a businesslike tone, 'I don't suppose Dr. Katz is back yet.'

'He set out for Port Kaituma at daybreak. I don't suppose he'll be back 'til after midday.' Rosaline doesn't know if her instinct to mimic Eve is courteous or the exact opposite. For good measure, she clucks her tongue. 'Is there something I can help w—?'

'Father is asking for Dr. Katz,' Eve interrupts. 'I suppose he'll just have to wait.' She purses her lips and stares off in the direction of Jim's cabin, eyes slate-blue, dark rings beneath them. 'If you could tell the doctor to check up on Father as soon as he returns.'

'I'll tell him.'

'It's just Father's stomach condition is giving him so much grief.'

Rosaline offers another tongue-cluck. 'Did you give him anything for the pain?'

'I gave him *something*,' Eve replies. In the morning light, the worry lines between her brows are clear-cut, shocking. It occurs to Rosaline she isn't accustomed to seeing Eve up close, away from her usual shadowy indoor habitats. It occurs to her that Jim was never an easy man to live with, and that jungle life hasn't made him any easier.

'If only he'd agree to see that specialist in Venezuela,' Rosaline sympathizes.

'*Venezuela can't be trusted,*' Eve snaps. 'If Venezuela had their way, Father would be dead in the ground and this land would be theirs for the taking.'

'Be that as it may …' Rosaline sighs. 'There's only so much Dr. Katz can do.'

Eve peers back at the path, at the isolated thicket beyond which lies

Jim's cabin. After a while, quietly, she agrees: 'There's only so much Dr. Katz can do.'

Perhaps embarrassed to have admitted so much, Eve lowers her eyes and plucks an invisible speck of lint from her blouse. Raises them, now in the direction Phil took Soul. But Soul's squeals have faded and Phil is surely out of sight.

'Your folks'll be here soon,' Rosaline tries. 'If I'm remembering right?'

Eve nods. 'Tomorrow.'

'That'll be nice for you and Sally-Ann. Not to mention Soul.' Eve smiles politely but doesn't take the bait. 'A nice birthday gift for Jim, too. Your folks have always been sympathetic to the Cause. He appreciates that, even if he doesn't say it.'

'Yes. Well.' Eve's eyes dance ironically. 'Father doesn't like to make a fuss on his birthday, but I suppose one of the first things he'd ask for is something to counter the vicious lies of the media. I hope Tom and Margaret will deliver.'

Rosaline keeps a straight face, despite the absurd stiltedness of *Tom and Margaret*. 'That's true,' she agrees. 'Jim never likes a fuss on his birthday.'

'Forty-seven is still young, of course.'

'Of course,' Rosaline echoes, and she supposes it's true, for a man anyway. She shifts from one foot to another, peering down at the mousy-dark blaze of Eve's head, and has the sense they're probably both thinking the unspeakable: old or not, the way things are going, forty-seven could well be Jim's last year.

At that moment, the gardener girls sashay out of the pharmacy, young and pretty, swinging their hips and their baskets. Eve turns to watch them and so does Rosaline.

'Have you seen Polly?' Eve asks after a while, in a newly bright, acquisitive tone.

'No,' Rosaline answers warily. 'Why?'

Eve just raises her brows blandly, as if such scruples are cruder than the implication. Disgusted, Rosaline shakes her head.

'I haven't seen her. You'll have to find her yourself, Eve.'

Without another word, Rosaline turns her back on Eve, wishing she had the gall to call her something worse than *Eve*, simultaneously glad that she doesn't. Smug, even. Smug, and not the slightest bit guilty about it. But Eve isn't done yet.

'Rose,' she calls softly, 'I hope you know that we appreciate everything you do.'

And looking over her shoulder at Eve — her white hands clutching her file, her paleness against the pale sky — Rosaline has to wonder: that *we*, does it mean Eve and Jim? Or is it just a word Eve uses to feel less alone?

2.

When the rain bullets the pavilion roof and the workers come in from the fields with a smell of wet dog, Evelyn's meeting with the Agricultural Department heads breaks up. Ike Dickerson takes the opportunity to upbraid the sorrel farmers for letting the weed problem get out of hand — 'Sorrel? Who's in sorrel? You got a trowel? You know how to use it, huh?' — and Evelyn finds herself drifting toward the edge of the pavilion, the edges of conversations, watching with folded arms for signs of treason. Beverly Watson huffs and rolls her eyes. Ninette Lewis, a fresh arrival from Los Angeles, blames the sorrel plants for looking too much like weeds. Martin Luther, one of Jim's sons, comes in, rain-slick and tall as a tree, and starts tickling his girlfriend Sheila, but folds his muscled arms and puts on a poker-face when Joseph Garden asks about the bulldozer. A trio of girls in wet T-shirts are giggling, evidently about their wet T-shirts, but stop when they notice Evelyn. Evelyn moves along and the giggles resume, and though they do not hurt her, there's a certain blunt awareness where hurt might be, as if the organ of hurt has been removed yet is remembered by the surrounding nerve endings. Phil Sorensen wanders over from the radio shed, his polo shirt spotted with rain, droplets in his light hair.

Evelyn has matters to discuss with Phil, but none urgent. She will not go to Phil.

Evelyn goes toward the radio shed, passing conversations and turning them over in her mind; silencing conversations with the mere tread of her foot, the flash of her pale profile. Was there really a time when she was well-liked, popular? When girls confided in her and boys asked her to dance? If there was, that time is prehistoric, its details no more than faded hieroglyphics on a buried tablet. She doesn't think of that time.

Evelyn passes Phil, who is consulting Oscar Hurmerinta about a prospective visit from the Minister of Agriculture. Phil turns his face slightly in her direction.

The radio shed smells of stale farts, though Mona at the controls looks too pretty to have produced them: dark bowl of chestnut hair, large hazel eyes, sweating décolletage, pouty lips transmitting code in her soft Jersey accent. '… 8-R-1, we read you loud and clear. Abigail, tell Scarlett to bring the shortbread to Rex's house tomorrow. Over.'

Scarlett: Terra. *Rex's house*: the US Embassy. *Shortbread*: tape recorder.

Evelyn smiles neutrally at Mona as she retrieves a clear plastic umbrella from the hook by her head. The radio hisses and crackles before Joya 'Abigail' Mendelssohn's voice breaks through, demonically distorted.

'8-R-3, I copy. Do you want the raisin shortbread? Over.'

'8-R-1, affirmative. Tell Scarlett to serve Rex's friends the raisin shortbread and ask them to repeat what they told us about bringing home the fishermen. Over.'

Bring home the fisherman: shoot down the planes. Namely, spy planes spotted flying low over the settlement some nights. Of course, the US Embassy is responsible. Of course, the Embassy is a puppet of the CIA. Of course, the CIA would like to provoke them to do something so extreme as shooting down a plane. Why else would the US consul, Morris Whitehead, have made such a suggestion during his inspection of the settlement yesterday? This latest attempt at sabotage must be captured on tape.

Evelyn slips out of the radio shed, opens her umbrella.

Phil has finished with Oscar. Phil is crossing the walkway toward Evelyn. 'Very resourceful.' Phil points at her umbrella, and Evelyn smiles politely, notes the outline of his pectorals through his damp polo. 'Are you heading to the Letters Office?'

'West House,' she corrects. West House is the official name of Jim's cabin. Everyone knows that she lives there with Jim — everyone who knows things, anyhow.

'Same direction.' Phil gestures at the path. 'I'll take you halfway.'

'… Said the drowning man.'

'I'm a pretty good swimmer.' A raindrop slides comically down Phil's long, fine, very Scandinavian nose. 'But if you're offering to share your boat …'

They are flirting. Or getting dangerously close to doing so. Aware of this, Evelyn hands Phil the umbrella. He holds it above them both.

Evelyn watches her sandals, ignoring how tall Phil is, how close.

'Terra should have the Whitehead tape by this time tomorrow,' Phil informs her. 'When do we want it leaked to the Soviet Union?'

'Not until relations improve,' Evelyn replies. 'At this stage, they're likely to see it as a threat, not a cry for help. I wonder if they'll ever stop thinking of us as Americans.'

'When we shoot down an American plane, maybe,' Phil quips, though he's perfectly straight-faced, eyes pale and bracing. Gray eyes, lighter than her own, a ring of golden-brown at the center. He is too good-looking. Evelyn doesn't laugh.

'We are a peaceful people, born out of due season,' she says. 'Even Gandhi believed in self-defense.' A breathtakingly lanky youngster powers past, face clouded, skin blue-black in the rain, shirt plastered to his narrow chest. Evelyn feels the old white guilt, yet continues: 'Nobody will question our right to bear arms once we have it on tape. Assuming Terra succeeds in getting Whitehead to talk.'

'She's always been good at getting men to talk.'

The office building comes into view. Evelyn has the sudden feeling that her chest is a cliff her heart might leap off.

'Don't forget to hand in the schedule of activities for our visitors tomorrow,' she instructs Phil, slowing on the path. 'If you could have it by dinnertime.'

'I'll have it before then,' Phil assures her. 'Actually, I wanted to ask whether you'd like to do a final check of the Guest House with me this evening. If you have time.'

'I'm busy,' Evelyn responds instinctively. It's the truth, after all.

'Of course,' Phil says, with a faint shake of his head, a faintly fatalistic smile. 'What was I thinking?' He stops, looks past her, lowers the umbrella. Looks into her eyes. 'Gauguin to Turner and back again in ten minutes. It always amazes me.'

Evelyn turns her gaze to the landscape. 'Van Gogh's wheatfields,' she offers.

Phil folds up the umbrella, shakes it dry, his forearms sinewy and sun-kissed.

'Thanks, Evelyn.' He hands it back and takes a step toward the office. Evelyn steps away and nods. Purses her lips at his turned back: broad shoulders, tapered waist. Perfect ass.

'Phil,' she hears herself say. 'Perhaps … early tomorrow. After my radio shift.'

'Early tomorrow.' Phil smiles. 'Sunrise?'

'Early,' Evelyn repeats, unsmiling.

The cabin is dark, blinds lowered. Jim is sitting up in bed, wearing his Mao hat with his nightshirt. Even before she has entered, Evelyn can see he's in a better mood than when she left. '—The freezing don't kill 'em? How's that?'

'Inevitably, some die. But the freezing process is controlled, see,' Dr. Katz, kneeling at the bedside, explains in his Arkansas drawl. 'Slow programmable freezing. And there are substances to protect the sperm from freezer damage. "Cryoprotectants".'

'*Astounding*,' Jim marvels. Noticing Evelyn, he cranes his neck to view her from his cloud of pillows. 'Ever hear of this? "Cryopreservation"? Preserves sperm?'

Dr. Katz smirks at Evelyn. A morosely handsome Jew built in the mold of her high school boyfriend, Elliot Goldberg: pale complexion, bruised-looking under-eyes, teardrop nose. He wears his greasy dark hair past the ears to conceal a missing chunk of earlobe, the result of a failed attempt to impress or terrify a girl from his hometown.

Evelyn blinks noncommittally. 'I have some documents for you to sign, Father.'

Jim opens his hand.

'Could be, fifty years' time, a woman ain't even born yet giving me a son.' As Evelyn passes him a pile of papers, he brushes her flat backside. '2028. What d'you think?'

'It's an idea …' Evelyn slips a pen between Jim's fleshy olive fingers. '… But I fear our enemies could get hold of your highly advanced DNA and misuse it.'

'Oh, yes.' Jim frowns. 'That's a point. Yes, yes.'

He signs a letter to the Minister of Education, another to the editor of a left-wing San Francisco paper — one of the few still sympathetic to the Temple after the bad press that has made continuing in America impossible. Since Eugene Luce went and got himself hit by a train, no accusation has been too outlandish for those rags to print: murder, embezzlement, child abuse, you name it. All without a whit of proof, let alone consideration of the innocent people being harmed by such accusations. Under that kind of scrutiny, *anyone* would look guilty, whether they stayed or fled. At least here in the jungle, their people don't have to listen to anti-socialist propaganda every day.

'Harry, I want more research on this cryopreservation.' Jim shoos Dr. Katz. 'It's very interesting, but Evelyn's concerns are legitimate.'

So much for getting to her afternoon lessons with time to spare. Dr. Katz rises, still smirking. 'Yes, Father.'

'You look like you need to be fucked,' Jim tells Evelyn matter-of-factly once Dr. Katz has let himself out of the cabin. But he loses interest in the thought almost immediately, puckering his lips at the next letter. 'What's this? *Dear Mr. Whitehead ...*'

'A thank-you letter to the consul for coming out to the settlement yesterday.'

'*No-no-no-no-no ...*' Jim groans. 'Honey, this is horseshit, frankly. Doesn't say anything 'bout what we know. Get the typewriter.'

'We can't very well accuse him of being the CIA chief of Guyana in writing, Jim.'

'Ain't gonna let you put words in my mouth. Get the typewriter.'

Evelyn flounces out of the room. Peeks her head outside the cabin and whispers to Billy, the guard on duty, '*Please fetch Frida immediately.*'

She hauls her typewriter out of the cabinet next to the bunks. Flounces back to Jim.

He smiles sweetly. 'Thank you, darlin'.' Patting an empty space on the bed, he looks at her with soft concern. 'What's the matter, sweetheart? You look tired.'

Warily, Evelyn perches on the edge of the bed, lets Jim compress her bony white hand. 'It's nothing ... I'm just a little stressed about my parents' visit, that's all.'

'I'm gonna need you to stay strong, honey,' Jim reprimands her gently. 'They'll be applying pressure. Don't make me regret trusting you to withstand it.'

'I won't, Jim.'

Evelyn pulls her hands away, tucks her hair. Jim re-tucks it, then traces down from her earlobe to her jugular, the pale triangle of bones at the base of her throat. 'Beautiful revolutionary,' he murmurs. 'We'll be at peace soon.'

Evelyn gazes steadily past his sunglasses. '*Dear Mr. Whitehead ...*' she prompts.

Jim is still dictating the letter to her when Frida steals inside, so thin it seems to be her bones and not the keys around her neck jangling. While jungle life has improved Phil's looks, it has wreaked havoc on his sister's: pimples sprouting from her square jawline like mushrooms in nuclear darkness; orange freckles across her face and chest; orange tinea joining with the freckles and disappearing into the paleness beneath her tank top. Yet Frida is still young and clear-eyed; still cute with her long hair in pigtails; still knows how to handle Jim.

'Father,' she breathes, approaching the bed. 'You're awake.'

Jim inclines his head. 'Frida, darlin'. You here to help us whitemail Whitehead?'

Frida looks at Evelyn, who flits her eyes down at the letter she's typing, blinks twice for no, raises her brows at the correspondence by Jim's pillow and blinks yes.

'Yeah, Father,' Frida says confidently. 'We're gonna nail his crooked white ass at the Embassy tomorrow. Terra got your instructions.'

'Oh, Terra ... Terra,' Jim laments. 'She's a good soldier, but she's been gone from the fold too long. She needs to be near my aura, or she'll weaken. I can already sense it.'

'She'll be back next week, Father,' Frida reassures him. 'As soon as Phil is done here and can take her place in Georgetown.'

Evelyn straightens her papers, nicks her finger, brings it to her lips, blood stinging. 'You should radio Terra,' Evelyn suggests. 'It'll do her good to hear your voice, Father.'

'*Yes*,' Frida enthuses. 'She should be back from her YWCA lunch by now.'

Evelyn rises, typewriter in arms. 'I think it's a very good idea. In fact, I think it would do everyone good to see you up and about. Your presence is an inspiration to the people.'

Emboldened, Jim swings his legs out of bed. 'My people need me.'

In the next room, Evelyn checks her watch: two minutes to get to her Political Science class. They will be discussing Jamaican politics:

Manley, Seaga, the joining of hands at One Love last month. Frida joins her by the wardrobe.

'Make sure those documents go out with tomorrow's mail shipment,' Evelyn whispers. She glances at the mini refrigerator. 'And try to get some food in his stomach.'

3.

Evelyn's only concession to her date with Phil is a splash of water to her tired face, a flattened palm to her clothing. She cracks the door of the radio shed — mosquitoes be damned. A pleasant morning breeze to dispel the miasma of her and Frida keeping themselves awake with too much coffee and dried cutlass beans. Naturally, Frida has been dismissed early. Phil raps on the door at exactly five-forty-five.

'Oh, of course.' Evelyn looks up from her paperwork. 'Let me just finish this.'

Phil obediently sits his long body on the daybed, waits in silence. She would never keep Jim waiting, but it feels right with Phil; his eyes on the back of her neck, thoughts wandering.

'Sanitation report,' she explains, after five minutes have elapsed, no more. She stands and retrieves her attaché case. Phil stands with her, slinging his camera bag.

'No problem.' He smiles.

Outside, smelling the morning dew, observing the mists rising from the jungle canopy, Phil smiles again and says, 'Just look at that. Beautiful.'

Platitudes. Only, Phil has more to him than platitudes. Phil can speak three languages; can devise and crack codes with as much skill as she or Frida; has intelligent ideas not just about world events, but philosophy, poetry, artistic theory. A conversation several months ago, working late at the headquarters in Georgetown, in which they had discussed his combat-zone photography: thatched huts burning; women floating face-down in rice paddies; G.I.s pointing guns at toddlers. The purpose of great art, like *Guernica*, like *The Scream*, to alert one to human suffering, human madness.

He is good with her child.

'How's the little Man of Peace?' This is one of Phil's nicknames for Soul, along with *Little King, Shalom, Sunny.*

'He's been calling all animals "doggy", lately.' Evelyn feels a sweet tightening at the corners of her mouth. It is easy for her to speak of Soul, when asked. Not many people ask, though. 'The other day, he came up to me in the yard and said, "Little doggy for you, Little Mother." Then he stuck the world's largest beetle on my trousers.'

Phil laughs. '"All animals are doggies." I like it.'

'"But some animals are more doggy than others."' Evelyn smiles crookedly. 'He's quite a character.'

They pass the bakery with its smokestacks; get a whiff of burnt cassava flour. The banana shack. The path branches, narrows.

She watches the sky lighten, Phil's features taking shape.

The Guest House, for obvious reasons, is some distance from the town's center. Sheltered by trees: palm, titi, tamarind, Surinam cherry, frangipani. A chattering of blue-headed parrots. Phil stops on the path; touches Evelyn's shoulder. Points upward.

Monkeys. A family of three. Up in the titi tree, tails twining.

Phil takes out his camera, shoots: *shoom-shoom-shoom.* 'Hey, doggy doggy,' he calls up the tree, then grins at Evelyn over his shoulder.

She walks past Phil. Up the path to the boxy cabin on stilts, up the porch, the chemical sweetness of the paint edging her nostrils like a drug. She pushes the door open — no lock on the door, no *need* for locks; no material possessions; no crime.

Phil follows her inside.

Evelyn feels Phil at her back. His eyes on her, even as he keeps his distance. His eyes, as she treads the jatoba floorboards, inspects the twin beds, mosquito nets. Handicrafts by their seniors. On the wall, a watercolor by Sally-Ann depicting a Promised Land of flowers, birds, monkeys, multiracial faces smiling from the greenery as a rosy dawn bleeds overhead.

'Everything seems to be in order,' Evelyn says. She looks at Phil and his face is so good-natured and attentive that she has to add, 'It's beautiful. Truly.'

Phil smiles wide. 'I'm glad you think so.'

There's a moment. His eyes. Her eyes. Phil leans his back against the doorframe.

'You must be looking forward to seeing your parents.'

'Yes,' Evelyn admits, and is surprised by her honesty.

'A long time?' he asks. 'Since you last saw them?'

'About a year and a half.'

'Soul has grown a lot.'

'Yes,' Evelyn says again, trying not to linger on Phil's lazy limbs, the forward tilt of his pelvis. 'He's really a little boy now, not a baby.'

Phil continues to look at her with interest, yet she has run out of things to say. She averts her eyes and straightens purposefully.

Phil straightens, too. Shuffles out to the porch and announces, 'Yolanda! Great timing.'

He isn't speaking to Evelyn, of course, but to the beautiful young woman coming up the dirt path with a basket of flowers.

'We thought it would be nice to have some flowers,' Phil explains to Evelyn, though he isn't looking at her anymore; he's looking at Yolanda.

Evelyn looks at Yolanda, too. Stares, really, with a kind of shell-shocked neutrality at the tight corkscrew curls, the round young breasts, the itty-bitty waist. Evelyn recognizes her as one of the wet-T-shirt girls from the day before; recognizes the body. Not the body of a thirty-two-year-old woman. Not the body of a thirty-two-year-old *white* woman.

Yolanda stares back, doe eyes unfazed, like she's used to being stared at.

Phil steps down from the porch. 'You look straight out of some pastoral idyll,' he tells Yolanda. He looks into her basket. 'Those ones with the red stripes are out-of-sight! Are they from your grandma's garden?'

'They're not from any garden.' Yolanda smiles slyly and lowers her voice. '*If you walk toward the falls, there's this little place …*'

As Yolanda launches into a description of where the rarest wild orchids are to be found, Evelyn concentrates on keeping her face a polite blank. 'Righteous,' Phil enthuses, and Evelyn is sure he's never looked at her as he's looking at Yolanda. 'You'll have to show me sometime, Yo'. I'd love to take some photos.'

'Sure. "Sometime",' Yolanda says archly, and gives an incxplicable little laugh.

'I mean it.'

'*Sure.*'

The two laugh together. Evelyn checks her watch pointedly and refolds her arms.

Phil notices. Gallantly, he offers, 'These orchids are really something.'

Evelyn ignores him. To Yolanda, she says, 'Make sure you put those in water.'

Yolanda nods with such vacant-eyed courtesy, she may as well be saying *yessum*. She sneaks a glance at Phil and they laugh again.

'I'm sorry,' Phil tells Evelyn. 'But this light …' He gestures helplessly at the sunrise, Yolanda. 'It's perfect. Do you mind?'

Who is he talking to? If Evelyn, she doesn't answer. If Yolanda, she throws her head back, showing white teeth, the fuchsia inside of her mouth. 'Ohmygod, Phil. Are you serious?'

'It's *perfect*,' Phil repeats. Then, to Evelyn, 'I'm like a moth: always chasing the light. Thanks for letting me keep you up so late … early? You probably want to catch some z's, I bet.'

Offended by the implication that she needs sleep, Evelyn blinks fast, murmurs, 'Yes. Well.' She checks her watch again. 'Honestly, this *has* taken longer than I expected.'

At that, Evelyn steps down from the porch like a queen vacating her throne.

'Please don't leave those orchids without water too long. It would be a shame for something so beautiful to die.'

It is better once she is out of Phil's sight, walking the luscious path back into town alone. Better, to walk alone. Better, not to dwell on things that are essentially unsurprising. Brown skin. White teeth. Fuchsia mouth, laughing. High ass and tiny waist and pert breasts. Why wouldn't Phil look? Phil is a man, and men are shit.

Men are shit; she has known this since Percy, who took her virginity on the sand dunes at Santa Cruz but never called her back for a third date. Since Jean-Claude, who let her fly from the country she had grown to love and back to the one she hated, without ever thinking to follow. Since Lenny Lynden, who accepted Terra as her replacement as easily as pancakes instead of French toast. For as long as she has been a woman, Evelyn has understood the fundamental indifference of men.

Evelyn passes a crowd of male workers, dispersing loudly from the Dining Tent. Her nose wrinkles, as if she is indeed smelling shit. Further down the path, she sees a flock of children being shepherded to breakfast. Her nose unwrinkles — Soul is among them. Soul, who may someday be a shit man, but who for now strikes her as the most perfect creature in the world.

'Mmmmom!' Soul bursts out in his froggy little voice. He jumps up and down, waves his arms above his head. Evelyn smiles, waves back. Soul turns to one of his friends, a kinky-haired girl called Tenille, and boasts, 'That's my mom: Little Mother.'

Her child. Her child by Jim. Evelyn clings to this thought, for it is everything.

Inside Jim's cabin, Frida is already snoring like a lumberjack on the top bunk. Mona is on the bottom bunk lacing her boots, but scoots to the floor when she sees Evelyn. '*I'll be out in a minute.*' Evelyn nods, puts down her attaché, and begins to remove her own shoes. In a hush, Mona adds, 'Sally-Ann took Soul to the nursery on her way out.'

'Yes. I saw him.'

'We had to put him in odd socks. One black, one navy.'

'Odd socks for an odd little boy.' In fact, Soul is a reassuringly normal child.

Once Mona has left, with a rustle of her straw bag and a creak of boots on jatoba, Evelyn strips down to her tank top and underpants and pads into Jim's room. He is asleep. A rounded form under the covers of the queen bed, wide mouth parted, sunglasses in place.

Evelyn removes the sunglasses carefully. His face in repose still has something doglike, bearlike, warmly mammalian in its handsomeness, which makes her want to draw close and stroke it. She lifts the covers and climbs into bed.

Jim stirs, without waking. She strokes a dyed sideburn and whispers, '*Is this okay?*'

'Mm-hmm,' Jim groans. His eyelashes flutter like dark moths. '… The tsar's agents are plotting to kill us, darlin'.'

'We are well-armed,' Evelyn reassures him. 'And we have many troops.'

Jim murmurs something in Russian, reaches blindly for a breast.

'There's a young woman who wants a personal relationship with the

Cause.' Evelyn continues to stroke the black sideburn, the black hair. 'Yolanda.'

'Yo-lan-da,' Jim repeats, moistening his lips.

It could almost be his idea; perhaps it will be when he awakens. She kisses him gently.

'You're the most loving man on earth. We would die without your love, Father.'

It may be the other way around; maybe *he* would die, if she left him. Or he would have her killed. Certainly, he would not be indifferent.

Whatever he is, he is not indifferent.

Evelyn keeps stroking, kissing.

4.

'There she goes again, leaving us with the dirty work,' Elly Bud taunts, flashing her eyes at Sally-Ann from over Sister Corazon's foot fungus.

'Sayonara, Elly-phant!' Sally-Ann waves theatrically. Actually, Elly's the opposite of an elephant: skinny legs and smoothest skin you ever saw. 'Corazon, I owe you a foot-rub.'

'Whassat?'

If it were up to Sally-Ann, Elly would be in the meeting party with her. Mom and Dad had liked Elly, the times she brought her to the Berkeley house to eat ginger snaps and talk shit around the walnut dining table. And, of course, Elly liked Mom and Dad; *everyone* does.

But Martin Luther and Jin-sun are already monkeying around with Soul in the playground, where they agreed to meet. 'Auntie! Watch me!' Soul yells from the top of the slide, then leaps straight over the edge and onto Martin Luther's back.

'Whoa! Is it a bird? Is it a plane? Is it a … *Soul*?' Sally-Ann rushes over; grabs hold of her little nephew's ankles and suspends them as Martin Luther charges around, Superman-style.

By the time they set Soul down, his face looks like an apple. 'Grandma-grandpa are coming on a plane. From America,' he informs them.

'Do you know where America is?' Jin-sun asks, bouncing his baby son, Bam, on his chest. Soul points at the sky.

'*Up.*'

It's not long before Phil Sorensen shows up with Billy Younglove. Like Jin-sun, Billy's got a wife coming home from Georgetown; he looks ready to burst, he's so excited. Phil, well, he just looks like he's ready to read the news or something. But that's enough to get Soul throwing himself at Phil's leg. 'Brodder Phil!'

'I think he's in love with you or something, Phil,' Sally-Ann says. 'Where's Evie?'

'She's just finishing up some paperwork.'

'She *is* coming?' Sally-Ann tries not to sound annoyed, but it'd be just like her sister, missing something like this for *paperwork*. Instead of waiting for an answer, she turns to Billy, digs him in the ribs. 'I know you're real excited to see Alice ... just don't pee your pants, okay?'

'I don't think it's gonna be *pee* in his pants,' Martin Luther swoops in, and all the guys laugh. Guys are pretty gross, most of the time. That's something she and Elly agree on.

By now, Soul is climbing Phil's leg. 'That's enough, Sunny. You're gonna trip me up.'

'*That's enough,*' Evie repeats in her sharp schoolteacher voice, coming up behind them.

One thing about Evie is, she's always coming up when you're not expecting her, and a lot of people don't like that. Another thing, people don't talk as much when Evie's around. As the guys stand around swatting flies, Evie tugs Soul away from Phil, crouches down and starts fussing with his clothes, his hat with the flaps. Sally-Ann sucks her lips. Sometimes even *she* finds herself going quiet around Evie. Was it always like this?

'You wore the black top,' Sally-Ann says, for want of anything better. 'I like that top.'

'It's a nice top,' Phil echoes, admiring Evie as she straightens up. Evie ignores him.

A bit of red shows like a wound through the trees, then the flatbed truck emerges. Sally-Ann hoists Soul up to see it better. 'I spy Grandma and Grandpa!'

'Grandma-grandpa?' Soul gapes. 'Where?'

'Right. *There.*' Sally-Ann points to the peak of Dad's balding head, Mom's dyed champagne-blond hair.

Soul swivels to regard Phil. 'Grandma and grandpa came on a plane. From America.'

'So did you,' Phil says. 'When you were a baby.'

'I wasn't a baby!' Soul argues. 'I *remember.*'

'Do you *really*?' Evie asks skeptically. 'What do you remember?'

Soul starts talking crap about flying over the fires of America until they reached the clouds, the clouds wrapping them up like a blanket, putting them asleep until they reached the Promised Land. Even Evie laughs. Then the truck is so close Sally-Ann can see her parents waving, and the guys are stepping up to help with the luggage, helping the women down. Jin-sun smooches his wife Carrie, shows her the baby. Billy smooches Alice.

'*Oh!*' Mom makes a hilarious face as Martin Luther lifts her, places her down where the soil is less likely to muck her sandals. Dad jumps down, and then, since he's tall, lends a hand to a young black girl with a lumpy little body and big scared eyes. Sally-Ann has never seen the girl before. Her parents look older and whiter than she remembers.

'Welcome to the Promised Land!' Sally-Ann grins, just the same.

Behind her, quieter but smiling, too, Evie says, 'Welcome to Jonestown.'

The best thing about that night isn't that they get fried chicken for dinner, or wearing the new blouses Mom gave them (orange with red-and-white flowers for Sally-Ann, blue with white-and-gold flowers for Evie), or even the after-dinner entertainment of African dancing and Jamaican steel drums and a steady flow of jazz, rock, and soul. The best thing for Sally-Ann is seeing all her favorite people in one place, how easily they fit together: Mom deep in conversation with Mother Rosaline, making her laugh, rolling their eyes at the pavilion roof; Dad listening patiently to Father, in his papaya-orange shirt, talking about the freighter they're in the process of buying, how they'll use it for commercial runs to Trinidad; Evie and Phil nodding along with Father, inserting comments, data, but also talking to each other in a grave, tentative way, too quiet to hear over the entertainment. Carrie breastfeeds baby Bam while giving Sally-Ann the latest gossip from the capital: how Joya Mendelssohn ran around like a headless chicken trying to find a bottle of vodka to bring to a last-minute meeting with the Russian consul's wife; how the Guyanese women are always blowing kisses at Roger Luce, he's so tall and *so blond*; how Terra Lynden has been real uppity, a bitch to live with. At one point, Father gets up to praise the African dancers on their performance, taking Dad with him, and Sally-Ann pulls goofy faces at Elly Bud and beautiful Yolanda

Greene, both in full costume. Phil gets up to go to the radio shed, and Mom waits until he's gone, before leaning across the table and marveling, 'Phil is very good-looking, isn't he?'

'Also, grass is green,' Sally-Ann retorts, with a smug swallow of her fruit punch.

Evie laughs, high and tinkly like a musical triangle; touches her earrings and starts telling Mom tomorrow's schedule of activities in unnecessary detail.

Tomorrow is Father's birthday, Sally-Ann knows, but also that he doesn't want a fuss. Father is really a very humble man, and Sally-Ann doesn't understand those people saying he's the opposite. It'd be one thing if they were strangers, but the fact Sally-Ann used to be friends with some of them makes her wonder if she could've done things better, been a better friend and made them stay. Like Bobbi Luce — didn't they have fun on the buses, helping with the healings? But now Bobbi's telling the media how the buses were too crowded and the healings were fake, and even that she thinks the Temple ordered a hit on Brother Gene! Then there's Wayne and Tish Bud, saying their family are being kept in Jonestown against their will, though Sally-Ann knows *for a fact* that Elly loves it here, laughs with her every day.

Thankfully, Sally-Ann doesn't have to worry about anything like this with Mom and Dad. Sure, they were creeped out when they first learned about Father and Evie; and sure, they thought Evie had gone nuts, divorcing cutie-pie Lenny Lynden for a married preacher; and sure, they used to call Father 'Rasputin' all the time, in the years between that first meeting and when Sally-Ann finished high school and went down to the valley by herself to see what all the fuss was about. She was supposed to go live with Vicky in New York straight after, try her luck busking and selling street art, but New York seemed overrated once she saw what a big thing Evie was part of — even if Evie took it *too* seriously. Now, six years down the line, there's this little boy, Soul, toddling over from the kiddie table, getting his hair ruffled by Father then Dad; continuing to Mom and Evie, clambering between their laps.

Phil returns just as Soul is burying his face in the folds of Evie's new blouse. 'Brodder Phil!' Soul chirps.

'Hey, Little King,' Phil smiles, then bends to Evie's ear. Her expression shifts from tender to taut. She kisses Soul's forehead, rubs the wetness left by her kiss, and rises.

'Excuse me,' she tells Mom. 'I'll be right back.'

Evie marches out of the pavilion after Phil. Soul starts to cry.

'Hey, kiddo. Don't cry,' Sally-Ann sing-songs. 'You've still got us, right?'

'Oh, *poor baby*,' Mom frowns tragicomically, smooths Soul's dark hair.

'Is that my son crying?' Father booms. 'Why's my son crying?'

Mom says he's probably just tired, but Father lumbers over anyway, scoops up Soul.

'Sweetheart, c'mon now. Peace, *peace* ...' Despite Father's ministrations, Soul keeps howling, kicking. 'Son, why're you doing this to me? Don't do this, baby. *Please.*'

Sally-Ann notices the dull look on Father's face, which flickers to pain the more Soul screams. She notices people turning to stare. A few more babies start squalling in sympathy. With forced glee, Sally-Ann rushes to Father, relieves him of Soul.

'*He's such a baby sometimes,*' she laughs, rolling her eyes.

Father nods solemnly, turns to Dad. 'It's getting late, for the babies.'

'That makes sense,' Dad obliges. 'I'm told you all rise with the sun.'

Mother Rosaline joins Father, says a few words about the sun. Mom helps Sally-Ann quiet Soul. Soon he's cuddling her, babbling, 'Grandma, I want to sleep with *you* tonight.'

'That's not such a bad idea,' Evie says, reappearing in her sudden way. 'There's plenty of room in the Guest House. Would you mind?'

'Mind bunking with this snuggle-bug? Heck, no.'

'Well, he's used to sleeping with Sally-Ann, that's the only thing.' Evie looks at Sally-Ann pointedly, and Sally-Ann knows, for sure, something's up.

'Slumber party?' Sally-Ann grins. 'Hey, I don't mind sleeping on the floor.'

'Don't be silly.' Mom waves her hand. 'You can have one of the beds.'

Evie smiles. 'I'm sure you'll all be very comfortable.' She kisses Mom, then Soul. 'Be good for Grandma and Grandpa. They came all the way from America to see you.'

As quick as she came, Evie is leaving again, stopping to bid Dad goodnight, to pull Father aside. Father shakes hands with Dad, and then follows Evie to the radio shed.

'Evie's all business, isn't she?' Mom says. 'What do you think she's doing?'

'*Crisis control.*' Sally-Ann mimics Evie's poker-face. 'Probably someone ordered the wrong kind of fertilizer.'

Just then, Father's voice comes over the PA:

'*THE CHILDREN ARE VERY SLEEPY. PLEASE PACK UP AND RETURN TO YOUR CABINS, PEOPLE. SWEET DREAMS.*'

Mom smiles at Sally-Ann, a crooked-pretty smile a lot like Evie's. 'Well, I guess if the children are sleepy, the jetlagged over-fifties club must be too. Let's hope the fertilizer crisis doesn't keep Little Mother up all night, huh, Soul?'

The watercolor on the wall of the Guest House isn't one of Sally-Ann's favorites. She thinks the happy faces look two-dimensional, their smiles too fixed, and there's a bit of sky that bothers her every time she looks at it, red and green paint muddied together in a shitty crust. But of all the pictures she presented Phil Sorensen with when he asked for something to hang, this was the one he chose.

Soul is already awake when Sally-Ann opens her eyes, staring into her face with peaceful attentiveness. She smiles at him and he giggles, feigns sleep. 'You big old fake,' she teases, tickling him. Soul giggles again, a sound like a million tiny rainbow bubbles bursting. He's so damn cute, it hurts sometimes. 'Shhh, you're gonna wake Grandma and Grandpa.' But actually Sally-Ann doesn't mind if he does; sun is already dotting their skin through the mosquito netting. She smiles impishly, 'Hey … want to wake Grandma and Grandpa?'

Soul slips under the mosquito netting and over to their bed. A minute later, Sally-Ann hears them groaning awake, Soul exclaiming, 'Auntie said to wake you!'

Evie and Phil show up on the porch while Mom and Dad are still in their PJs, noisily reading Soul the barn-animals book they brought for him. Evie signals for Sally-Ann to shut the door. She has on a layer of makeup and a different outfit, but her shaky hands tell Sally-Ann she hasn't slept. Neither has Phil, by the looks.

'I brought a change of clothes for you and Soul,' Evie says, tremulously handing them over. 'Come to West House once you're ready.'

'Harry doesn't need me in the clinic?'

Evie lowers her voice. '*I need you to watch Jim today. He's had another heart attack.*' At Sally-Ann's concerned glance, Evie rolls her eyes, sighs like a bitch. 'Mona is with him now, but, as you know, she's useless.' She touches her temple, blinks deeply. 'I need coffee.'

'If you have any more coffee, you'll be climbing the walls, Evie.' Phil half-smiles.

Evie sighs again. 'I suppose you're right.' She looks at Phil. 'You may as well just meet us at breakfast. It looks like everyone here is still in pajama-party mode. Get some rest.'

'Wishful thinking.'

'Well … I'm going to lie down,' Evie says cautiously. She turns from Phil, looks surprised to see Sally-Ann still there. Scowling, she pushes her to the door, closes it on Phil.

'*Moooo!*' Soul bellows as they re-enter the Guest House.

'Moo,' Evie answers flatly. 'Enough reading, Soul. Come lie down quietly with Mama for a while.'

'You look very pretty today, Evie,' Mom says, without a trace of irony.

Sally-Ann doesn't look forward to spending the day cooped up in West House with Father's unconscious body, but she runs there anyway, as soon as she's dressed. Mona, who's clutching a glass of water by Father's bed, squeaks when Sally-Ann enters and vacates her seat. Sally-Ann doesn't ask about the red marks on Mona's neck, or why she starts clacking frantically on her typewriter in the next room a minute later.

Times passes in minutes, breaths per minute. The slow rise and fall of Father's chest.

Once Mona leaves the cabin, Sally-Ann takes out her sketchpad and works on her half-finished drawing of an angry sun. Sally-Ann has more half-finished drawings than finished ones.

At lunchtime, Phil's sister, Frida, comes in with a plantain sandwich for Sally-Ann.

'Dr. Katz said to give him another half-dose of morphine,' Frida says. She watches with unnerving interest as Sally-Ann prepares the hypodermic, pulls down the sheets, then Father's pants. As the needle dents his sallow flesh, Frida crouches by the bed and tells him, 'We should've killed that whore when we had the chance. She doesn't deserve your love.'

'Who …?' Sally-Ann asks, but Frida just glares. Like Evie, Frida's not the easiest person to talk to. It's a relief when Frida finally stops staring at Father and goes back to work.

Sally-Ann knows it's an honor to be Father's nurse, but she yearns for the clinic, the patients, the other nurses, Elly. She starts drawing a picture of Elly as a skinny-legged elephant, but puts it aside when Evie comes in later with a bag of oranges. She gives one to Sally-Ann, instructs her to feed it to Father, when he wakes.

'Mom and Dad are resting after the orchard tour, but they agreed to babysit again tonight.' She glances at Sally-Ann. 'Honestly, the more exhausted they *all* are, the better.'

Maybe this is another time where it would be better to stay quiet, but Sally-Ann has had no one to talk to for most of the day, and there's something sinister about the feeling of plans being changed all around her. A terrible thought pops into her head, flies out of her mouth just as quickly. 'Evie … will there be a White Night? With Mom and Dad here?'

'At this stage, it's unavoidable. The people need to be prepared for an invasion.' Evie looks at Sally-Ann apologetically. Goes to the bag of oranges and takes another one out, making a few neat incisions and rolling it into a caterpillar, the way Sally-Ann liked when she was a little kid. 'I don't like it either, but they're hardly going to be straying far on their own after dark. Not with all the stories the boys have been telling them about jaguars and vampire bats.'

'What if something happens to Soul?'

'They'll have a radio. Besides, they know what they're doing. They're good parents.'

'But …'

'Eat this.' Evie hands her the orange caterpillar. 'You need your strength.'

Part of Sally-Ann wants to argue, to demand answers to all the questions crowding her head: who betrayed Father? Is it *really* so bad they need another sleepless night full of floodlights? Will it be like

'Dwight Night' — that terrible night after Dwight Mueller defected last fall, where they wound up arming themselves with machetes and waiting for mercenary soldiers to spring out of the jungle? She knows she'll get no answers from Evie. Instead, she smiles weakly and wiggles the orange caterpillar in Evie's direction. '*Please don't eat me, human! I want to be a butterfly.*'

Evie laughs, and then goes into the next room to pack an overnight bag for Soul. Sometimes Sally-Ann wonders if what Evie likes most about motherhood is all the extra stuff it gives her to be anal about. Evie comes back in wearing a billowy long-sleeved blouse and watches Father breathe for a while. 'Oh, Jim,' she says softly.

It's too dark in the cabin for Sally-Ann to draw, by the time Father opens his eyes. Anyway, she has a cramp. '*She left me,*' Father moans, clutching his heart, and for a moment Sally-Ann thinks he means Evie. He rasps for water. After soothing his throat, he continues, 'That balmy-eyed blond bitch. Took off with that spook, Whitehead.'

Blond bitch? So probably he means Terra Lynden.

'On my fucking birthday. Knew it'd break my heart.' Tears start rolling down Father's face. Sally-Ann finds his sunglasses. 'She's trying to kill me, sweetheart.'

'That's not gonna happen. You've got the world's best nurse,' Sally-Ann reassures him. 'And Terra's got some real bad karma coming, I bet.'

'Terra, Terra,' Father repeats tragically. 'I gave her *everything*. Goddamn bitch in heat. Think I wanted that? Over and over, I give myself. Can't help it. I'm too damn *loving* …'

Sally-Ann has never been in love. Even before the Temple, it always seemed like more trouble than it was worth: all that time Evie used to spend in front of the mirror, making herself pretty for pimply boys; how nasty and depressed she was the summer after she split up with the French fiancé she'd barely told them anything about; the weird letters she used to send their parents after first getting together with Father — *Jim this*, and *Jim that*, and even saying what good sex she was having and what good friends with Mother Rosaline she was. Sally-Ann used to sneak peeks at those letters with Vicky, laughing about Evie's nutty new church, but when Vicky moved east for college and got married to some guy, Richard Levin, mostly Sally-Ann just noticed how neurotic Mom suddenly was about boys. One time, before Sally-Ann went to a Country Joe gig with her friend Glen — just a gig and just a friend — Mom hugged her and asked, '*You'll tell me if you ever decide to have sex, won't you?*' Sally-Ann didn't want to be like Evie with all her secrets, and she appreciated that Mom wasn't expecting her to wait for some marriage that probably wouldn't last. So she told a year later when she did it with her friend Dave, but anyway, Mom still cried, and Sally-Ann couldn't see the point of upsetting Mom over something so stupid as boys again.

'That whore, y'know, she kept asking me to impregnate her. I kept telling her: Terra honey, I'm not bringing any more children into this world. Take them outta this world, that's kinder. But she was a bourgeois slut. Rich white lawyer daddy. Can't change 'em …'

Secretly, Sally-Ann and Elly have a dream of having a baby together. It started as a joke but somehow turned into more: how they'd build their own cabin and adopt a Guyanese baby from one of the villages. Only, Sally-Ann doesn't know how she'll ever get permission to move out of West House — or 'White House', as Elly calls it.

'Never had to change you, sweet Sally-Ann,' Father croaks. 'I trust you. Can't trust nobody in this life, but I trust *you*. Never had to sacrifice my body to you to keep you loyal.'

Sally-Ann wishes this were true. Except there *was* that one time, way back when she first joined the Temple, when she must've sent out signals or else he wouldn't have done it. She was still living with Evie then. Evie never mentioned it, which Sally-Ann understood was her way of forgiving her. She guesses forgetting it ever happened is Father's way.

'Give me a l'il something, hm?' He reaches for Sally-Ann's wrist, his morphine-weak hand sticking to her like something amphibious.

'You know the drill, Father.' Sally-Ann smiles, or tries to. 'First you have to eat.'

'Terra knows too much. Knows our radio codes, knows where our money is …' Father resumes as Sally-Ann slices an orange for him. When she comes back to his side, he looks at her guilelessly. 'Sally-Ann, sweetheart. Do you like being my nurse?'

'Sure I do. It's the best work.'

'Sally-Ann,' he says again, and his face reminds her of Soul's a bit, the open mouth, the upraised eyes, just visible through his dark glasses, 'Do you love me?'

'You sure ask funny questions today, Father.' Sally-Ann laughs nervously and pats his hand, which is also a bit like Soul's, soft and pudgy. 'Of course I love you. We're family, right?'

5.

Rosaline Jones can't remember the last time she saw her husband's eyes without first having to look through dark glass. But she doesn't need to see Jim's eyes now to know he's high.

'We have been betrayed,' Jim announces to the nine hundred or so people gathered in the pavilion. 'One of our members in the capital has defected. They've stolen official Temple funds and gone to the US Embassy. They're presently revealing *everything they know* to enemy agents.'

The uproar is immediate. Rosaline watches Jim lean back, a slight curve of satisfaction to his lips, buffeted by cries for the traitor's blood, or at least their identity.

'*Roger Luce!*' someone accuses, and abuses rain upon poor Danny, until he rises.

'If it's my brother, I'll kill him,' he volunteers, tears in his eyes.

'Thank you, Danny, for your commitment.' Jim waves him down. 'People, this is not a time for speculation. For your safety, I cannot disclose the traitor's identity tonight. What I can tell you: this traitor was a longtime member; *trusted*; knows a great deal about our finances, our security arrangements. They will, *without a doubt*, bring scrutiny and persecution upon us, of a magnitude we've never seen before. Attack is imminent.'

Jim isn't slurring or jabbering. His voice is a goldilocks-just-right cocktail of command and sensitivity. If Rosaline didn't know better — didn't know about last night's crisis in the radio shed, about him strangling Mona until the boys pulled him off her, about him clutching his heart and demanding morphine — she'd almost believe him saner than herself.

'We have an important decision to make, people. At any moment, our enemies will be coming through that jungle with their weapons, and we know, sure as we know they're coming, they ain't gonna show us no mercy. Cause the lives of people like us don't mean nothing to them.' Jim pauses for the inevitable cries of outrage, despair. 'Proud, black socialists. We're just trash for the burning. Ain't a matter of *if,* but *when.*'

Rosaline knows where this is going. She doesn't know, but she believes, *has to believe* it's just words. She looks down at the cauliflower-whites of her knuckles, remembering the time, decades ago, when Jim threatened to kill himself if he ever saw her praying. Well, here she is praying now, right under his nose.

'There's only one solution I can see, and I'm gonna call for dissenting opinions, but I've looked at this from every angle; I've *agonized* with searching for another way we can all get the peace we deserve. There's only one solution, and that's revolutionary suicide.'

Nine hundred, reacting: it's a strangely dull sound, like a massive beating of wings. Rosaline wishes she could unhear the words; unsee the certainty on Jim's face; turn the clock back to a time when it would've shocked her more, hearing him talk this way. '*This is bullshit!*' Martin Luther looks ready to jump onstage and throttle Jim. '*Fucking bullshit!*'

But Jim just smiles equably.

'I hear some dissenters. Martin Luther, I heard that. It's alright, I don't mind some dissent. Show yourselves.'

Most of the young people, all four of her boys included. Rosaline stands with them and feels the numbers rise at her back: mothers with children, mid-lifers, seniors. She'd like to think there's strength in the number of them. Only Jim seems more pleased than anything to see them all.

'I see many freethinkers here tonight, and it don't surprise me one bit. You're a free people. You take your destinies into your own hands. Nobody can tell you what to do with your lives, not even your leader, who knows you better than you know yourself; who's been your best friend and father; who's crucified himself every day trying to make a better life for you … I can't tell you what to do. Your freedom is too precious to me. I'll die a thousand deaths before I see a single one of you robbed of your freedom.' Jim rubs his lips together. 'Now, y'all don't believe in revolutionary suicide. Alright. I've turned this over in my mind, but I'm ready to have my mind changed. You got another solution? I wanna hear it.'

Russia! Cuba! Self-defense! The people yell their alternatives, and Jim cocks his head.

'… Self-defense. Who's for self-defense? Sister Eunice?'

At Jim's invitation, Eunice Mosley steps forward, solid-thighed in her tight jeans and work boots. 'I'll talk about self-defense, but first I wanna say, I don't think *any* of us should have to die because of some weak-ass traitor who can't hack living in socialism!'

The cheers seem loud enough to rip Rosaline's ears off. Even so, Jim's still cucumber-cool. 'Too right, sister. If life was fair, we wouldn't be discussing it. But fact stands, this weak-ass traitor got the US government onside. How're we gonna defend against *that*?'

'Guerilla warfare,' Eunice answers confidently.

A long discussion ensues of guerrilla tactics. Jim listens as Eunice talks about the strength they'd showed as a community on 'Dwight Night', banding together to guard the settlement against mercenaries; about using the jungle to their advantage; about the Guyanese villagers to whom they've been offering free medical care, forming safe houses among them; about their people outside Jonestown, ready to act at any moment. 'We don't have to be a sitting duck,' Eunice declares. 'We're socialists, and the socialist uprising is everywhere. We're more united than our enemies.'

'Hmm … But let me ask, sister: what does it mean to be united, when we got so many babies and seniors? What can they contribute to the uprising, without being a burden? Seems to me, we got a minority who can fight, and a majority who *can't*.'

'I c-can't fight,' rasps Liesl Lynden, hollow-cheeked from her stage-four lung cancer. 'But if there's some way I can help the struggle to go on without me, dead or alive, I'll do it.'

'We can take care of each other,' says Cornelia Fitch, another senior. 'And the babies.'

Just as Rosaline is about to add her voice to the chorus, she feels Phil Sorensen's hand on her shoulder. '*We've got Su-mi on the line in San Francisco. She wants to talk to you.*'

Rosaline had been getting her lungs checked by a specialist in San Francisco last Fall when Su-mi's husband, Dwight, had defected. She wonders now if things would be different if she'd been here instead; if she could've kept Jim from dragging *everybody* into the crisis with him. She'd been shocked to see how many weapons had accumulated in her absence; how many youngsters knew how to use them. Inside the radio shed, Eve and Frida are hunchbacked and headphoned, madly scrawling notes. Mona, neck ringed with bruises, pulls up a seat and hands Rosaline a set of headphones. 'Su-mi? It's Mom here,' Rosaline creaks into the microphone.

'Hi, Mom. Listen, there's no sign of her yet, but we're monitoring the airports, we're monitoring the embassy, we're monitoring the Concerned Relatives.' Su-mi sounds calm, but then, she's always been good at that; even during her divorce from that two-faced Dwight Mueller, Rosaline never saw her shed a tear. 'Don't do anything drastic.'

'Your dad ...' Rosaline begins, sobs clogging her chest. She feels the glisten of eyes, Phil listening at her back. 'Your dad loves you all. He's trying his best for all of us.'

Su-mi's sigh says more than words can. 'I know, Mom. Just ... hang in there, okay? Do your Mom-thing, comfort people. Don't get too emotional.'

'Okay.' Rosaline breathes deep; how is it that children wind up telling their parents what to do? 'I love you, sweetie. Want me to put your brothers on?'

As Phil starts out to fetch the boys, Eve slips off her headset. 'Oh, Phil. Can you find Meyer too? Joya needs him.'

It's a moment before Rosaline realizes why Eve's words sound so odd. *A question, not an order.* But Eve is quick to move her gaze from Phil to Rosaline. 'The Greeting Party has gone to meet Lenny Lynden's flight. He'll be on tomorrow's boat to the interior.'

Sending for Lenny was one of the first orders of business, when they heard his wife had flown the coop. Rosaline nods. 'It'll be a comfort for Liesl to have him here.'

Eve gathers up her notes, makes way for Phil as he comes back in with Meyer and the boys. Meyer starts blubbering to Joya. Jimmy Jr. fits on his headset and tells Su-mi, 'It was nice knowing you, sis,' and even if it's just a young man's bravado, it gets Rosaline teary all over again. Mona, with a panicked expression, leads her to the sofa, fills a glass of water.

'Father needs you to stay strong,' Mona coos. 'The mothers need your example.'

Looking at Mona's necklace of bruises, her bugged hazel eyes, Rosaline wonders what this girl could possibly care about motherhood. Yet, as she raises the glass to her lips, her glance snags on Eve: talking low in the corner with Phil, her cheeks almost rosy.

'They're killing us. They're killing their brothers and sisters,' Antonia Bud weeps, stroking the head of her young son, Ignatius. 'Every lie they tell. It's killing us.'

Onstage, Meyer is laboriously reading out a report, undeniably negative, on the progress of their Russian classes. Under the bright lights, only Jim looks alert. *Words, just words.*

'Words can't kill us.' Rosaline squeezes Antonia's rope-veined hand. 'Words can't kill *this boy*. He's so full of life; you've given him a good life, and we're gonna keep fighting—'

'*He looks so peaceful*,' Antonia sobs. 'I wish they were never born.'

Rosaline doesn't know if she means the huddle of weary kids around them — ranging in age from Ignatius, eight, to Elly, twenty-one — or the treacherous grown ones back in the States. 'You raised them beautifully. No matter what, no one can say you didn't give them your best. Someday they'll understand that, and thank—'

'*Spasibo*, Comrade Meyer!' Jim interjects, uncrossing and recrossing his arms. '*Spasibo* — means "thank you", for all you who don't know, and seems that's most of you. Most, seems you don't think you need Russian lessons to up and move to the Soviet Union. What, you think they're gonna welcome with open arms a bunch of Americans who can't even speak a word of Russian? You think they're gonna take us seriously as socialists?'

There's a stirring among the people, but it's weaker than it would've been, a couple hours ago. Still, like a spring dandelion, one of their young fieldworkers rises to the floor.

'I'm grateful for the Russian lessons, Father,' says the girl, strikingly beautiful, though her doe eyes are raccooned with sleeplessness. 'Sometimes I find it hard to concentrate after working in the sun all day, but I believe in socialism, and I believe the Soviet Union will welcome us as socialists, if they see how hard we can work; if they see what we've built—'

Jim's sunglasses flash as he smiles down at the girl.

'I know you work hard, Yolanda. I'm sure they *would* welcome a young, able-bodied sister like you. But, ah, what about your grandma there? You think they'll have a place for her to grow her zinnias in Siberia? You think she's gonna have Dr. Katz personally coming by her cottage for her weekly checkup?' Jim heaves a sigh, droops his head. 'Someone's always gonna be left behind. That's the point we keep coming back to. No matter where we go, no matter how many times we go over it, someone's always gonna suffer. Cause no place in the world compares to this piece of paradise we've carved for ourselves outta the jungle.'

It's that nightmare time of night when the lights have a hospital quality, bugs flinging themselves at bodies too tired to shoo them away. Even so, there's authority to that word: *paradise.*

'Talks I've been having with the Soviet Embassy, ain't so encouraging. *Comrade Jones*, they tell me. *We can set you up. Wife, kids. Put you in a nice country house by the Red Sea. But you got too many people …* My wife there's shaking her head. She knows that ain't our way. Right, Ro'?'

'Th-that's right.' It's true, Rosaline did shake her head, though mostly because she's never heard a thing about any country house. Spine twinging, she hobbles to his side. 'I know you'd never turn your back on your people, Jim.'

'You got something to say to the people, Ro'?' Jim caresses the whorl of baby-fine hairs at her nape.

Whatever she says, it must be couched in sweetness. She forces herself to smile through the caress.

'I wanna say … it hasn't been easy for us. We've attracted a lotta harassment over the years. My husband has never been … *conventional.* Never hidden his beliefs, and that's earned him his share of enemies. Sometimes I wonder …' The words rise to her throat like saccharine vomit. 'I wonder if I've been selfish, clinging to Jim's love, Jim's leadership. I wonder, maybe, if he did go to Russia, someplace our enemies can't reach him, maybe we could make do here for a little whiles. Maybe, y'know, with less scrutiny—'

It's a small thing, but it's there: an immediate tightening of the hand on her nape, a twitch in the smile by her ear. Small, but enough to make her aware of Eve, leaning against the radio shed with folded arms, her face a locked safe.

'Listen to my *good wife*,' Jim takes advantage of the falter in her speech to intone. 'She don't know how *selfless* she is.'

And if there was a glimmer of hope in the crowd before, it's extinguished by the sight of them: her pale, damp, and rumpled as a used tissue; him golden, full-faced, supporting her weight.

'Mother knows you won't never find a love like mine, leadership like mine. You'll never find a father like me. Ain't selfish, Mother clinging to what she knows is true, hmm?'

Tears plop from Rosaline's eyes like jungle rain. Antonia Bud rises, hugging Ignatius.

'We don't care about Russia, Father! We just want *peace*.'

The door to the radio shed creaks open. Phil strides out with a tape recorder, nods at Jim, who zeroes his gaze on Antonia.

'Sister, thank you for coming forward. Would you care to tell the world your reasons for taking this final stand …?'

It's dawn by the time the tape recorder is switched off, the people having been granted the good news that they won't have to die just yet; the traitor has been spied in Miami.

'We sleep 'til noon today,' Jim announces benevolently. 'Sunday — day of rest.'

Clarisse Luce jogs past Rosaline with a look of intense concentration, her bump seemingly bigger than a couple days ago. 'Clarisse, don't run!' Danny calls ineffectually; then, in an aggrieved tone, to his stepmother, Juanita, 'Can you tell her not to run with the baby?'

'Girl, don't run!' Juanita hollers. When Clarisse fails to obey, Juanita grumbles to her friend Corazon, 'Girl's gonna run if she wants to.'

Jim steps offstage, followed by Phil with the tape recorder, and then by Eve.

'See? It's Elly-phant!' Sally-Ann Burne giggles over her sketchpad with Elly Bud and Yolanda, that pretty fieldworker. Yolanda leans forward, then rears back laughing, shaking her curls.

Jim eyes Yolanda, says something to Eve. She stiffens, nods.

Smirking, Jim shambles inside the radio shed. Phil and Eve stare at each other for a moment, faces flushed. Then they drop their gazes, stalk in opposite directions.

'Mom, want us to walk you to your cottage?'

Rosaline wrests her gaze from whatever drama is unfolding between Eve and Phil, and turns to Jin-sun. He looks like he's aged ten years in one night, but his eyes are wide, solicitous. Carrie yawns into the crown of Bam's head.

'Don't worry about me, sweetie.' Rosaline kisses all three of them. 'Make sure your parents get some sleep, baby boy.'

As the young family shuffles out of the pavilion, Rosaline watches Eve issuing commands to Yolanda. 'If you can't find any orchids, cut some zinnias. Bring them straight to West House.' Yolanda nods and Eve waves her away, marches toward the Education Tent.

Though she knows her aching bones will hate her for it, Rosaline follows. Slowly. Inside, Eve is spraying blackboards with a bottle of vinegar like her life depends on it. She stops when she sees Rosaline. 'Yes?'

In response, a new ball of pain fires up Rosaline's spine. With a strangled cry, Rosaline flaps her hands, wincingly sits herself on the nearest wooden bench. She can't speak for at least a minute, by which point Eve is standing over her, clutching her spray-bottle.

'I'll sit too,' Eve says helpfully, and does.

'I'm sorry,' Rosaline says, and hates herself for apologizing where she shouldn't.

'You're tired.'

'It's *tiring*,' Rosaline admits. Then, because she's too tired to skirt around the issue, 'It's not right. *He* isn't right. Hasn't been in a long time, Eve.'

Except for a blink, in profile, Eve doesn't react.

'*Please*,' Rosaline insists. 'You can help him.'

Eve looks at Rosaline impassively. 'Really, Rose, I don't know what you're talking about. You shouldn't get so worked up. It's not healthy.'

'*He* isn't healthy!' Rosaline fires back. 'He's ...' Unable to find the words, she sighs. 'Soul, he deserves to live a long and happy life, dontcha think?'

'Of course he does,' Eve responds coolly. 'Are you suggesting Soul isn't a happy boy?'

'You *know* that isn't what I mean.' Rosaline dashes a blood-hot tear. '*Jim*, I mean. He's not in a position … so many lives in his hands …'

Eve gets up abruptly. Walks to the blackboard and surveys it with crossed arms.

'I meant what I said onstage,' Rosaline tells the dark knot of hair, the sharp shoulders. 'If there's somewhere Jim could go for a little whiles and get better, or, well, live out the rest of his days in peace … we could keep things going, I think.'

'*We?*' Eve says with a pitiless jerk of her eyebrow, which brings Rosaline back to her own pain-wracked body.

'Well, a committee of us,' Rosaline downplays. 'You. Phil, of course …'

Eve turns her back again. 'No,' she says quietly. 'That's not an option.'

'Eve, please—'

Over her shoulder, Eve flashes a look of undiluted contempt. Resumes cleaning.

Not crying seems like such an impossible ambition, Rosaline concentrates on crying silently. And, aside from a few sniffles, she succeeds. Once she's done with the blackboard, Eve puts away her spray-bottle and looks at Rosaline patiently. 'You're tired,' she repeats.

'Aren't *you?*'

Eve bats her eyes and fetches some tissues. 'No, not really.' She looks away as Rosaline blows her nose. 'I guess I'll rest when my time comes.'

'It doesn't have to be like that. You're young, still. You could have a whole 'nother life without—'

'I really think you should stop talking now.'

Eve's eyes, though shinily alert, have a shuttered look. That earlier rosiness is gone, cheeks as pale as a corpse's. '*Your poor parents*,' Rosaline says, out of nowhere.

'I'm sorry.' Eve looks down. 'But that's just the way it is.'

Rosaline shudders, hiccups. In a fury of self-righteousness, she raises herself, attempts a couple of angry steps, but the pain is too much; her body wasn't built for all-nighters.

'Rose. You're struggling,' Eve says soothingly. 'Let me—'

'*No*,' Rosaline says firmly. '*Thank you.*'

'Rose.' Eve comes to her side. 'It's the least I can do.'

Years ago, there'd been a day when Eve had caught her struggling with some boxes in the Temple parking lot. The failure of Rosaline's body — it's always the elephant in the room with Eve. It strikes her that she doesn't like or understand Eve any better than she did that day.

'The least you can do. *Maybe* ...' Rosaline sighs, looking at the pale hand hovering before her. '... But don't you want to do more?'

6.

If it weren't for them being such good, intelligent people, Evelyn would probably smirk at the ironies her parents keep spouting. Like her mother, yawning indulgently over a late breakfast of rice, sweet potato, and pineapple, their final morning in Jonestown. 'Really, I think we're going to have to invest in one of those "rainforest relaxation" tapes! I never sleep so well in Berkeley.'

'You could try unhooking the phone,' Evelyn suggests; her mother's attachment to the phone is legendary, the one thing — other than Evelyn — that she has in common with Jim.

'Those relaxation tapes are cool,' Sally-Ann enthuses, spearing a hunk of pineapple. 'But I bet we could make one ourselves. It'd be way more authentic.'

'I'm sure it will be "authentic", if you girls are making it,' their father says. 'But "relaxing" … I have my doubts.'

'*Ee-ee*,' Sally-Ann chirps. '*Brep-brep! Krahk-krahk! Bzzz … CAW!*'

They laugh. Soul, who's been placidly following one of the dogs around, trying to touch the tip of its tail without disturbing it, beams at the commotion and, after considering for a moment, toddles over. '*Silly* Auntie,' he chastises Sally-Ann.

'Geez, kid, when did you get so condescending?' Sally-Ann laughs and pinches Soul's pudgy brown arm. Soul is an undeniably white child, but he tans easily, like Jim. 'C'mere, I need to tell you something.' She lifts one of his hat flaps. '*Ca … CAW!*'

Soul giggles. Then, at the top of his tiny lungs, shrieks, '*Ca-CAW!*'

'Whoa-oh.' Phil approaches with a nervous look. 'What have I walked into?'

'"Rainforest Relaxation",' their father answers calmly. 'A Burne family original.'

'… Right.' Phil looks from Evelyn to her mother and Sally-Ann, who are cawing at each other as Soul rushes around the table, flapping like a bird.

'You've known us an entire five days now, Phil,' Evelyn's mother pipes up. 'It's time you stopped looking so surprised to see us acting like a bunch of crazy coconuts.'

'I guess Evelyn didn't prepare me.' Phil smiles in her general direction, without meeting her eye. *Evelyn*, not *Evie*. He clearly hasn't forgiven her for turning Yolanda over to Jim.

'Oh, Evie may look perfectly sweet and sane,' her mother says. 'But she's one of us.'

'*One of us, one of us!*' Sally-Ann chants.

Evelyn feels herself blush. She avoids looking at Phil, but makes room for him at the table. He stays where he is. 'How're you liking that pineapple, Tom?' he asks her father.

'He *loves* it,' her mother responds. 'Tom's got the palate of a hummingbird.'

'Best I ever tasted,' her father confirms.

'We'd give you some to smuggle home, but I'm afraid we can't afford to piss off Customs,' Phil says good-naturedly. 'If you want more, though; more of *anything*—'

'Mr. Sorensen! I refuse to let you make a glutton of my husband,' her mother cries in mock-outrage. '*No*. We can't spend all morning stuffing our faces. It's our last chance to be obnoxious American tourists, after all.'

Phil laughs. 'Got any film left?'

'I've got precisely half a roll, and I'm *determined* to get a clear shot of Antonio.'

Antonio is the resident anteater, a surprisingly evasive fellow. Phil laughs again, and Evelyn can't help comparing the easy warmth of it with Jim's high-pitched cackle.

Evelyn is disappointed when Phil doesn't accompany them on their last walk around the settlement; even more disappointed by her disappointment; even more disappointed, still, when Jim appears and makes a great show of greeting every person they meet, bombarding her father with agricultural projections, taking Soul to the playground and cavorting with exaggerated hoots, claps, and cackles. At midday, they return to the pavilion to wait for their ride to the airstrip, and Phil is there with a packed bag, but so, too, is Mona, who will travel on to Panama to move around some of their finances, and so, too, is Rosaline, whose face is a silent reproach, and Martin Luther and Jimmy Jr. with her parents' luggage. Conversation doesn't flow so much as crackle; sentences like radio noise. '... *I hope you'll tell the world about us,*' she hears Jim tell her father, faux-humble, but not the actual farewells they exchange before Jim retreats. 'Oh, you haven't seen the last of us!' she hears her mother cry, flinging her arms around Rosaline, though she wasn't even aware they were friends. Her father presses her hand and says, 'No reason we can't make this trip an annual thing,' and Sally-Ann loudly interjects, 'Vicky and Richard the Second, too! If she's not too much of a *New Yawka* for us guys ...' (Vicky is on her second marriage, to a second Richard, and working at a publishing house in Manhattan.) At the same time, Soul is demanding attention with the insistence of a fire alarm, *Phil-Mom, Phil-Mom,* until Evelyn picks him up and asks, '*What,* Solomon Tom?'

Soul points to the red flatbed truck driving up. 'I spy.'

Rosaline makes herself scarce. Martin Luther and Jimmy Jr. race each other to the truck and throw in the luggage, give Mona a leg-up. Phil tells her parents, 'Here's our limo.'

Hugs are exchanged. Soul's face is plastered with kisses, his pug nose pinched. '*Don't grow up too fast, Soul-baby,*' Evelyn's mother sighs, and Evelyn finds herself wishing for the same: no growth, no passing time, just the world exactly as it is now, down to the blades of grass beneath her feet.

Phil, on the outskirts, seems unsure how to proceed, until Sally-Ann grins and loops her lanky arms around him. 'Hey, Phil. Don't let these geezers get lost in Georgetown, okay?'

'I'll look after them like they're my own,' Phil replies gallantly and turns to Soul. 'Little King Solomon. Will you be good to all the doggies while I'm gone?'

'... Yeah.' Soul hides his face in Evelyn's neck in a sudden daze of shyness.

'Good man. That's my little Man of Peace. *Shalom,* Sunny.' Phil peaces Soul, then pulls the brim of his hat low over his face like a beak, kisses the top of it. In the same sweep of movement, almost incidental, he curves an arm around Evelyn's back, grazes her cheek.

'Bye, Evelyn.'

Soul giggles. Evelyn's insides writhe, a sweet nest of vipers.

She watches Phil jump onto the truck — broad shoulders, tapered waist, perfect ass — and instantly start up a conversation with Mona. Her parents turn to her with broken smiles, and there are more hugs, jokes from Sally-Ann, which she doesn't hear but knows to laugh at. *I will never see my parents again*, she thinks, and accepts the thought, as she accepts that she will die someday, probably soon. They board, and she gives Soul to Sally-Ann, who has more energy to run alongside the truck, to shout and wave, to pretend the parting isn't what it is.

As soon as the truck is out of sight, Soul throws a tantrum.

'I'll take him to the nursery,' Sally-Ann says.

'*I'll* take him,' Evelyn snaps. 'Go to work.'

Sally-Ann looks startled, but does as she's told; saddles Evelyn with the red-faced, recalcitrant tangle of limbs that is her child, her child by Jim.

Though the nursery is closer, and Soul is heavy, Evelyn chooses to take him back to the cabin instead. The cabin is empty, thank God. 'That's *enough*, Solomon Tom,' she scolds him, setting his thrashing little body on the lower bunk, plonking down beside him. She feels an unexpected tranquility, as if nothing in the world could possibly harm her, ever. Then, like a disemboweling, the feelings come tumbling out — raw, loud, ugly.

Soul stops crying; looks at her in awe. '… Little Mother?'

She is bitchy that day. Not just in a routine, getting-things-done way, but in a way that makes her ashamed. Provoking Polly, her pretty young teaching assistant, to tears for doing a poor job with the worksheets. Taking Meyer to task for the slow progress of his Russian classes, until his glasses are foggy, his bald head bowed in defeat. In the haze of late afternoon, catching sight of Lenny Lynden among the newest boatload of people clumped outside the Supply Tent, she makes no effort to wipe the *ugh!* from her face.

That evening, she and Frida dine alone with Jim in the cabin, spend slow hours going over the new radio codes, before giving him the day's infraction report, to be referenced during that night's confrontation. The report is unusually long. Jim is amused by this.

Jim is amused, too, when, seeing Frida touching her pimply jaw, Evelyn remarks snidely, 'The pigs may not be breeding, but the pustules are.'

But soon after, Jim dismisses Frida with an indulgent smirk, a poorly concealed nod in Evelyn's direction. 'Honey, go check in on the Clearing Committee, will you? I've got things to discuss with Evelyn.'

Evelyn starts clearing the coffee cups. Obediently, Frida rises from her rattan stool.

'Alright, Father. See you tonight.'

Evelyn keeps tidying, even after Frida leaves. There are always things to be tidied, living with a man, a toddler, and three women in their twenties. She takes up the vase of withered orchids from Jim's nightstand. 'I like those,' Jim protests, shaking some pills from a bottle on his bookshelf with a sound like one of Soul's silly rattling toys. Evelyn dumps them in the trash, water and all.

'You're not being objective,' Jim gripes. 'Do I need to get you to write yourself up?'

'If you think it's necessary.' Evelyn plonks the empty vase on the nightstand.

'That ain't what I asked.' He slouches over to the mirror, puckers his lips and squares his jaw. '*I* don't need it. *I* can read your thoughts without seeing 'em on paper.'

'Well, then, if you ask me, it sounds like a waste of time and resources. We go through enough paper as it is.' She plucks a sock from the floor, makes for the doorway.

'Bitch. Look at me when I'm talking.'

Evelyn stops. Leans against the wall with folded arms. Jim keeps peering at his reflection. 'What do you think? Time for another haircut?'

'Hardly.'

'I want to try another rotation with our PR team,' he changes subject. 'Two weeks here, two there. People stay too long, they get soft. That's where we failed with Scarlett.'

It's easier for him to speak about Terra when he uses her alias.

'I agree. We need more structure.'

319

'Write me up a proposed schedule for the next two months, and don't waste no paper doing it.' Jim roams over to the bed, sits, bounces. Stretches out. His bare feet fidget. 'And I want you over there later this week. Soon as Mona gets back here with Roger.'

'Fine.'

'You can work with Phil.' He rolls onto his side. 'Fuck him, too, if you want.'

Evelyn doesn't flinch. Jim continues pragmatically: 'Phil's a good socialist. And he's got a pretty big dick. Not as big as mine, mind, but sizeable.'

'Phil is a mannequin,' Evelyn rejoins. 'Looking into his eyes is like looking at glass.'

'If you say so, honey … Do what you want. I know you can't live without me.'

'I don't mind dying.'

'You bitch.' He laughs. 'C'mere then and let me blow your brains out.'

Evelyn doesn't particularly feel like playing games with Jim, but when she sees him fumbling in his nightstand for his .38, she comes to roost on the edge of the bed. He waves the pistol at her. She looks skeptical.

'Take it,' he says.

'I have my own. Thank you.'

'Take it,' he repeats. 'Show me what you can do with it.'

She takes it. Feels the weight of it. Checks that it's loaded, then points it at her temple.

'Close your eyes,' he says. She does, and there's nothing but a whisper of calm; the disorder of her life, reduced to a single, fulfillable order. After a while, Jim says, 'Open up.'

She opens her eyes. Sees his pinprick pupils needling her through his dark glasses, and the old questions stir: *do you love me? Have I given your life meaning? Would you die for me?*

'Good.' Jim nods. 'Other way, now.'

She knows what he means. Scooting closer, she leans across his lap and presses the muzzle to his own dark temple. He closes his eyes.

Rosaline would want her to pull the trigger. Rosaline wouldn't have the courage to pull the trigger herself. Evelyn is not Rosaline. *Open your eyes*, she thinks, and he does.

'Good.' He smiles. 'Good soldier.'

She hands him the pistol. He returns it to the nightstand, pats her bony hip. She rises. Swinging his legs off the bed, Jim pulls her back to him by the belt of her rather ugly drawstring trousers. 'That's how I want it, when my time comes,' he murmurs. 'My right hand.'

Evelyn watches him pick up her hand.

'When they come for me. Cause they're comin' …' His black head tilts from side to side, as if listening for hooves, trumpets. 'I die with a bang. There'll be nothin' left for you to live for. Promise me.'

Whichever way she winds her mind, it is destined to come full circle, to snag on the same small comforts. The dog-whistle of nothingness. The shelf of household poisons. The ghost of herself, reflected in his gaze. There is only one answer, and she knows it.

'I promise.'

Eve of Destruction

1.

There are mornings, lying in bed in his parents' mansion in the Berkeley Hills, when Lenny Lynden dreams Jim Jones's voice in his ear, Jim Jones's hand reaching under the covers and taking out his cock. Jim tugging at him good-naturedly, talking all the while, until he wakes with damp sheets and a stickiness in his shorts. So ashamed he could die, or maybe kill.

These are the mornings Lenny swims to forget. In the kidney-shaped pool, back and forth, holding his breath, skimming the floor. Swims until the stickiness dissolves and there's nothing but stinging blue, a nullifying coldness. A woman's drowned voice, calling his name.

'*Mister Lenny!*'

Lenny doesn't respond to the woman right away. The older Lenny gets, the slower he is to respond to voices, partly because he has more trouble telling the real ones from the imaginary ones. He stays underwater until his lungs start to burn.

'*Mister Lenny!*'

The woman's legs are sturdy in white sneakers, a brown skirt to the knees. Danila doesn't wear a uniform like the maids of Lenny's childhood — this was his mother's doing, after she became a socialist but before she left his father. Lenny blinks at Danila's white shoes.

'Mister Lenny!' Danila repeats. 'Phone for *you*.'

The early sun coats the water with a slick, dirty scrim of gold. Dust on the surface. Broken brown leaves. A leggy brown bug, propelling itself forward with tiny ripples. Lenny slides his palm under the bug. '… Who's calling?'

It can only be work or the Temple, calling him to do more work. But the longer Lenny can delay this knowledge, the longer he can stay in the pool.

'A lady.' Danila scowls at the bug inching up Lenny's wrist, then fetches his towel from the recliner and brandishes it. Obediently, Lenny sets the bug on dry land.

The phone is shiny and black, like a beetle. Lenny presses it to his left ear while digging the water from his right. 'H'lo?'

'Lenny, a car's coming to take you to the airport,' Su-mi Jones's voice is on the other end, low-pitched and impatient. 'Be ready with your bags in twenty minutes.'

'Airport? You mean I get to go to—?'

'Yeah, Lenny. You're going to the Promised Land.'

Tank tops. Tube socks. Snot rags. Work boots. Fatigues. A clear-plastic rain poncho that makes him look like a jellyfish. Noxzema. Talcum powder. Insect repellent. Flashlight and batteries. A dozen or so other things Lenny wouldn't remember, if it wasn't for the Temple buying them in bulk, divvying them up with instructions to pack in advance, to be ready to leave *at any moment*. He's been waiting almost a year for his moment to come.

Lenny's dream has dried to an off-white patch on his navy bedsheets. *Sorry, Danila.* He makes his bed. He looks at the M.C. Escher picture overhanging his bed: black birds flying in one direction, white birds in the next, black and white birds morphing into an aerial view of black and white fields. Lenny won't miss the picture, or the shelf of outdated encyclopedias, or the study desk with its hard chair and donut-shaped pillow, prescribed to him in the winter of eleventh grade, when he got hemorrhoids from sitting in the hard chair too long. Lenny changes into white jeans, a madras shirt, linen jacket. No time to shave. Not much to be done about his hair, except comb it over the increasingly Dr. Lynden-like expanse of his forehead. Lenny slings his carry-all over his shoulder, makes for the door with his suitcase.

King Henry VIII is dozing on the donut pillow like a fuzzy orange croissant. 'Take care of the old man, King Henry,' Lenny says. King Henry says nothing.

Downstairs, Danila is making breakfast for Dr. Lynden, which means Dr. Lynden must be awake somewhere in the mansion's polished entrails — probably in his office, probably working on his latest book, the one he hopes will win him a Nobel. Lenny isn't in the habit of disturbing Dr. Lynden when he's working on his book. He scratches out a note, grabs an apple from the fruit bowl, mumbles, '*Do svidaniya, Danila,*' and places the note in the apple's place:

Gone to Jonestown.
Peace,
Lenny

Hair still damp, Lenny leaves the mansion without looking back.

2.

There are black people on the flight to JFK, but none Lenny recognizes from the Temple. In the Pan Am lounge, waiting to board for Guyana, there are more black and brown people than whites. Lenny spends some time watching everyone, trying to figure the Temple members from the regular tourists, businessmen, Guyanese going home to their families. He sees some old ladies in their finest church clothes. A teenage girl reading *TigerBeat*. An older guy in sagging chinos and a mod-knit shirt in the style of fifteen years ago, pacing. The guy picks up a discarded banana peel and puts it in the trash. He finds a newspaper in the trash, takes it out and unfolds it, catches Lenny looking. He gives him a cheesy grin. 'Howdy, fellow traveler!'

'Hey.' Lenny doesn't know if the guy recognizes him or is just friendly. He plays along; points at the paper. 'What's new in the world?'

The guy shows Lenny the front page. 'Carter's weak. Ain't news to *me*.' He tosses the paper aside and comes to sit by Lenny. 'It's all lies anyway. They never tell the whole story.'

'Yeah.' Lenny thinks of the newspaper articles last year that drove Jim out of the country, and almost everyone else with him: *Former Temple Members Speak Out*; *Humanitarian of the Year or False Prophet?*; *Peoples Temple Cop's Daughter Calls for Inquiry into Accidental Death*.

The guy holds out his hand. 'Norman Coleman. Friends call me "Norm" … and I say we friends if we flying outta the US of KKK together.'

'Lenny Lynden.'

Norm's shake is over-eager. Close up, Lenny can see his eyes are downturned, at odds with his cheesy grin. His taupe cheeks are flecked with black freckles.

'Yep. I'm flying today. Pan Am to *Guyana*.' From the way Norm swallows and slaps his knees, Lenny can tell he's nervous. 'Renetta and the kids, they bona-fide Guyanans by now. Flew out last *August*. You got a wife, kids, Lenny Landon?'

'Wife. No kids, yet.'

'Mrs. Landon, she'll be wanting some, better don't keep her waiting! Don't *ever* keep your woman waiting.' Norm laughs hectically, darts his eyes around at the women in the area. Then he looks sidelong at Lenny. 'You don't have any kids? Not *any*?'

'No, sir.'

It's come up before, of course, between him and Terra. But it's not an easy thing to get permission for, and anyway, he's always had the sense it'll happen eventually.

'You should get to it, don't wait. My Pauly's seventeen this November! Same age we was when we *made* him.'

Lenny does the math and is dismayed to realize that the chatty fellow in the outmoded shirt is just a couple of years his senior. This happens more and more lately; his old man's colleagues, doctors at the clinic where he works, even stout Danila — all his unexpected peers.

'So what do you do with yourself, Lenny Landon, if you don't have kids?'

'Well … I work as an X-ray technician at—'

'X-rays! Hot damn! That must be a good job? Pays good?'

'It's a pretty good job,' Lenny confirms.

And it would be, if Lenny was anything other than a Lynden. If his old man hadn't been personally acquainted with Albert Einstein back in Princeton in the forties. If his brother wasn't earning six figures a year as a neurosurgeon. If his sister wasn't balancing a biotech research fellowship with motherhood and the kind of home that gets featured in *House & Garden*.

'What do *you* do?' he deflects.

'Used to work at a bowling alley. Maintenance.' Norm's grin droops to match his eyes, then fixes back in place. 'Only, I slipped and threw my back last year? Couldn't walk for a while? Lost my job … but they's been sending me this disability check every month.'

'Oh … Sorry.' Lenny watches Norm's mouth twitch, feeling bad for the guy, but also like his desperation might be contagious. 'So … when did you join the Temple?'

'See, Father Jim healed my ma-in-law of cancer back in, whatwasit, '74? Pulled this red blob right outta her mouth! Smelled like *death* ...' Norm natters on a bit about the healings, how it's too bad he didn't hurt his back before Jim left the US — healing from a different country would be too much to ask, he guesses; how he's been attending on-and-off for a few years, but the women are 'real faithful'. 'I've never been one for Bible-thumping. I'm a real independent thinker, see. Renetta's always telling me, "Norm, you gotta quit questioning every little thing. Have *faith*." But I like to have evidence, that's me. That's what I like when I come to Peoples Temple. You get healed, you get fed, you get flown to Guyana, even!'

Norm lets his enthusiasm fade to a whimsical chuckle, a joggling of his knees and feet. Lenny nods, repeats, '*Guyana*,' smiling. The silence is companionable until it's awkward.

Across the lounge, the teenage girl flicks a page of *TigerBeat*, recrosses her legs. They're nice legs. Lenny notices and so does Norm, and when they notice each other noticing, the forlorn longing on each other's faces, they both look away.

'Yep. I'm really looking forward to seeing my Renetta,' Norm says.

Though Lenny doesn't mean to fall asleep on the plane, he does, head sailing across an ocean of lilac-blue clouds. When he wakes, there are no clouds, just the spiked dark shapes of trees, *jungle*, and some of the churchy old ladies, rows ahead of him, are singing spirituals.

'I can see my house from here!' Lenny's new friend Norm whoops from across the aisle; if he was nervous about flying, the nerves are gone. 'My *new* house!'

Last time Lenny flew overseas was the winter of sophomore year: England, for his sister Beth's wedding. He'd slept on that flight, too. He'd been slapped by the cold as soon as he got off the plane; England in January, everyone's faces pink, mouths fogging.

He's not in England now. The black mass of the jungle confirms this, the sparse lights breaking it up, the hot snag of the wheels on the tarmac.

'*Welcome to Georgetown, Guyana*,' a sexy voice, belonging to a bullet-breasted woman in Pan Am blue, announces. '*Local time is 22:45. Local temperature, 82°F ...*'

The night air is soupy, diesel-scented. Lenny huffs it, feels his head grow pleasantly light. *Guyana.* Legs stiff, as if shackled, he shuffles down the rickety metal stairs, eyes pinballing from the swishing palm trees to the banded fluorescence of the terminal.

It's stuffy inside. Dark skin everywhere. Dark men in uniform, who seem to look through his whiteness like it's translucent. Lenny keeps his eyes averted as he waits for his suitcases, wades through customs … so it takes him longer than it should to notice the cute blonde, flirting with a customs officer nearby.

'Hi, Lenny!' The blonde waves, beams. 'You made it!'

It isn't Terra. It's Dot Luce.

'Hey, Dot.' Lenny checks around for her mother, Joya, who's a scary lady, then hugs Dot swiftly. '… I thought you were Terra.'

For a second, Dot's face looks weird. 'Nope, just me. Dot *Jones.*' She waggles her hand.

'Oh, hey, you married Paolo?'

'Paolo married *me.* I'll tell you all about it, but first I've gotta help these guys.' She gestures at the old ladies. 'If you walk that way though, you'll find Johnny and Donna.'

Lenny walks *that way.* He finds Johnny Bronco and his wife, Donna. Johnny has grown a moustache. Donna has on a batik sundress and a headwrap that almost hides her dolphin forehead. They both hug him, seem so excited to see him that he doesn't ask where Terra is.

Neither does he ask when Dot returns with the other passengers — Norm, the *TigerBeat* girl, the four old ladies, a teenage boy called Irving, a big guy in his early thirties called Bruce — and leads them out to a mud-spattered Temple van. 'Get comfy! It's a *long* drive.'

Sometime well after midnight, the farms and factories give way to flaky colonial buildings, dingy Christmas lights, pumping swirls of reggae. Then oceans of darkness, until they pull up to a massive cream-colored building. 'Here's the halfway house!' Donna announces.

Roger Luce comes out to help with the luggage. Roger is perfumed, dressed in a form-fitting floral shirt and skin-tight off-white pants. As he moves to take Norm's bag, Lenny notices Norm purse his lips fastidiously. 'No, thanks … I got it.'

Roger shrugs, moves on to help one of the old ladies. As soon as Roger's back is turned, Norm points and asks Lenny earnestly, 'He a *fairy?*'

'I … don't think so,' Lenny answers, though Roger's pants make him wonder.

The bags are huddled on the porch when a shiny black car comes purring along the dirt road, windows tinted. Roger strides to the car and gets in. It drives off noiselessly.

Joya Luce — no, 'Mendelssohn' now — opens the front door wide and waves them in.

'Ooh, that night breeze is *divine*! Who wants to sleep on the porch?' When no one answers, she barks a laugh. She still has those chiclet teeth, chipmunk cheeks, but she's got a scarf over her hair and is thinner, deeply tanned. She presses the liverspotted hand of an old lady. 'We've got a full house tonight, sisters, but I've made up some nice soft beds for you in the den!'

Dot turns to the *TigerBeat* girl. 'Daisy, you'll be bunking with me and my baby sisters!'

'And y'all get the basement!' Donna Bronco winks at Lenny, Norm, Bruce, and Irving. 'Nice and cool down there. Lucky *you*.'

Johnny starts moving some bags downstairs, smiling at Donna as he goes. Lenny feels a pang of envy for the married couple.

'But …' he hesitates, not wanting to seem ungrateful. 'Where's Terra?'

'Terra?' Joya scoffs. 'Terra's not *here*.'

'Mom!' Dot looks frantic, then apologetic. 'Sorry, Lenny. Terra is …' She glances at Donna, who swallows, nods solemnly.

'Terra is on a mission, Lenny. I'm sorry.'

'Oh.' The disappointment parches Lenny's lips, numbs his tongue. 'When will she—'

'It's a *mission*, honey. Top secret,' Joya intervenes. She takes a step toward Lenny, squeezes his arm. 'Sorry you didn't get the message. Our radios are under constant surveillance, y'know? But soon as you get to Jonestown—'

'Terra will meet me there?'

Joya looks into his eyes and smiles. '*You'll* love it there, hon. *Everyone* does.'

3.

There's no voice in Lenny's ear that night, no hand reaching into his shorts, just an unrelievable tension, lying awake on the cool rubber mat on the basement's cement floor. Around him, the darkness swarms like something living. He listens to his racing heart, the other guys' snores, and his cock grows hard, soft, hard again.

Lenny touches his cock, and tries to think of Terra, but all he can think of is how long it's been since he last saw her; so long, he'd need a photograph to remember her face.

Lenny thinks instead of his sophomore-year girlfriend, Marianne Glover. Necking with Marianne to 'A Taste of Honey' with all their clothes on, until the revelation of her brown-tipped white breasts. Missing Marianne's breasts during Beth's boring wedding in Cambridge and the subsequent week of touring Europe with his mother. Telling Marianne he loved her as soon as he got back to Davis, and convincing her to spend a weekend with him at the family holiday house in Napa. Having sex with Marianne in the four-poster bed in Napa without a rubber, and afterward Marianne crying, because of course she'd wanted to wait for marriage. Buying a paper bag full of rubbers from the drug store the next day, and convincing Marianne to do it again, and again, until they were seldom together and not doing it …

One of the guys lets out a soft, sizzling fart. Lenny stops touching himself. His eyes water. His throat yearns for water. He pictures vast bodies of water, planets of water, his body absorbing water like a sponge. His bladder prickles.

Lenny feels his way upstairs, trips on a piece of luggage, mistakes the luggage for a body and almost cries out in horror. He stumbles into a room where actual bodies are snoring and bumps against a sofa, causing one of them to moan ghoulishly. Somehow, he finds a bathroom.

In the bathroom, Lenny pees, flushes, washes, cups handfuls of water to his mouth and drinks. He's had several handfuls before he registers the water's brownish hue. Spits.

There's a strip of light under a door down from the bathroom. Lenny goes to it, hoping that someone will hear his footsteps. When nobody does, he knocks softly. He hears voices, radios crackling. Minnie Bellows-Luce opens the door.

'Lenny?' Minnie asks, her face sober. 'Are you lost?'

In the room behind Minnie, Joya and Dot are hunched by the radios, listening. Lenny hears Jim's voice, eloquent even through the crackling: *Tell the world your reasons for taking this final stand.* Minnie notices him noticing and shuts the door.

'I ...' Lenny feels stupid, embarrassed of his stupidity. 'I drank tapwater. Is that bad?'

'*Oh*, Lenny.'

How many times have women said his name like that? How many women? It must be a few, because he finds it oddly reassuring. Minnie sighs and grabs his arm.

'It's not good, I'll say that ...' She steers him past some curtains, touched with grayish light: sun or moon? Flicks a switch, unbolts a door, and ushers him onto the porch. '*Sit.* I'll be right back.'

Lenny sits on the rattan recliner. Watches Minnie walk back into the dim glow of the house: white dress, dark legs, yellowish soles of her feet. In the deep purple sky, black shapes flit. His stomach flits.

When Minnie returns, her arms are full: blanket, bucket, lighter, bottle of rum. She hands him the blanket, sets down the rum in the bucket. Unpins a veil of white netting from somewhere above his head and lets it fall.

Beyond the veil, she lights some candles. 'For the mosquitoes,' she says, crossing over.

Lenny just stares. Minnie is very beautiful.

'You know, we usually only break out this stuff for the diplomats.' She perches on the edge of his recliner and uncaps the rum. 'Oh, *shoot.* I forgot to get a glass.'

'I don't mind.'

She smiles. 'The alcohol should kill off any bugs in your tummy … hopefully.'

He accepts the bottle. Swigs. Rum dribbles from his chin to his chest hair, and he remembers that he's only in his underwear. Quickly, he pulls the blanket up.

Minnie laughs. 'Enjoying your medicine?'

Already, Lenny feels dizzy. Then again, it may be the tapwater. Or jetlag. Or Minnie. He shrugs. 'Want some?'

'No, thanks.' She gestures politely. 'It's *good*, though. Demerara rum. They make it with sugar cane, along the banks of the Demerara …'

'*Demerara*,' Lenny repeats, touching the bronze lettering on the label. He raises it to his lips once more. It tastes good, he decides, like burnt sugar.

'Oh …' Minnie hesitates as he offers it again. 'Oh, *fine*.'

He watches her long lashes lower, casting shadows on the tired puffs beneath her eyes. Her full lips encircling the bottle. Her long neck rippling as she swallows. *Beautiful.*

Minnie dabs her mouth. 'Have you seen my folks lately?'

'Oh … yeah.' Burning, he bunches the blanket strategically over his groin, tries to think of something to say about Minnie's folks, still in the US. 'All the time. They're proud of you.'

'Prouder of Alice, though.'

She may be joking, yet he can't be sure. Though he's never considered it before, it's possible Minnie feels the same about her younger, law-graduate sister as he does about Beth.

'Proud of you both,' Lenny says, then remembers Ursa, the white sister. 'Proud of you all.'

Minnie nods, grateful for the correction. 'Ursa loves Jonestown. *Loves* the animals.' She passes the bottle. 'She's been working in the piggery. But Antonio Anteater is her favorite.'

Lenny laughs, drinks. 'Antonio.'

'There's no place in the world like it, Lenny. Everyone has a purpose, regardless of their handicaps. It's a society completely free of prejudice.'

Of course, Lenny has heard all this before. In Terra's rare letters home. His mother's letters. Phil Sorensen's films. But for Minnie, he nods like he's hearing it for the first time.

'It's the best place in the world. I'd give anything to keep it going.

I'd give my *life*.'

She looks sad. Lenny wonders if he should kiss her; wonders if Terra would mind.

He leans forward, blanket slipping a little past his chest hair. But Minnie just looks to the side. 'Uh-oh. We've got a friend.'

Lenny looks, too: a cockroach, scuttling into the empty bucket. It has orange stripes, like a tiger. '*Don't kill it*,' he urges, awestruck.

Minnie throws back her head and laughs. 'Well, I wasn't planning on it, Lenny.' She laughs some more; he didn't know he was so funny. '*Oh*, Lenny.'

Then she takes the bottle from him and swigs. He inches closer.

They're sitting *very* close, taking turns on the bottle, when a thump sounds somewhere beyond the porch. 'What the …?' Lenny looks vaguely in the direction of the thump; his head feels heavy and lit up as a chandelier. Minnie stifles a snort. Minnie is *drunk*.

So's Roger, it seems, when he shambles onto the porch a moment later, blond hair tousled, cheeks red. He takes in the rum bottle, his wife's shiny face, Lenny's shirtlessness.

'Hey, Roger,' Lenny says, trying hard not to giggle.

'Hi, Roger,' Minnie echoes, failing.

Roger takes a few steps. Spies the cockroach in the bucket. 'That's fucking *disgusting*.'

'Don't … don't kill it,' Lenny objects weakly.

Minnie sputters helplessly. Roger sneers, shakes his head, and strides indoors.

'Oh, *shit*,' Minnie says, wiping her laughing eyes.

Lenny laughs, too, joyfully lets slip what he's always thought: 'Roger's kind of a dick.'

'Oh … he's not so bad,' Minnie demurs, then sobers. 'He's had a hard time with what happened with his dad, that's all.'

'Oh … yeah.' Lenny feels a shockwave of profound awfulness, remembering Gene Luce, found in two pieces on some railway tracks. 'Poor Gene.'

'*Poor Gene*.' Minnie sighs. 'Roger says he's glad he's dead. But it's still his *dad*, you know? Even if he was a traitor.'

'Yeah.' Lenny wouldn't normally ask, but with Minnie, it feels okay. 'Do you really think it's "bad karma"? How Gene wrote that letter saying he was leaving, then gets hit by a train the same week?'

'If there is such a thing as karma, there are people way more deserving of a moving train than Brother Gene.' Minnie scowls. 'Robert Chambliss. Bobby Cherry. Don't ask me to write a list; I'll be writing *forever*.'

Lenny feels bad for his dumb question. 'I guess it's just bad luck.'

'Bad luck — I'll drink to that.' Minnie swigs, passes Lenny the bottle. 'It was a bad way for Gene to go. In some ways, I don't blame Bobbi for lashing out; it's obvious she's grieving. But to say we could do *that*, to one of our own ...' Her eyes gloss over. 'I still remember one time, back in Indianapolis, he took Roger and me to the precinct for the day, let us do our fingerprints. He was telling us all about the different types: loops, whorls, arches. I thought it was *magic*. We must've been six, seven.'

'I don't think I know anyone I knew when I was seven.'

Minnie smiles sadly at the white curtains. Then, out of the blue: 'He's in love with this Guyanese woman. Odessa.'

'Roger?' Lenny tries not to look too excited when she nods. '... You don't mind?'

Minnie shakes her head. 'We haven't had that kind of relationship in a *long* time.'

Lenny considers how to respond: *That's too bad*, or, *You can do better than Roger anyway*, or, *Neither have me and Terra*. Thinking this, it sure seems true, but he doesn't want to admit it aloud, any more than he wanted to admit to things souring between him and Evelyn all those years ago. Before he can say anything else, Minnie starts to cry softly. So he just says, 'Hey.'

'It doesn't bother me,' she repeats. 'So long as Roger doesn't forget his commitments.' She dashes a tear. 'There's this "confirmed bachelor". Old money. He owns a lot of the newspapers here. Roger spends a lot of time with him ... for the Cause.'

'Oh.' Lenny thinks of the shiny black car, Roger's tight pants. 'Right.'

'It's not forever.' Minnie puts her hand on his arm. 'Please don't tell him I told you.'

Lenny looks at her hand. 'I won't.'

'There's just so many things ... It's good to talk. You're a good listener.'

'So are you,' Lenny says clumsily. 'I mean, I like listening.'

He puts his hand on hers. It feels good. She looks good, really good …

'*For shame! That's our best rum!*' Joya storms onto the porch. Lenny and Minnie jerk apart, mumble apologies. Joya snatches up the depleted bottle. 'I'm writing you *both* up!'

'No. It's my fault …' Minnie rises, smoothing her dress. Lenny thought the dress was white before, but now he can see it's a dusty rose color. 'Lenny's new here.'

Joya scoffs at Lenny's shirtless chest. 'He's not *that* new.' Then she notices the roach. 'Yucky-yuck-yuck!' she cries, and empties the bucket over the porch. She returns it to Lenny. 'Use that if you have to vomit. *Is there anything else Mister needs?*'

Though her tone is sarcastic, Lenny is thirsty enough to ask, '… Maybe some water?'

'I'll get it,' Minnie offers.

'You will *not,*' Joya cuts in. 'Go to the radio room. We're recording testimonies.'

With drunken composure, Minnie goes in. Lenny watches her go: dust-pink dress, dark legs, yellowish soles of her feet. Joya watches him watching.

'*You should be ashamed of yourself,*' she spits.

She tightens the cap on the rum and flounces inside after Minnie, leaving Lenny alone on the porch. He looks at the white netting, touched with first light. Hears a rooster crow and, further off, men chanting, marching … soldiers?

Head splitting, he settles into a new day's shame.

4.

Meet here in two hours. The boat for Jonestown leaves at five, Dot Luce-Jones instructs them as she parks outside the town hall, and though she isn't as scary as her mom, Lenny still has every intention of obeying. He piles out of the van with Norm, Bruce, and Irving. Donna and Nikki, an auburn-haired white chick with mousy teeth, follow with sacks over their shoulders like Santa Claus.

'The market is a couple of streets over.' Donna points, then steps into the traffic with Nikki. Nikki is wearing Minnie's rose-colored dress. It looked better on Minnie.

Cabs and buses honk as they shadow Donna and Nikki across the road. They pass a statue of Queen Victoria. A big wooden church, still smattered with Sunday worshippers, though it's past lunchtime. Lenny's stomach is clogged from the fatty soul-food lunch cooked up by the old ladies. When they enter the market and are hit with food smells, his stomach turns.

'They got Coca-Cola here too! Hot damn,' Norm notes enthusiastically.

Bruce mumbles something about wanting *his* Coke with rum and shuffles off. The chicks weave ahead with their sacks. Irving strides into the swell of bodies like a surfer without a board.

'Five finger!' A hand grabs Lenny's arm. He instinctively looks at its five fingers. Then another set of fingers slip a slimy star-shaped fruit onto his palm. 'Try.'

'Oh, no. Thanks,' Lenny tells the owner of the fingers, feeling rude in spite of his politeness, for she's skinny and old and brown.

'Five finger. Starfruit!' the woman insists, making a twinkle-star motion.

'Yeah, cool …' Lenny nods and smiles. Tries to give the fruit back.

She won't let him.

'*Try.*' She pats her flat midriff; she's wearing a sari. Lenny looks around, but even Norm is beyond reach, crowded up to a drink vendor. He gives in; pops the fruit. It's firm yet oily, like a grape, tart to taste.

'Good!' she exclaims joyously. She casts around for more fruit. 'Try, try ...'

Again, Lenny refuses; again, she persists, feeding him tiny bananas, guava, breadfruit, laughing at him. Then she starts gathering fruit into a plastic bag. 'Sorry, I can't—'

'*Very* good,' the woman stresses. 'Good for you.'

'Yeah, just ...' Lenny shakes a stream of pennies from his wallet. 'That's all I have.'

Her expression grows taut, calculating. Wordlessly, she removes all but one starfruit from the bag, scrapes the change from his palm, waves him away.

Strange fruits. Fruit drinks. Flower drinks. Tree-bark drinks. Alien-esque vegetables. Mounds of spices like bright dirt. Hands dart at him. Women with black hair and nose studs smile at him, and he's torn between smiling back and knowing he's both broke and married. From afar, he sees Donna and Nikki negotiating with a toyseller, and his instinct is to avoid them. He smells something sweet, skunky, and is buoyed by a Pavlovian wave of euphoria.

He follows the scent to a stall, hung with beads, woven baskets. Two dreadlocked dudes with a glass pipe. They look at Lenny with unfazed dark eyes.

'Yes, sah?' says the younger one, a powerfully-built guy in a Harley-Davidson T-shirt.

'Hey.' Lenny looks around. 'Cool store.'

'It cool,' Harley agrees, then looks at his pal, a fat guy in a Yankees cap and dashiki. They laugh. Yankees takes a hit.

'Hey ... smells good.' Lenny signals at the smoke hopefully.

'It *good.*' Yankees passes the pipe on to Harley. They laugh again.

'Is it ... legal here?' Lenny asks, wide-eyed.

'We pay small fee, police don't mind.' Harley looks at him sidelong. 'You want?'

'I spent all my money,' Lenny confesses, showing his starfruit. They laugh more.

'*Whereyoucomefrom*, man?' Yankees volleys with almost aggressive cheer.

'California.' Lenny watches the smoke curl. 'I'm going to Jonestown. You know it?'

Both guys mmm, nod, don't elaborate. Lenny looks at the beads: shells, seed pods, red-yellow-green. 'That's some nice jacket you wearin', sah,' Harley remarks.

'Yeah?' In fact, the jacket is new, chosen by the lady who does Dr. Lynden's shopping.

'Very nice. Made in America?'

'Yeah.' Lenny shrugs it off, shows the label. Passing the pipe to Yankees, Harley examines the stitched lettering, the little polo player.

'Jacket like this, you won't be needing in Jonestown ... We keep this jacket. Okay?'

Lenny smiles. Yankees is already offering up the pipe.

It's good weed. The best he's had in years, which isn't saying much, since it *has* been years. So many years, it's almost like that first time in college, getting high with those guys from his Philosophy class who Marianne would later (not incorrectly) accuse him of spending too much time with. But Harley says, 'We don't smoke to get high like Americans. We smoke for meditation,' and Lenny likes the sound of this, as he likes the sound of the beads playing through his fingers. He notices a purse with pretty woven patterns, and his heart swells, his mind strains longingly. Then a hand reaches through the beads to give Yankees a bowl of saltfish. *Salt. Fish. Ocean.*

'I have to be on a boat ...' Lenny panics. 'The boat leaves at five.'

Yankees checks his watch through a mouthful of saltfish. 'Four-thirty only.'

Lenny stands; the floor reels like a boat's deck. 'Thanks ... Nice to meet you ... Peace.'

It's anything but peaceful, finding his way back to the meeting point. Hooting traffic. A man in uniform he crosses the street to avoid. A black dog with an untethered eyeball. When the van screeches up beside him, his instinct is to shrink away.

'Lenny! Get in!' Dot orders, sounding a lot like her mom.

He gets in. It's crowded. Both Norm and Bruce reek of liquor.

'Irving isn't with you?' Nikki asks anxiously. 'You didn't see Irving anywhere?'

Lenny manages to shake his head. The girls hiss, '*He's gonna have to get the next boat out,*' and, '*We're in deep shit.*' Relieved, Lenny sits back.

Somehow, while Lenny is focused on camouflaging himself with the upholstery, they arrive at the port. The sky a hazy peach-scape, flung with white birds. Raw-edged shipping containers. Dock cats he longs to pet. The *Rosaline* is being packed with supplies.

On jelly-legs, he waits for the call to board, then does.

By nightfall, he's puking his guts out.

Puking, and shitting, and when he isn't puking or shitting, strung out in the moaning twilight of the deck. Lanterns turn faces Halloween-orange, fizzle out as new waves crash onboard. Someone comes by with waterproof jackets, and then, as the night wettens, life jackets.

Lenny wonders if this is how he'll die.

He closes his eyes and tries to pretend he's dead, but there's too much going on, inside and outside. He's unable to distinguish inside from outside, the churning of the ocean from his churning guts and mind. Drowned bodies. Woven purses. Minnie. Evelyn. Marianne, crying. The pool in the Berkeley Hills, with Marianne, with Evelyn, with his siblings, with the uniformed maids serving lemonade on ice. X-rays. More crying. His mother, Liesl, taking him to a Jewish ghetto in Salzburg and crying over aunts, cousins he knew nothing about. Gassed bodies. Liesl's long cigarettes, curling with smoke. Patterns swirling, containing all the meaning in the world, if only he could hold still enough to see everything at once.

Maybe he sleeps. It's a new day; someone brings rice. The *TigerBeat* girl, Daisy, teeters across the deck on coltish legs, leans over the edge, sweet-cheeked in tiny terry shorts, and throws up her rice.

Lenny throws up again. Someone brings water, clear but salty, or maybe it's his lips that are salty. He sleeps, and dreams he's a dying soldier — white sails, black sails.

He wakes. The *Rosaline* has moored, and people are rising. 'Are we in Jonestown?' he asks hopefully, but no; someone gives him a crate of rum to carry. Off the boat and into a village clearing, where Jorge Harrison from the boat crew is bartering with some locals. Lenny places the crate down. Brown girls with startlingly smooth, pretty faces peek out at him from behind shanties, and he looks at the red dirt rather than back at them, they're so young. After a while, some men haul out slabs of meat, cut slices. The meat is smoky, fishy, surprising. A rum bottle is opened, and the village men smell the contents, taste, nod. An exchange is made.

'Shark meat,' Jorge explains, as they trek back with the meat on their shoulders. 'We're approaching the mouth of the river. The waters will be calmer from here.'

Lenny sleeps. He wakes, cotton-mouthed and foggy, to Coca-Cola waters, hanging vines, views like something out of Evelyn's old *National Geographic* magazines. He wishes he was high.

Someone brings rice. 'Mekong River, '68,' Bruce says, and Lenny nods, feels evasively respectful, like he always does when guys his age compare scars and locations.

Jorge walks around shirtless, back muscles glazed and rippling. Bruce takes off his shirt, too, lies supine and barrel-chested, dark skin dappled with greenish light. Even Norm, pasty-brown and flabby, strips off. Lenny follows. *Jonestown*, he thinks, and the thought feels like sunshine, like fanning feathers, like the best thing that's ever happened to him.

When he next wakes, the river is a sludgy piss-yellow, his skin tight and itchy: sunburn. The old ladies are singing again — *Deep River, My home is over Jordan* — and others are joining in, and soon so's Lenny, voice weak but happy, so happy to be here. Thatched roofs. Brown legs running. Smoke. 'Port Kaituma: six miles from Jonestown.' The *Rosaline* docks.

There's a red flatbed truck, waiting. They pile on. Lenny stands looking over the edge, until it becomes clear there's nothing to see, and the journey will be long.

He slumps down. Closes his eyes against the truck's jolts, the metallic red *thunking* in his brain. Until a siren cuts the air, and a sign appears:

WELCOME TO JONESTOWN
PEOPLES TEMPLE AGRICULTURAL PROJECT

Lenny is silent, gaping at the observation tower above the canopy. Everyone is. A silence that widens as the view does; fields, black workers in fields, an occasional red-tan white person. Then barns, cabins, small and spartan, huddled together. 'V'ry nice,' an old lady mumbles. Some army-green tents emerge and, in the distance, the pavilion. The truck churns to a stop.

They form a line outside a tent with their luggage. In line ahead of Lenny, Daisy is having her possessions rifled through, a tube of lipstick confiscated, her *TigerBeat* magazine — 'Only good for toilet paper.' Sister Regina comes around with a clipboard and starts telling people their assigned cabins; Single Males C-17 for Bruce, C-23 for Norm ...

'Sister, I think there's a mistake?' Norm panics. 'I should be in a cabin with my wife?'

'Who's your wife?'

'Renetta Coleman. Kids are Pauly, Vivienne, Irene—'

'No "Renetta Coleman".' Regina frowns, adjusts her rimless glasses. 'We've got a "Renetta Dixon" ... Wife of Claudius Dixon. Mother of Paul, Vivienne, Irene, Louis.'

Norm turns whiter than Lenny's ever seen a black man turn. 'No ... That can't be ...'

'You can take it up with the Relationship Committee.' Regina makes to move away. Norm reaches for her round brown shoulder, begins pleading. Her nostrils flare.

'Mister, don't you lay your hands on *me*. That ain't my area, alright? *Take it up with the Relationship Committee.*'

Lenny figures Norm might cry, so he stares away; the green-black canopy, the dusty yellow sky. He feels nothing but blunt inside: blunt to the cruelty; blunt to the newness; blunt to the stinging, the salt, the dirt, the flies. That is, until he sees his ex-wife.

Walking alone, in drawstring pants and a lace-edged tank top; that same fast walk; hair in that same boring bun, flashing dark as plumage. Back in college, there were girls Lenny would see some days and those days felt improved, lucky somehow. With Evelyn, the feeling was strongest. It's still strong; a flight of rare birds in his chest, a clear blue wonder.

Lenny stares at his ex-wife.

She notices him staring, and all the beauty flies from her face.

5.

There are mornings, lying in his bunk in C-25, when Lenny dreams Jim Jones's voice in his ear, Jim Jones's hand reaching across his sweaty thigh and taking out his cock. Jim tugging at him furiously, talking through clenched teeth, until he wakes with damp sheets and a stickiness in his shorts. So ashamed, he could open his veins, drown in red.

These are the mornings Lenny rises before the sun, blindly laces his boots and ties his hair with a snot rag. In his blindness, following the scent of routine, he can sometimes convince himself that he's back at the commune in Red Creek — that there's a warm, wifely body waiting for him just out of sight, just out of reach. He tries to keep up the fantasy as he lines up for his morning rice and syrup in the tent that smells of iodine. Eats at a long table, elbow-to-elbow with other workers in boots, snot rags. But it's not easy when Jim's voice keeps beaming through the speakers. *Flies. Everyone with a flyswatter, I want you out there swatting. These fuckers, they get immune to pesticides; don't get immune to being splatted!*

It's still blue-dark when they set out, by the dozens, for the fields. Jim's voice fading, mercifully, the farther they range.

In the fields, they break into crews, take up hoes and cutlasses. Split soil. Pull weeds. Slice through dense intrusions of vine, which bleed green like slaughtered aliens.

Lenny pretends he's on another planet. A hostile place of red dirt, blistering sun, giant bugs. He doesn't kill the bugs, though they land, sting, feast on the nectar of his sweat. Doesn't kill, though he wields sharp tools, and there are new muscles in his arms that scare him.

He's on another planet. How'd he get here? *By moving through space.* Why was he sent? *For the Cause.* When will he return? *Never; earth is*

345

ruled by fascists. What's for lunch?

'Gotta be kiddin' me!' Rondelle, a big, mouthy girl he remembers from San Francisco, opens the sandwich inside her lunch bag. 'They forgot the filling.'

Matty, an effeminate white guy with shoulder-length dark hair, peeks over her shoulder. 'See that brown stuff, sweetie? *Syrup.*'

Rondelle mutters under her breath, then jabs Matty. 'Show me yours, twink.'

Matty shows her. 'You kiddin' me? You got banana bits! You're kiddin' me, man—'

'Give it up, Rondelle,' bird-boned Taysha intervenes. 'You could skip lunch every day and it wouldn't hurt you one bit.'

Rondelle looks ready to smack Taysha across the mouth. Quincy — one of the guards assigned to oversee their crew — comes past and she decides against it; settles in the shade and starts munching with a holier-than-thou look.

Lenny opens his own sandwich. There's a smear of syrup on one slice of cassava bread, two rounds of banana on the other. He closes it and bites in, eyes averted. Quincy jabs his arm.

'Get to the radio shed. Father wants you.'

'*Wants* …?' Lenny squeaks, but Quincy has already moved on to flirt with Yolanda, the prettiest girl on the crew.

'Hey, Yo'. You gonna watch us play ball this Sunday?'

Yolanda rolls her eyes. 'You know I don't got time for that.'

'What gives? You still on orchid-duty for them in the White House?'

'Drop it, Quincy.'

'Miss seeing you 'round, that's all. Maybe I can help you pick flowers sometime? Two's company, right?'

'I said, drop it,' Yolanda says, but she's smiling as she nibbles her crusts.

On the trek back into town, Lenny chokes down the rest of his sandwich, midday sun hard at his back. When he reaches the radio shed, Phil Sorensen beckons him in. 'Lenny.'

Lenny follows Phil's broad back. Jim is inside. So's Evelyn. So's his mother.

Liesl looks bad. So bad, the sight of her distracts from both Evelyn and Jim. When did she get so skinny? Whenever she got cancer, probably. She gives him a feeble smile.

'Mom?' he says; then recovers and looks at Jim. 'You wanted to see me, Father?'

Jim doesn't look up. He's frowning into his shirtfront. He looks fat; skin an unhealthy pale yellow. He makes a weak curly gesture in the air.

Evelyn seems to understand the gesture. She turns and fetches some papers.

'Sit,' Jim says. Lenny joins his mom on the daybed. Jim hands over the papers. 'Read.'

It's a facsimile of a newspaper article. On the first page, a photo of Terra. Her hair is shorter than Lenny remembers, chin-level and shaped like a mushroom. Her eyebrows are different, too, plucked into fashionably thin curves. Eyes wide. Lips parted. Big hoops in her ears. She looks pretty and sexy. Briefly, Lenny feels proud to have such a pretty, sexy wife.

'*Read,*' Jim repeats.

Lenny reads the headline. '"Escape From Jungle Hell: Ex-Temple Aide Bares All".' He stops; glances at the date at the corner of the page: *June 12.* A month since he left the US. 'Is this … new?'

Jim glowers. Lenny keeps reading.

'"The Peoples Temple mission in northern Guyana has come under scrutiny from US government officials as alarming reports emerge of starvation, sleep deprivation, public beatings, and illegal weaponry. The reports were provided by Miss Teresa Jane Day, 29, a top aide of Temple leader Rev. Jim Jones, during a press conference last night. Day, daughter of a prominent Oceanside attorney—"'

'"Attorney's daughter". Didn't take her long to go back to her bourgeois roots.' Jim catches Lenny's reflection. 'Didn't take her long to forget her marriage, either.'

Is that what she's done? Lenny doesn't have the words for it, so he just nods. Jim motions for him to keep reading.

Armed guards. Cruel and unusual punishments. Twelve-hour workdays. Rice for every meal. Meetings, long into the night, in which the paranoid leader rants about enemies …

'Do you believe these things your wife's saying? Your daughter-in-law?' Jim booms. 'Why would she say these things? After all we've given her?'

'I — don't know,' Lenny offers.

'Tell me, darlings — *do you believe what she's saying*? Do you believe — be honest now — you're underfed? Overworked? Our punishments are too harsh?' Before they can answer, Jim squeezes up to Lenny. 'You *know*, darlings, self-sufficiency don't happen overnight. We all gotta work hard, make sacrifices … Sometimes, for the good of the group, individuals gotta be made examples of. It don't please me. When I see one of my people hurtin'? Hurts me ten times more. So if you're unhappy, if you'd rather go back there where they're puttin' blacks in concentration camps and experimenting on them like in Nazi Germany, *you tell me.*'

There's a long silence. Then Liesl says, 'I do not ever want to leave here.'

Lenny looks at his mom. She's got her chin held high, fists bunched tight. Cheekbones like billiard balls. He feels Jim's eyes crawling along the back of his neck.

'I want to stay.' He swallows. 'I love it here.'

'Course you do,' Jim says gently, placing a plump hand on Lenny's knee. 'I *know*.'

Lenny looks at his own hands. Runnels of dried dirt-sweat. Orange blisters. Grime under the nails. He feels dirty. He wishes Jim would remove that hand.

'Your wife's a traitor,' Jim tells him, caressing his knee. 'How's that feel?'

'Bad.' Evelyn turns away and starts sorting through papers, her movements contained. Lenny knows better than to watch her. 'She's not my wife anymore.'

'And you, sweetheart?' Jim turns to Liesl. 'Terra, wasn't she like a daughter to you?'

In fact, Lenny doubts his mom would've joined the Temple if it wasn't for Terra. For sure, he never invited her; never encouraged her to give up her jewelry, her art collection, her six-figure divorce settlement. *That* was all Terra.

'She is dead to me,' Liesl says adamantly.

It's a relief when Jim sends them off to the Letters Office with Phil. A relief, to walk in the bright sun, away from the dark corridors that always seem to open up in him, around Jim.

'In a way, it's better Terra talked,' Phil says, offering Liesl his arm before Lenny can. 'Her claims are so exaggerated, they shouldn't be hard to refute.'

'With letters?' Liesl wonders.

'Our letters are good, but not *that* good.' Phil laughs. 'We're organizing another press conference: supporters and detractors, together. The last thing we want is to look defensive.'

They reach the office. Brother Tobias, a gay guy Lenny's age who's weirdly fond of Liesl, stops typing when she crosses the threshold with Phil. 'Well, look what the cat dragged in!'

'Cat? No, Phil is a *lion*,' Liesl says admiringly, patting Phil's arm in thanks.

Lenny wonders what King Henry VIII is doing now; dozing, licking his paws? Tobias sits Liesl at the typewriter next to his. Phil says, 'I'll put Lenny next to you, Min'.'

Minnie?

'Hi, Lenny.' Minnie's wearing a yellow blouse through which he can just make out the shape of her bra, and she's got her hair in two cute dumplings atop her head. 'How *are* you?'

'Oh … You know …'

Minnie nods. 'I'm sorry. Is it a shock?'

'Yeah. I mean …' There'd been talk of a traitor, when he first arrived. Within days, he'd stopped asking about Terra. *Had* he known? Suspected? Or just been exhausted? Suddenly, he feels he could cry; the depths of his not-knowing. 'Her picture was in the newspaper.'

Minnie nods again. 'I haven't seen it yet. But I heard she told some awful lies.'

'Yeah.' Lenny looks at his boots. They're dirty. He goes to the porch and tries to stomp off more dirt. When he returns, Minnie has turned back to her typing.

Phil pulls out a chair for Lenny. 'Ready to write a letter to your old man?'

Lenny writes. Trying not to bump his sun-damaged white arm against Minnie's smooth brown one, but also thrilling when he does. He finishes a letter to Dr. Lynden, another to his brother, Ned. Liesl writes to Ned and Beth. Phil reads all four letters, praises them, marks them up in red and explains the markings. They type up second drafts, which Minnie and Tobias read. After a while, Evelyn comes in.

'This paragraph about the cassava bread is overkill. Strike it.' She skims, then looks at Lenny starkly. 'Wasn't there a nickname you and your brother had for Beth? Something cruel?'

Lenny racks his brain. '"Bad-Breath-Beth"?'

'Use that.' She returns them to Phil. 'Finish these letters soon. The boat is going out.'

'I won't miss the boat.' Phil half-smiles.

'Don't,' Evelyn says, and flounces out.

Phil gets them to rewrite their letters by hand. He steps out, and when he returns, Lenny's flexing his cramped hand, hoping for Minnie to notice his fieldwork muscles.

'Stop the presses.' Phil grins; hands out watermelon slices. 'Nice work, comrades.'

Lenny returns to the fields feeling, actually, not too bad.

But it happens that night: sirens, slicing his sleep, and not just sirens. Guards. Banging on the cabin doors. Over the speakers, Jim's voice yammering: *White Night! White Night!*

Lights form halos against the isolating blackness of the sky. Lenny imagines UFOs, beaming him to another planet, back to sleep. Every bench is packed with weary asses, kids on laps. Standing room only. He can't see past the shoulders to Jim taking the stage; just Jim's authoritative voice, like a hand gripping his hair by the roots.

'The traitor has spoken,' Jim declares. 'She's gone to the press with her vicious lies and ruined our name. It's time for you to know *her* name.' He clears his throat loudly. Hocks. Spits. 'The traitor is Terra Lynden. Wife of Lenny Lynden.'

6.

Sometimes, for the good of the group, individuals gotta be made examples of.
Lenny tries to keep this in mind as he stands before the group, taking
their insults. Weak. White. Bourgeois. Lazy. Junkie. Homosexual. Only
a homo could be married to a traitor-bitch so long without realizing
it. Only a homo would need Father fucking his wife on the regular to
keep her loyal. Only a homo would get drunk in Georgetown and try
to overcompensate with a married woman.

'Where's the woman?' Jim barks. 'Where's Minnie Luce? Get up
here.'

Minnie rises, eyes round and mortified. Her sister, Ursa, rises with
her, and Minnie frantically pushes the air, shakes her head. Clarisse,
Minnie's pregnant sister-in-law, tugs Ursa back down to the bench and
diverts her with the kicking in her belly.

'Lenny, are you interested in fucking this woman?'

There's no point denying it. 'Yes, Father.' People jeer.

'Minnie, are you interested in fucking this ... "man"?'

Minnie looks at Lenny. 'No, Father.' More jeers.

'But you broke the rules for him, hmm? Rum on the porch? Batting
them nice eyelashes? Felt good, didn't it, this whiteboy lookin' at you
like you the Queen of Sheba?'

Minnie doesn't dignify this with an answer for a long time; so long,
in fact, that Jim's smirk slips.

'It felt good to be distracted,' Minnie confesses eventually. 'There'd
been a lot of talk of death that night, but Lenny wasn't part of it. He
was a nice distraction.'

'Nice you can be *distracted* from death, sister,' Jim taunts. 'Rest of us,
we livin' it. I'm dyin' every day to keep y'all alive. But drinking, white

351

boys? Them's nice distractions ... Just don't you go getting *distracted* from how they been keeping you enslaved for centuries.'

The mob kicks in, calling Minnie 'uppity', 'race traitor', 'negro princess'. She stands tall, arms at her sides. Jim asks again if she's interested in Lenny. Again: *No, Father.* Why not?

'I'm not interested in any relationship. Socialism's my only reason for living. I don't want to die if there's a chance for socialism in this life. And I don't want to be distracted.'

Jim softens. 'Well, *don't* be, honey. You ain't no use to us if you distracted. I want you to keep death in your mind *always*. If you ain't ready to face death every day, you're no better than that traitor-bitch.' He waves Minnie down, saying he's feeling merciful; at least she recognizes sex is *only* a distraction. To Lenny, he says, 'You still wanna fuck that woman?'

'No.' His ears burn. 'Not if she doesn't want me.'

'*Not if she don't want him.*' Jim laughs, prompting the crowd to do the same. 'What'd you think she'd want? Your body? Your bitty white dick? Cause sure as hell you don't got a *mind* to give. Can't even string a sentence together.' Jim waits for Lenny to disprove him. 'Think that's what a proud, black socialist woman wants?'

'No,' he says; the only answer.

'You got anything else to give her? You got anything to give *any* woman?'

Peace? Love? Loyalty? None of these things are articulable, against Jim's scorn. 'No.'

'*Nothing?* Well, sisters, he's offering. Don't got nothing, but he's *offering*. Any takers?'

The pavilion buzzes with the disinterest of every woman present; shifting legs, averted faces, hands cupping whispers. A few stray cheers, whistles. Lenny feels a searing hate: for Minnie, for Terra, for Marianne Glover, who broke up with him for coming to bed with red eyes; for his mother, who gave him life. But not Jim. Hating Jim is too much hate to live with.

'Sheila, what d'you say? Would you fuck him?'

'*Hell* no.'

'Ninette?'

'I don't fuck faggots.'

'Gail? Elly? Sally-Ann?' As an endless lineup of women shout their rejections, it takes all Lenny's willpower to keep his arms at his sides, instead of covering his groin like he wants to. Finally, Jim growls, 'Not a single sister out there wants you, and you better get used to it, 'cause you ain't getting *nothing*. Any sister goes near you, she's a traitor-whore. Already proven you can't keep a woman faithful. Pussy. Piece-of-shit. What are you? Say it.'

Words, the power of speech, have evaporated from him completely.

'Say it, pussy. Say what you are. Say what you're good for.'

His self — something small, a glove, a pebble, dropped off the side of a mountain. Someone hooks him, jarringly, in the ribs. Someone else deals him a shin-kick. Someone else, a knee to the groin. He's on the dirt, the faces surprising: Johnny Bronco, with his cool moustache; Eustace, his old buddy from the Red Creek commune; Irving, who was badly beaten for missing that boat to Jonestown a few weeks ago. Jim laughs amiably into the microphone. 'Don't hit him too hard; he's still gotta work,' then, in tender wonderment, 'He's not fighting back? Course he isn't. Little peace-dove. Bless him.'

Lenny feels himself hauled up by the armpits. Wetness on his cheek; his own blood, clean and sweet as watermelon. 'What are you, Lenny Lynden?'

Lenny still can't see Jim for all the people, the UFO lights in his head.

'Nothing.'

7.

Living without a woman, the promise of a woman's touch, smiles, glances, is a bit like living without hot showers, or privacy when shitting, or enough sleep, or morning coffee, or sugar, or meat — juicy hunks of hamburger or chicken and not just a few scraps dissolved in gravy — or weed; *especially* weed. It's a life without softness or luxury; a life of bare necessity; a life that sometimes has Lenny looking at the sharp tools in his hands and wondering.

When he sees Minnie weaving among tables in the Dining Tent a couple of nights after the confrontation, he drops his gaze as though searching for a lost earring. Keeps his gaze down if he so much as senses the presence of a female over fifteen and under forty; the jelly of a walk, the shadow of a breast, the tangle of an armpit; sweet, hot zones absolutely forbidden to him.

It's a relief when Yolanda is taken off the sugarcane crew for getting too friendly with Quincy. Still, there are days when Lenny's blood seems so close to the surface, it's all he can see. Blood-hot visions. Terra, at the edge of the sugarcane field, telling him, *Lenny, you're sweet.* Before he knows it, in full view of the crew, pacing Quincy, he's breaking a stalk, crunching the sweet-wet; and before he knows it, Quincy's fist is crunching against his cheek.

'Fucker! That's *stealing*. You're gonna steal from the rest of us?'

'Sorry,' Lenny bleats, heart hammering; the pain dizzy, exhilarating. 'Sorrysorry.'

When, one afternoon, they stop work to listen to the press conference broadcast, Lenny sits on the pavilion floor picking at his scabs.

In one word, 'impressive' — Rev. Burne, his former father-in-law, tells the reporters.

Jones brainwashed my teenaged daughter and married her off to a divorced junkie — his other father-in-law, Mr. Day.

It concerns me as a father, it concerns me as a man of law, and it concerns me as an American. Jonestown needs to be investigated — Mona's dad, who owns all those factories in New Jersey.

After serving his country, my son became a dedicated peace activist. He wouldn't be in Jonestown if it didn't align with his values — Phil's mom, a nice-sounding lady with a Southern accent.

I was Jim's son-in-law for seven years. He's a crook — Su-mi's ex, Dwight Mueller.

I'm critical of communalism, but the fact stands, Peoples Temple has given my mom and brother a sense of meaning and direction — Ned, miraculously dragged away from his job as a neurosurgeon.

After the press conference, instead of going back to work, they get fried chicken. After chicken, there's a screening of *M*A*S*H*. After *M*A*S*H*, Jim has them entertain him with revenge fantasies: blowing up Dwight inside his fancy car; crushing Mona's dad with his own factory machinery; cutting off Terra's tits and shoving them inside her traitor-bitch mouth.

Lenny feels like vomiting up his chicken. But he doesn't. Days later, the image of Terra's mutilated body appears to him so calmly, he steals more sugarcane just to feel the fists.

Others steal, too. Others are beaten, and not just for stealing. Rondelle, one day in the fields, starts singing slave songs at the top of her lungs. Paolo Jones — who replaced Quincy after he got his guard privileges stripped for trying to sneak off with Yolanda — tells her to quit it. Rondelle sings louder. Paolo cracks her in the nose with the butt of his rifle. Everyone stares at the rifle, Rondelle's bleeding nose. Then they lower their heads and keep working.

Every couple of weeks, Lenny is called to the clinic to help with X-rays. A kid with a broken arm from a failed slam-dunk. A senior with a shadow on her lungs, still operable, not like Liesl's. Clarisse Luce, eight months pregnant, with an impacted wisdom tooth. 'Poor kid: not even born and she's meeting the dentist!' she jokes through her pain, face cheekbone-y, heart-shaped.

Lenny prefers the cool, sterile air of the clinic to working in the dirt and sun. Yet it doesn't occur to him to ask for a transfer.

Likewise, it doesn't occur to him to get back into bed when he falls out one night, dreaming of gunshots in the jungle. He wakes to boots stepping over his body.

Another stormy night, returning from a meeting in the pavilion, head crashing with news of bloody wars in Africa, race riots in the US, Klansmen patrolling state lines and murdering with impunity, it doesn't occur to Lenny to protest when a guy pulls him into the bushes, unzips them both, takes out both their dicks. They pull at each other for a confused minute, then it's over, and the guy's pushing him away, coughing, 'Faggot,' fleeing.

A life without softness or luxury. A life of bare necessity. Not a life he especially wants, but did he ever want life? Did he ask for it? 'Every child has the right to feel hostile for being brought into this world,' Jim tells them one night. 'Living is agony. Nobody *wants* it.'

There is no other life. He wants no other. He wants nothing. *What are you, Lenny Lynden? Nothing.* And when you're nothing, nothing can be lost — or that's what he thinks, until Brother Tobias comes running up to him in the field one afternoon.

'Lenny: your mom just had a seizure,' Tobias tells him. 'She's asking for you.'

The first thought Lenny has, seeing Liesl on her deathbed, is how thin she is. Holocaust thin. His next thought is, *people didn't get deathbeds in the Holocaust.* Or drugs to ease their pain.

He sits. Then, because it seems like the thing to do, clasps her cold, blue-mottled hand.

When Liesl wakes, she pulls her hand away, wipes it on the sheets. '*Lenny*,' she says in a wispy voice. After a while, she asks, 'Bethy and Neddy?'

'They send their love.'

He listens as Liesl talks at length about his siblings, Beth especially. Beth's Edwardian-era wedding dress. Brother Ralph, who works with Liesl in the library, comes in and says, '*Again* with that wedding dress, Liesl?', tries to get her to drink water. She refuses.

Dr. Katz checks in; says if her body doesn't want water, don't force it.

Liesl appears to go into a trance, or to fall asleep, eyes open. A gurgling comes from her throat. Ralph, seeing Lenny's discomfort, offers to watch her while he gets some air.

'No … I'll stay.'

The ladies who share Liesl's cabin sleep elsewhere that night. Lenny sleeps in the chair by her bed, and, later, on a spare bunk. Over the PA, Jim's voice is slurred, soporific.

Lenny wakes before sunup; habit. Liesl is awake too, making agitated little noises like a cat that's lost a mouse. He goes to her. It takes him a while to realize she's speaking German.

'Mom?' he says. 'It's me … Lenny.'

Ralph and Tobias come by later with rice. They're both gay, but not a couple. Lenny wonders if his life would be easier if he was gay; if his mom would like him better. He tells them she was speaking German. Ralph says, 'She does that sometimes.'

Lenny eats some rice. Liesl won't eat, but this isn't surprising.

Lenny supposes there are things he should ask his mother. He's relieved when she falls asleep. Phil comes in. 'Heard the little patient was speaking *Deutsch*?'

'Yeah,' Lenny says; then, in case it wasn't evident, 'She's sleeping now.'

To his surprise, Phil stays.

Phil is good-looking. Lenny always figured as much, but it's obvious, confined in the cabin with him. Phil pacing. Phil leaning. Phil sitting on a bunk. Phil asking innocuous yet disorienting questions: 'How'd you like UC Davis?' and, 'That's where you met Evelyn, right?' and, 'I had a buddy at Davis. Maybe you knew him? Jake Nash, class of '66?'

Lenny doesn't know if Phil is gay, but he suspects he might be.

Waking to find Phil, Liesl's eyes light up, as much as a half-dead woman's can. They start speaking German. Sporadically, Phil translates: 'Uncle Franz's grand piano,' or, 'Cycling with Clara down the street with the linden trees.' At one point, Liesl lapses into poetry; at another, a wavery-sounding German. 'Yiddish.'

Later, Liesl looks directly at Lenny. Phil explains, 'She says she stopped being Jewish when she married your father.'

'Oh.' Lenny guesses he knew this.

Liesl speaks again. '"My children aren't Jewish. They're American,"' Phil translates.

Lenny nods. It's true, he's never considered himself even half-Jewish.
'"I thought if my children grew up American, they'd be protected."'
Phil smiles sadly. '"The older ones, yes. Lenny, not so much."'

'Oh,' says Lenny. 'So … does she wish I was raised Jewish?'

Phil asks. Liesl shakes her head firmly.

Suddenly, Lenny remembers that cruel thing Beth told him, all
those Thanksgivings ago. He asks, 'Does she wish I wasn't born?'

Phil doesn't need to translate. Liesl nods.

Lenny's mother dies that night. After receiving her last rites from Jim,
pledging her undying allegiance to socialism. Jim stays to comfort
Lenny. 'She was a beautiful revolutionary … Could've healed her, if it
wasn't for your traitor-bitch wife draining my psychic energies.'

In that moment, Lenny hates Jim with a celestial clarity. But, next
moment, he starts crying, and Jim hugs him, calls him, 'My son.'

Dr. Katz signs the death certificate: *Lynden, Liesl. March 14 1914,
Salzburg. Austria. September 30 1978, Jonestown, Guyana.*

Voices low, but not so low as to exclude Lenny, Jim and Phil
discuss the burial. A jungle burial, far from their water supply. ASAP;
decomposition sets in fast in this climate. Can Carpentry whip up a
headstone? No religious crap, something for a good socialist?

Lenny is back at work by lunchtime.

At work that day, among the dirt and beetles, Lenny finds the
broken head of a trowel, and doesn't think anything of slipping it in his
pocket. Doesn't think anything, either, of sharpening its edges with a
bit of granite he finds by the shower block that evening.

Two nights later, with animal deliberateness, he slits his wrists.

8.

There are mornings, lying in his cot in the Special Care Unit, when Lenny dreams Jim Jones's voice in his ear, Jim Jones's hand reaching under the sheets and taking out his cock. Jim working at him desperately, weeping as the cock slips, over and over, like a bar of soap from his grip. Weeping, slipping, until Lenny wakes with a feeling of joyous limpness. Dead; it's peaceful, being dead.

'You're lucky you didn't get tetanus.' Sally-Ann Burne, streaked with morning sunlight, confirms he isn't dead. 'That thing was like ninety per cent rust.'

'… Tetanus?'

'Don't worry, we gave you a shot.'

Lenny looks down. He's shirtless. Bandages on his wrists.

'Try not to mess with those. We don't want your stitches coming undone.' Sally-Ann checks the bandages; squeezes his fingertips like she's trying to juice them. 'Your circulation's good … No damage to the tendons, either … *Oh*, Lenny. You really scared us.'

'Sorry,' Lenny mumbles.

'You scared Father,' she adds. 'You know, he cares so much. And you know what he says about individual suicide; it hurts us as a group—'

But Lenny can't listen to this. Just … can't. He watches Sally-Ann's lips move, tries to remember who she is to him, or who she once was. Davis. Thirteen years old. Playing guitar at his first wedding. Always drawing, painting, making faces, kicking him under the table.

'Do you still draw …?' he asks once she's finished talking.

Sally-Ann looks surprised. There's a hint of Evelyn in her oval face,

359

small gray-blue eyes, but so what? Why should he care?

'Yeah.' She smiles faintly. 'I'll show you my sketchpad sometime.'

Lenny closes his eyes.

There are drugs. Drugs that keep him soap-slick, cotton-headed. Watching the world through a dusty netting, dust-moths beating their wings. A tall young guy walking in the green beyond the netting with a dark-haired boy on his shoulders, the boy pointing at the trees.

'Dat you!'

'What? You sayin' I'm green and leafy?'

'No! Dat you! Big-as-sky!'

'Yeah, that's me,' the guy mutters. 'I'm the son of God. Big as the fucking sky.'

Martin Luther Jones. On his shoulders, Evelyn's child, Soul. Lenny feels nothing for the child ... but, again, why should he?

Another day, Sister Diane comes by and asks about his wrists, his mother, his feelings. He tells her nothing, or things like nothing: 'I don't know,' 'I don't remember,' 'I'm tired.'

He's tired. So tired. Like he's just traveled through several dimensions, tired. Like a hibernating creature, dug up before its time. Like the ability to not be tired was drained from him, along with those two pints of blood.

He sleeps. Sleeps. Wakes. To Sally-Ann lathering his face and wearily singing, '*Shaving cream! Nice and clean ...*' To beautiful Yolanda, sleep-creased and floppy-armed, protesting, 'But I don't wanna go to White House ...' as Elly Bud gravely helps her into a robe and slippers. To fiery walls at sunset, Jim calling a White Night.

Around Lenny, the nurses whisper: 'Do we *all* have to go?' '*Somebody's* gotta stay here.' He goes back to sleep. Is stirred in the dead of night by Janet Lakshmi. 'It's *time*. Get *up*.'

In the pavilion, Jim is crooning, 'It's all over. They're coming to kill us. Step over now; step over.' The queue worms all the way to the radio shed. Guards outside the queue.

'What's happening?' bellows Brother Garnet, an older white guy, put in the Special Care Unit for threatening someone with a machete.

No one answers Garnet at first. He keeps bellowing until Eustace, rocking his little son Kwame in his arms, sighs, 'Just drink it, and maybe we'll all get some sleep.'

Laura Kana, a few places ahead, gives Lenny the stink-eye. 'It's your wife's fault. Her lawyer daddy convinced some congressman to come here with a TV crew.'

'Congressman?' Lenny can't quite fathom what a congressman is, but it sounds bad.

'*Congressman Theo Hanson.* Big Democrat hero,' Laura says in a la-di-da tone. 'He thinks he's going to save us like those baby seals in Alaska.'

'Baby seals?' Lenny definitely can't fathom what baby seals have to do with anything. Crying babies, though, he can hear them.

'Mothers, keep those babies quiet,' Jim orders. 'Clarisse? No need for that baby to be crying. Death ain't fearful. If you want a successful reincarnation, you gotta face death bravely.'

Outside the queue, seniors sit drinking from paper cups. One lady empties hers stealthily behind a bench. The lady beside her yowls and a plump young nurse, Junie Crabb, bustles over with a new cup, looms over the first lady until she drains it.

Beyond the pavilion, bodies are playfully twitching, rolling. When Lenny finally gets his own cup, he downs the sweet, dark liquid like it's cough syrup. Jim notices him from the stage. '*You.* Why're you still here? Get outta my sight.'

Obediently, Lenny skulks out to the fields to die.

He doesn't die, though. Just sleeps. Wakes to stamping feet, war cries.

The next day, back in the Special Care Unit, Sally-Ann removes his bandages. The cuts are grayish-pink, tingly, but no pain. 'It's been a month. You can probably work again.'

'Fieldwork?'

'Not fieldwork.' Sally-Ann looks at him sadly. 'We'll find you something else.'

After lunch, he's given some paint-flecked fatigues, a T-shirt, brought out to the playground by Quincy, who's a janitor these days. Quincy shows him how to clean the big tires, scrape graffiti: *leave us in* ⊕; *Tera is a traytor whore*, *fuck Congressman Hanson*.

He cleans until his wrists hurt. Then he lies on a tire, squints at the cloudy belly of sky, and pretends not to hear Quincy asking, 'You done? You gonna do the rest? Or … not?'

Later, the playground floods with children. They're cute. Striped T-shirts. Overalls. Sun suits. Flappy hats. He sees Evelyn's child among them and, again, feels nothing … until that nothing transforms into a great, gaping something like the sky falling in.

'Lenny? Are you alright?' Sister Phyllis, a sweet old Indiana lady who works in the nursery, peers down at him from a backdrop of doom-clouds.

'Yeah … I'm alright.'

'Just, it's getting dark? And it looks like rain any minute?'

'I'm alright,' he repeats. 'Just cloudwatching.' Then: 'Do you think it's falling?'

'What's that?'

'The sky … Do you think it's falling?'

'Well … it's never done it before. Don't see why it would now,' Phyllis humors him. '*Rain*, though. Looks like rain, for sure. I'd hate to see you get wet, honey.'

In response, Lenny closes his eyes. Keeps them closed until Phyllis trots away with a herd of small children; until the rain begins plopping, people yelling and rushing for cover.

Bodies of water. Planets of water. Ships on the water with white sails, black sails.

It's dark when Lenny opens his eyes. His body like a wet sponge, slopping as he stirs. From the mud, strange mists rising. He trudges toward the glow of the Dining Tent.

Rice. 'Th-thanks,' he swallows, not looking at the sister serving, clamping his wrists together so she won't see his scars. Shambling with clamped wrists, mumbling a little. *Crazy*, someone whispers. *Ever since his mom died — crazy.*

'It's alright,' Lenny answers the whispers. 'Alright … I said I'm *alright.*'

He notices Norm, his Pan Am buddy, seated at a long table. Nods and sits. 'Lenny Landon!' Norm says, then points to the woman to his right. 'This's my new girl, Bessie.'

Bessie is heavyset, but her eyes are nice and she has a nice shy smile, dimples. Lenny nods again, avoiding Bessie's nice eyes. He looks at his rice, his spoon, his clamped wrists.

'Bessie works in the soap factory. That's why she smells so nice, ha-ha.'

Lenny shivers. His clothes are wet. If only he could take them off? But that'd be *crazy*.

He picks up his spoon between two crabbed fingers, scrapes it along the inside of the bowl. Hands trembling, wrists still clamped, he raises the spoon to his mouth. Rice drops.

Over the PA, Jim burrs: *Don't forget — I want it to be a matter of course now — when you're walking by each other, take the time to smile, give a friendly greeting, a pat on the shoulder ...*

Lenny fills his spoon again. Again, tremulously lifts it to his lips. On the back of his neck, something large lands. Prickles.

He lowers his spoon. The thing crawls from his neck to his collarbone; then, with apparent deliberateness, nosedives into his rice.

He sees legs, six of them. Antennae. Wings. A body, seemingly metallic in its hardness and sheen. He sees, and then he doesn't see, because he's killing it.

'Kill it,' he mutters, flipping the bowl, pounding his fist on the table. 'Kill it,' his voice not his own. The bug's body crunches, squelches. 'Did you kill it?' he growls and someone chimes in: *Yeah, I think you killed it, man.* Lenny looks at the brown slime on the side of his hand. 'That's fucking *disgusting.*'

He wipes the slime off. Dirty. Starts hitting again. 'Kill it. *Kill it.*'

... Show some love and kindness, wherever you go. Nobody can say we ain't a loving people.

Bessie shrinks away as he dents the table's wood. So does Norm.

'Killed it,' Lenny announces. 'I killed it.' His fists are torn, leaking. 'It's alright ...' He swipes a bloody hand across his forehead and smiles. 'Don't touch me, or I'll kill you.'

There's silence inside him, blue and sweet, like standing at the center of the universe, patterns swirling around him. The back of his neck prickles again.

Lenny turns. Looks through the shrinking crowd and sees:

Evelyn and her gray eyes, watching him.

Beautiful Day

1.

When she heard the doorbell ring on that smoky blue evening in the Fall of '66, in the house she shared with her many girlfriends, Evelyn had been ready to fall in love with whoever might be standing on the other side of it. A bone-deep readiness bordering on boredom: she *was* bored, she could admit it; after Bordeaux, Jean-Claude, those miserable weeks staying in hostels without Jean-Claude, the weeks after those weeks back in her parents' house not knowing why she was there, how she could've given up the world for the slow drip-trickle of church, relatives, everyone tiptoeing around her broken engagement like she'd die if it was mentioned; yes, *bored.* She was bored of those girls she lived with — Joan, Linda, Marilyn, Mary-Kay — and the little house they'd taken such pains to beautify. Bored of how she acted around those girls, like a pinwheel desperate to spin faster, brighter than the rest; sharing stories of lanterns along the Pont de Pierre, recipes for *Crêpes Suzette*, spurning cosmetics and prim shift dresses to go about fresh-faced, in flouncy gypsy skirts. She'd even mastered talking about Jean-Claude without getting upset, and if anyone dared to ask what they were all wondering, *why?*, could summon the perfect tone of worldly resignation: 'Honestly? The better my French got, the less interesting he was.' Yet this didn't change the fact that she was bored by the sound of her own voice; that her life, for all its grand intentions, had never seemed so trivial. It was enough to make her want to — well, maybe not kill herself, but join the Peace Corps maybe, spend a year on the Ivory Coast, or maybe, just maybe, fall in love again.

So she was the first to jump at the sound of the bell, to abandon the canapés they were fussing with, to wipe her hands and chime, 'I'll get it.' The canapés were her idea, but already it was clear they'd overdone it; some grad students had cancelled last minute and, to make up the numbers, Joan and Mary-Kay had spent the afternoon inviting random cute boys while the rest of them cleaned and shopped. Yet so far, the only guests to show up were Linda's cousin Judy and Cronkite, a neighborhood cat whose visits coincided with the evening news.

There was a wine glass in her hand. A barrette in her hair; over the summer, she'd decisively grown out the chic French-girl bob she'd worn since sophomore year. Sipping her wine, tucking her hair; feeling the glitter of wine in her eyes, the warmth on her cheeks. That's how she was when she opened to the smoky blue evening, the beautiful blue-eyed boy whose name she didn't yet know was Lenny Lynden.

'You're here.' Evelyn beamed at him. 'I'm *so glad*.'

2.

They're ready, or as ready as they'll ever be. The paths have been swept, the toilets scrubbed, the bushes pruned, the dogs deloused, the children's hair combed and braided, ribbons to match the girls' dresses. Cooking smells stir the air like weather, an incoming storm of meat, dough, gravy. They're all ready, except Jim.

'The Congressman has arrived,' she tells the shadows. 'We need you at the pavilion.'

Jim, from his pillows, chokes out a tangle of cusses and objections.

'You know we can't turn him away. The lawyers have given him permission to be here.' They've hired and flown in a pair of famous civil rights attorneys; Bertrand, who worked extensively with the Black Panthers, and Marshall, who has authored several books about government conspiracies. 'We just need to get through the next twenty-four hours. Then we'll have peace.'

An anxious crackle rises from the radio: Mona, asking if the Congressman's Party can be given a tour.

'*No tours,*' Jim croaks, and gestures for water. Evelyn brings it, holds the cup to his lips; he snatches it away, spilling half down his front. '*Never had a moment of peace. Never—*'

'*No tours,*' Evelyn tells the radio. To Jim: 'The longer we keep him waiting—'

'Bitch. Who're you working for?' Jim barks, then crumples his face and clutches his heart. '*Harry.* Call Harry. I'm having another heart attack. Oh God. Quickly—'

Evelyn sighs, retrieves Jim's oxygen mask from the bedside. '*Breathe,*' she tells him. She fetches a tiny amber bottle from the fridge, fills a syringe. Jim peers at her warily with his underwater face as she locates a vein, penetrates it. Once the needle is out, he lowers his mask.

'I want Harry,' he says obstinately.

The afternoon is thick, yellow, idle. A picturesque game of basketball on the court. Children swarming the playground, clambering skyward. She notes Soul's glossy dark head but doesn't stop. She does stop, however, for a putty of fresh green bird shit on the walkway.

'Excuse me,' she calls to a white man idling nearby. 'Could you clean this?'

She doesn't realize it's Lenny Lynden until he turns, so skinny and unshaven it's hard to keep the shock from her face. He shuffles over, peers down at the shit. 'Yeah,' he says.

'Ask the kitchen for a cloth and bucket,' she instructs. Lenny nods so morosely, she's compelled to justify: 'We can't have the guests getting it on their shoes. Unfortunately.'

Lenny nods again, avoiding her eye. Shaken, she stalks off to the pavilion.

She's calm by the time she reaches the gathering of officials. Congressman Hanson, a hawk-nosed Democrat about her father's age, dressed down in a maroon polo and chinos. Hanson's doe-eyed aide, Luísa, gold-shouldered in a spaghetti-strap dress. The lawyers, Bertrand and Marshall. Rosaline, Joseph, Frida, Phil. A platter of untouched pastries between them, jungle fruits buzzing in the heat.

'Jim is counseling a young man with schizophrenia,' Evelyn lies. 'He'll be here soon.'

'Usually, when I'm late for a meeting, it's because I pressed the snooze button one time too many,' the Congressman jokes, then leans against the table. 'I'll wait.'

It's over an hour before Jim shows up. Mincing across the pavilion with lamblike steps, black head huge on his shoulders, red shirt untucked, legs short in beige slacks. She'd selected the outfit. A bad choice? Certainly, it's painful to see him in broad daylight. It's a relief when Rosaline steps forward, steers Jim toward the Congressman.

'Pleasure to finally meet you,' Congressman Hanson says, offering Jim his hand.

'Wish I could say the same.' Jim shakes the hand; weakly, it seems. 'But, ah … I'm a humble man. Don't enjoy the attention. Just me, walkin' the jungle, talkin' to little old ladies, that's my — Didn't come here for *attention*.'

'I understand that,' Congressman Hanson replies, 'And last thing I want is to disrupt your way of life. From what I've seen, you've got a good thing going here ...' The Congressman gestures expansively at the fruit, the green beyond the pavilion. '... But it's no secret, there are people out there who are concerned about their relatives in Jonestown. Seems to me, the easiest way to dispel those concerns is to let them see you've got nothing to hide.'

Jim rolls his tongue over his lips, clenches and unclenches his jaw. Evelyn's stomach ices over; her heart refuses to beat. She pictures knives, guns, deviations from order.

'Of course,' Jim murmurs diffidently. 'We've got nothing to hide.'

They're ready, and they're eager to please. It's there in their quick-flash smiles, their Friday-night best, the friendliness of the kitchen staff, bearing plates of pork and biscuits, jugs of fruit punch. They'll sing on command. They'll make nice with their treacherous relatives, the same ones whose throats they've vowed to slit. They'll have fun and look spontaneous doing it.

'It's a misconception to think we hate America, just because we're socialists.' Evelyn courts Don Gonzalez, NBC correspondent, after Sister Cassandra's soulful rendition of 'The Star-Spangled Banner'. 'There are many American values we continue to hold dear. Liberty. Democracy. Equal opportunity ...'

Don Gonzalez nods distractedly; dabs his mouth and peers down the table at Jim, who's attempting to tell the Congressman much the same, tripping over his words.

'... America. Pains me, leaving behind — Had *ideas*. People many times told me I could do the — Congress? *President*, even. Well, ah, ain't worth now, ah, dwelling ... Too humble. Wouldn't survive the bigwhite — big white houseonahill. But *ideas* ...'

A cameraman swings by, getting a wide angle of the stage, the children giggling and mimicking Sister Fantine's jiggling backside. Jim ducks, as though the camera is a swooping pterodactyl, and stares around: lips pale and slack, eyes like jelly behind his sunglasses.

'*Rude*,' Jim mutters. '*Rude*. Wasn't that rude?'

'He could walk into someone that way,' Evelyn agrees.

'He could've walked into a *senior*,' Frida chimes in, disgusted.

'Walked into a senior,' Jim repeats. 'Could've … Who did that? Who—?'

'That's Rand Carlo from NBC.' Phil leans forward, silver-gold eyes on Jim's. 'He's *good*. He'll get some great footage.' Phil leans back, scans the stage. 'Fantine, isn't she great?'

'Great,' Evelyn and Frida chorus. *Great*: the lawyers, the newsmen, and Luísa, who's been giving Phil the eye all night. *Great*: Jim and Congressman Hanson.

At Evelyn's side, Don Gonzalez rises. 'Excuse me.'

'Can we get you anything?' Evelyn widens her eyes, touches his wrist. 'More punch?'

'Just stretching my legs,' he says tersely, and strays into the crowd.

Evelyn sits back; toys with the silver rose at her ear, drums her fingers to the music. Jim's gaze slides across her chest, the pussybow at her neck. He doesn't need to beckon.

'*You couldn't keep him?*' he growls, swirling his punch. '*Uptight cunt, you need me to pour this up your vagina?*' He slurps down the contents, places the cup pointedly on the table.

'Well, I think we could use another jug.' Phil stands. 'Anything else while I'm up?'

'Yes, actually,' Evelyn purrs. 'Could you check on Solomon Tom?'

If Phil is surprised by the request, being asked in front of everyone, he doesn't show it; just smiles cleanly, nods, strides off. 'Will you ever return to America, Reverend Jones?' Mike Yi from *The Examiner* prompts Jim, who's chewing and sucking on his lips in a silent funk.

'Is this on the record?' Frida retaliates. 'If it is, Jim hasn't consented—'

'America,' Jim obliges. 'America, the beautiful. I love Guyana … but I ain't Guyanese. Pains me, being torn from my homeland.' He wipes his face mournfully. 'No, I don't think I'll ever return to America. Guyana. I'll die in Guyana, among my people.'

Evelyn and Frida trade an uncomfortable glance.

'Sometimes I feel like a dying man,' Jim moans. 'What can I do? My people need me.'

'He's had some heart trouble,' Frida intervenes. 'But Dr. Katz ..,'

They trot out a well-worn rhapsody to Katz's genius, Jonestown's world-class medical facilities. Jim falls silent, stirring only to repeat salient points, loudly enough to make them sound like his own; slurring suggestions — 'Did you ever have a prostate exam, Congressman? Harry can do you, right now.' Phil returns with a fresh jug of fruit punch just as they're extolling the healing powers of papaya. He takes the seat beside Evelyn.

'I've been snubbed by a three-year-old,' Phil informs her with a quiet smile, refilling Jim's cup, the Congressman's, her own. 'He said "I cand dance when you liff me, Brodder Phil".'

Evelyn takes up her cup. Lowers her eyelashes and sips.

'*Matty Nieubaker was seen passing a note to the NBC correspondent,*' Phil lowers his voice another octave. '*Ike and Oscar are questioning Matty now.*'

Evelyn's pulse quickens. Her lip curls in contempt. '*Keep it contained,*' she murmurs behind her raised cup, stealing a glance at Jim. Sips again, sweetness coating her nerves.

'Congressman, I've been trying to think of a way to get you to give up your seat by Luísa all night,' Phil says brazenly. 'This is the best I could come up with: how about a speech?'

'Phil! Don't be a chauvinist pig,' Frida hisses. 'She's here to *work*.' She turns to red-faced Luísa. 'Sorry about my brother. He thinks he's Robert Redford.'

'Speech?' Jim rasps dolefully. 'Speech …?'

'It might be worthwhile,' Evelyn muses. 'People are curious. At the very least, it would comfort them to know you're not a Republican, Congressman.'

The Congressman chuckles. Jim squirms, starts one of his rants: '*Told you 'bout that Republican wanted me—*'

'Your musicians are a hard act to follow,' Congressman Hanson speaks over Jim. 'But I wouldn't want anyone to go to bed tonight thinking I was a Republican.'

The table bristles with laughter. '*Rosaline can introduce him,*' Evelyn tells Jim in a soothing undertone. Jim just nods, sulks. Minutes later, Rosaline rises from her place at the next table, where she's keeping peace between the Concerned Relatives and their people: Wayne Bud and his large family, Mona's rich Italian-American parents, Bobbi Luce holding her brother's new baby in her lap. The music stops and Rosaline sidles onstage.

'Thank you, brothers and sisters … Can we get some quiet now? Thank you … and I just wanna say before we introduce our guest of honor, thanks to our very talented musicians—'

Don Gonzalez, NBC correspondent, creeps back to the table. Phil sacrifices his place by Evelyn; he goes to Luísa's side and smiles down at her. Evelyn smiles up at Don Gonzalez.

'How are your legs?' she asks coquettishly. 'Are they stretched?'

They're ready, but they're getting restless. Instruments clang. Seniors nod. Children bump into each other, cry, collapse on benches. A white fieldworker, Matty Nieubaker, is pushed from the radio shed by Ike and Oscar, shaking on his feet. A sister from his crew, Rondelle Mayberry, is hustled in, emerging later with a stony expression, sweat on her brow. Ike storms up to the relatives' table and, unprovoked, calls Bobbi Luce a 'traitor-bitch-dyke'. Wayne Bud and Eric Hurmerinta shoot to their feet in her defense. Rosaline, pink-faced, places her body between them, scolding, 'Ike, that wasn't *necessary!*'

'Ro'?' Jim bleats. 'What now? Ro'?'

'Just a misunderstanding!' Rosaline calls brightly, leading Ike away.

'Alcohol is strictly prohibited, but the natives have been known to trade fermented beverages with some of our people,' Evelyn bluffs. 'It's a problem we're anxious to resolve.'

Phil gets up to talk to Oscar. After some time, Rosaline and Ike join them. Then Rosaline takes to the stage again:

'Seniors and those of you with little ones, please take this moment to say goodnight and return to your cottages. Adults, please pick up any trash you see on your way.' She smiles wanly. 'The Congressman's Party will be back bright and early tomorrow.'

'*Two rats in the house: white male, black female,*' Phil murmurs in Evelyn's ear as Rosaline wishes the people peace, sweet dreams. '*They've requested help from the Congressman.*'

The pavilion gradually stirs, clears, until only guests and a few guards remain.

'We can stay overnight,' Don Gonzalez suggests as they mill around, awaiting their ride. 'Save you trucking us back to Port Kaituma.'

'We don't need beds,' Mike Yi affirms. 'These benches here are fine.'

'*There's no place for you here!*' Jim barks, startled by their nerve. 'Not possible. No, no.'

They back Jim up, and the matter is dropped. Hands are shaken. Rosaline makes a First Lady-like show of ambling away, arm-in-arm with Jim, though they only go as far as the radio yard. 'I dunno … It really seems like they like it here,' Bobbi confides in Wayne Bud.

'What a disappointment that must be for you,' Evelyn taunts, coming up behind them. 'I'm sure you were hoping for something exciting like a concentration camp.'

'I'm just glad my family are *safe*.' Wayne shoulders his backpack and stalks toward the flatbed truck.

In the shadows beyond the headlamps, Phil is conversing with the NBC cameraman.

'Off the record? I don't think he'll be around much longer …' Phil nods toward the pavilion and, in so doing, catches Evelyn's eye. Half-smiles.

Stomach snaking, Evelyn makes her way to the radio yard, where Jim is ranting softly to Rosaline. '*Benches … I ain't stupid … They be bugging them benches … Probably bugged already …*' He lurches; notices Evelyn. '*I want every bench checked! Check 'em, now! Vulture bastards—*'

Evelyn helps Rosaline steady Jim, walk him inside the radio shed.

'We'll get security to do a full sweep of the pavilion,' Evelyn assures Jim as they lay him on the daybed. From Rosaline's harassed look, it's clear she hasn't mentioned the defectors.

Jim is still ranting about bugs, Congressman Hanson's phony-progressive entourage of 'spics and chinks', when Mona and Frida let themselves in. Mona, looking the part of the good daughter in a full-skirted white sundress, unclips a gold cross from her neck.

'Papa tried to give me Nonna Sofia's crucifix,' she says. 'I don't want it.'

The offering calms Jim. 'What are those, rubies?' Mona nods, and Jim closes it in his fist, smirks. 'Pawn it in Georgetown … Them rich Guyanese love Catholic shit.'

Evelyn steps back out to the radio yard. Phil and Danny Luce are discussing Bobbi, what a train-wreck she's become since leaving the Temple. 'Please do a security sweep of the pavilion,' she instructs Danny.

To Phil, she says, 'Find Dr. Katz. We'll need him on hand when we tell Jim.'

'*Where'd you go? Who you talking to?*' Jim booms upon her return to the radio shed.

'I was arranging an inspection of the pavilion, as you requested. Father.'

'Don't think I don't see y'all whispering … Talking circles around me … Don't think I can't read your *minds*,' Jim grumbles. 'Tell me what you got. I can *see* you. Tell me.'

Evelyn exchanges glances with Frida, Mona, Rosaline.

'There's a situation. Two potential defectors.'

'They're just fieldworkers,' Frida offers gently. 'They're *nothing*.'

'They know nothing,' Mona reassures him. 'They can't hurt us, Father.'

'Two outta nine hundred, Jim,' Rosaline says. 'We're doing *good*.'

The door squeaks open; Phil and Dr. Katz.

Jim sits forward, gaping. Droops his head and vomits on Mona's dress.

3.

'It went okay,' Phil tells their people in Georgetown over the radio, and it's true; no White Nights, no stranglings, Jim sedated and spirited back to West House by Mona and Frida. Okay. He smiles at Evelyn; no, Rosaline; he's smiling at Rosaline. 'Want to talk to your sons?'

Rosaline nods, gets on the radio to Jimmy Jr., Martin Luther, and Paolo, who are in the capital for the week playing basketball; they just lost to the Guyanese national team.

'Well, the important thing is that you had fun,' Rosaline coos as Evelyn shuffles papers.

Once the call is concluded, Evelyn hands Rosaline the next day's running order.

'I think it's best if you start with the nursery. Show them the babies in the sunroom.'

Again, Rosaline nods. 'I'll do that.' She studies the paper, then hands it back. 'All those beautiful babies. We've got everything to live for.'

'Right,' Phil says. 'You're so right. We'll make sure they see that.'

Rosaline rises. Looks from Phil to Evelyn. 'Well … I guess I'll turn in.'

'Let me walk you to your cottage,' Phil offers, and though Rosaline refuses, he won't take no for an answer.

In Phil's absence, Evelyn changes the wavelength, speaks to an operator, waits through the static for word from San Francisco. Phil comes back in, starts rubbing her shoulders.

'You're going to end up a hunchback, Evie.'

The radio continues to whirr and snow. Phil takes off her headset.

'We're ready. Whatever tomorrow brings,' he says in her ear. She closes her eyes and leans into the dig of his fingers, tension dissolving.

'Seriously, Evie … Watch how you sit. It's gonna take me hours to work through all these knots.'

'We don't have hours.'

'How long do we have?'

She doesn't answer. Phil turns her chair around, tilts her chin upward. She opens her eyes to his belt buckle; her reflection in it, gray and small. 'How long do we have?' Phil repeats.

'I don't know.'

On the bottom bunk, Soul sleeps with Sally-Ann, starfished on his back, fat cheeks aflame. Too cute to wake. On the top bunk, less cute, Frida snores with her long white feet in Mona's face. Evelyn takes off her sandals; tiptoes into Jim's room.

The bed is unmade. Jim isn't in it.

A ghost of relief rises up in her, only to be smothered by a pall of dread. Sandals in hand, Evelyn exits the cabin.

Around the back of the cabin, Mona's white dress flutters on the line. Beyond it, in last night's clothes, Jim watches Dr. Katz squeeze a syringe of liquid into a dog's mouth.

He sees her, she's sure, though nothing in his attitude indicates it. Just the general supposition that he *always* sees her.

She treads across the dewy grass to Jim and Dr. Katz, just avoiding the lifeless body of another canine, flakes of red at its mouth.

She crosses her arms and watches Jim and Katz watch the dog: walking in circles, panting, whimpering, vomiting blood. Retreating under a titi to yelp, roll, spasm.

'Th'other was faster?' Jim grumbles. 'This a weaker blend?'

'It's the same blend,' Katz explains. 'The first dog was a juvenile.'

Jim nods, puckers his lips. 'Any way to make it the same for everyone?'

'There are always going to be variations based on individual physiology. But we can keep it under five minutes for everyone.'

'Bring that dog.' Jim points to the dog under the titi tree. 'Lay it next to its comrade.'

Katz, no doubt inured to odd requests, starts dragging the dog through the early blue-dark. High in the sky, a chalky three-quarter moon. The morning star, laser-bright.

Jim crouches next to the dogs; stroking one, then the other. 'Darlings. My darlings.'

Evelyn watches Mona's dress dance in the breeze. Katz clears his throat.

'Peace, my darlings.' Jim looks at Katz. 'Thank you, Harry ... You may go now.'

Katz skulks away. Jim keeps petting the dogs, talking to them in a childlike hush.

Evelyn takes a step backward, listing on her feet. She looks at the sandals in her hands. Her pale toes flecked with dirt. *Objective*, she thinks. *Be objective.*

She steps toward Jim. 'Why aren't you sleeping?'

Jim ignores her. She repeats the question. Still, he ignores her. She takes a step closer.

'Father,' she coaxes, hand on his shoulder. 'Come to bed.'

Jim looks up at her. 'No, I don't think so,' he says mildly. 'No, no, Evelyn ... Why don't *you* come down *here?*'

Evelyn, too, is inured to odd requests. With a sigh, she crouches beside him. He takes up her pale hand and places it on the nearest dog. 'Feel,' he says. 'Isn't she peaceful? *Feel.*'

'Yes. Very peaceful.'

It isn't an American dog, soft and well-fed; the bones are stark, the fur coarse. A ridge of leathery teats. She can smell the toxin, clean-bitter beneath the clamminess of blood, sweat.

She drops her hand. Wipes it off on her trousers and rises. 'Come to bed,' she repeats.

'*Why?*' Jim snarls. 'You think I want you? You think you got anything to give me?'

When she doesn't answer, he laughs; staggers to his feet.

'You think I want *this?*' He makes a grab for her crotch. 'Think your boyfriend wants it?' As he pokes and prods beyond her waistband, Evelyn wills herself not to think of where his fingers have just been. 'Honey, you ain't twenty-three no more. Hell, even when you were ... weren't exactly turning heads in the street. He could have *anyone*, and he chooses a humorless bitch with a bastard child? It don't line up.'

Jim withdraws his fingers; dries them off on the pussybow at her neck.

'Soon as he gets a taste of power, my kinda power, he'll throw you under the bus. Your baby, too. I'm sorry, darlin'.'

'You're not sorry, you lying shit.' Evelyn draws back, sneering. But she can't keep the hurt from her voice, completely. 'Soul is your baby, as much as mine.'

'Course he is. They're all my babies.'

'You're a worthless father.'

'You're a worthless cunt.'

Evelyn crosses the yard. There's a red wagon belonging to Soul, an inch of brown water at the base. She pours the water out, repositions the wagon. Surveys it with crossed arms.

'You think you got power, pushing papers around, crossing your arms like a bitch?' Jim berates her. 'You *don't*. Never did.'

Evelyn drops her arms to her sides.

'You ruined my life,' she says.

'You weren't alive 'til you met me.'

Evelyn's chin wobbles. Jim comes toward her. She closes her hands into fists.

'Why don't you—' Evelyn sobs, hearing the Rosaline-like waver of her voice. She swallows and summons her classroom cadence. '*Why don't you just die already?*'

Jim comes up behind her, shushing, stroking.

'Beautiful revolutionary,' he croons. 'It's a beautiful day.'

She stays in the garden, to agonize, to organize. As the sky pinkens, the moon fades, the sun rises; as the first flies bead the dogs' mouths — she stays. Walled off from the sound of Soul's froggy little voice, somewhere beyond her sight.

'Doggy!' he burbles. 'One doggy … two doggies!'

Soul runs around to the back of the cabin, straight toward the lifeless dogs, Sally-Ann straggling behind him. Evelyn stands to attention.

'The doggies are sleeping,' she says sternly, snatching him up. 'Don't wake them. It's not nice to wake somebody when they're sleeping, *don't you know that?*'

Something in her tone must rattle him, since he begins to wail inconsolably. 'Sorrymommy… SorryImsorry…Imsorrymommyplease…'

'*Stop it*,' Evelyn hisses. 'Stop it, Solomon Tom. That's *enough*.'

She sees her sister's face blossoming with tears; feels irrationally envious. Scowling, she pushes toward the front of the cabin.

'His socks are odd,' Evelyn bitches, crouched on the jatoba floorboards and yanking off Soul's tiny tennis shoes. 'Why is he in odd socks?'

'I don't know,' Sally-Ann answers. 'I don't know.'

'Get him some new socks. Matching socks. *Now*.'

4.

It doesn't matter that Lenny Lynden's socks don't match; it's too dark in Single Males C-25 to see them anyway. Too dark to see he hasn't showered or shaved; his hair a malodorous mass of sheepish brown curls. He's looked better ... but who's looking? A sunbeam cuts his arm as the cabin door creaks open; he huddles against the wall.

'Hey, Dracula!'

'Don't call him Dracula, man.'

'Hey, Count Dracula, sir?' Brother Jerome, a plucky kid with a downy moustache, peeks over Lenny's bunk. 'Weren't you on sugarcane crew with Rondelle and Matty?'

'What?' Lenny mumbles. 'Yeah.'

'Sorry, man,' Brother Seb, a few years older, chisel-jawed and soulful-eyed, sympathizes. 'That's rough.'

'What?'

'Judases. Fucking Judas rats, jumping ship, talkin' shit about Father ...' Jerome rants boisterously. 'You *know* them? You fucking *friends* with them?'

'Cool it. Does it look like he is?' Kindly, Seb offers, 'You've got the right idea, Lenny. It's wild out there. Better stay where it's peaceful.' Seb snatches a baseball from the shared shelf, drags Jerome doorward. Stops. 'Uh, want us to crack a window or something?'

'They're not my friends,' Lenny mutters in response. '*They're not my friends.*'

They're not his friends, Rondelle and Matty from the sugarcane crew. Not his friends ... Judases, rats, bugs to be squashed, that's all. Where are his friends? His wife, mother? Lenny curls closer to the wall. Smell, his smell; like a rat, bugs on his skin.

'*They're not my friends.*' He kicks his sheets.

There's cameras in the pavilion. A huddle of people around that Congressman, the one who's famous for saving seals or something. Rondelle. Matty. Four generations of Harris-Harrisons: Grandma Gertie, Bob and Kay, Jo with her mixed-race daughters, Amali and Nylah. Another white family, the Fowlers, low-key Indiana people he's never paid much attention to. Joey Dean and his pregnant wife, Carmel. Carmel's teenage sister Eileen and her part-Pomo boyfriend, Otis. Jim in the midst of it all, puckering his lips, cupping shoulders, swaying his head like it's too heavy to hold up.

'They're not my friends,' Lenny tells a group of surly-looking guys, all hanging around the pavilion's edge with crossed arms. They seem to agree.

'Slack-ass counterrevolutionaries. They'll be *sorry.*'

'Lookat that white bitch. What kinda life she think Amali and Nylah are gonna have back in the US?'

'Course it's mostly white folk. Why am I even surprised?'

Lenny nods vehemently. Scrapes his hands through his hair. Crosses his arms. Not his friends. Not like them. Show the world, he isn't like them.

Evelyn.

She's sat on a bench some distance from Jim, talking to one of the lawyers. Across from them, Sister Molly in a purple muumuu, mopping her brow. Molly looks stressed. So does the lawyer, thin mouth frowning, feet twitching in mud-spattered brogues. But Evelyn looks relaxed, like she's at a party.

Like she's at a party. Exactly like that. Leaning back. White blouse unbuttoned at the neck. Legs outstretched in plain black trousers. Sandals. She's talking with one arm, who knows what about — Bert the Turtle, her thesis on Marcuse, working for the UN, changing the world? Her other arm is curved around the back of the bench, as if to embrace some Lenny-shaped hole in the universe.

Lenny moves toward her with more certainty than he has ever had in his life.

He bumps into Phil Sorensen.

'Oh, sorry, Lenny,' Phil says, sounding more dead than sorry. He looks a little dead too, less handsome than usual. He places a hand on

Lenny's shoulder. 'I'm really sorry, Lenny.'

For what? Lenny doesn't stop to ask; the words are already flying out like bullets.

'*They're not my friends*,' he blurts. Then: 'I want to help. Please.'

'Why do you want to leave Jonestown?'

The Congressman's secretary Luísa holds a tape recorder under Lenny's mouth, and it doesn't hurt that she's cute: big brown eyes, full mauve lips, streamer-like dark curls in a high ponytail. Her shoulders bare, goldy-brown. She looks maybe Mexican.

'My wife left.' Lenny thinks. 'My mom is dead. I don't like working in the fields.'

'Anything else?'

Lenny thinks some more. 'I just want to leave.'

'We're going to need a second plane,' the Congressman tells Luísa, a little worried, a little proud, once she's done interviewing Lenny. He extends a big white hand. 'We'll get you out safely, don't you worry, Mr. Lynden.'

It rains. Hair-raising, thought-drowning rain. Luísa sources clear-plastic ponchos, gives one to Lenny, tells him to board the red flatbed truck with the others. Jim, flanked by Danny Luce and Billy Younglove, beckons Lenny over.

'Soldier of peace.' Jim squeezes Lenny through the sterile skin of his poncho. 'You'll have a hero's reincarnation. Anything you wanna be. What you wanna be?'

Lenny says the first thing that pops into his head. 'A bird.'

'Alright. You'll be a bird soon.' Jim smiles and squeezes him tighter. 'Sweet dove. You were always my favorite.'

Billy slips Lenny a pistol under his poncho, gives him a shove and, loud enough to be heard over the rain, shouts, '*Traitor shit! Get outta here!*'

'You didn't have to go over there!' Luísa frets. 'You didn't have to talk to them!'

'It's alright.' The pistol slithers against his skin, the skull-horns of his hips. 'I'm alright.'

Otis's mom, a tall lady with gray-threaded braids, tries to drag the boy from the truck. His sneakers come off in the mud. Cameramen swarm. Some kids throw rocks.

'Don't throw rocks!' Sister Diane cries. 'That's not — not *helping*!'

Luísa bustles over to the Congressman. Phil comes up to Lenny, slips him a palmful of pills. 'This stuff got me through 'Nam.' He looks at Lenny with his pale eyes. 'I was crazy to want to die for America. But Jonestown … it's the most beautiful place on earth.'

Lenny glides toward the flatbed truck, it seems to him, on white wings.

'Are you for real?' Matty asks him nervously. Lenny doesn't answer; he's thinking about his gun. Then about the swell of bodies in the pavilion. Then the smell of the Congressman's blood as he climbs aboard, shirt spattered red, silver chest hair showing.

'Just a nick,' the Congressman tells the cameras, looking more annoyed than scared, though his big white hands are shaking. 'Nothing to worry about.'

Lenny leans in to get a better look at the Congressman's blood. Kay Harris, out of nowhere, points and screeches: 'Don't let Lenny Lynden ride with us! Don't trust him!'

'Nothing to worry about,' the Congressman repeats, banging on the side of the truck. 'Can we get a move on?'

The newsmen jump onboard; Luísa, mermaid-wet. The truck heaves and Luísa's breasts bounce, nice. Minnie — no, Alice, just as pretty, same oblong face, long lashes — runs across the playground and starts kissing Billy Younglove; wet kisses, rain-shimmery kisses, Billy wiping rain or tears from her cheeks. More kids, undeterred by Diane, chase the truck with sticks, stones, clods of mud. Angry women beat their breasts, work their mouths.

Lenny's head pounds, in time with the truck's jolts, the women's mouths, the metallic hard-on. The shouts of hate, which he knows in his immortal dove soul are really love, love, love.

5.

She watches Phil's arms. Sunkissed sinew, blond hairs like Van Gogh wheatfields. Shadows of effort as he struggles to compress a mountain of cash inside a suitcase.

'It doesn't fit,' Phil admits, sweat on his brow. 'The bullion takes up too much space.'

'Remove the bullion. It'll weigh you down, anyhow.'

Phil starts removing the bars of gold. She goes back to typing. Roger Luce shows up at the cabin door. 'Mona said you have a mission for me.'

Frida hands him his passport. '*Zhivi khorosho*, Roger. You're going to Russia.'

Roger looks aloof. He's standing like a cop. Frida points out two more suitcases, one big and one small. 'Can you lift those?'

Roger lifts them. His face turns tomato-red; his arms quake.

'That won't work,' Frida says. 'Who else can we trust?'

Roger puts the suitcases down. 'I can ask my brother,' he puffs. 'Danny's strong.'

Frida looks skeptical. 'Didn't he go to the airstrip with security?'

'I saw him in the pavilion,' Roger says. 'With Clarisse and Libya Eugenie.'

Evelyn finishes the letter she's typing. Checks the clock. On the radio, at low volume, Jim is ranting about crazy Lenny Lynden, how he's going to shoot the pilot of that plane and bring great violence upon them. 'Find Danny,' she says.

Evelyn hands the letter to Phil, along with his passport. *Sorensen, Philip John. 6'1½'. 8–17–1945.* He looks up at her, then puts them in his pocket. She takes up a box of documents, takes it around to the burn barrel they've rigged up in the yard, throws it on the flames, coughing as the smoke tickles her lungs. She sees Mona's dress still on the line, still stained with a pale rose of vomit; on impulse, she feeds it to the fire as well. She returns to the front of the cabin just as Roger and Danny Luce stumble up the garden path. Danny is weeping.

'What's wrong?' Evelyn asks.

Roger glares. Danny keeps weeping, tells her about Clarisse, baby Libya Eugenie.

'Well, you know, Danny, it had to be done,' Evelyn replies reasonably.

But the Luce boys are looking at her in a very unreasonable way, making her fear for the bones of her neck, her skull. She skitters back inside the cabin; goes straight past Phil, Frida, and the radio. Lifts the queen bed's covers.

He's still there. Cheeks pink. Chest rising, falling. Baby-blue baseball T-shirt, a gift from her parents. Navy socks. She strokes the silky dark hair, tucks him in again.

'Don't get caught,' Frida warns her brother and the Luce boys as she hands out pistols. 'If you're caught alive, shoot yourselves. Got it?'

Evelyn returns to the lower bunk, her typewriter.

'Got it.'

The Luce boys haul their suitcases past the cabin porch. Phil hangs back, cups Frida's shoulder. 'Be brave, sis.'

'You're not my brother,' Frida says inexplicably, and follows the Luce boys outside.

'Right,' says Phil. 'Right …' He hoists his suitcase onto his shoulder; appears to listen for a moment to Evelyn's fingers typing.

'The Congressman will be dead soon.' Evelyn doesn't turn her head. 'What are you waiting for?'

Nothing, it turns out. Without another word, Phil walks out of the cabin, and her life.

6.

It's alright. You'll be a bird soon. Don't forget your clean uniform.

Lenny watches the planes buzz over the jungle canopy. Two planes, but only one gun. Two planes, but only one Lenny. Will his body, at the vital moment, split into two? Will his body, high in the sky, have powers this earthly body doesn't?

'Don't trust him!' Kay Harris says for the millionth time. 'Don't trust Lenny Lynden!'

She's not the only one saying it. Others are, too; shrinking from Lenny like he's contagious, a circle of dead space forming around him.

He can't think why. But then, he can't see his jaw clenching and unclenching, his twitching fingers, darting eyes. Is this how it feels to be Jim Jones? To be God?

The truck rolls forward to the airstrip, parks a short distance from two small aircraft. Lenny jumps down from the flatbed and starts striding toward the rickety metal ladder of the nearest plane, ignoring the hysterical cries at his back. Luísa chases after him.

'You can't get on that plane yet!'

Lenny looks at her hand on his chest. 'Yes, I can.'

'Theo!' Luísa calls the Congressman. 'This man's insisting—'

Lenny keeps moving toward the plane, stopping only at the sound of a tractor zooming onto the airstrip, filled with armed brothers from security. *Friends!*

'We need to go!' pregnant Carmel yells. 'We can't stay here!'

'Don't let Lenny fly with us!' Jo Harris-Harrison screams, hands covering her daughters' ears. 'Don't trust him!'

'Oh, for crying out loud …' The Congressman walks up to Lenny and frisks him through his poncho. 'He's clear.' He points from Lenny to Rondelle, Matty, Eileen, Otis, Joey Dean, and Carmel. 'You seven, take the Cessna. Everyone else, line up for the Otter. We can make it back to Georgetown before dark, if we all work togeth—'

The tractor rumbles closer, blocking the path of the larger plane. Billy Younglove, climbing onto the hood with a rifle in his arms, peaces Lenny. Lenny peaces him back.

'What the *hell* are you doing, Lenny?' Rondelle gives him a shove as they board the Cessna. Mutely, Lenny stumbles into his seat. Eyes the back of the pilot's head and fingers his gun.

In Jonestown, the mothers and children will be lining up to board the helicopters to Russia. Or boats … some of them will go by boat, he guesses. He's not sure of the exact plan, but there is a plan, he's sure of that. '*Stay away from us,*' Joey Dean warns Lenny, bolting shut the door of the Cessna. '*I don't know what you're on, man, but you're giving us the creeps.*'

Lenny shrugs, smiles. Seconds later, outside the Cessna, the shooting starts.

Pink spatter on the window. Screams like boiling water. The pilot's capped head ducking for cover, but anyway, the plane's not in the air yet, forget the pilot. *Not his friends.* Lenny whips the pistol from his belt, blood singing in his ears, shouts of hate, love. *Pop-clang! Pop-clang!* He sees a bit of flesh fly off Rondelle's arm and stick to the seat across the aisle. Matty falling to the floor, white skin blanching whiter. Carmel backing into a corner, clutching her pregnant belly. Eileen's face freckled with blood. Joey Dean and Otis jumping to their feet, wresting the gun from him.

'*Don't touch me,*' Lenny says as boots press between the wings of his back, pin him to the aisle. His heart bounces like a rubber ball in his chest. '*Don't touch me, or I'll kill you.*'

But already, his voice is losing conviction, watching the blood soak the carpet like a bad trip, screaming patterns, melting walls. Rondelle lets out an improbable howl, clutches her spurting arm, begins to tremble all over. Matty is mannequin-still, skin like fogged metal. The whole cabin stinks of exposed guts.

It occurs to Lenny that this is the worst thing he's ever done.

Pop-clang, the shots continue on the airstrip. *Pop-pop-clang.*

7.

'Can we turn it down a bit?' Frida nods at the radio, and Evelyn knows it must be bad, if even Frida is getting squeamish. But of course it's bad; of course she knows this.

'We can turn it down.'

As Frida crosses to the radio, adjusts the dial, Evelyn resists the urge to check on Soul. There are still reports to finish; even now, they must uphold the appearance of a thriving community. She keeps typing, studying figures, typing harder to cover the cries on the radio. Hard like rain on a tin roof. Hard enough to bruise her fingertips black and blue.

'Oh, go to hell, you fucker,' Frida growls out of nowhere. 'Fucker! Fuck *you.*'

She slams the side of her typewriter, gives a yelp of pain or frustration. Seeing Evelyn's questioning glance, she explains lamely, 'The ribbon ran out.'

'Really, Frida, you need to keep it down.' Evelyn nods toward the room where Soul is sleeping.

They keep working in silence, or near-silence. Evelyn finishes the Education Report.

'It's a pity we won't get to see the results of Meyer's new methodology,' she tells Frida. 'But I've made some predictions. Who knows, maybe some group somewhere will be inspired by our example.'

'I can't wait to die,' Frida says.

After some time, the cries on the radio get quieter. *Legacy,* Jim is saying. *What a legacy.* Footsteps approach the cabin, and Evelyn and Frida look at each other, scramble for their pistols. But it's just Jin-sun Jones and his white wife, Carrie, holding her baby in her arms.

'Bam!' Frida coos, getting up to stroke the baby. 'Oh … You did it already?'

Carrie nods tearfully. Jin-sun says, 'Dad said it was okay if we came here.'

'There are some things in the fridge,' Evelyn offers. She thinks of asking Jin-sun about his brothers, whether they've had any success getting revenge on their enemies in the capital, but Jin-sun doesn't look much in the mood for talking and, really, she isn't either.

Carrie climbs onto the top bunk with her baby. Jin-sun gets some cups, fills them with fruit punch, and joins his wife. Evelyn keeps typing as the couple whisper to each other.

When the bunk begins to rattle above her, she moves to the floor.

'It's been quiet for a while,' Frida says, after the cabin grows frigid with radio silence, the stillness of the young family. 'Do you think Father—?'

'I doubt it.'

'Do you think we should—?' Frida closes her fist, holds it out. 'Rock-paper-scissors?'

'Don't be ridiculous. I'll go.' Evelyn rises. 'Finish the Maintenance Report.'

'If Soul wakes—'

'He *won't*,' Evelyn snaps, taking up her pistol, the flashlight. 'Just, don't — don't do *anything*. Don't touch him.'

Evelyn concentrates on the dance of the flashlight, ducking her head for curtains of foliage, low-flying bats and insects. Shapes in the dark, which could be sandbags or logs; yes, logs. But after a while, she has to look down; there are so many, she'll trip if she doesn't. She doesn't want to trip. She doesn't want to fall … fall on somebody.

Why did she wear sandals?

'*No*,' an older woman in a red hat is saying to Sally-Ann, trying to fend off her hands. 'No, no, *no*.'

'*Please*.' Sally-Ann draws up the woman's sleeve. 'Please, just … it *won't* hurt.'

Evelyn tautens her nostrils against the smell: an intense human clamminess, overlaid with something sickly-sweet, like pineapple. A few more nurses are struggling with recalcitrant adults; dead-eyed guards along the perimeters, holding their guns like toys. But most of the people, the ones still living, are huddled quietly, swallowing quietly.

'*No,*' the woman says as the syringe goes into her arm. '*Why?* No.'

Sally-Ann notices Evelyn, looks at her with overbright eyes, cheeks flushed like she's been playing a spirited game of tag, jumping rope. She opens her mouth to say something.

Evelyn stops her.

'Finish it quickly,' she tells Sally-Ann. 'It's almost done.'

She continues toward the stage, stepping over the fallen.

'Why's it taking so long?' Jim, slumped in his chair, scolds Dr. Katz. 'Why — you said they wouldn't struggle, you lyin' quack; *why*—' He notices Evelyn. 'Honey. We *tried.*'

Evelyn nods. Her eye is caught by a crop of reddish-gold curls, a few feet from Jim's chair. Jim notices her looking. 'My good wife,' he explains.

Evelyn nods again, touches her ear; she's missing an earring. She resists glancing down in search of it.

Mona scurries out of the radio shed, tape recorder in hand. She takes one of Jim's arms; Evelyn takes the other.

They help him offstage.

'Did you hear me on the radio?' Jim asks. 'How'd I do …?'

8.

Lenny's shirt is open when they snatch him from the airstrip, flapping around his wasted torso like wings. White wings. White jeans, slipping to his pubic hair. Did he have a belt before? Belts for tourniquets, yeah. A pair of Guyanese men in snappy green berets take hold of his arms. They both have belts. Badges.

'You're not my friends,' Lenny says.

'Not your friends,' the men agree. 'No, Mister. We are not your friends.'

The sun is a dusty fireball, sinking low into the jungle's dark haze. His heart screams for the old life, the new life, evergreen.

'Can you take me back to Jonestown?' he asks. 'I want to go to Jonestown.'

'No Jonestown. Too dangerous in Jonestown.'

They pass the shot-up Otter, wires dangling from its wings. The Congressman's body, wrapped in a soaked red sheet. An Asian newsman's shattered skull. Amali and Nylah, Jo's girls, huddled outside the green army tent, sucking their thumbs.

'I want to go to Jonestown,' Lenny repeats as he's loaded into the back of a Jeep. 'Please? I want to see my friends.'

The cell is small, dank, friendless. No sharp objects to cut his skin like he wants to. He scratches his skin until it bleeds, slaps away at bugs, real or imaginary. He detaches the metal circle from the front of his jeans and, joyously, rolls it along the cell walls, the metal piping. Hides it in the flat of his hand when a guard shows up with three mud-spattered blond men.

'Here you go!' the guard announces cheerily. 'Friends for you!'

Roger, Danny, Phil. They've looked better.

'*Don't touch my friends!*' Lenny leaps to his feet. '*Don't touch them, or I'll kill you!*'

'Shut up, Lenny,' Roger says.

Lenny hugs Roger, then Danny, who's crying, then Phil. '*My friends!*'

'Alright, Lenny,' Phil says. 'Alright … we know we're all friends.'

'Sorry I didn't shoot the pilot,' Lenny blabs. 'I tried to shoot him, I did, but the plane didn't go in the air. I tried, Phil. I tried—'

'Alright, Lenny.' Phil looks into his eyes. 'Can you do me a favor? A favor for a friend? *Keep a lid on it.*'

'Hey! Can I make a phone call?' Roger shouts. 'I want to call my wife in Georgetown. Hey! Don't I get a phone call?'

The guard stalks away. Roger starts rattling the bars.

'Hey!' Lenny yells helpfully. 'That's my friend! He wants to call his wife!'

'*Shut the fuck up, Lenny!*' Roger charges at him with clenched fists. Phil blocks him.

'Guys, can we keep it friendly? We're all friends here. Keep it friendly … and *quiet.*'

Obediently, Lenny retreats to a corner, starts sharpening the metal circle again. Roger sits by his brother, lets him drench his shirt with tears. Phil paces like a caged lion. When the guard opens the door, beckons, 'Sorensen,' he seems unsurprised.

'Don't hurt my friend,' Lenny mutters uncertainly as Phil is led from the cell.

Phil is returned unharmed, perhaps a half-hour later, seemingly on good terms with the guard. The guard looks from one Luce to another. 'Which one got the wife in Georgetown?'

Roger stands tall, follows the guard out. Danny starts weeping anew.

'Mom's dead, that crazy bitch,' Roger says dully, upon his return. 'Her and Dot slit the kids' throats, then each other's.' He closes his eyes and thumps his head against the wall. 'They did it. Those crazy bitches.'

Danny cries harder. Phil reassures him. 'They were good soldiers. All of them.'

After a while, Lenny squeaks, 'Minnie?'

'Minnie's safe, but she's losing her mind. Alice, Ursa—' Roger shakes his head, looks Lenny square in the eye. '*Everyone*. They were killing *everyone*. Don't you get it?'

Phil walks to the center of the cell, pale and serene.

'They were committing revolutionary suicide,' he corrects. 'It was beautiful.'

Danny keeps crying inconsolably. He has lost Clarisse and baby Libya Eugenie.

9.

It is not a perfect legacy, but it's one to be proud of, they agree, listening to the recording of Jim's final sermon. The worst parts, Mona ensured to stop the recorder for. Everything else, well … it's understandable that they should grieve a little at the end of the world.

'What a beautiful little family,' Jim says, peering over the top of the bunk at Jin-sun and Carrie's tadpoled bodies, their swaddled baby like a shared heart between them. He looks at Evelyn. 'Have you taken care of Soul?'

'Not yet.'

Sally-Ann, Frida, and Mona avert their faces as Jim follows Evelyn into the next room. Dr. Katz hovers on the threshold, preparing a syringe.

Evelyn lifts the covers.

'Beautiful baby,' Jim says ceremoniously. 'Beautiful Soul.'

Evelyn knows from his tone that he hasn't changed his mind.

Yet there's always a chance he will. Always a chance. Just let her keep him like this; never to wake, never grow, just breathing; the shine of his hair, the pink of his cheeks.

'Ready.' Katz hands her the syringe. 'Ready when you are.'

Evelyn sits cross-legged on the bed, adorns Soul's sleepy head with a garland of feverish kisses. Inhales his powdery little boy scent. She lifts the pudge of his forearm. *No.*

'Little Mother,' Jim prompts. 'Be objective.'

Objective. Only a push of her finger. Only a prick. Only a fine layer of skin. Only a deeper kind of sleep. Only a birdlike peep, escaping his lips.

After all, he's had a good life … a life of mostly play, puppy dogs, people giving him rides on their shoulders.

She holds the rage tight in her chest. Holds Soul tight as the sweating starts, the rash-like red, the choking, spasms. Stillness.

'Brave mother. Brave soldier.' Jim puts an arm around her, grazes the gloss of her temple. They sit like that for a time, smelling the bitterness, dead flames. Then Jim picks up her right hand. 'It's time, darlin' … There's nothing left.'

Mechanically, Evelyn tucks Soul in again. Follows Jim.

Follows him into the next room. The glow of his red shirt in the cabin's dim; yesterday's shirt, she chose it. He pulls the pistol from his pocket, beckons her with it.

Evelyn stops. 'No,' she says.

Katz looks up from the punch he's pouring. The girls, from whatever they're doing: scrawling notes, tearing up sketches, putting on jewelry.

'C'mon, now,' Jim says. 'A promise is a promise.'

'No,' Evelyn repeats. 'I don't want to.'

Jim mugs at her, expression thick, skin gray. *That's how I want it. My right-hand.* Sally-Ann catches Evelyn's eye; jumps to her feet in a sudden bolt of understanding.

'Father,' she says. 'It's better if a nurse does it, don't you think? Someone with medical experience?'

'Yeah, Father,' Frida agrees. 'It'll be quicker and cleaner if Sally-Ann does it.'

'We don't want you suffering, Father,' Mona chimes in.

Jim stares at Evelyn a moment longer, her blank white face, crossed arms.

'Alright, Sally-Ann,' he murmurs, holding out the pistol. 'Th'nk you, darlin'.'

Sally-Ann takes the pistol, takes Jim's arm and helps him out the door, giving Evelyn a last bright look over her shoulder.

Evelyn smiles wanly, dashes a tear. Too little, too late, like everything.

'Excuse me,' she says, reaching past Katz to take a cup.

There are things she would've liked to live for, of course. Nothing revolutionary, just things. Spend more time with Soul. See her parents. Vicky and Richard the Second in Manhattan. Visit France again. Work in France. Perhaps work for the UN. Perhaps … a haircut.

New earrings? She is missing an earring.

She is missing an earring. Rose earrings given to her by Lenny Lynden, who was her husband in another life, her beautiful blue-eyed boy-husband with the smile that made her wince, but not this life. This life is stepping over. This life is a shimmering blood-sunrise over jungle so beautiful, like a fairytale, MomandDad, I must finish this letter soon, the boat is going out. This life is the new life. This life is the dawn of revolution and she is ready to meet it in a necklace of thorns, sprouting black feathers, adorned with the reddest roses.

Author's Note

On November 18 1978, a US congressman, three members of the media, and a Peoples Temple defector were assassinated on Port Kaituma airstrip — seven miles outside the Peoples Temple Agricultural Project of Jonestown, Guyana. Meanwhile, in Jonestown, over 900 Temple members ingested a fatal mix of potassium cyanide, tranquilizers, and fruit punch. A third of the victims were minors. Over two-thirds were African-American, with African-American girls and women making up approximately 45% of the population. The leadership of Peoples Temple, however, was predominantly white.

Prior to 9/11, the Jonestown massacre was the largest loss of American civilian life in a single, deliberate incident.

Beautiful Revolutionary is not the all-inclusive story of Jonestown and its victims. At most, it is the story of some (mostly white) characters who become involved with a fictionalized version of Peoples Temple, and who are instrumental to the final tragedy. While these characters were often inspired by real individuals, and informed by years of research, they are ultimately fictional.

My fellow researchers sometimes speak of 'the Jonestown vortex' – a whirling mass of information that pulls you in, until you're drowning in details. Possibly, my novel may draw some new readers into this vortex. If so, I encourage you to keep reading.

Alternative Considerations of Jonestown & Peoples Temple (jonestown. sdsu.edu) is a website sponsored by San Diego State University. It's totally free, and comprehensive in documenting, presenting, and memorializing Peoples Temple and its members.

Dozens of books have been written about Peoples Temple, but some reputable general nonfiction titles include: *The Road to Jonestown* by Jeff Guinn (2017), *Stories from Jonestown* by Leigh Fondakowski (2012), *A Thousand Lives* by Julia Scheeres (2011), and *Raven* by Tim Reiterman (1982).

Memoirs by Jonestown survivors include: *Jonestown Survivor* by Laura Kohl (2010), *Slavery of Faith* by Leslie Wagner-Wilson (2008), and *Seductive Poison* by Deborah Layton (1998).

For a perspective on the teenagers of Peoples Temple, see *And Then They Were Gone* by former schoolteachers Judy Bebelaar and Ron Cabral (2018).

For a LGBTIQ perspective on Peoples Temple, see *A Lavender Look at the Temple* by Michael Bellefountaine (2011).

Black Jonestown (www.blackjonestown.org) is a new website devoted to the African-American victims and survivors of Jonestown, with an emphasis on the history and experiences of black women in the Temple. Founded by author and educator Dr Sikivu Hutchinson, together with Jonestown survivors Leslie Wagner-Wilson and Yulanda Williams, it is a key resource for anyone interested in learning more about Jonestown's largest demographic.

Acknowledgements

The people of Peoples Temple — whether I was speaking to you directly, reading your words, watching your interviews, or searching for you in the documents of forty-plus years ago — you're the beating heart of this book. I will always cherish the time I spent with you, and I hope that this story does you justice (or, failing that, entertains you a bit). Thank you for making me feel like I was part of your world.

Rebecca Moore and Fielding McGehee III – aka, Becky and Mac – aka, my 'America parents'. Thank you for welcoming a random Australian into your home three years ago, and for everything since then – the emails, the Skype sessions, the anachronism prevention efforts, the friendship. Thank you for *Alternative Considerations* and your commitment to preserving the history of Peoples Temple and its members. I don't know how I would've navigated 'the Jonestown vortex' without you as my trusted guides.

Thank you, further, to Becky and John Moore for sharing your memories of Carolyn and Annie.

Kathy Sparrow, for showing me the Carolyn you knew at Davis.

The nonfiction authors who investigated Jonestown before me, and particularly those who took the time to meet and/or correspond with me: Judy Bebelaar, Ron Cabral, Jeff Guinn, Julia Scheeres. Also, to all the contributors to *Alternative Considerations of Jonestown & Peoples Temple* and *The Jonestown Report* over the years.

California Historical Society, for opening your archives to me.

Ukiah Library, likewise.

Dave's Bike Shop in Ukiah, for aiding me in my pilgrimage to the old Temple building. (Sorry if I was weird.)

Mary Lee Fulkerson, for Pyramid Lake and your stories of being a bad-ass artist, activist, and army wife.

Katharine Susannah Prichard Writers' Centre, for providing me the perfect cabin in which to write out those frenzied 'Eve of Destruction' days.

The John Marsden / Hachette Prize for Fiction 2014, for helping fund my research. Melbourne Writers Festival 2015, for giving me a platform to talk about it.

Scribe Publications, and especially Marika Webb-Pullman, for believing in this book before it was a book. Our talks always leave me feeling clear-headed, and your advice and edits have taken *BR* from strength to strength. Also, Laura Thomas, for yet another stunning cover.

Grace Heifetz — it's so great to have you in my corner.

My family, for being incredibly proud and patient. *Finally*, you can read the damn thing.

Kirill Kovalenko — best friend, bringer of Pepsi, boy of my dreams. Thank you for being with me for the writing and, more importantly, the aftermath. Without you, it wouldn't mean so much.